With Wanton Disregard

With Wanton Disregard

Gwen Banta

In the California Penal System, California Penal Code # 187 states:
Murder is the unlawful killing of a human being, or a fetus, with malice aforethought.

Murder With Wanton Disregard:
In the Criminal Justice system, The Thomas Test states that when a person acts with a wanton disregard for human life, malice is implied.

Chapter 1

Tim Mulrooney gripped the steering wheel of his unmarked Crown Vic as his excitement overcame his anxiety. The Belmont Shore area of Long Beach was the high-rent district—known as "The Shore" to the locals—a refuge of sunshine, bikinis, and trendy eateries. He couldn't help wondering what in the hell he was doing in beautiful Belmont Shore at 12:42 A.M. on a Wednesday morning chasing down a Code 187.

Mulrooney forced himself to relax and enjoy the welcome change of scenery. He liked his job, although lately the depravity he so often encountered had been burning a hole in his gut. In recent months he had found himself struggling with both self-doubt and a growing inability to dissociate from the horrors which were part of his daily routine. Mulrooney had long sensed that he was at some sort of crossroads in his life. But right now there was a corpse that needed his attention, so he stepped on the gas and cautioned himself to leave the self-analysis to the tofu eaters.

Barely twenty-four hours had passed since he had returned from his first vacation in four years—a jaunt to sunny Puerto Vallarta, Mexico. While south of the border Mulrooney had hit every fishing spot he could find and had consumed enough spicy food to make his stomach protest, in Spanish and in English. Now he was back—tan, attractive, and quite fit for his forty-eight years.

The vacation had been long overdue. His ex-wife, Isabella, had often complained that his work consumed him. It was something Mulrooney deeply regretted but never knew how to change. Mulrooney recalled a quote by Kipling that had always struck him as memorable: "More people are killed by overwork than the importance of the world justifies." He tugged at his ear and grunted. *Shoulda read Kipling before my heart attack.* Nonetheless, Mulrooney knew he didn't have to justify his job dedication to Isabella anymore. She was gone. And Kipling was too dead to give a rat's ass. So Mulrooney shoved them both out of his mind and focused his attention back on the job.

After he turned onto Second Street, he lowered his car window and sucked in the sea air. *I've gotta get me a little hacienda down here someday,* he told himself. Mulrooney had long admired the mission-style architecture introduced by the Spanish friars who had come to California to spread the word of

God among an increasingly hard-of-hearing populace. And the 1950's innocence and hospitality of the Belmont Shore area always plugged him into his youth with a soothing continuity. It was like watching an old commercial of a dancing Alka-Seltzer tablet. When Mulrooney realized he was grinning like the village idiot, he self-consciously instructed himself to close his yap.

After cutting down Glendora, Mulrooney then turned east and followed the moonlight to Alamitos Bay. When he arrived at the crime scene, he automatically appraised the area. Road barricades were already in place. On the small bridge that traversed the bay, a crowd of locals was gathered to watch the action. Several black-and-whites had blocked off the south end of Bay Shore Avenue and the Belmont Shore fire trucks had secured the north end. An Emergency Medical vehicle was parked at the scene in no apparent rush to go anywhere. Not a good sign, he concluded.

Another group of bystanders was gathered in front of a majestic Mediterranean-style villa that stood guard over the bay. The lights of at least ten squad cars illuminated the area like Cirque du Soleil while the onlookers watched expectantly as if waiting to witness a death-defying high-wire act.

Mulrooney recognized the pale officer handling crowd control. It was Officer Kate Axberg's new sidekick, Sanders. Sanders appeared to be about fifteen years old, which made Mulrooney feel older than mold. He had dubbed the new crop of recruits the

"Embryo Patrol" for good reason. As he watched Sanders tentatively admonish a reporter who had slipped under the police tape, Mulrooney could see the tension pulling at the rookie's jaw. The veteran cop still remembered the stress of his first homicide case; and he knew Sanders would harden fast. The kid had no choice. Suck it up or fuck it up.

"Get statements from everyone, Sanders," he directed as he exited his car and headed for the villa. Mulrooney pretended not to notice the beads of sweat that had collected above Sanders' furrowed brow. "You're doing just fine, Officer," he shot back over his shoulder as he approached the door of the villa.

Mulrooney paused to look around and listen. From somewhere inside the residence, the moody notes of Gershwin's *Summertime* seeped out into the night air. The contrast between the soothing music and the ghoulish crowd made him feel as if he were in the middle of a Coppola film. Please, no horse head party gifts, he thought as he straightened himself up to his full height.

Mulrooney shoved open the door and stepped into a spectacular living room. Raising an eyebrow in admiration, he went to work, his photographic memory taking in every detail. There was a superb collection of original art including some aboriginal pieces and a Frederic Remington oil of the American Southwest. A bottle of Cristal champagne with balloons attached rested on a silver tray atop a Steinway.

While he was examining the champagne bottle, Officer Kate Axberg entered the room. Mulrooney noted the strained look that tugged at Kate's usually congenial face. Kate and Sanders had been first to arrive at the crime scene, and no 187 was ever pretty. It occurred to Mulrooney that Kate had probably never been first in on a homicide before. In Belmont Shore, a rainy day was a felony.

"You okay, Kate?" he asked.

"Yes, but I'm glad you're back, Tim," she nodded.

"Thanks. So, you want to break it down for me, my pretty?" he cackled in his best wicked-witch voice. Although Kate usually smiled when he did his impersonations for her, her mouth remained hard. Mulrooney loosened his tie. He knew this one was going to be ugly.

When he looked up again he saw his partner, Brian Clarke, stride into the house with Sanders trailing close behind like a uniformed cocker spaniel. "Hey, Smokey," Mulrooney greeted his partner. Clarke's wife Karen had nicknamed Clarke "Smokey" because of his resemblance to Smokey Robinson. However, Mulrooney was the only other person allowed to use the moniker without incurring Clarke's wrath, which was never a wise choice.

"I can't believe the timing of your phone call, bro," Clarke groused. "You interrupted the wife's lo-o-ve machine."

"So your brother is visiting again?" Mulrooney baited. He laughed as Clarke scratched his brow with an erect middle finger. "Well let's just have Katie give us the tour so she can go home," Mulrooney said, "and then you can drag your sorry ass old 'love machine' back to Karen." Mulrooney then turned to Sanders. "Keep at it outside," he directed.

Sanders obediently complied as Kate gestured for Mulrooney and Clarke to follow her. "One victim," she pronounced as she led them through the hall. "Stabbing. No vitals upon arrival. Victim is Dr. Scott Connolly. Caucasian, forty-five. Wife, no kids."

Mulrooney raised his brows when he heard the name. He had once seen an interview with the prominent Long Beach gynecologist on the local news. Connolly, dressed in Gatsby style, had oozed wealth and confidence, although he had appeared distracted during the interview. And Connolly's eyes had shown signs of stress, accented by inky depressions just below the rims. "Whoa," Mulrooney whistled, "he's the safe-keeper of the Shore's finest resource!"

"Was," Clarke corrected.

As they climbed the curved staircase, the hypnotic notes of Gershwin's *I Love You, Porgy* threw off Mulrooney's sense of the scene. Kate read his exasperated look. "The music was on when we arrived, Tim. I'll '86' it when Fingerprint wraps."

When they reached the top of the stairs, Mulrooney made a mental note that the upstairs speakers were out of order; then he turned back to Kate as she continued her brief. "No weapon," she reported, "and no signs of the assailant. We did the visual search, but Sanders got queasy so I had to send him outside."

"That explains the barf in the bougainvillea," Clarke muttered.

"Yeah," she winced, "he was really embarrassed. I backed out last and secured the area. Two women are downstairs in the den, so you'll want to question them. They were in the house together when we arrived, but we took their explanations separately of course."

As they reached the large master suite, Kate hesitated then turn away. Unlike her to do that, Mulrooney noted. He suddenly felt the familiar anxiety he had often felt as a kid when staring down the dark cellar stairs fearing some faceless intruder lying in wait. As he stepped into the bedroom, his eyes immediately lighted on the bed. "Jesus Frickin Christ!" he sputtered.

"Whoa, Mama!" Clarke yelped from behind.

The renowned Dr. Connolly lay completely naked on his back with his legs spread eagle. His eyes were open and his arms were outstretched as if nailed to a crucifix. Connolly's mouth was agape, as though the life in his body had crawled out the face hole, leaving nothing behind but a brutalized carcass. The victim had been slit from pelvis to sternum. But worst of all, his insides were no longer inside. He was gutted like a fish.

Most of the viscera lay next to the corpse. However, the intestines, still attached to Connolly like an umbilical cord, were strung across the bed, and bits of tissue and fecal matter were splattered about in an eruption of gore. The odor was sickening.

"Jesus!" Clarke groaned as he looked around for footprints. "There's gotta be a Bruno Magli print here somewhere."

"His wife got into bed and found him like that," Kate winced.

Clarke grimaced. "Christ-on-a-cracker! She crawled into bed with THAT?"

"Yep," Kate nodded, "and in her hysteria she ran out of the house naked and screaming. Her best friend arrived immediately thereafter. Interesting timing."

Mulrooney examined the blood splash patterns closely. A blood smear on the closet door intrigued him. The wood bore superficial scratches, and there were fingerprints near the top of the frame.

"What do you make of those prints?" Kate asked.

Mulrooney and Clarke exchanged glances. "Correct me if I'm wrong, Smokey," Mulrooney answered, "but I'd say that's a nipple print."

Clarke pursed his lips and nodded. "Looks like a terrified woman tried to exit straight through the closet door, Kate."

"Do you need me up here anymore, guys?" Kate asked as she backed further away.

Mulrooney shook his head. "No, Katie, not unless you brought a bigass sewing kit."

* * *

When forensics finally arrived, Mulrooney gave orders as he and Clarke inspected the crime scene meticulously, maneuvering around the pieces of corpse. There were no signs of forced entry. One wall was lined with cabinets that contained a television, a DVD, an old VCR, and a rare book collection. Nothing had been disturbed. A telephone, a lamp, a digital clock radio, and two remote controls lay atop the nightstand. Mulrooney, while mentally photographing every detail, noticed that the mattress had drawn most of the blood to the victim's side of the bed.

"Rest in pieces, Doc," he whispered, giving in to his old habit of talking to the victims whenever he felt anxious. The sour taste in his throat indicated that his anxiety level was rising. Not a bad thing, he reminded himself. In Iraq he had learned that a healthy dose of anxiety kept one's senses on maximum alert. His sergeant had repeatedly cautioned his platoon, "A fool acts without fear, but a brave man acts in spite of it." *Semper Fi*, Mulrooney mentally saluted, determined to be nobody's fool. As he stared at Dr. Connolly's gaping mouth, he took out a tube of Blistex and coated his sunburned lips before continuing.

While Clarke inspected the corpse, Mulrooney focused on a pile of clothes on the floor near the blood pool. In the pocket of a pair of Armani trousers, Mulrooney found Connolly's wallet with three hundred dollars hidden in the inside flap. An 18 karat gold money clip was empty. "See if you can lift a print off this money clip," he directed a technician.

After further inspection Mulrooney discovered a small glass ampoule wrapped in cotton knitting in a back pocket of the trousers. He held it aloft for Clarke to see. "Lookee here, partner," he said with a raised brow.

"Poppers!" Clarke exclaimed. "I haven't seen those in awhile. Either the doc had a heart problem, or a hard-on problem."

"That's not his worst problem," Mulrooney mumbled as he turned to inspect the blood on the dresser. Judging by the blank area in the pattern, the perp had taken much of the blood spatter. The blood pattern indicated the doctor had been lying on his right side when killed. The victim's body must have somehow been turned and the intestine yanked out afterward. But how...and why, he wondered?

Above the dresser was an etching of Duke Ellington at his piano. A drop of Dr. Scott Connolly's blood was still clinging to the flesh fold beneath the Duke's eye like a bloody tear. Mulrooney leaned closer to read the title of the etching: *Mood Indigo,* the name of a tune Ellington had composed for the film, *Anatomy of a Murder.* The irony didn't escape him.

"Hey, buddy," Clarke called, interrupting Mulrooney's thoughts, "did you notice how the Duke's eyes follow you like the friggin' Mona Lisa?"

"So do the doc's," Mulrooney grunted as he moved to the dressing table on the south wall. He gazed at an angora robe that was draped over the vanity chair. Several birthday cards were jammed in the edge of the mirror and a box of face powder rested on a silver tray. Mulrooney examined a pair of sheer panties and a bra that were in a pile on the table. When he looked up, he saw Clarke grinning.

"Don't you wear lingerie like that?" Clarke teased.

"Only when I'm on a date with your dad," Mulrooney jabbed back. Mulrooney welcomed the easy repartee. Their sparring was a verbal barrier against the savagery. He was still staring at the vanity when something else caught his attention. Reaching down, he pried a photo out from under the opaque glass top. It was a snapshot of a man lounging near a hotel pool. The man had dark good looks and an easy smile. "MY LOVE ALWAYS, SAM" was written across the back of the photo in bold, assured handwriting. Mulrooney handed the snapshot to his partner. Clarke let out a low whistle as he bagged it into evidence.

Mulrooney then turned his gaze to a thin film of dust on one area of the vanity. It struck him as odd that the dust was much thicker around the area where the panties lay. He wondered if the perp had been looking for something specific. Or was it something very personal? "See what you can make of this, Smokey," he said to Clarke.

He watched as Clarke snorted several times to clean his nasal passages before bending down to inhale the dust particles near the lingerie. Mulrooney waited expectantly, knowing his partner had the nose of a bloodhound. One time Clarke had even sniffed out a suspect because of the type of alcohol on his breath–Guinness.

"It's sure not the face powder," Clarke pronounced. "It's drywall."

"Drywall? Damn, you're good, Smokey!" Mulrooney said.

"That's what Karen tells me," Clarke grinned as he checked his watch. "And she's keeping my spot warm. I'm going down to wrangle some witnesses. You ridin' shotgun?"

"In a minute," Mulrooney answered. "I need some air."

After Clarke left, Mulrooney stepped out onto the deck. He could see the Queen Mary, illuminated by lights from the offshore oil islands as she reclined majestically in the water. The ship was a tranquil contrast to the din of the police chopper hovering overhead like a mutant praying mantis. Viewing the surroundings, Mulrooney noted that the bungalow next door was too far away to make a safe jump, and the two-story Connolly home offered no footholds for climbing. The assailant must have left through the front door, balls to the wind, he figured... unless the killer had never left the premises at all.

Mulrooney sucked in the ocean air and tried to scrape the taste of death from his tongue with his teeth. He was craving a drink for the first time in ages, but he hadn't touched alcohol since his heart had given out on him. Thus, there would be no wasting away in Margaritaville tonight.

After unconsciously glancing over his shoulder into the shadows, Mulrooney took another look at the strewn remains of Doctor Scott Connolly. He sensed that the killer's intimate contact with the victim had been motivated by more than hatred or passion. The rage was almost palpable. As he headed down to the den to join Clarke, he once again felt like a kid descending the dark cellar stairs into the abyss.

Chapter 2

When Mulrooney strode into the den, he knew immediately which woman was the widow. Lauren Brandeis Connolly was sitting on a straight chair, leaning on its arms for support. There were streaks of blood on her face, and strands of her tawny shoulder-length hair were matted to the right side of her face. Her eyes were unfocused and her body shook uncontrollably. Lauren clutched an afghan that was draped around her back. Her bare feet grasped the floor as though attached by ground wires.

"Mrs. Connolly?" Mulrooney said as he walked slowly toward her. Lauren showed no sign of response other than to lick her lips as if tasting something unfamiliar.

Mulrooney glanced toward the door of the den to see if Clarke had come back in. Usually their routine was for Mulrooney to calmly question the suspects before Clarke came in to apply the thumbscrews. After seeing Lauren Connolly, Mulrooney knew Clarke would really have to muster up some attitude to follow up as the heavy on this one.

While he waited for Lauren to relax, Mulrooney studied a collection of photos of Lauren in some jungle outpost. In each image she looked strong and self-assured. Now it seemed that her stunned expression was the only thing holding her beautiful face together.

A striking woman sat next to Lauren clutching her hand. Mulrooney observed faint blood stains on the woman's jeans and on the front of her beige linen jacket. Her hair reminded Mulrooney of sunsets in Puerto Vallarta. Its fiery color contrasted with the serenity of her patrician features–regal nose, wide-set eyes and full lips.

"I understand your name is Anya Gallien?" he asked Lauren's friend, unconsciously running one hand through his dark curly hair.

"Yes, I am Anya Gallien," she said quietly.

"And you were the first to arrive to assist Mrs. Connolly?"

"That's right, I was here. I just happened to be in the neighborhood." Mulrooney caught a hint of irony in her voice. Before he could reply, Anya cut him off. "And you want to know why I was in the neighborhood at 12:30 A.M., no?"

Mulrooney noted her odd word placement. Was that a slight accent he detected? He said nothing, knowing his silence would provoke her to continue. Anya played neatly into his hand.

"Around midnight I drove through the parking area at Alamitos Bay and I saw Lauren on her boat at the dock. She was working... she's a writer, you know. I didn't want to disturb her, so I decided to drop by here a bit later because I wanted to be the first to wish her Happy Birthday. It's today." Anya placed her hand against her chest and took a deep breath. "She was running out just as I arrived, and she was hysterical. After she told me what had happened, I brought her inside and called the police."

"So she wasn't expecting you?" he asked. While Mulrooney stared at Anya, he eyed a birthday card sticking out of a flap in the purse at her feet. There were three balloons hand-drawn on the envelope.

"No, I've been in Mexico. I got back around seven o'clock, and I wanted to surprise her. That's why I brought the card I assume you have already noticed," she replied without averting her eyes, "and the bag of confetti."

"Mexico? I just got back from Mexico myself," Mulrooney responded in his most pleasant party voice. "Nice, huh?" When he saw Anya let down her guard a bit, he fired another question at her. "If you weren't planning a little get-together, why do you suppose the stereo was on when she went to bed? I'm just trying to understand the sequence of events, Ms. Gallien."

"Obviously she must have forgotten to turn it off," Anya responded. "She loves music, especially Gershwin. May I put on another CD to calm her?" She glanced at Lauren, who sat motionless.

"I'd prefer that you not touch anything else, Ms. Gallien," Mulrooney firmly instructed.

He then squatted to face Lauren and spoke very quietly. "Mrs. Connolly, I'm Detective Tim Mulrooney." When he held forth his hand, she tentatively offered hers. He noticed that Lauren's teeth had punctured her lower lip, which was now beginning to swell. Dry blood discolored her broken fingernails; and her left arm, which protruded limply from under the afghan, was coated with blood. When he shook her hand, he stroked her palm with his fingertips. No signs of abrasions or indentation from force.

"Before I get a complete statement from you, Mrs. Connolly, I need to know if you saw anything that might help us with our investigation."

Lauren abruptly pulled her hands back under the afghan just as the L.B.P.D. helicopters passed overhead. The noise from their engines jolted Lauren's body like artillery blasts. Anya took Lauren in her arms, shielding her from the racket as the chopper lights pummeled the windows with a strobe-like effect.

Lauren suddenly startled them both by speaking. "I didn't see anything. It all happened before I got home," she said in a voice that sounded like radio static.

As Mulrooney leaned in, he smelled wine on her breath. "Were you drinking tonight, Mrs. Connolly? I know it's your birthday."

"I had some wine on the boat...not much," she whispered.

"How much would you estimate you had?"

Anya held up her hand and interrupted, "Detective-".

"I'm not addressing you," Mulrooney snapped, rendering Anya silent. "Mrs. Connolly how much alcohol did you drink?"

"Just a little. I had to drive home."

"What time did you get home?"

"Shortly after midnight," she replied mechanically. "I went upstairs and undressed in the bathroom. Then I showered."

"Did you enter the bedroom prior to that?"

"No."

"So you left your clothes in the bathroom?"

"Yes," she stammered, "and when I stepped into the bedroom for the first time... I... I got into bed in the dark-"

Mulrooney waited as her voice trailed off. "And you didn't turn on the light?"

Lauren hesitated then shook her head.

"You're sure?"

Lauren nodded and stared straight ahead, now engrossed in her own silent horror movie.

"If you had not yet entered the bedroom and you undressed in the bathroom, then how did your underwear get to the vanity?"

Lauren continued to stare without focus. Finally she whispered, "They were already there. I wasn't wearing panties this evening."

While he plastered a professional look of disinterest across his face, Mulrooney's mind drifted to places he knew he shouldn't go. He buried himself in the notes Kate had given him before he continued. When he looked up, Anya was pressing a cup of water into Lauren's hand. Both were right-handed, he noted.

Suddenly the cup slipped from Lauren's grasp and spilled down Anya's leg. While Anya dried herself with her sleeve, Lauren sank back into the safety of her chair, completely unaware that the afghan had slipped off one shoulder, exposing her naked body.

Mulrooney made a mental note of the blood stains on her body while trying not to stare at her firm figure and long legs. At ease, Marine, he admonished himself as he looked away. If nothing else, Mulrooney was still an officer and a gentleman.

He could feel the perspiration rush to his temples as Lauren made no attempt to cover her exposed body. She remained completely still like a delicate wax figure. Anya's attention was still elsewhere, so Mulrooney respectfully averted his eyes and reached out to wrap the afghan tightly around Lauren.

"Thank you very much, Detective Mulrooney," Lauren whispered softly. "You're a kind man."

Just as his breath caught in the back of his throat his defense system kicked in. Mulrooney quickly turned his attention back to Anya, who was rubbing her fingertips together as if saying an invisible rosary. "May I take Lauren to my home now?" Anya asked. "She needs rest."

Before Mulrooney could respond, Clarke strode into the room and called Mulrooney aside. As Mulrooney listened intently to Clarke's report, he studied Anya's face. He abruptly changed demeanor and turned back to the women. "Ladies, if you don't mind, we'd like to take you to the station for further questioning."

Anya bolted upright, "I certainly DO mind! Can't this wait?" she glared.

From what Mulrooney could see, Anya Gallien was one tight coil. "It would be much easier for us all, Ms. Gallien," he condescended. "You see, my partner was outside, and he found some witnesses who saw you run down here from Division Street just as Mrs. Connolly exited the house. However, your car is parked right out front. Apparently you had been in the neighborhood for a while prior to coming to her aid." He raised one brow and added, "...No?"

Anya flushed at his direct attack. She unconsciously rubbed a spot behind her left ear. "So am I under arrest?"

"At this point we only wish to question you further," Clarke said tersely.

"Does Lauren have to go, too?"

"Yes," Clarke said. "Officer Axberg will help Mrs. Connolly dress." He signaled to Kate before turning to Lauren. "Can you manage, Mrs. Connolly?"

Lauren nodded, but continued to sit.

"Officer Axberg," Mulrooney said formally as he pulled Kate aside, "please call for a female photographer to get photos of Mrs. Connolly first. And we'll need close-ups of her breasts."

"Yes, sir, breast shots."

When he caught Kate's sardonic smile, he made a face then looked away. "Purely professional, I assure you," he whispered.

Mulrooney watched Anya with interest as she helped Lauren stand up. Anya's willingness to confront him suggested a sense of fearlessness. Or was it recklessness? When she tossed her mane of red hair, she reminded him of Ginger on the old TV show, "Gilligan's Island."

But it was Lauren Connolly who intrigued him most. Even in shock, she moved with the grace of a deer. There was something warm and solid about her, something that intrigued him. He quickly checked himself. "Wait for the photographer and then please dress," he directed.

As Anya guided Lauren toward a downstairs guest room, Lauren stopped to adjust the afghan over her bare shoulder. She sighed before looking back at Mulrooney. Suddenly Lauren dropped the afghan to the floor. She stood with her naked back to him and lifted her arms away from her body as if to be free of the blood-stained cover. Anya noted Mulrooney's stunned expression before leading her friend into the bedroom. Kate hustled in behind them and closed the door.

Mulrooney stood for a moment, staring at the door, knowing that on the other side was a woman - a potential suspect - who had gotten under his skin. He shook his head and then focused on his work.

Sanders had returned and was standing near the doorway next to Clarke. "Sanders, please find out the asking price on the bungalow next door with the For Sale sign," Mulrooney directed. Sanders shot him a puzzled look then dutifully retreated.

"A house in this 'hood?" Clarke snorted, "are you on the take?"

"A guy can dream, can't he?"

"Gotta sleep first. Let's ride, pal."

As they exited, Mulrooney noticed the balloons in the living room had worked loose from the bottle of Cristal. They were now hugging the ceiling, trying vainly to escape. "Happy Birthday, Lauren Connolly," he said grimly. "Some sick bastard threw you one hel-luva surprise party!"

Chapter 3

Mulrooney's eyes were burning. He knew he was getting too old to pull all-nighters. He seldom drank caffeine, but he knew he could use a double espresso today. After he and Clarke had extensively questioned Lauren Connolly and Anya Gallien, the two detectives has combed the area for witnesses. When he had finally arrived back at his small clapboard bungalow near Cal State twenty hours later, he had lain awake mulling over the case before he met Clarke again at the autopsy of Dr. Connolly at 8:00 A.M.

The prompt autopsy was unexpected, but there had been no back-up of corpses at the coroner's office to delay attention to the late doctor. The timing was unusual for a place that Mulrooney often credited for hosting more stiff bodies than an Irish Pub on payday.

As a result of his nonstop movement, Mulrooney was now too wired to sleep, so he headed back to Belmont Shore. When he veered off on Livingston to

Second Street, he noticed the familiar road sign, "Belmont Shore Welcomes You." An imaginative street artist had already tagged it with a neon-colored skull and knife-like crossbones. Obviously, the grim news had already hit the streets.

Mulrooney parked in front of Surf's Up and went inside. The restaurant always cheered him with its decor of old surfboards and fixtures the colors of beach umbrellas. On one wall was a huge mural of Belmont Shore in the 1950's, replete with grinning Texaco servicemen. Was there ever a time that carefree he wondered. Suspended overhead was a stuffed shark with painted bloody teeth. That shark had better have a solid alibi he mused as he took a counter seat.

After Mulrooney nodded to several locals, he pulled out his folders to discourage conversation. He wanted time alone to relax and to organize the thoughts that ricocheted like buckshot through his sleep-deprived brain.

"Well, it's Tim-sum-and-then-some," the waitress called as she sauntered up with a coffee cup and a pot of decaf.

"Good morning, Sophie," Mulrooney smiled.

"How's my favorite hunka dick?" Sophie laughed bawdily as she leaned her ample frame on the counter, flashing her assets like a midshipman's ring. She loved to flirt shamelessly, but all her customers knew the ol' girl was a devoted wife. Five times over.

"The paper says you and Clarke got yourselves a grisly case," she said as she pulled a chewed pencil out of her upswept straw-gray hair as if plucking a feather.

"Yep. I'm gonna need the high octane brew today," Mulrooney grunted as he waved away the decaf, "and a breakfast burrito."

"Maybe I should leave you the pot," she laughed as she reached for a pot of regular. "You look like you've been partying with the Stones. You better get yourself some sleep before I trade you in for something that's still breathing - not that that's a requirement." She shot him a devilish grin before strolling off.

Mulrooney looked at himself in the mirror above the service bar. He had often been told he looked like Harrison Ford. More like a rehab drop-out he thought. He took a large swig of coffee and laid out the preliminary autopsy report.

Since the moment Mulrooney had begun the investigation, everything felt out of sync to him, like when the dialogue in a film didn't match the characters' movements. That always pissed him off. This was pissing him off, too.

Currently Anya Gallien and Lauren Connolly were the only people under suspicion, but he and Clarke had barely begun the investigation. Unfortunately, the bonehead mayor and the chief were already pressing them to make a fast arrest.

Mulrooney winced as he thought of the meeting he had with the chief and Mayor Charles Howe directly following Connolly's autopsy. Mulrooney and the mayor had been at odds since Detective Carlos Atilla had publicly accused Mulrooney of being a racist, the flavor-of-the-month tactic used to call another officer's integrity into question. Everyone who had been familiar with the situation knew the bogus allegations were motivated by Atilla's personal animosity toward Mulrooney. Mayor Howe had inflamed the situation by pontificating about Mulrooney to the press in order to flaunt his politically correct image. It was also no coincidence that Detective Atilla's brother had been a major contributor to Howe's mayoral campaign. Since the incident Mulrooney could barely sit in the same room with Howe. Or Atilla.

While he sipped his coffee, Mulrooney became even more agitated as he thought about the racism accusations. Hell, Clarke was his partner and also his best friend. And Clarke was black. Mulrooney didn't hate Latinos either...just Atilla. Atilla was a mean cop. He was known to fire his weapon with as little provocation as he fired off his big mouth, which is why Mulrooney had nicknamed him "Atilla-the-Gun." Now Atilla was trying desperately to move in on Mulrooney's territory, and Mulrooney wanted to send Atilla packing back to his former division, or back under whatever rock the slime bag called *mi casa.*

Mulrooney sighed and tried to concentrate on his notes. As he gnawed on a calloused knuckle, he reviewed the facts: After the coroner's investigator had taken the doc's liver temperature reading at the crime scene he had set the time of death between 11:15 P.M. and 12:15 A.M. Earlier that evening, a witness had overheard the couple arguing at 7:30 P.M., at which time Lauren had left the house. She went to her boat at the Alamitos Bay Marina, a refuge she used as an office to do her freelance writing.

Mulrooney recalled the slow, almost robotic way in which Lauren had related the evening's events when she gave her detailed statement at the station. She claimed she had called home at 11:55 P.M. to smooth things over with her husband and to let him know she was coming home. Scott had sounded groggy, but at least he did answer the phone. Mulrooney concluded that if her recall of the events was accurate, then the estimated time of death had definitely been narrowed.

Anya Gallien had confirmed Lauren's alibi, swearing again that she had seen her friend on the boat around midnight. Mulrooney had maintained a necessary degree of skepticism until an investigation at the marina turned up a corroborating witness. Mr. Armstrong, a colorful, lascivious old duffer living on a boat in a slip adjacent to Lauren's, had reluctantly admitted to Clarke that he had continually "glanced at" Lauren Connolly most of the evening from his boat. He confirmed that she had left at midnight and she had appeared to be sober.

According to Lauren's account, she then returned home, poured another glass of wine, and showered. She finished her wine as she dried her hair. After she returned the glass to the kitchen, she went upstairs and crawled into bed to discover her slaughtered husband.

Anya, however, had experienced a sudden shift in recall. She claimed she had left the marina and arrived at the crime scene just past midnight. Although she knew Lauren was not there, she had decided to wait around to wish Lauren a Happy Birthday. She finally remembered some forgotten details: Having already parked, she had decided to walk to Midnight Espresso for a cappuccino at approximately 12:05 A.M. When she returned some twenty minutes later to Lauren's house, she walked into a horror show.

Mulrooney figured it was definitely possible to walk from the Connolly home to the coffee house in seven to eight minutes. Anya said she had a habit of scalloping Styrofoam cups with her thumbnail. She also recalled having tossed her cup into the trash, where it was later located. Interestingly enough, one possible witness had also been found.

However, Mulrooney was still bothered by several details. Of at least twenty people at the coffee house that night, only one person remembered seeing Anya–at around 12:15 A.M. But the male witness admitted he had been trashed ever since the basketball game earlier in the evening and couldn't even remember who had won the game.

Mulrooney circled 12:15 A.M. on his pad and did some mental calculations. Anya could be telling the truth. It would be tough to off a guy, get home, clean up, return to the scene and park, then walk down for a soothing cup of java in just twenty minutes, which was the amount of time that would have passed since Lauren allegedly last spoke to her husband. And thus far, Anya's prints had not been found anywhere in the house other than where she remembered being after bringing Lauren back inside.

Mulrooney recalled Anya's frank response when Clarke had asked her why she had taken Lauren back into the house, considering that a brutal assailant might still be on the premises. "The murderer had left," Anya explained matter-of-factly, "or Lauren would not have gotten out alive, would she?"

Nonetheless, something told Mulrooney that Anya knew more than she was letting on. He rubbed his brow and reached for his coffee just as Sophie set his breakfast in front of him.

Mulrooney had been ravenously hungry but was now feeling nauseous. He couldn't get the smell of death out of his sinuses, and his body wasn't used to the caffeine rush. "Better switch me back to decaf, Sophie," he said. "I feel like a herd of ponies took a dump in my stomach."

"Ah, I remember when detectives were real men," she teased.

"And now waitresses are," he shot back.

As Sophie made a face, Mulrooney flipped to his autopsy notes. There had been one wound, entrance point midline at the base of the sternum. The weapon had entered the xiphoid process then extended downward. It severed the abdominal aorta before exiting two inches right of the midline. According to the coroner, who had about as much spark as his clients, death probably occurred within minutes of the assault due to exsanguination. Mulrooney

29

thought about the curve of the wound relative to the position of the body. He jotted in the margin: *Left-handed assailant.*

The robotic coroner had estimated the knife blade to be 5" long. Entrance and exit points indicated a serrated tip, double-edged blade, extremely sharp, such as a skinning knife. Bone fragments from a chipped rib indicated some strength behind the thrust. The wound was clean and expertly executed. There was no indication of struggle, probably due to the victim's altered state. The M.O. was an interesting choice. A slash across the throat would have been just as effective. And infinitely easier. It was apparent that this killer really enjoyed his work. Or was it *her* work?

The toxicology report would take some time, but the coroner was sure four partially dissolved pills in the doctor's stomach were Percodan. The intact state of two of the pills indicated ingestion very close to time of death. The lab had already identified the tobacco residue from the doc's shirt pocket as reefer. But the most interesting find in what was left of the doctor's stomach was an undissolved worm, bitten in half. Mulrooney had immediately recognized the hapless agave worm. He had swallowed a few too many in his day from the bottom of a tequila bottle.

The doctor had obviously found some time to party on his last night alive. The lab was running D.N.A. tests on several black hairs found on his clothes which suggested companionship beyond that of tequila and the assorted pharmaceuticals. Connolly was so medicated he probably never knew what hit him. However, Mulrooney knew that Lauren would never be able to forget the horror she found in bed that night. He remembered Lauren's vacant account of how she crawled into bed in the dark, reached for Scott, and unwittingly thrust her hand inside his gut pulling his viscera on top of her. Mulrooney shuddered involuntarily.

He examined the police photos of Lauren. There was a heavy blood coating on her left arm. No spatter pattern. As he studied a close-up of her breasts, he wondered if a nipple had specific I.D. markers. Mulrooney scribbled a note for Annette in Fingerprint to lift a print of Lauren's nipple to run a match with prints from the closet door. He also imagined how in a parallel universe Annette would need his attentive assistance on breast detail.

He abruptly shoved Lauren's photos back in the file. As he pushed his partially eaten burrito aside, a familiar voice boomed in his ear. "Mulrooney, shouldn't you be out humpin'?"

Fuck me, Mulrooney thought. He knew without looking up that the voice was Atilla's. Atilla spoke with the hit-and-run emphasis of a sports announcer. The solid, ruddy-skinned detective plopped down on a counter seat and whistled to Sophie as if calling a dog. While Mulrooney pulled out his wallet he avoided looking at Atilla, who always looked like he was sweating Vaseline.

"Sophie, can I get a check, please?" Mulrooney pleaded as she approached.

"Of course. And what can I get you today, Detective Atilla?" Sophie asked in a saccharin voice.

"Coffee, lotsa cream, and a sticky bun to go," Atilla ordered curtly before turning his charm on Mulrooney. "You and Clarke better solve the Connolly case fast. This one's hotter than a jalapeno Pop Tart. The doc was very well-known."

"Tell me something I don't know, Atilla," Mulrooney snapped. It was all he could do to be civil to Atilla. Besides accusing Mulrooney of racism, Atilla had mouthed off to the media about Mulrooney "crossing boundaries with broads" after Atilla had witnessed an embarrassing incident outside the station involving Mulrooney and a woman. The prick had then spread the gossip without knowing any of the details. Mulrooney had never set the matter straight because the situation was very private. And very painful. It would have required more conversation than he ever wished to have with Atilla, or with the media.

Sophie brought Atilla his food and left two checks. When Atilla put down the exact change, leaving no tip, Mulrooney pulled out an extra bill and slammed it onto the counter.

Atilla shrugged and stood up to leave. "I've been talking to Chief Clemente about me coming in on your case," he announced.

Mulrooney glared at him. "I'd chew the hair off an orangutan's ass before I'd let that happen, Atilla," he snapped.

"You might want to re-think that. Another fuck-up could cost you your shield." Atilla picked up his food and turned to leave.

Mulrooney's face was burning, but he watched in silent anger as Atilla sauntered out. "Fuckin' gargoyle!" he mumbled as the door slammed behind Atilla.

Sophie shook her head as she scooped the money off the counter. "Everyone says you're the best detective L.B.P.D. has ever had. So why do you put up with his crap, Tim?"

"He'll get his due, Sophie. All in good time."

"That *would* be a good time," she smiled. "Before you go, I've got somethin' to tell you that you may find of interest. I saw Doc Connolly in here last fall. He was with his wife's girlfriend. You know, that sexy redhead, Anya Gallien. They all used to come in here a lot, but that night it was just him and her. No wifey."

"Did you see or hear anything?"

"That's why I'm talkin' to ya, boy genius. I wasn't waitin' on them that night, but at one point in the evening Anya nearly mowed me down when she suddenly jumped up from the doc's booth. She was glaring at him. I heard her say, 'I'll kill you if you go back to Lauren after this.' She sure had a bee up her butt."

"You're positive she said that, Sophie?"

"You'd question my memory? When was the last time I screwed up your order?" Sophie fluffed her hair for emphasis then continued. "And I've got more for you, doll. Several months after that, I was loading some goodies onto the pastry racks when I noticed

Dr. and Mrs. Connolly sitting on the bench up front waiting for a table. I got a creepy feeling like I sometimes get. I looked out the window and I saw Anya standing there, purple in the neon light. She stared at the Connollys for the longest time, like some kind of stalker. It gave me the willies. That's it, but it stayed in my mind."

Mulrooney leaned forward and kissed her on the cheek. "Sophie, you're just what I needed today."

"I'm what every man needs every day," she grinned. "Gotta go. I've got an order up. Take care, doll."

Mulrooney grabbed his papers and walked out into the sunlight. He breathed deeply but even the sea air couldn't lift the weight that was pressing down on his chest.

Chapter 4

Trenton, New Jersey
Same Day

Clarence Smolley wadded the greasy C-notes into a large ball. "Money well spent, my man," he told his buyer. "This thumb drive is the hottest thing I've ever scored. You ain't never seen me though, man, or you're history. I'm talking PAST TENSE. You got it?"

Clarence waited for the fat man named Scab to nod before he continued. "Somebody big at the top is makin' a lotta noise. I'm told the chick they got on camera is some fat-cat dude's private property. So I suspect this is really worth something."

"So this comes from Long Beach like the others?" Scab asked.

"Yeah. It came from my man, Flint, but now his connection is tryin' to recall these babies. They're hot motherfuckers."

35

Scab picked his nose then wiped his hand on his pants. "Righteous, man," he grunted. "You gonna take time to check out one of the girls in the back before you head back to Cali-hornya?" Scab laughed at his own joke.

"I ain't got time to burn in this fuckin' dump."

"Jus' thought you might want to see the new girl. Goes by Rikki," Scab said, licking his lips for effect. "She's hot. Room four."

"Ummm, Rikki-Licky. That name does have promise." Clarence checked his Rolex. "What the fuck, I got time. Gimme some fives."

While Scab opened the money box, Clarence thought about Flint, his Long Beach friend who had followed through on his promise to set Clarence up for a rosy-assed future by letting him distribute porn for him on the East coast. But apparently Flint had pissed off his connection, and now he was desperate to get the merchandise back. But there was no way Clarence was giving the zip drives back now, no matter who was bent out of shape. In two hours he'd be off to Florida with a suitcase full of cash. He grinned. *Scorin' in the free world, Clarence my man.*

After Clarence accepted a stack of bills from Scab, he turned and walked down the dimly lit passageway to the back. The light from the bare yellow bulb overhead cast ominous shadows on the dark paneled walls. He could smell booze and sweat and semen. He sucked in the smell through wide nostrils savoring its pungency.

Clarence slowed his pace in an effort to prolong his arousal. While he stood outside booth number four, he relished the growing pressure in his groin. When he felt as though he might explode, he stepped inside the small booth.

The seedy room was dimly lit, but as his eyes adjusted to the darkness he spotted a bench with a box of tissues and a plastic waste basket nearby. He closed the door behind him and paused for a moment before unzipping his pants. He was going to enjoy this bigtime.

When he began pumping bills into the machine in the booth, lights came up behind a glass partition. He could see into the cage, which was bare except for the worn leopard-print carpet and the shiny pole in the center. He ran his tongue under his lip. *Come on, sweet thing...come to Clarence.*

After several seconds, Rikki entered through a small door in the back of the cage. Her long bleached hair caressed her breasts as she walked toward the pole and squinted out toward Clarence. He backed into the shadows where he couldn't be seen.

"Whatdaya like?" she purred into the darkness.

"Don't talk," he said while she adjusted her G-string. "Just dance, Rikki. And pleasure yourself while you dance."

"That'll be extra," she cooed. "Put twenty bucks through the slot if you want it, hon. I'll make it real nice for you."

"Show me what you can do, Rikki. Maybe I got even more than that for ya, baby."

An old Donna Summer tune suddenly throbbed from the speaker mounted over the door. Rikki aimed a crooked smile into the darkness, and then she began to move slowly, sensually. She draped one long leg around the pole and arched her back as her body fell backward like a rag doll. Then with one movement of her pelvis she pulled slowly upright while grasping the pole with her thighs. She writhed against the pole and swung her hair as she felt the pole between her legs. Finally she thrust her bare buttocks toward the glass.

Clarence licked his lips. *Bull's-eye, babe! Ahhh, an ass I could grease and ride.*

Rikki grasped the pole with her hard thighs and began a rocking motion. She closed her eyes and let the friction lead her slowly into her own world of pleasure.

Clarence groaned as he stroked himself. *Don't rush it, man. She's fuckin' juicy.* He loved the way her crimson pasties with the black tassels shimmered in the light. They reminded him of Shriner hats, the way they swayed and bobbled. *Dance, Rikki-Licky, dance. Dance for Clarence.*

Rikki was really getting into her performance now. She slipped her hand inside her G-string. Her lips parted while her eyes remained tightly closed. Her face was flushed and the sweat on her forehead glistened in the pink light of the booth.

Clarence was hip to the routine. *Don't quit on me now, Rikki.* He quickly reached into his pocket for his roll of bills and pulled a C-note out from under the rubber band. "Keep going, baby," he said, shoving the bill through the slot. "Don't stop."

Outside the booth, footsteps silently approached. In the shadows of the hallway a grisly heap of carved flesh lay on the floor in a pool of blood. Scab lay on his back, struggling in vain to hold his guts in. He could smell his own viscera. His vacant eyes watched in horror as the intruder's feet moved slowly toward Rikki's cubicle. Scab's assailant stopped to twist the light bulb overhead, plunging the hall into near darkness. As Scab struggled for his last breath his killer turned back to observe him. He smiled at the grisly carnage with satisfaction. Then the stranger quietly turned the knob on door number four.

In the cubicle, the pressure Clarence was feeling was delicious, overwhelming. His stroked himself and closed his eyes as the sensation crawled over him covering all his senses with steel wool. *Now, Rikki-Licky. Now, baby.*

He didn't see the reflection in the glass as the intruder soundlessly entered the booth. The cold eyes watched as Clarence writhed in ecstasy.

Here it comes, Rikki. Clarence resumed his stroking motion slowly, deliberately, his closed lids forever sealing the image of Rikki into his catalogue of erotic fantasies.

The steel-like eyes watched Clarence from the shadows. Slowly the gloved hand moved toward Clarence's throat.

"Here it comes, honey," Clarence panted. "I'm the pole between your hot thighs."

"What you are is a dead man, Clarence," the voice whispered in his ear. The quick hand yanked Clarence's neck back, stretching his esophagus like an accordion. "You and your friend Flint shouldn't have fucked with us."

Clarence opened his eyes as he struggled to escape from his attacker's powerful grip. The reflection of his assailant was superimposed over Rikki in double exposure. The stranger smiled with satisfaction while Rikki humped the pole wildly. The Shriner hats shot upright as Rikki arched her back and groaned with her own private satisfaction. All at once, the black tassels vibrated with the rush of her release.

"Lovely," the intruder said as he struck. The sharp knife sliced across Clarence's throat, opening it like a bloody gill. The gill sucked frantically at the foul air in the booth as the wound dropped open into a lecherous smile. The killer then opened Clarence's gut. The last of Clarence's life erupted as Rikki writhed against the pole.

Rikki continued to dance, not knowing she was performing for the very last time.

Chapter 5

As Lauren sat trance-like in the beautiful garden her fingers mechanically punished the fibers of her black crepe suit. She stared at a small mahogany table with a jade green urn on top. The urn contained the remains of her very dead husband.

Although she had honored her husband's request for cremation upon his death, Lauren shivered involuntarily at the idea of Scott's gruesome reduction to the contents of a jar. To her it was a means of disposal almost as barbaric as his violent death.

She smiled sadly as she remembered an evening long ago when she and Scott had discussed cremation. "Bake me into brownies, and then send them to the IRS," he had stated with a wicked grin. "Tell them I said to 'eat me.'"

She had always been drawn to Scott's humor and boyish appeal, but she had discovered in him a desire for acquisition that nothing could satiate. Until he became a doctor Scott's life had been one of continuous economic struggle. Although Scott fell in love with Lauren, money was always the primary focus of his life, and it had created a painful distance between them.

Eventually Lauren numbed herself with the solitude of the sea. When Scott began spending endless hours supposedly at the office, she had turned to Sam out of loneliness; and her sense of failure and guilt had punished her ever since. Now as Lauren stared at the urn she longed to tell Scott that she had never stopped loving him—not even after Sam came into her life. But it was too late...for so many things.

Anya sat next to Lauren. She stroked Lauren's back with one hand while clutching a rosary in the other. Both sets of parents sat to Lauren's left. Their bodies remained rigidly upright as though the slightest movement might shatter them into pieces.

Lauren watched as each friend or patient of Scott's entered the meditation garden for the brief memorial. Detective Tim Mulrooney stood near the honeysuckle bush silently observing the crowd while Clarke mixed with mourners near the back. The two detectives stood out like vigilant centurions.

"The cops are here," Lauren said to Anya, breaking the silence. As they both looked toward Mulrooney, he smiled and nodded. When his eyes met Lauren's, he adjusted his dark tie. She sensed he was uncomfortable, but she also suspected he would stop at nothing to do his job well. And something told her he was exceedingly good at what he did.

Lauren remembered his treatment of her the night of Scott's death. He had been respectful, but he had also been skillful, subtly returning to each question like a dog with a chew-toy and keeping Lauren slightly on edge. She knew Mulrooney was a skilled hunter, yet it was his gentleness that had both comforted her and disarmed her.

Lauren watched as Mulrooney walked to his car. He spoke to someone in the passenger seat before turning his attention back to Lauren. She was embarrassed when he observed her staring at him. Mulrooney smiled self-consciously and looked the other way. Lauren averted her eyes as she wrestled with her own conflicting emotions. Anya took in every detail of their silent exchange.

* * *

On the opposite side of the memorial garden, Mulrooney and Clarke studied the crowd. From inside Mulrooney's car, Paul, the L.B.P.D. photographer, recorded it all on camera.

"Gorgeous blond," Paul said through the open window as he adjusted his lens.

"Ummm," Mulrooney agreed. "Lauren Connolly–the widow. Still under suspicion.

"Hmmm...who's the redhead with her?"

Clarke spoke as Mulrooney recorded the license number of a late arrival. "Person of Interest. Anya Gallien. Before the Romanian Revolution she was imprisoned for stealing food. A year later she seduced a border guard and then escaped while he grappled with his trousers. Although he fired shots, she made it to the other side. When she realized she'd been shot, she plugged the hole in her shoulder with a sock until she could get help. According to her immigration records, after she was free she tried to get her family out, but it was too late. Her family had been brutally executed as payback."

"That's harsh!" Paul exclaimed.

"Yup, that can twist ya up pretty bad."

Mulrooney watched as Anya hugged Lauren again. "But Anya's unusually devoted to Lauren," he noted, "She's a bit of an enigma, that one."

The men stood quietly while the minister made a few closing comments. As he spoke, he moved his arm back and forth like a chain saw. "The good pastor looks like he's about to auction off the urn," Clarke sneered.

Mulrooney's eyes were elsewhere. A woman in an expensive black suit and matching hat was tentatively making her way through the crowd. A black veil obscured her face and most of her dark hair. "Heads up. Morticia just arrived." Mulrooney watched as the woman moved to the edge of the crowd.

"She looks dodgy," Clarke observed.

"Get some shots of her, Paul," Mulrooney instructed. "I'll check her out." Mulrooney was already moving.

* * *

Anya leaned in closer to Lauren. "Doesn't that minister remind you of Bill Murray?" she asked.

Lauren chuckled, grateful for something to talk about besides the reason they were there. Anya was like a sister to Lauren - something Lauren had never had. As they watched the mourners, Lauren studied Anya. She loved the way one of Anya's front teeth sneaked lazily over the other, forcing her lips into a perpetual, childlike pout. Her exotic face hinted at her European ancestry. But her jaw, although delicate, was often set in defiance.

Lauren had always been in awe of Anya's courage. She knew about her imprisonment and ultimate escape. And she knew her deepest secrets. Lauren remembered Anya's frighteningly simple answer when she had asked what Anya had done upon hearing about the execution of her family.

"I found the guard who shot me, and then I put a bullet through his head and watched him die," Anya had coldly replied. "They were all collectively responsible. They took my family." Anya's hands had clenched into fists just as they were now as they waited for the memorial service to end. Lauren reached out to hold Anya's hand.

"Help me with names," Lauren implored, stroking Anya's hand to relax her fist. Anya had a good memory. She spoke four languages, her accent nearly nonexistent except when she was nervous. "Do you know the woman in black crepe over there?" Lauren asked, indicating the veiled mourner who was now partially obscured by a yellow hibiscus.

45

Lauren noticed that Mulrooney had moved in for a closer look also. The woman moved away as he sidled closer to her.

"She looks like a guy in drag," Anya sneered.

Lauren smiled. Anya could always lift her spirits. Her thoughts drifted back to the night when she had first met Anya at the Marina Towers. Lauren had meandered out of a staid event into a nearby room to look out at the moonlit Pacific. She was there several minutes before she noticed the tall, elegant woman with a set of binoculars trained on the harbor.

"It's so dull in there," Anya told Lauren. "This is much nicer." She offered Lauren the binoculars. As Lauren was scanning the coastline, Anya directed the binoculars toward a hotel room. Lauren burst into laughter when she realized she was staring at two naked men doing the tango. Anya winked and strolled off.

After a few inquiries Lauren found out that Anya was new in town, so she invited her to dinner. To Lauren's delight, Anya showed up with her binoculars and the two women talked and laughed into the morning hours. Over the years they had created an intimate bond of friendship. But in spite of her sharp wit, Anya was not able to hide her sadness at being completely alone in the world. And now Lauren finally understood Anya's all-consuming sense of loss.

Lauren turned from Anya to the scene around her. Many of the mourners were leaving when a tall, well-built man suddenly approached. His piercing eyes were set off by his tan skin and silver-streaked hair. "Lauren," he whispered as he reached out for her.

"Michael!" Lauren shook with emotion as she grasped him and pulled him close to her. "I thought you were still in South America!"

She hadn't seen Michael for months since he left for Buenos Aires on business. They had been friends many years, and Lauren's brief separation from Scott had been hard for Michael, just as it had been for family members and other close friends. Nonetheless, when she and Scott were separated, Michael had stood by her while keeping a respectful distance.

"I just returned," Michael said as he kissed her forehead. "I tried to call you on your birthday. When I couldn't reach you or Anya, I started calling around. I took the first flight out when I heard what had happened. God, Lauren, I just don't know what to say."

"No one does, Michael," she rasped. "It's painful for all of us."

"I'd never let you go through this alone," he smiled sadly.

"I'm so glad you're back. Thank you for coming." As Lauren leaned into Michael she felt the familiar burn in her eyes, but she didn't have enough strength to cry.

Michael turned to Anya and took her hand in his. Anya acknowledged him with a controlled response before pulling away. Lauren found it curious how Michael always seemed to unnerve Anya. Anya had once complained that she felt as if Michael could see right through her. Anya was strong, yet she had obviously met her match in Michael Ryan.

Lauren felt a hand on her back and turned around. "Detective Mulrooney," she said as she took his hand.

"I'm very sorry about your husband, Mrs. Connolly," he said. He gently squeezed Lauren's hand as he turned his gaze on Anya. "Hello, Miss Gallien." Anya nodded then quickly looked away. Mulrooney fixed his gaze on Michael.

"Michael Ryan," Michael said, offering his hand to Mulrooney.

"Tim Mulrooney, L.B.P.D. Do any of you know the woman over there by the hibiscus?" As they all turned to look, the woman pulled her veil closer to her face.

"It's Jackie O. She's here to light the eternal flame," Anya grunted.

Lauren's low rumbling laugh broke the tension. Anya and Michael were chatting quietly when Lauren suddenly froze in place. Her eyes were riveted on the walkway beyond the garden. She abruptly turned and rushed toward the walk as Mulrooney watched her closely.

At the edge of the garden, Lauren paused. Her body trembled as she gazed around the garden in confusion. She was sure she had seen Sam Bennett. Or had she convinced herself it was Sam because she needed him more than anyone right now?

She thought of the photo of Sam underneath her vanity top. The image of Sam's smiling face lingered as she stared blindly at the mourners. She had never meant to fall in love with him. He had been sitting on the dock by the Rusty Pelican one day as she moored the boat. When she walked past him, he silently nodded and took the heavy bag of boating gear from her hand. He tossed it over his shoulder and followed her to her car. "You're beautiful, you know," was all he said as he leveled her with his gaze. He took in every detail of her face before turning abruptly and sauntering off.

She began to plan her work at the boat so she could run into Sam each day. His passion for life and his respectful trust in her opinions made her feel needed. But their intimacy led to a sexual excitement each of them found more and more difficult to resist.

One day on the boat Sam touched her hand as he spoke softly to her. She could see his mouth forming words, but she heard nothing. She was only aware of an all-consuming desire to feel him inside her.

Now as Lauren stood in the garden she could almost feel the weight of Sam's muscular body lowering onto hers. She longed for something familiar, something safe. But would anything ever feel familiar or safe again?

Someone tapped Lauren on the shoulder, interrupting her thoughts. She reeled around and was face to face with Anya. "Are you okay, Lauren?" Anya asked.

Lauren stood perfectly still as she stared at the empty clearing. "Anya," she whispered hoarsely, "please catch up with Detective Mulrooney and tell him I need to talk to him about something important. Get his cell number so I can reach him as soon as I return. I'll come by your place when I get back." She kissed her friend on the cheek. "And Anya, please stay calm. Try not to say anything that will incriminate us."

Lauren watched Anya walk away. She saw Anya unconsciously scratching at the hidden scar behind her left ear as she reluctantly made her way toward Mulrooney and Clarke.

Lauren then returned to Michael's side. "If you want to help me, Michael, please bring the urn and come with me," she said quietly. Michael looked at her curiously. "Please, Michael. I just can't do it." Michael nodded and walked to the table. He hesitated, and then he picked up the urn. Michael cradled Scott Connolly's remains in his arms and followed Lauren out of the garden.

Lauren could see Mulrooney watching every move she made. His eyes, dark and intense in the light, drew her in like a magnet. She noticed him pull his broad shoulders back and hold his head erect. As Lauren closed her eyes against the sun, a slight smile spread across her face.

Chapter 6

Mulrooney sprinted as fast as he could. His heart pounded in his chest as dribbles of sweat ran down his muscular neck. When he lunged and stretched his arm forward, he felt his leg buckle. "Fuh-uck!" he yelled as his abdomen smacked the floor. He heard the ball land one foot beyond where he lay.

He looked up to see Officer Kate Axberg prancing around the racquetball court, arms raised in a victory dance. She then jumped over his prone body and pirouetted before taking a dramatic bow.

"Oh God, I just got my ass kicked by Peter Pan," he grunted as he rolled on his back to massage his knee.

As Kate straddled him she pressed her racquet into his stomach and smiled triumphantly. "Whooped by a girl! Is that dinky piece of shrapnel in your knee still tripping you up, old man?"

"No, it's my long johnson that constantly trips me up," Mulrooney groaned as he struggled to get up.

Kate laughed and offered him a hand. "When are you going to get that thing fixed?"

"Are we still talking about my willie?" he smiled devilishly.

"You wish," she grinned. "Com'on, I'll spring for a drink and a shot of B-12 in the pub after we shower." She ran down the stairs to the showers, two at a jump.

Mulrooney got dressed then waited on the balcony of Murphy's, the restaurant that was part of the Belmont Athletic Club. From there he could catch a breeze and watch the action below on Second Street, which was bustling with shoppers and businessmen in casual garb. *Ah, California— the illusion of endless youth,* he mused.

While he stretched his calf muscles, he mulled over his conversation with the chief earlier that morning before he and Clarke attended the memorial service for Scott Connolly. Chief Clemente admitted he was considering bringing Carlos Atilla in on the investigation. The Mayor's Office and local businessmen were applying intense pressure because no suspects had yet been charged.

According to Clemente, the citizens were fearful of a homicidal maniac in their midst. Based on that, Mulrooney couldn't see how Belmont Shore was any different than the rest of California. He had been able to hold the chief at bay on the Atilla matter temporarily; but this was turning into a political watershed. He knew he had to produce. And fast.

Mulrooney was aware that since being involved in the ugly scene Atilla had witnessed in the station parking lot, he had been on shaky ground. His temples tightened as he remembered the incident. He had not only lost control, but the object of his anger was a woman. He could still see her dark angry eyes, too proud to cry. He forced the painful images back into the dark recesses of his memory and tried to focus his attention on his notes.

The phone records had verified that Dr. Connolly, or someone, had answered the phone the night Connolly was murdered. However, Mrs. Connolly's call from her cell phone on her boat had not been made at 11:55 P.M. as she stated. The call was placed at 11:42 P.M.

Long distance records indicated that another call had come in at 11:58 P.M. They had traced it to Lauren's parents in San Diego, who said they had called to wish their daughter Happy Birthday. Lauren's father was sure it was a sleepy Scott who had answered. He said Scott groaned before the call was suddenly disconnected. When Lauren's parents called back they got a busy signal.

On a hunch, Mulrooney had dug up a valuable piece of information that morning. The Connollys' alarm system connected to the phone line and recorded disconnects as well as calls, even when the alarm was not engaged. Records indicated the phone had been taken off the hook at 11:58 P.M. after the San Diego call. But, it had been replaced in its base at 12:02 A.M. The bonus was that the phone had been wiped clean of prints. Apparently all the perp had needed was four minutes of silence to strike.

If Connolly was killed sometime before Lauren returned, which was just after midnight, the window of opportunity was rapidly narrowing. This sounded a helluva lot like a midnight hit to Mulrooney.

Forensics was still at work on the evidence, but it had been established that the black hairs found on Connolly's clothes were from a high-quality hairpiece. There was also a hair found on the victim's testicles. The coroner determined the victim had ejaculated within an hour of his show stopping demise.

In addition to the Percodan, the doctor also had a lot of Tequila surging through his veins at the time they became fast frozen. The crime team had found Clase Azul Anejo Tequila in Connollys' bar–Montezuma's gold at more than six hundred bucks a bottle–but not the kind of tequila that came with a worm. So where in the hell did Connolly swallow a worm? The doc had certainly depleted himself that evening. No wonder there was no struggle, Mulrooney noted. It's a wonder he wasn't already dead.

Mulrooney looked up to see Kate entering the restaurant. He signaled for a waiter and ordered a root beer for her and a diet Coke for himself. "Have we met?" he slurred in his best bar-drunk impression as he pulled out a stool for her.

Mulrooney smiled at the way Kate's energetic curves were trying to squeeze out of the men's-cut, standard issue police uniform that was wearing her. Her hazel eyes crinkled around the edges as she smiled up at him. He had seen those eyes drill through more than one man twice her size who had been foolish enough to challenge her.

He examined the small 'K' on the key chain she placed on the bar. "Is the 'K' for 'killer'?" he grinned.

"It's for 'kiss my ass,' smart guy." Feigning a shoulder punch, she jabbed his belly playfully.

"Ow! I liked you better out of uniform!"

"You should try taking yours off once in a while," she smiled.

Mulrooney didn't respond. He knew what she meant. He never crossed the line in an attempt to be any more than friends with her. The word games in their long relationship were safe and posed no threat. They both valued their friendship too much.

Mulrooney self-consciously shifted on his stool and looked down at his hands. The white mark from his wedding band had long ago blended into the golden tan of his rugged skin. He inspected the finger, expecting the mark to still be there.

Kate smiled at his gesture and said, "You're definitely one of the good guys, Tim."

When their drinks arrived, he poured her root beer. He drew out the process until the foam swelled above the rim but held.

"Bravo!" she saluted. "Jack-off of all trades, masturbator of none."

"I love it when you get salty."

"I know. So, how were the funeral festivities this morning?"

"Enlightening. Dr. Connolly was in a jar."

"A JAR?"

"Yeah, mayo. You know–a friggin' urn. Very appropriate for a guy who looked like he'd been through a food processor."

"Have you arrested pretty little Mrs. Doctor C. and her sidekick yet?" she asked abruptly.

"Wow, you really cut to the chase, girl!"

"Well, I've been doing a little detective work of my own, so I'm curious."

"Oh, yeah? A Belmont Shore cop like yourself doing some investigative work–you been checking the surf reports?"

"Dr. Connolly used to be my gynecologist."

Mulrooney raised one brow. "Really?"

"Uh-huh. But I switched doctors. He made me uncomfortable."

"Why, Kate?" Mulrooney asked as he set his drink down.

"I'm not sure. He was okay when I first went to him. He was professional and very nice. But he became increasingly distracted, and he was always in a hurry. Sometimes he repeated himself. When he started getting a bit flirtatious, I didn't go back."

"I don't blame you," Mulrooney nodded. "We're questioning his patients and friends now. By the way, does anyone in his office wear a dark wig? Forensics didn't find one in the victim's house."

"Not that I recall. Anyway, my sister works at Metro Mortgage. It seems the Connollys were consistently late on their house payments."

"I know. I pulled their credit reports," he answered, treading slightly on her triumph.

"Ah, but did you know they had never been late until eighteen months ago when the checks started coming in at random, despite the hefty late charges on a mortgage the size of the national debt? When the checks did come in, they were no longer from her personal account but from his."

Kate was one step ahead of him now, and Mulrooney was listening. "I sense there's more."

"Yep. He tried to re-fi their home a year ago, but he was turned down because of his huge debt ratio. He had greatly increased his debt from the time they originally took out their home mortgage and the loans for his practice. It seems he got deeply involved in that never-completed complex down by the docks in Long Beach Harbor. He had no cash flow."

"That hasn't shown up on his credit report yet," Mulrooney nodded, "but I discovered he owes everyone money except me. When some of his loans were called in, he borrowed more money against his medical practice. Lauren Connolly couldn't have been too pleased about the steady depletion of their financial security."

Kate nodded. "Especially if, as the rumor mill in Belmont Shore has it, she was planning to divorce him," she said.

Mulrooney let out a low whistle.

"I'm not officially on the investigation, Tim, so we never had this conversation about the mortgage," Kate grinned. "Or I'll have to dispose of you by violent means."

"Death by racquetball?" Mulrooney grinned.

"Too easy. Com'on, you owe me some dirt. So why haven't you picked up the lethal ladies yet? I saw you fixated on those two beauties."

"Fixated? That's harsh. Like I keep telling the Chief, they had alibis, Kate. Everyone needs to chill and let me do what I do best. Mrs. Connolly claims she was working on her boat until midnight. And an old sea dog named Armstrong who lives on a boat near hers corroborated her alibi. And Anya Gallien was at Midnight Espresso sipping cappuccino. She returned and called for help. Then you and your posse showed up. You know the rest."

"Something isn't right there, Tim." Kate traced the roughened varnish on the counter top with her finger tip.

"I agree." He knew he couldn't underestimate Anya - or Lauren. Although this kind of homicide was not usually perpetrated by a woman, there had been known cases of women offing their victims like bottles of Bud. "I'm just not ready to move in on them yet, Kate."

"Don't take too long, okay? The shore is my beat, you know. These streets are my responsibility. The people here have trust in me, so I have a stake in this also. Besides, Sanders thinks I'm a law enforcement goddess. I don't want to blow my image."

Mulrooney stared at his friend as she flashed a smile. Her teeth reminded him of Chiclets, but he always told her they looked like little headstones. "Why did you do it, Kate - become a cop?"

Kate finished her root beer before she answered. "I couldn't stand the corruption I saw all around me. This is my way of fighting it, one slime ball at a time. How 'bout you, Tim?"

"Same reason. I guess the question is, why do we stay?"

"I'm in it for the satisfaction. But you, it's your life. You need it." Kate stood to leave. "Well, I've got to dash." She paused long enough to call over her shoulder, "Hey, Tim, I hope your work isn't really what you do best."

"It's been too long to remember, Katie," he smirked. Mulrooney picked up his gear and threw a tip on the table. He looked over the balcony railing while Kate exited out onto Second Street below.

As he stared down the street, thoughts began to flutter through his brain like persistent mosquitoes. A row of balloons at a nearby clothing store danced in the breeze, creating a chorus line of Tootsie Roll Pops. When he looked again, a mosquito in his brain suddenly landed.

It had almost gotten by him. Anya Gallien had shown him a birthday card she had planned to give Mrs. Connolly. She had painstakingly drawn colored balloons on it. The balloons were exactly like those attached to the bottle of Cristal. He was sure the champagne must have been a gift to Lauren from Anya also.

Mulrooney remembered that the label was marred. There was also an accumulation of moisture on the silver tray beneath it, an indication that the champagne must have been cold. It couldn't have been there for long. If his hunch was correct, Anya Gallien had been inside the Connolly home earlier that night, prior to the murder. He pulled out his phone and dialed Annette in Fingerprint.

"Lynwood," said the voice on the other end of the line.

"Annette, Tim here. Did you lift any prints off a bottle of Cristal entered as evidence on the Connolly case?"

"Hi. Yeah, we got prints, but we're just now matching them against the elimination prints you got from the ladies. I also lifted an areola print off the widow's breast as you requested. I used food coloring. Got a match. She wanted you there, but I couldn't reach you."

Mulrooney heard muffled laughter. "You're enjoying yourself at my expense, aren't you, Annette?"

"Completely."

"Happy to be of service. I'm going to lunch. Even Doc Connolly's funeral and a racquetball pummeling by Kate Axberg can't ruin my appetite. Call me when you've got something."

He hung up just as another text alert went off. He read the number and dialed immediately, very aware that a pair of binoculars was trained on him from the alley across the street.

Chapter 7

Detective Dave Killackey picked up on the first ring.

"What's up, K'lack'?" Mulrooney kept his attention focused on the adjacent alley as he spoke. He couldn't make out the person with the binoculars who was still watching him from behind a dumpster. Mulrooney moved away from the edge of the balcony and automatically placed his hand on his weapon.

"I'm gathering that info for you on the Trenton, New Jersey, peep show homicides you picked up on the computer. I put in a call to the lead detective as you requested. And I'm checking one of the victim's Long Beach connections for you. I'll call when I've got something. In the meantime, I've also got good news."

"I could use some. Lay it on me."

"Clarke got two more witnesses that turned up about a half hour ago. He's talking to them over near the Connollys' house on Bay Shore right now, so he asked me to call you."

"Thanks. Oh, and check on any local liquor stores who sold a bottle of Cristal in the last month. Get the times of all sales and find out if the champagne was chilled at the point of sale. Start with Morry's Liquor in Naples. It's the closest liquor store to the Connollys' house. It can't be an everyday sale. Tell them it had a torn label. I'm outta here," Mulrooney said. As he hung up, he peered back down at the alley. His tail with the binoculars had disappeared.

* * *

Mulrooney drove down Division Street to Bay Shore and pulled up behind Clarke's car. He automatically grinned when he saw his partner. At 6'3", Mulrooney towered over Clarke, but Clarke's smarts made up for his size. Clarke had an I.Q. higher than L.A.'s smog levels and a dependability quotient to match.

Clarke was sitting on the sea wall with two boys around the age of twelve. Both boys were holding skateboards and wearing the ubiquitous skaters' Rip-n-Dip tee shirts. They appeared to enjoy being the focus of attention of the beach crowd.

"This is Detective Mulrooney," Clarke said to the boys as Mulrooney exited his car. "This is Eric Tierney and Steven Bush. I thought you'd want to ask them a few questions." The boys looked excited at the prospect of being part of a criminal investigation.

Mulrooney shook each boy's hand. Steven, the taller of the two, grinned and glanced across the street at two women who were sitting on a porch at rapt attention. Mulrooney pulled the short boy,

Eric, aside. He noticed how the kid's wedged hair-cut made his head resemble the front end of a Boeing aircraft. "Okay, Eric," Mulrooney asked, scanning Clarke's notes, "how come we're just now hearing from you?"

Eric was obviously nervous. "Well, sir, I didn't know I saw anything important till I told my mom today. She's the one who called the cops." He gestured to one of the women across the street.

"You were smart to tell her, Eric. I understand you saw something the night of the homicide?"

"Yes, sir."

"Can you tell me what you saw?"

"Yes, sir. I saw a white car pull up in front of the house next to the Connolly's house." He pointed in that direction.

"It was a new Beemer."

"A sedan?" He was testing.

"No, sir, a convertible. Cool, huh?"

"Cool. Where were you at the time?"

"We were over there skating." He pointed to the strip of asphalt that led from where they were standing to the tennis courts at the edge of the beach. "It was like, five minutes before twelve, sir. That other detective told me that part was important."

"Yes, it is. How do you know what time it was?"

Eric raised his arm to show his watch. "I have to be in by midnight. I was in bed when everything happened, so I missed all the good stuff," he said with obvious disappointment.

"Too bad. May I see your watch, Eric? Hey, that's cool." Mulrooney looked at the Lakers watch. He then checked his cell phone. Eric's watch was within twenty-six seconds of being accurate. "Did you see the driver of the BMW, son?"

"Just for a second when I skated by. It was that friend of Mrs. Connolly's."

"Which friend?"

"The pretty one. Tall with like reddish, like, kinda longish hair." Eric gestured with his left hand, palm side up, like a pint-sized waiter struggling to balance a shaky tray.

"Do you know the name of Mrs. Connolly's friend?"

"Yeah, it's 'Anya.' I've seen her a lot. She's real nice to me. She said I could drive her car someday." Eric's runaway hand suddenly flipped into a stop position as the pint-sized waiter became a crossing guard. "But not until I get my license, sir. Honest!"

"I believe you, son. Did you see Mrs. Connolly that night?"

"No, sir. But Steven saw Anya after I went in."

"He did?" Mulrooney turned to look at Steven who was leaning against the sea wall, basking in his own importance.

"Yes, sir." Eric looked abandoned as he felt the attention slipping from his grasp.

"You've been a great help, Eric. Maybe you can show me how to skate sometime."

"You're on, dude!" His hand once again flipped heavenward, holding up the sky like Chicken Little.

Mulrooney laughed and shook his head. "Thanks, son. Let me talk to your buddy." He signaled to Steven, who sauntered over as Eric walked back to Clarke.

"Do you want to tell me what you saw when you two boys were out here the night of Dr. Connolly's death, Steven?" Mulrooney asked.

"A new Beemer convertible, white, 6 Series, convertible, a good-looking chick driving. Got here just before midnight, 'round 11:55 P.M.," he rattled off.

"How old are you, son?" Mulrooney asked, trying not to stare at the purple streaks in Steven's hair.

"Twelve," he said cockily. "I'm older than Eric." Steven ran his hand through his hair, inadvertently adding wings to his sleek aircraft hairdo.

Mulrooney's cell phone alerted him to an incoming text. "Hey, Smokey, call Lynwood in the Lab, will ya?" he yelled. He turned back to see Steven grinning at a prepubescent girl sitting nearby on the seawall. Mulrooney placed himself between Steven and his quarry.

"Where did Anya park her Beemer, Steven?" he inquired. Steven indicated the same spot where Ms. Gallien's car was parked when the officers arrived. Mulrooney remembered that the lab had found no traces of blood in the car. "Did you see her get out of the car?"

"Sure. She walked up to Mrs. Connolly's front door."

"Did you see her go in?"

"She must have," he answered with certainty. "Cuz after Eric went home, I skated some more. He has to go in early cuz his mom is, you know, real strict. I stayed out longer cuz of no school the next day due to a teachers' conference. When I was cutting down First Street to go home, I saw Anya come out the front door. After that, she cut down the side alley to the back alley."

"Wait a minute, son," Mulrooney crouched down to get in Steven's face, "you actually saw her exit from the front door?"

"Yeah, man."

"At what time?"

"Just about twelve."

"Could you see her well?"

"I could see her face pretty good. She went 'round the back and whistled."

"Whistled?"

"Uh-huh. Well not at me!" He looked embarrassed. "Just, you know, like a whistle to call somebody." Steven emitted a sharp whistle to demonstrate. He grinned impishly as Clarke, Eric, and the two women all jerked their heads to look.

"Did she have any balloons with her?"

"No, man," he exclaimed. He looked at Mulrooney as though he had dropped his pants and exposed himself.

"How about a bottle of champagne?"

"Sure man, that would be epic! I love champagne-"

"NO, Steven!" Mulrooney said, cutting him off mid-illusion. "I mean, was Ms. Gallien *carrying* a bottle of champagne?"

"Oh. Well I didn't see any," he pouted in disappointment.

"What happened after she whistled?" Mulrooney prodded.

"Nothin', so I went on home. I live on St. Joseph."

No wonder they'd missed him on the door-to-door search for witnesses, Mulrooney noted. St. Joseph was about ten blocks from the bay. "Thanks, son. Which one is your mom?"

"I live with my Aunt Lisa. She's the one in the red sweater." His aunt waved when he pointed to her. "She's a babe, don't ya think? And she's single."

"Steven, this isn't an interview for Match.com. I'm going to ask your Aunt Lisa to save me a trip and bring you to the station. Okay?"

"Sweet! Am I done?"

When Mulrooney nodded, Steven dropped his board on the pavement and pushed off. As Eric hurried to catch up, their skateboards rumbled on the asphalt like jet engines. Mulrooney mouthed "thank you" to the ladies before heading back to Clarke, who was involved in an animated discussion on his phone.

Clarke hung up as Mulrooney walked up. "Lauren Connolly is out on her boat with Michael Ryan. And Killackey traced the Cristal to Morry's Liquor–same marred label. It was purchased the night the Doc was killed. Fingerprint confirmed the prints on the bottle are Anya Gallien's."

Mulrooney nodded. He now had Anya where he wanted her. The bottle of Cristal in the living room and a witness who saw her exit the Doc's house were enough to establish that not only had she been lying, but she had also been at the crime scene *before* the murder. "It's time for another little chat with our red-headed seductress, "he said.

Clarke nodded. "Hmmm, you know every time I look into that face, I feel like I am staring at the sun during an eclipse."

"Yep, Anya Gallien is mesmerizing… and blinding."

"You forgot to mention dangerous, bro. That woman is freakin' dangerous."

Mulrooney nodded and instinctively reached for his weapon. "Then I hope your affairs are in order, Buddy. Time to boogie."

Chapter 8

Michael Ryan had always felt like a displaced person. Being half Jewish in a predominately Italian neighborhood, he had never really fit in. On this March day, however, as he stood on the deck of Lauren's boat, his early life was little more than a faded memory.

Michael's father Tomas had been of Italian parentage, and his mother was a Polish Jew. When both died in a TB sanitarium, their young son Michael was shipped off to Aunt Grazie from the Italian side of the family, a ruthless woman who took Michael in only because of the savings Tomas had left for the boy's care.

Michael was mostly on his own, and he learned early that physical strength earned respect. He never backed down from a fight, and there were plenty; but by the time he entered high school, the astute teen had learned that there was even more power in money. He concluded from studying the neighbor-

hood bosses that the man in charge got the most respect.

After the age of fifteen, he never fought with his
fists again. Instead, Michael developed a quiet and
shrewd style. Already instinctively refined, he im-
mersed himself in his education. He studied finance
like a game of chess, and Michael hadn't been beaten
at chess since he was twelve.

Michael returned to the old neighborhood because
Angie Le Marca was waiting. He set up an investment
business and was doing well by the age of twenty-
six, investing internationally for the neighborhood
kingpins who admired his cunning mind. At last the
"Yid Kid" felt important. He felt a sense of belong-
ing among the Italians who had earlier refused to see
him as one of their own.

At twenty-eight, Michael decided to marry Angie,
and Angie said yes. She said it, however, to someone else. Her parents would not give their blessing
to marry Michael because he was half Jewish. Mike-
the-Kike was still the Yid Kid ... *persona non grata.*

Michael never knew how much he needed Angie
until he lost her. Their intimacy had been something
he had longed for all his life. But he refused to cry
on the day she walked out on him. Instead, he closed
his business and borrowed heavily to set up a new
company in nearby New York City, distancing himself from the only soft touch he had ever known.

Michael vowed never to lose again. Before he was
thirty, he had made his first million by purchasing
struggling businesses. He and several silent partners

set up a division in Los Angeles where his fortune continued to grow.

Money was safer than emotions, and he never confused the two. He knew his remoteness often pushed people away, and he liked that, until the day when he realized he was a lonely man. Michael Ryan was finally ready to let someone in.

Now, as Michael leaned against the rail of Lauren's boat, he was glad he could be there to support Lauren as she had so often done for him. When he met Scott and Lauren, he had found something else he had missed out on during his struggle to the top. They offered friendship, and he was grateful.

When Scott and Lauren separated he was not only sad, but he also was angry with Lauren for seeking solace in Sam Bennett, a reputed playboy. Michael knew that although Lauren was a strong woman, Sam had some kind of power over her. And all Michael's senses told him that Sam Bennett was a dangerous man.

Michael had the same gut feeling about Anya Gallien. Anya was possessive of Lauren; and Michael's life had taught him to sense the moves and motivations of those who protect their territory to the exclusion of others. Michael sensed that Anya was not a woman who would, or could, share Lauren, who was the object of her enigmatic affection.

While Michael stood on the foredeck of Lauren's boat watching her, he knew Lauren would have to find her own way to cope, just as he had. But he was determined to protect her. Michael knew what he wanted, and he would wait.

* * *

Lauren expertly maneuvered the "Seduction," her classic 45' Symbol, out of its slip. She smiled at the sound of the still-powerful twin CAT 375hp engines that piloted her to freedom on the open sea. As she opened the throttle, the front of the boat lifted like an open jaw and chomped hungrily through the swells toward Catalina.

Lauren turned to the water whenever she needed solitude. From aboard her boat she loved to watch the sun rise and set as it glazed the interior in creamsicle hues. While she and Scott were separated, she lived aboard the boat while Scott resided at the house. The sounds of the water lapping against the boat were soothing to Lauren, and the sea air was a sedative. Today she needed her place of refuge more than ever.

When Michael handed her a Scotch, she took a long swallow, allowing the warmth to soothe the raw lump in her throat. "Thanks for coming, Michael," she said. "Scott's parents needed to rest. And I couldn't ask Anya. You know how terrified of the water she is."

Lauren was grateful for Michael's help. Their long friendship allowed for the silence she needed. Now as Lauren piloted the Seduction further out to sea, she sipped her drink and tried to relax. She planned to anchor briefly off Avalon and would need another person to guide the anchor chain from the hold as she worked the new winch. Today she was too depleted to do it alone.

Before Michael arrived, Lauren had considered asking Detective Mulrooney to accompany her. As she pictured his warm smile, she had an odd sense of comfort, which was a feeling she had lost with Scott. Perhaps it was because Mulrooney had come to her rescue. Or was it the vulnerability beneath his tough shell she found so compelling? Whatever it was, his presence made her feel safe.

Lauren suddenly sat upright and drove the image of Tim Mulrooney from her mind. Even though she and Scott had been emotionally separated for months, even years, before he was murdered, she could not allow her deep needs to surface. Not now.

Lauren looked up as Michael turned on the stereo and refilled her glass. "This is nice," he smiled. Michael briefly watched two dolphins frolicking off the port side of the boat before addressing her again. "Lauren, I want to hire some people to protect you until this is all over," he said quietly.

"You're a great friend, Michael, thank you. Let me think about it. How long do you plan to be in town?"

"I'm supposed to leave for France in a week or so. Why?"

"Scott left a financial mess. I need someone to advise me."

"Okay, I'll arrange to stay around a bit longer. I also want to offer you my penthouse for as long as you need it." Michael gently placed his hand on hers. "I'm worried about you, Lauren."

Lauren exhaled slowly. She felt as though her body parts were connected by one, long, raw nerve. She studied Michael's earnest face and striking looks. "Thank you for your offer, Michael, but I'm going back to my house as soon as I can. I can't let fear rule my life."

Michael winced. "Please don't do that, Lauren. What if someone comes back?"

"They can take whatever they want. I don't care anymore."

Michael set his glass down and stared at her. "What do you mean? Robbery wasn't the motive. The newspaper reports said the police ruled that out. You know that, right?"

Lauren sucked in her breath. Her eyes were riveted on Michael as she clutched the wheel tighter. "They must have wanted money, Michael. I'm sure our house was just selected randomly."

Lauren watched Michael as he shook his head almost imperceptibly. "Why else would they do it? Why else?" she demanded. "I just didn't arrive home soon enough. And then Scott must have awakened-" As she cleared her throat, her strangled sounds changed to a low moan.

Michael set down his glass and put his arms around her, pulling her into him. She buried her face in his neck as he stroked her hair. While Lauren clutched Michael, she wondered if she would ever stop smelling Scott's blood on her or feeling the warm, sticky tissue of his butchered body clinging to her skin.

74

"Make it go away, Michael," she shuddered.

"Come with me," he said as he reached to cut the throttle. Michael took her hand and led her down to the stateroom. He guided Lauren to the bed and arranged the pillows behind her.

"Try to relax, Lauren," he whispered as he sat down and slipped his arm behind her. "Put your head on my shoulder and rest while I rub your temples." Blanketed by Puccini's *Turandot*, she slowly leaned back into Michael's arms and closed her eyes. For whatever fleeting period of time the day would allow, she was able to separate herself from the pain. Her heavy lids pushed against her eyes until she slept.

* * *

When Lauren awoke, she looked out at the calm Pacific. In the distance she could see Avalon, the little town on the island of Santa Catalina. The hillsides were dotted with houses and flowers providing a lovely backdrop to the quaint turquoise pier that gaily greeted its visitors.

Michael was on the bridge piloting the boat when Lauren went above. He smiled and turned off his cell phone when she appeared. Lauren noticed how Michael's smile was handsome and boyish at the same time, and his hair had gotten more silver during the time he had been away. "I've arranged to stay," Michael assured her, "and I'm having an alarm system installed in your house as soon as the authorities lift the seal," he said. "I'll do everything I can to help you."

75

"We already have an alarm," she said. "I know, I know! Don't say it, Michael," she pleaded, holding up her hand as he started to respond. How many times in the past few days had she sat up in bed, screaming silently because Scott had left the alarm off for her that night? Michael turned away and looked out to sea.

They sat quietly for a long while as the sun began to dip behind the hills of Avalon. "Why were you gone so long, Michael?" she finally asked. "I thought maybe you were avoiding us. Avoiding me... because of my relationship with Sam."

"No, Lauren, it was none of my business. If I seemed remote, it's just because I never felt Sam Bennett was good enough for you."

Lauren felt her face flush, but she knew she couldn't explain to Michael feelings she was still trying to explain to herself.

"Anyway, to answer your question," Michael continued, "I tried calling many times when you and Scott separated, but I knew you were with Sam. Eventually I had to go to South America to handle real estate transactions for the corporation. I did talk to Scott a few times. I missed you both, Lauren," he admitted.

Michael noticed Lauren's sad smile and wondered if he had said too much. Perhaps he should have done what he planned to do, which was to attend the memorial just long enough to offer his services, then leave. However, it was inherent in him to take control of a situation when needed. And when he had seen Lauren at the funeral that morning, he was shocked at how fragile she seemed. "Lauren, I'll stay long enough to get you through this," he assured her.

Lauren kissed Michael on the cheek before abruptly walking to the tackle box on the aft deck. She raised the cover, removed a jade-green urn, and then slipped off the lid. While Michael solemnly watched, Lauren closed her eyes and whispered, "I'm so sorry about everything, Scott. Please forgive me. I never meant to hurt you." Michael looked at her curiously before politely turning away.

As she tipped the container over the side of the boat, the cool breeze lifted the contents of the urn. Lauren and Michael blinked away the stinging ashes that dusted their eyes. They both stood motionless and watched while the remains of Dr. Scott Connolly were buffeted by the evening winds in search of a final resting place.

Chapter 9

"Yup! Yup! That's the one." Mulrooney smiled as Stanley Kelley, the clerk from Morry's Liquor Store, sat in the station loudly smacking his lips with each "yup." Stanley was pointing to one photo among the six-pack. It was a photo of Anya Gallien, who was staring curiously at the camera. "Yup, she bought my last bottle of Cristal. It was warm, so she said she was gonna chill it. Label was scraped up so I offered her a discount, but she didn't mind. 'Said it was a memorable day for her friend."

"Ain't that the truth," Mulrooney muttered.

Clarke quickly snatched the photo from under the nose of the drooling clerk and made a photocopy for Stanley to sign and date.

Steven and Eric, accompanied by Steven's voluptuous Aunt Lisa, had arrived at the station around noon. Both boys were as certain in their identification of Anya as the clerk had been.

Afterward, Mulrooney and Clarke gave the boys a tour of lock-up. Steven said the place was "pretty rank" and wrote his name on a cell wall when he thought Mulrooney wasn't looking. The boys were also impressed by the stories Clarke told of his and Mulrooney's feats as detectives, each colored with enough hyperbole to spin off a television series. Mulrooney blushed the entire time, knowing Clarke was also pitching him to Lisa like a car salesman selling a Chevy.

Another witness, Dan Mason, who had identified Anya as the woman he had seen at Midnight Espresso around the time of the murder, arrived after Lisa exited with the boys. Dan was oddly dressed in a suit and open-toed sandals and was more sure-footed than he had been the night of the homicide when he was trying to sober up. His memory, however, was as confused as his clothing when they laid the six-pack of photos on the table in front of him so he could corroborate his prior statement.

"Yes. No. Well, maybe. Damn!" he uttered alternately. "The chick I saw that night isn't here," he finally concluded after staring at each photo. He picked up the snapshot of Anya taken at Dr. Connolly's memorial. "This is Anya? Well, she's not the one I thought I saw. Sorry. I was pretty tanked. So I guess I was mixing her up with some redhead that works at Sonny's Cafe. They could be sisters."

"One is plenty," Clarke intoned.

"Well, this definitely isn't the one I saw at Midnight Espresso the night the doc was killed. Did I fuck you guys up?"

"Not at all, Dan," Clarke said. "But Anya won't be thrilled."

Mulrooney picked up the phone. "Get me Clemente," he sighed. As he prepared to tell the chief that Anya's alibi had been blown, he steeled himself for what lay ahead.

* * *

Mulrooney slammed down the phone. "Shit!" He reeled around so fast he rammed his wrist into the file cabinet, which enraged him even more.

"Smokey, the chief just ordered us to arrest Anya Gallien based on the circumstantial evidence we have. AND, based on the fact that she failed a polygraph!"

"What the fuck?" Clarke sat upright in his chair.

"Which *he* personally arranged and she agreed to several hours ago! He said he couldn't reach us so he moved forward with it. He thinks she had a relationship with the victim."

"Then why in the hell would Anya agree to a polygraph? She's too damn smart for that!"

"My thoughts exactly."

Clarke scratched his head. "She failed, huh?"

"That's right."

"Shit."

"Yep. But in my all-too-often ignored opinion, we've still got squat. We've got no weapon or motive. And a good defense lawyer could manipulate the time of death enough to cause reasonable doubt about Anya's presence at the crime scene."

"True. Chief Clemente didn't do us any favors. We need to get more solid evidence, and we need time to let our perp trip up."

"I don't get it, Smokey. Usually the chief requires so much evidence we have to prop up the corpse as an eye witness. Why do you think he's ignoring our input on this one?"

"That pusbag mayor must be pushing this. He wants this case solved in minimum time 'cause it's an election year. You know what a media whore he is."

Mulrooney nodded. "And Mayor Howe thinks he can control the chief. There's some good-ol-boy shit going on there. Clemente wants to be sure Mayor Howe will keep him around."

"Yeah, and bad press lingers like a whore's perfume."

"D.A. Perry will just toss the case back in our faces."

"I don't know about that. My sources at City Hall tell me Mayor Howe has strong-armed the D.A. to run with any case they give him. Howe needs the publicity now, and he'll funnel money from his contributors into D.A. Perry's coffers."

"This whole thing will blow up in everyone's face."

"Sure but the trial won't happen until after the election; and by then they'll all be secure in their positions, at least for some time. I'm telling you, bro, Mayor Howe is behind this. One of these days he's gonna find my shoe shoved all the way up his grand-standing ass."

"Move over, Bruno Magli," Mulrooney muttered. Every part of him was feeling the squeeze. "If I don't go along with the chief on this one, I'll lose my shield. Clemente already cut me some slack after Atilla talked to the media about my parking lot in-cident. But Jesus, Smokey, what if Anya Gallien is innocent?"

"Then we'll have to prove that, too, buddy. Did I hear you mention Lauren Connolly when you and the chief were talking?"

"Yep. He thinks she was an accessory. When I told him I had my doubts, he nearly chewed my ass off. He said I was thinking with my dick."

"You still got one of those?" Clarke teased.

"Yeah, and Chief Clemente can suck it!"

"We've got nothing on Lauren Connolly."

"I know," Mulrooney nodded. "Howe and Clemente are going to have to drag Lauren Connolly in them-selves. I'm not budging on that unless something solid turns up."

Mulrooney noticed Clarke's grin. "What? You're looking at me like my nuts are dangling in your soup. It's not just that I'm *hoping* Lauren is innocent. My gut tells me she's clean. And this case is not the slam-dunk it appears to be. I can feel it."

"I'm with you all the way, buddy."

"Thanks, partner," Mulrooney said as he tried to suppress his nagging self-doubt. He clasped both hands behind his head as if to keep the back of his skull from exploding.

"Look, let's at least go through the motions just to cover our asses. After that, we'll run the rest of the case our way, on our own time. We've done it before. Clemente and Howe can conduct their own shit show while we catch us a killer."

Mulrooney nodded and rubbed his eyes. He was exhausted. He glanced at his chewed knuckles and unconsciously patted his 9mm Sig/Sauer. "Okay, we'll go through the moves, but I'll need you to cover my tracks. Otherwise you'll be shopping for a watch for my retirement."

He wondered if retirement would really be such a bad thing. He had asked himself many times in the last year if his heart was still into it; and the self-doubt was starting to eat at him. Mulrooney suddenly checked himself. *Don't get weak now, fool. Weak cops get killed.* Mulrooney jumped up and made a move for the door. "Let's book, Smokey," he grunted. "We've got a pretty little fish to fry."

* * *

Mulrooney and Clarke headed for the picturesque section of Long Beach known as Naples Island via the small bridge on 2nd Street that crosses Alamitos Bay. The exclusive enclave of Naples, situated on the east side of the bay, was directly across the water from Bay Shore Avenue where Dr. Connolly had been murdered. As the sun was crouching low in the late day sky, they cut down The Toledo to the Rivo Alto Canal, which was part of the unique canal system that made Naples Island famous in Southern California.

After they parked at the scenic Rivo Alto Bridge, they walked along the canal, which was lined with exquisite homes and boat docks. A young man in Venetian gondolier garb guided a gondola along the tranquil canal as a couple enjoyed their sunset ride under arched bridges covered in ivy and bougainvillea. They were drinking wine as sounds of Sinatra wafted from a stereo aboard the gondola.

Mulrooney recalled the evening he and Isabella had rented a gondola. Two months later she went away. Isabella didn't leave him solely for another guy; that would have been a passion he could understand. It was for money. He just didn't make enough damn money. *At least I have power and prestige.* Mulrooney smiled at his own private joke. Now it seemed as if he had watched it all happen to someone else.

When he and Clarke got close to Anya's residence, Mulrooney could see it was smaller than some of the neighboring homes, but every bit as charming. Anya was sitting alone on the tiled patio of the Spanish-style house as they walked up.

"Ms. Gallien?" Mulrooney said politely. As he approached, Clarke lingered by the gate. The lights on the patio came on automatically just as the sun dropped out of sight.

Mulrooney noticed that Anya was wearing a black slip dress. Her shoes had been kicked aside, and she had draped a shawl over her shoulders to buffer the spring breeze. The patio lights backlit her hair, creating a frame of firelight around her face. Anya let out a deep sigh. She looked tired, but beautiful.

"Hello, Ms. Gallien," he said, "It's been a long day for all of us. But I think you know why we're here."

"Yes, I do," she said quietly.

"We're placing you under arrest for the murder of Scott Connolly."

"Couldn't it have waited until Lauren returned?"

"I'm sorry, Ms. Gallien," Mulrooney said. He glanced at Clarke, who was pretending to study the water. Mulrooney knew Clarke was watching Anya closely.

"Please, Detective Mulrooney, if I'm to be your sacrificial lamb, we may as well lose the formalities. I insist you call me Anya."

"Okay, Anya. And you can still call me Detective Mulrooney." They sat for a moment, watching a large New Zealand sailboat pass by. "Nice neighborhood," he said. "Which boat is yours?"

Anya's laugh resonated like a low guitar chord. "How subtle, Detective! This is as near as I get to water," she replied. "I almost drowned once in Europe when I was a child. I cannot swim. That's why I am not out on the boat with Lauren this evening."

"I'm sorry to hear that, Anya. And I'm sure you'll be sorry to hear we have two new witnesses," he said with an abruptness he hoped would rattle her.

"Oh," she replied softly. She clutched her hands together and shifted back to face the water.

"Are you sure you weren't in the Connollys' home earlier the evening Doctor Connolly was murdered? Maybe you can try to recall the events better than you did during your polygraph test," he said wryly.

Anya's blush was visible even in the dim light. "No, as I said before, I did not return from Mexico until 7:00 P.M. I was home until I drove by Lauren's boat slip at midnight. So what is your point?" she said defiantly. "Haven't we been through this already?"

"The two witnesses we found are sure they saw your car arrive at the crime scene at 11:55 P.M. That was just minutes before Dr. Connolly was murdered. You want to try this one more time, Anya?" He smiled again, throwing her off balance.

Anya was obviously very uncomfortable. She frowned at Clarke, who was leaning against the rose trellis as the courtyard lights glinted off the shield at his waist.

"Can you tell us again what time it was when you parked your car that night?" Mulrooney asked.

"No," she said quietly as another gondola passed by. "Who can remember at exactly what time they do something so ordinary?"

"Nothing was ordinary that night, Anya."

"Touché, Detective."

Mulrooney observed Anya carefully as she clutched her shawl. She was sending mixed signals. Her back was straight and proud, but that faint accent was creeping into her voice ever so slowly.

"But someone verified I was at the coffee house, no?"

"The man who confirmed your alibi was drunk at the time, Anya. It seems he had confused you with another lovely redhead, so he recanted his statement. The other witnesses, however, were able to make a positive ID. We know you purchased champagne around 7:30 P.M. on the evening Scott Connolly was killed; and the same chilled bottle was found at the crime scene."

Anya reeled around, obviously confused and surprised. She appeared to have had the wind knocked out of her.

"It had your prints on it. And also the doctor's," Mulrooney said as he studied her reactions. "You did not have the champagne upon your arrival at the Connolly home at 11:55 P.M., nor when you came to Lauren's rescue after the murder was committed, so we know you were there earlier. You've been lying to us, Anya."

Anya uncrossed her long legs and exhaled. "Shall I pack a bag, Detective? Will I be spending an evening at your fine hostelry?"

"I hope you'll find it comfortable, Anya."

Anya's eyes connected with his. He kept his gaze steady until she finally looked away. While he waited, Anya slipped her feet into her slinky black heels then fastened the thin ankle straps.

Mulrooney glanced up to see if Clarke had noticed her movement. Clarke nodded. "Ah," Mulrooney smiled, "you used your left hand. I see you're ambidextrous."

She turned to smile at Mulrooney with restrained emotion. "Yes, I am. And all you ever had to do was ask."

He laughed aloud. "It's more of a challenge this way."

"Mulrooney, I like you in spite of the fact that you're making an arrest you don't believe in. But as long as you and Clarke are here to do the bidding of your chief, can you tell me what my motive was for heartlessly butchering my best friend's husband and returning later to relish the gore?"

Mulrooney looked into her clear, intelligent eyes. "Did you love him?"

Anya shook her head and laughed bitterly. "I didn't even like him, Detective. I'm glad the bastard is dead." She suddenly held her arms out to him, prisoner-style. "Do you wish to handcuff me?" she asked, almost coquettishly.

"Not for long, Anya. You'll need a free hand to dial your attorney."

Chapter 10

Mulrooney rolled sluggishly out of bed before the shrill alarm could enjoy its unique brand of sadism. Minutes earlier, at 6:00 A.M., Clarke had called and, with the articulation of a train conductor, said his wife was taking him in for an emergency root canal. Mulrooney stared at the ceiling for several minutes. *Waking up alone sucks. I should get myself a stuffed dog and name it Freeze.*

After he showered and fed his Lion Fish, Houdini, Mulrooney sat at his easel and tried to finish a watercolor he had begun before his heart attack. Art was the only passion he allowed himself these days. Usually painting helped him get his head straight, but after ten minutes he decided he could probably get in touch with Jimmy Hoffa before he could get in touch with his muse. The avocados in his still life looked like steroidal frogs.

After he dressed, Mulrooney drove to Belmont Shore for breakfast and to garner any new info he could dig up. As he entered the Donut Depot, Officer Sanders was stuffing a cream pastry into his mouth. "Thanks for keeping the cop stereotype alive and well, Sanders," Mulrooney teased.

"I'm saving my kale salad for lunch. It's in the car under the fried chicken boxes, sir," He grinned.

Mulrooney laughed. "Did you pick up any information we can use?"

"Nothing new, but Kate and I are still combing the streets for you, sir."

"'Appreciate it." After Mulrooney downed some juice, he headed for the Connollys' villa. Starting at the crime scene, he once again timed the drive to Anya's house in Naples via the Second Street Bridge. It would require 2.45 minutes for Anya to get home from Lauren's. He carefully documented the time.

So much for Anya; now there was Lauren. Mulrooney was not so blinded by Lauren's charms that he was about to overlook details. He continued to the Marina boat slips by the Rusty Pelican Restaurant and timed the drive from Lauren's boat to her home - 4.58 minutes at normal speed. The 7:30 A.M. traffic was slower than midnight traffic flow on a week night, so he knew it could actually be done faster. But even at four minutes, Lauren Connolly would have had to leave her boat *before* 11:55 P.M. in order to arrive home in time to be a participant in the night's lethal festivities.

While he drove to the station, he mentally reviewed his notes. They were already accumulating copious amounts of information on everything from dry wall sales to black wigs, but so far all they had gotten was a few more hemorrhoids. And in spite of her lie detector performance, Anya was still maintaining complete innocence while backing Lauren's alibi.

Clarke was still out dealing with a tooth infection, and Mulrooney always felt vulnerable when his partner wasn't around. As he walked into headquarters, he had the sensation of watching himself in instant replay. His long days and truncated nights had commingled like Bernie Madoff's bank accounts. But whenever he entered the office, the day usually took on its own identity.

Today proved to be no exception. Mulrooney spotted Lauren Connolly from across the room, while the other detectives pretended to be too busy to notice their attractive guest. He suppressed a laugh when Killackey lowered his elbow into his coffee cup with the grace of a blind buffalo. Mulrooney walked by Killackey's desk and chuckled while Killackey frantically tried to sop up the coffee with a box of tissues.

As Mulrooney approached Lauren, her blue eyes zeroed in on him like the vivid cross hairs of a rifle scope. When she jumped up like a marionette being yanked by its arm strings, he sensed she wanted to punch him. "Easy, Mayweather," he smiled.

Mulrooney took her firmly by the elbow and guided her into his office. He closed the door of his cramped quarters, which had once been a storage closet. A desk and file cabinet had been shoved into the space to make room in the overcrowded Homicide Division when Mulrooney had first relocated to L.B.P.D.

"What kind of a moron are you?" she demanded as he pulled out a chair for her. Lauren refused to sit.

Clarke was missing a Kodak moment, Mulrooney mused. Clarke was always spouting his favorite line from *Butch Cassidy and the Sundance Kid*: "Morons! I've got morons on my team!" Apparently Lauren Connolly agreed.

"And how did I earn this pride-evoking sobriquet?" he inquired.

"For God's sake, Detective," she snapped, "do you really believe my best friend would kill my husband?"

"Evidence is evidence." *And you look lovely.* "Mrs. Connolly, we have witnesses, among other things. Look, I know how upset you are-"

"No, you couldn't possibly know how upset I am!" she asserted. "How could you? First, I lose my husband in a violent, hideous crime. Then, upon my return from Catalina, I find I'm losing the one person I need to get me through this–Anya!"

When her voice suddenly broke, Lauren cleared her throat and thrust her chin at him in defiance. She stood with both hands on her hips, her back as rigid as a palace guard. "I have been patient for days. Do I understand correctly that Anya's bail will be set by noon?" she demanded.

"One o'clock. It's up to the judge if she'll get bail. It would be unusual, but he may be merciful if he thinks it was a crime of passion."

"Well, I've already arranged to post whatever the bail amount is," Lauren said as she paced the floor. "I'm taking out a second mortgage as collateral."

Mulrooney's brows conveyed his surprise. "Well that's unorthodox, to say the least. Mrs. Connolly, I don't want to alarm you, but we're very concerned about you. Your friend may be an extremely dangerous woman."

"You obviously work out of books and live by statistics, Detective Mulrooney, but I know Anya could never hurt anyone without justification, especially me. She certainly would have no motive for killing my husband. They were friends."

"It's my understanding that Ms. Gallien did not like your husband."

Lauren's skin flushed. "It's complicated," she answered. "Anya liked him until Scott and I had some problems, then she took my side. Perhaps I told her too much. Naturally, she was protective, as most friends are in these situations."

"Protective enough to kill for you?" He noticed Lauren's shoulders draw back. "If that fist gets any tighter, I'm going to have to call for back-up," he smiled, completely disarming her. "Listen, Mrs. Connolly, I know you've been through tremendous shock and suffering, but I need to inform you that you have not been cleared as a suspect. I'm going to need your complete cooperation to clear you of all suspicion. Will you cooperate with me in this investigation?"

Mulrooney knew he could get more information if Lauren did not view him as an adversary. He also knew her anger was a cover for a lot of pain, a reaction he had seen many times before. He waited long enough for Lauren to collect herself. "Mrs. Connolly," he asked gently, "did your husband often take Percodan?"

"Yes, he had bad headaches."

"Did he usually mix Percodan with tequila?"

"He was a doctor, so he knew how much he could tolerate." Lauren leaned against Mulrooney's desk and stared at him. "I know my husband took too many drugs and drank too much, but he swore he wasn't an addict." Lauren pressed her fingertips against her eyes. "I admit, his drug and alcohol use really hurt us both."

"I'm sure it did. I used to be a drinker, Mrs. Connolly, like my father before me. I understand both sides. I also know drugs. Even lesser amounts can impair a person's judgment. And as far as sources go, even doctors have limitations as to how much they can self-prescribe. Scott might have had connections we need to question if you are correct in your belief in Anya's innocence."

"I have no idea who he would have bought drugs from."

"And he had no indication of heart trouble, did he?"

"No, why do you ask?"

"The amyl nitrite—do you know about them? They're vasodilators, often called poppers. There are much better drugs for the heart these days."

Lauren turned away, obviously embarrassed. "I've heard of them," she replied softly.

"Did he use them as a sex aid when you two made love?"

Lauren turned back to face Mulrooney. "I wouldn't know, Detective Mulrooney. My husband and I had sex only once in the last eighteen months."

When Mulrooney raised his eyebrows in surprise, Lauren answered the question he hesitated to ask. "He was not impotent, Detective. There were other reasons. I had planned to come in and talk with you even before I heard you arrested Anya. I wanted you to hear it from me. Scott and I were having problems. We grew distant."

"How distant?"

"Have you ever felt really lonely, Detective?"

Mulrooney didn't answer. He didn't dare admit to anyone that loneliness followed him around like an abandoned dog.

"I met someone. I'm not even sure how it all started."

"Were you planning to divorce your husband?"

"I thought about it. Something had to change. He knew about my affair, but he never said anything, which made it even worse somehow. It was as if he didn't even care. I think it was easier for Scott to keep up the pretense of being the perfect couple. But our life was anything but happy, so he just spent more money and did more drugs. And I got more discouraged and sad. I wanted so much to love him the way I once did."

95

"But you went back?"

Lauren sat down across from Mulrooney. "Eventually I broke it off with the guy I was seeing. I couldn't live with the guilt. I tried to get close to Scott again, but it was difficult being intimate. I wanted to the night I, the night he-" Lauren's husky voice dissipated like smoke.

"Let me get you some water," he said, excusing himself.

When Mulrooney returned, Lauren was turned away from him. He tried not to stare at her curved hips and narrow waist. He wished he could be her yellow suit, wrapped snugly around all her soft elegance. Her hair reminded him of buttered toast, and he wanted to eat it. Lauren was examining the photos on his bulletin board.

"Are they all criminals?" she asked.

"Well, the one on the lower right is my ex-wife, which makes them all criminals," he teased. Mulrooney noticed how even her laugh sounded gentle. He tried not to respond to the sultry pitch of her voice which made him feel as though he were being swept up in the warm Santa Ana winds. He took a deep breath. He had to shake it off. This woman might have helped slice up her hubby, or possibly hired someone else to do the honors. He studied her body language while he waited for Lauren to continue talking.

"I'm not seeing my male friend anymore, Detective Mulrooney. I haven't seen him for at least ten months. I'm not even sure where he is now."

"He's back in Australia," Mulrooney answered.

"Oh my God! You knew about Sam, and yet you let me grovel through true confessions like that? You're a sadist! I hope you enjoyed yourself, Detective." Lauren jumped up and stormed toward the door.

"Mrs. Connolly," he called after her, "it's my job to know, and it was wise of you to tell me. This sadist has enough sense to believe you're telling the truth." Lauren abruptly turned around.

Mulrooney pulled a photo from his file. "Samuel Bennett. Owned Jazzin' Night Club in downtown Long Beach until it was destroyed by fire. Suspected arson, but perhaps it was a result of organized crime if Sam's claims of being squeezed to pay mob protection were true. Fortunately, and coincidentally, his club was heavily insured. He returned to his native Australia and opened another club in Sydney, with the insurance money, I presume. The U.S. Department of State reports no activity on his passport within the past ten months, so we believe he must still be there."

Lauren moved closer to Mulrooney. She looked at the photo of a tall, athletic-looking man with black hair, a strong nose, gray eyes, and a mischievous grin.

Mulrooney read from the dossier. "'After leaving Macquarie Post in New South Wales, Sam attended the University of Sydney. He dropped out after one year, took out a loan, and started a pub, which became a popular watering hole.'

"The pub was named 'Panketye,' which is aborigine for boomerang. As Sam advertised in his ads, he wanted the customers to always return."

"And they did," she smiled.

"Probably in no small part due to the gregarious owner and his keen sense of business in offering everything from frog races to lobster crawls. And if I may go on: 'When an American entrepreneur bought Sam out, Sam set up Jazzin,' in Long Beach.'"

Mulrooney stopped reading and looked up. "Due to the annual blues and jazz festivals hosted by our fair city, Long Beach was a prime location for what was to become a popular nightspot. Successful guy. Does all that sound about right, Mrs. Connolly?"

Lauren nodded, but she knew Mulrooney had left out one thing: Sam never felt his success was complete until he met Lauren. He planned to stay in the States and marry her when she was free. And Sam was determined Lauren would indeed be free one day.

"Cocky Aussie," Lauren said aloud. As she smiled at the photo of Sam, she saw no signs of the anger he had displayed the night she told him she wanted to try to save her marriage. After a terrible fight, Sam had drilled his fist into the wall behind her. When she backed away in fear, he stalked off. The last she saw of Sam that night was a distant shadow as he smashed his fist against her car.

Mulrooney was studying Lauren's expression. "We were already watching Sam, Mrs. Connolly. The club fire was suspicious."

"If you think Sam would do that to his own club, then you didn't investigate him very well. That club was his life."

"No, Lauren Connolly was his life," Mulrooney replied.

As the words hung in the air, Lauren met Mulrooney's gaze. She felt her cheeks burning. "That is long over. Do you think I'm weak and immoral for turning to another man?" she whispered.

"Lonely people make desperate choices. The fact that you walked away from Sam Bennett when you were still in love with him tells me you're a good person, and a very strong one."

"Thank you for that." Her response was barely audible.

"By the way, Mrs. Connolly, I've read some of your articles in the Sunday magazine. You're a damn good writer and researcher."

"Thank you. Does that include my ability to research my friends?" A slow smile relaxed the tightness in her cheeks.

"I reserve the right to remain silent when not in the presence of my attorney."

Lauren smiled at Mulrooney. She noticed the quiet calm in his eyes. He was strong, but not hard. He was like Sam, but without the anger. She quickly averted her gaze.

"May we have permission to search your house again, Mrs. Connolly?" he asked as he thrust a paper at her.

"Yes, and please call me Lauren," she replied as she signed it.

"Thank you, Lauren," Mulrooney said. "Please call me Tim."

"Okay, Tim. About Anya–I know you're just doing your job..."

"Yes, I am. Incidentally, Lauren, I'd prefer that you not leave town."

"I promise," she smiled, giving him a Boy Scout salute.

"Can I trust you?"

"Yes, Tim, you can. You know, I'm not sure I've ever really thanked you."

Mulrooney smiled. "Aw, shucks, that's not necessary, ma'am," he said using his best Gary Cooper voice.

Lauren took his large hand in hers. "I'm sorry I was so hostile when I came in. You've been very kind, and I really am grateful." She held his hand a moment longer before turning to leave.

As she made her way through the room, Mulrooney watched the eyes of the men follow her. When she passed Killackey, he grasped his coffee cup as if it were a live grenade. After Lauren was out of sight, Mulrooney whispered, "You're drooling like a St. Bernard, Killackey. Do I have to turn the fire hose on you?"

"You look like you could use some cooling off yourself," Killackey grinned. As Mulrooney unconsciously rubbed his fingers along the back of his neck, he could feel the perspiration. She had done it again, and it was becoming a pattern. Lauren Connolly had left him feeling inside-out.

Chapter 11

Lauren left a trace of perfume and a room full of detectives fantasizing Walter Mitty heroics for the dame in distress. After Mulrooney watched her exit, he retrieved his iPad from his file drawer. He grabbed a newspaper, his phone, and the Connolly file before exiting his closet cubby hole.

Still sweating as he rushed out of the station, Mulrooney then got in his car and drove toward the ocean. As the sun burned off the morning fog, the day promised to be more like summer than late spring. Continuing along Ocean Boulevard, Mulrooney cruised leisurely down the small peninsula that jutted out from Belmont Shore like a paint drip.

At the tip of the peninsula, he parked in a lot near the channel that connected Alamitos Bay to the Pacific. With his gear in hand, he made his way out onto the jetty to the flat rock that was his refuge whenever he needed to think.

Spreading the newspaper on the rock, he glanced at the latest headline of the *Press-Telegram*: SUSPECT CHARGED IN SHORE MURDER. There were two photos: one of Anya and the other of Mayor Charles Howe. The photographer had caught the mayor in an unflattering, mid-blink head-cock suggesting mutant DNA. Recently Howe had been placing a lot of high-pressure calls to Mulrooney and Clarke. Mulrooney wondered if Howe gave his phone sex partners equal attention.

"In your face," he grunted, plopping down on the paper. Mulrooney turned on his music and hummed along as Sarah Vaughan sang "Someone To Watch Over Me." He recalled a quote of Nietzsche's that had always impressed him with its simplicity: "Without music, life would be a mistake." *Nietzsche must have anticipated the coming of Sarah.*

After a few brief minutes of bliss, he picked up the Connolly file and went to work. He didn't like the way the case was shaping up. Both he and Clarke had picked up mixed signals from Anya Gallien. Why had Anya been so forthcoming with them about her dislike for the doctor, he wondered? A slip-up perhaps? No, Anya Gallien was too smart for that. And too smart to park in front of the house of a guy she planned to carve. Passion, however, was always unpredictable. Was she jealous of Lauren? Sophie's tidbit about Anya and the doc at the restaurant would certainly support that theory. How much did Anya Gallien hate, or love, Scott Connolly?

Lauren had been mistaken, he thought as he remembered her accusation that he worked out of books and lived by statistics. He operated first and foremost on gut reaction. But he wondered if he could still trust his sixth sense.

Mulrooney thought about his broken marriage and felt the familiar pain. Had he really been wrong about Isabella, or had he always known she wanted more than he could give? His resultant anger had promulgated the incident that ended their marriage and nearly destroyed his future. But was it anger with her, or anger toward himself for ignoring the red flags? It didn't matter; he had no time to wallow in it. He had to keep believing in his instincts.

He was sure Anya was at the scene of the homicide earlier, even though she was vehemently denying it. The Cristal had been warm at point of sale, so she needed time to chill it and deliver it with the balloons sometime before the two neighborhood kids saw her return at 11:55 P.M. However, it couldn't have been too much earlier because there was still condensation on the bottle when Mulrooney arrived.

Mulrooney underlined a question he had scribbled in his notebook: *Did A.G. act alone?* The black hairs found on the doctor's clothing and viscera suggested Anya didn't act alone, if at all. She would have had to exit just before Lauren got home, and then cleaned up to return at about the time Lauren arrived home. Mulrooney was quite sure Anya's car hadn't been moved, therefore, she would have had to have gotten a ride or risk notice on the streets.

Lauren had asked the same question that continued to eat at Mulrooney: Why would Anya return? It didn't fit. Her survival instinct was too strong. Although circumstantial evidence implicated Anya, Mulrooney knew she was covering something, and he sensed she would go down before she'd talk. Mulrooney just couldn't figure out why Anya wasn't assisting in her own defense.

Mulrooney glanced at a print-out Killackey had made at his request. It was about a crime involving a porn dealer named Clarence Smolley, one of three slashing victims at a peep show in Trenton. The victim was a small time thug from Florida, and a sometime resident of Long Beach. As always, Mulrooney was keeping track of all cases that had elements in common. What interested Mulrooney was that the victim's throat wound had been enough to kill him, but the perp had slashed him again - vertically - for good measure. The peep show proprietor and a female dancer were hacked up the same way - an unusually vicious M.O. Mulrooney underlined the article before shoving it back in the file.

Sarah was singing the last notes of "Embraceable You" when he reluctantly removed his ear plugs and pulled out the written transcript of the interview with Lauren he conducted at headquarters the night of the homicide. She had insisted that she did not need an attorney present. As he reviewed the transcript, he remembered that her voice was soft and often shaky, sometimes muffled by her hand as she chewed her nail.

TM: Mrs. Connolly, can you tell me what time you left the boat?

LC: It must have been midnight.

TM: Are you sure?

LC: Well, I began securing the boat at 11:55, right after calling Scott. (LC pauses) Did I tell you that before? I checked the time on the coffee maker then secured the covers on the aft deck.

TM: How long did that take?

LC: A few minutes. Maybe five.

TM: Did you go directly home?

LC: Yes.

TM: Did you pull into the garage and use that entrance?

LC: Yes, I always do. Excuse me, Detective...I have a terrible headache. Can this wait? I would like to lie down.

TM: Mrs. Connolly, I know this is difficult. I'll only need a few more minutes of your time. What was the first thing you did after you entered the house?

LC: I picked up a glass and a bottle of Cabernet and went upstairs to the bathroom to shower. (coughing)

TM: Are you okay?

LC: Yes, but I'd like some aspirin.

TM: Okay, I'll have some more water brought in. Take some deep breaths and try to relax.

LC: Thank you.

TM: Do you recall anything unusual that night?

LC: The entire evening was unusual, Detective.

TM: Yes, of course. Excuse me, Mrs. Connolly. I meant when you first entered and went upstairs.

LC: No, not really. The light was off in the bedroom, so I undressed in the bathroom then showered.

TM: After you showered, then what?

LC: I dried my hair, and then I went downstairs to put my wine glass away before going to bed.

TM: Why didn't you turn off the music?

LC: What music?

TM: The stereo.

LC: I don't know. Are you sure there was music playing?

TM: Yes, ma'am. It was on when Officers Axberg and Sanders arrived. Do you usually go to bed with the stereo on?

LC: No, I don't. I don't believe I ever have.

TM: That's odd, don't you think? The music?

LC: Yes... but I just don't remember hearing it.

TM: So you don't remember turning on the stereo?

LC: No, I told you, I don't remember that at all.

TM: What happened after you put the wine away?

LC: You know the rest. I told Officer Axberg–is that her name? I also told your partner Clarke. Please don't make me say it again.

TM: We'll take a short break. One more question, Mrs. Connolly: Why did your husband leave the front door unlocked if you always use the garage?

LC: Did he? Are you sure?

TM: Yes, the front door lock had not been tampered with. Did someone else have a key to get in?

LC: No. No, of course not.

TM: No one else had a key, Mrs. Connolly? Are you sure?

LC: Yes, I'm positive.

TM: Let's take a break. I appreciate your cooperation.

As reviewed his notes, he tried to pinpoint what was eating him. He mentally replayed their interview, focusing his memory on Lauren's body language. Maybe her lies had thrown them all off, but Lauren Connolly's body language was a giveaway. "Red flags, you dumb mick!" he admonished himself. He hastily wrote *L.C. is lying - KEY evidence* in bold letters in the margin of his notes.

When he received an urgent text several minutes later, he had already gathered his gear and was rushing toward Anya's home across the bay.

Chapter 12

By the time Mulrooney reached Anya's house in Naples, the crime team had swept the house thoroughly and were now outside doing another sweep. Curious passersby gathered on the promenade that circled the canal while investigators questioned Anya's neighbors. Mulrooney looked down the canal for several minutes before entering through the carved gate that led to the patio.

The ambiance was even more beautiful by daylight. Many of the other homes were ostentatious, but Anya's small cottage had character. He could smell the blush roses and honeysuckle that adorned the wood trellis; and he noticed a family of birds watching the action from a bird feeder on a majestic birch tree.

Just as Mulrooney was about to enter the house, he was surprised when Chief Clemente intercepted him. "Mulrooney, I'm on my way to Laguna, but I wanted to talk to you in person first." The chief draped an arm over Mulrooney's shoulder as he led him to the side courtyard.

Mulrooney, sensing something was brewing, steeled himself. "What's up, Chief?" he asked.

"It's this business about Mrs. Connolly planning to make bond for the person accused of killing her own husband. It's highly irregular, and it suggests that the victim's wife believes Anya Gallien has been wrongly charged. We're looking worse than the A.T.F. at Waco." Clemente shook his head in disgust. "Look, I'm sorry about squeezing you and Clarke, Tim, but Mayor Howe is on my back like a malignant growth; and the city's movers and shakers are going schizoid on me." He scratched his balding head and looked around sheepishly. "Listen, just concentrate on making this as airtight for the D.A.'s office as possible. I don't need a debacle so close to my retirement."

"Hell, Chief, you've been dragging out this retirement longer than a dead man's nap," Mulrooney said with an innocent smile.

"I can drag, but you can't. Anya Gallien is starting to look damn sympathetic. Her attorney went public a half hour ago. Now I've got CNN and every magazine show on my ass. Next thing you know, it'll be Jerry Springer!"

Mulrooney knew Chief Clemente had skin in the game, but he laughed in spite of his anger. He had a love-hate relationship with Clemente, who had been willing to overlook the only blemish he'd ever received on his record. And even though Mulrooney was furious with Clemente for allowing himself to be manipulated by Mayor Howe, he understood politics. Now the chief was trying to straddle both sides of the fence as usual.

"I'm sure you've seen the newspapers, Mulrooney. Someone leaked about the scandal you were involved in, so the press is going to be up your ass like a proctologist. Do you want off this case?"

"You know me better than that."

Clemente shook his head. "Look, you and Clarke are the best I've got, but you're hard-headed as hell. I usually stay out of your way, but dammit, we've got a solid case against Anya Gallien. Don't fight me on this, Mulrooney. I can only give you and Clarke thirty days before I bring Atilla aboard, like it or not. I want you on Lauren Connolly like mold on cheese. All indications are that she set her husband up."

"We have no evidence of that, Chief."

"Well then get it. And get your brain outta your ball sack. If anything slips through the cracks, it will be the end for you. I want this tighter than an old maid's pussy!"

Mulrooney watched as the Chief turned and walked off. In spite of his tension, Mulrooney found himself chuckling at the way the bald spot on the back of Clemente's head resembled the great state of Ohio. The sunburn that was now setting Ohio ablaze was evidence of Clemente's passion for fishing.

One time Mulrooney had gone fishing with the Chief off Belmont Pier. He had learned a lot about the chief on that trip. He was a widower who had never

111

had kids, and he had nursed his wife through five harrowing years of cancer. Now, all he had left was his job. Mulrooney knew he was terrified of leaving office to face the end of his life alone. Mayor Howe knew it also and used it to his advantage.

As disgusted as Mulrooney was, he felt sorry for the crusty old chief. In every situation, Clemente's face was a map of emotions; and Mulrooney was sure of one thing now—Clemente was worried.

Mulrooney distractedly rubbed the cleft in his square chin, routing out the whiskers that always sidestepped his razor. He sighed loudly, wishing like hell he were fishing. When he walked around to the front courtyard, he spotted Kate talking with one of the investigators. She was in jogging clothes, and her dark hair was pulled back into a pony tail that bounced when she talked. She grinned when she saw him.

"I'm off duty, and we have a racquetball date, remember? I'll lend you some shorts," she teased.

"Oh, thank you," he lisped. "Sorry, Katie, but Clarke is having a root canal and I'm swimming in so much shit I forgot about our plans, but I'll make it up to you. Maybe I'll even spot you some points."

"I'm blessed. I dropped by because I thought you might like to have an update from the mean streets of Belmont Shore."

"I'm all ears."

"That's probably why you can't get a date," she grinned. "Anyway, I had a date last night. Are you jealous?"

"Of course."

"We were at Legends having a nightcap, and everyone there was talking about the homicide. It seems Dr. Connolly had a girlfriend, even though your hounds haven't turned one up. Or are you holding out on me?"

"Sit, darlin,' sit." Mulrooney led her to a table on the patio where they sat down. Just as Mulrooney was pulling out a pen and pad, an investigator brought a box of evidence out of Anya's house and set it on the table in front of him.

Mulrooney glanced at the box and nodded. "Thanks, Ed. I think the neighbors are afraid you and your team are up to no good."

"We are. Noodles is in there trying on her bras right now," he grinned. Mulrooney laughed heartily as he scanned the box of evidence.

Kate propped her feet up on a flower box and reached for the binoculars that were hanging on an adjacent bird house. She focused the lenses so she could watch birds that soared over the yachts and speedboats that were moored along the canal.

"Please continue your update," Mulrooney urged as he checked out a half-empty bottle of tequila.

"Well, we made love all night and he's hung like Godzilla.

"Chinaco Anejo Tequila. Doesn't come with a worm."

"Tim, you're not listening!"

"Yes, I am. You said your date looked like Godzilla. Go on."

She lifted the binoculars again and checked out a passing gondola steered by a buff gondolier before she continued. "Well, the woman who Connolly was dating when they were living apart drops by Legends and the Wharf Rat Bar once in a while for a drink. Apparently she was a patient of Connolly's. She also used to hang out downtown at Jazzin' before the fire, so she also knows Lauren Connolly's Aussie friend. I heard the woman is plain with dark hair, 5'5", mid-thirties, but I couldn't get a name. She works downtown at the World Trade Center."

"Dark hair, huh? Very interesting," Mulrooney said as he furtively grabbed a piece of evidence from the pile and shoved it into his pocket. Kate eyed him curiously. "No time for procedural bullshit," he whispered while looking around to make sure no one else had seen his move.

Kate trained the field glasses on him and smiled. "I see a spotted Mulrooney. A strange bird. An almost extinct species, I believe." She then turned for a view of the canal.

Mulrooney got up to leave. "Thanks for the info, Katie." Suddenly he hunkered down low and plastered a sincere expression across his face. "By the way, did you practice safe sex last night?" he asked, doing his best Dr. Phil impersonation.

She said nothing for a moment while she continued to peer intently through the binoculars. "By the way, yourself," she mimicked, Dr. Phil-ing right back at him, "did you realize one can clearly see Lauren Connolly's house from here?"

Mulrooney grinned in triumph. He knew she'd eventually notice.

Kate put down the glasses. "So you already figured it out, huh?"

"Yup - there was no need for Anya to drive by Lauren's boat the night of the homicide to see if Lauren had left for home. Without disturbing Scott with a phone call, and without leaving her patio, Anya would have been able to determine when Lauren had returned just by watching for Lauren's car."

"So she never drove by the marina..."

"Nope. She's providing an alibi for Lauren. Katie, it seems the mountain has come to *Mul*-hammed."

Chapter 13

As Anya paced a room at Sybil Brand Institute for Women, she pulled her hair over her temple then gouged the palms of her hands with her long nails. She was angry, but at least she was no longer frightened. She was sure no one had seen her with Scott the night he was murdered, but she would have to be careful. She wondered if Scott had told anyone he was meeting her.

Anya rubbed the thick scar behind her ear. The curved ridge of hard tissue, which was shaped like the edge of a gun butt, was a bonus from her last stay in a cell. But at least no one in this prison had put his filthy hands on her. And she had been offered food, which of course, she refused. She knew not to accept anything her jailers had to offer. If a prisoner accepted kindness from a guard, he would demand payback.

In spite of her resolve, she knew if she were forced to trade her dignity for freedom, she would. Dignity was not about pride, but about control. For Anya, freedom to live and to die for what or in whom she believed was the ultimate dignity.

Her papa had taught her that when he joined the resistance against the Communist regime in Romania. At the age of four, Anya was savvy enough to know something covert was taking place each time meetings were held in the basement of their home.

When she was young, the family had suddenly relocated from their home in Brasov to a small apartment outside Cluj. Even though Anya had two baby sisters, she missed her playmates, so her papa would amuse her by taking her for long walks along a nearby lake.

During their walk one day, she heard angry voices and loud popping sounds from behind a bank of trees. Papa scooped her up into his arms and started running for the lake. She felt his heart pounding as if it were outside his body. As he jumped into the icy water, he held fast to a clump of small trees, pulling a terrified Anya in with him. As the footsteps and shouting got closer, Papa went under the surface, still holding onto Anya.

When she opened her eyes in the gray winter water, she could see the fear in her father's face. She struggled to free herself from his grasp because she couldn't breathe. She tried to scream. As she looked at him beseechingly, not knowing why he was hurting her, he talked to her with eyes full of sorrow. At that point, Anya quit struggling. She decided she would never breathe again and go to heaven if it would make her papa not be so afraid and sad.

Papa suddenly emerged from the water, dragging Anya to the surface. His eyes were wild as they both gasped for breath. As he bent to look into her face, Anya heard a gunshot, and then her father's head exploded. Anya was dragged back down into the water as her father slipped below the bloody surface. Moments later a tall man in a uniform yanked her out of her papa's dying clutches. Anya held onto her father as long as she could, trying in vain to hold his head together.

Anya never remembered how she got home. For many days afterward she would run off, trying to find her way back to the lake. She was sure she could find her papa if she looked hard enough. After days of searching for him, Anya eventually gave up. She hid in a corner of their house and refused to talk. Anya had called for her papa until her throat was torn, and she had chewed the flesh off her knuckles. Although she had finally found her way back to the lake that had swallowed papa, she was too afraid to get close enough to the water to save him.

Now, however, Anya was determined to stop being afraid. Anya forced the memories back into the hiding places in her mind. She looked around the room and then glanced at her watch. She knew she needed to buy some time. She had fired her attorney when he suggested she accept a plea bargain to make it easier on everyone. Fortunately the prosecutor had asked for the arraignment to be continued in order to obtain more information. And they had set her bond, not expecting her to make the million dollar amount required.

She had asked her attorney to call Lauren because she was the only person in the world Anya was close to. She knew her friend was loyal, but how strong was Lauren now? Anya knew she needed to get out of there, and she needed to get Lauren alone.

Anya stared at the door then at a mirror on the far wall. She sat down and crossed her long legs before slowly lifting the hem of her dress high to adjust her silk hose. Her pink bikini panties outlined the tops of her firm thighs through the sheer hose. She re-crossed her legs then stroked them seductively from ankle to thigh with her graceful hand. After several moments she stood up and approached the one-way mirror. Suddenly Anya spit on the glass and jutted her long middle finger upward in defiance.

Anya held her head high. Fuck the perverts! They could put her in a petri dish and study her like some malignant cell, but they could never control her.

* * *

Mulrooney watched from the other side of the glass. Anya Gallien was definitely strong and proud, he concluded. And there was a lot of anger there. But was she angry enough to commit murder?

There was something else about her... it was an air of caution. He watched as Anya arranged a piece of long red hair over her temple, and then she rubbed a spot behind her ear. There it was again—that nervous gesture. Mulrooney knew for sure Anya was hiding something.

Chapter 14

As Lauren sat alone in a coffee house, she clutched her hands together to stop them from shaking. Despite her efforts to concentrate on her work, the images of Scott's ravaged body clawed at her mind incessantly. After trying to swallow a piece of muffin, she spit it back out into a napkin. Lauren then looked out onto Second Street, thinking back on the forces which had conspired to bring her to this moment in her life.

As a young girl, every profession she ever considered was one full of adventure. When she was seven, she played "Peace Corps" and built a hut in her back-yard in San Diego, equipping it with an aqueduct system of overturned Mexican roof tiles. Alone in her hut she would pretend she was in an exotic place where people ate with their fingers and listened to strange music.

By the time Lauren attended U.C.L.A., she was considering documentary film writing and producing. During her Senior year, however, she proved to be a skilled enough writer and researcher to become a recurring contributor to *The New Yorker*. Soon *Outpost Magazine,* based in Long Beach, was offering her the adventurous assignments she wanted, as well as a salary that was equally satisfying.

Just before Lauren married Scott, *Outpost* went out of publication. However, freelance work kept her busy, and she continued to cover topics which were challenging or controversial in nature. In recent years she had covered everything from the indigenous tribes in the South Pacific to the oil leaks from government pipelines throughout the U.S. But no assignment, regardless of its challenge, had ever prepared her for the recent events in her own life.

As Lauren stared at the passing traffic on Second Street, she considered her next move. She couldn't continue to stay at Anya's because she had seen police, including Mulrooney and Clarke, swarming the canal earlier that morning. Despite the fact that Lauren's boat was the most logical place where she and Anya could escape the scrutiny of the media, Lauren knew she could never convince Anya to stay on a boat when out on bail. And right now, it was time for Lauren to help her friend, just as Anya had helped her.

Lauren suddenly shivered and looked over her shoulder. Seeing nothing unusual, she turned back to the window. A young woman was looking directly at Lauren as she walked by. Lauren nodded and tried to recall where she had seen her before. She was sure the woman recognized her, too. When the blonde looked back over her shoulder, Lauren felt uncomfortable and turned away. She noticed her hands were shaking again and admonished herself for letting her own paranoia overcome her.

She was greatly relieved when Michael Ryan suddenly appeared at her table. He gently squeezed her shoulders and bent to brush his lips across her cheek.

"Michael," she exclaimed, "You can't imagine how happy I am to see you!"

Michael was darkly handsome in a charcoal suit and black silk shirt buttoned at the neck. His silver hair was smoothed back, and his aqua eyes were a vivid contrast to his dark brows. Lauren noticed several women admiring him as he seated himself. "It's great to see you, too, Lauren," he smiled as he took her hand. "I saw you in the window, but I didn't recognize you at first. I've never seen you in dark hair before."

"It's Anya's wig. I was hoping to avoid reporters this way."

"Well, you'd look beautiful with a cocker spaniel perched on your head. I tried to reach you at Anya's to check up on you. How are you doing?"

"I've been better, Michael."

"No doubt. That was a dumb question, I realize. I heard Mulrooney and Clarke arrested Anya and searched her place. Where do you plan to go now?"

"I don't know. But I'll be with Anya–I'm posting bond."

"Why in the hell would you do that?" he asked, making no effort to disguise his surprise.

"Anya did not kill Scott, so why shouldn't I?"

Michael shook his head in warning. "Lauren, we've been friends a long time, so I'm not afraid to speak my mind. You may be a very intelligent woman, but you're not thinking straight. I don't mean any disrespect, because anyone would be rattled after going through what you've been through. However, although I know you love Anya, you are ignoring the facts. Mulrooney and Clarke would not have arrested her unless they thought they had enough evidence to build a good case against her."

"She's innocent, Michael," Lauren said wearily. "It's all circumstantial. Anya wouldn't hurt Scott, and she'd never hurt me."

Michael settled back in his chair, sensing her resolve. "Then can I at least talk you both into coming to my place?"

"Thank you, Michael. But the authorities are lifting the seal on my house later today after they remove the mattress. Just before you arrived, I was trying to accept the fact that it's time to go home and deal with the media. And with my life as it now is."

"I was afraid you'd say that," he sighed. "Okay, I'll send a team of maintenance personnel to your place this afternoon. I don't want you to have to deal with anything that may have been overlooked during the cleanup."

"Michael, you don't need to-"

"Allow me to do this for you, Lauren," he said as he rubbed the pale laugh lines around his eyes. "I feel so damn helpless. I need to do something."

"Thank you, Michael." I'm very grateful." She slipped an extra key off her key ring and handed it to him.

As Michael took the key, he looked down at her hand. He smiled to himself as he remembered that her hands were the feature which had attracted him most when he first saw her. They were capable and talented hands, reflective of the kind of woman Lauren was.

He still remembered the first day he met her at the marina. She was wearing an ankle-length linen skirt split to the thigh, and she was barefoot. He had noticed her near the outside bar, laughing and gesturing. She was earthy and real, and when they first spoke, he sensed her remarkable confidence.

Michael Ryan tired of women easily because most could not see beyond his power and his money, but Lauren was the one person he wanted to spend time with. He loved her mind. Scott also became his friend, but Scott was never as necessary to Michael's life as Lauren was. Lauren was fiercely independent like Michael, and she was the only person with whom Michael could truly relax. In Lauren, Michael saw himself.

Lauren didn't know Michael compared all women to her. When Michael found himself fantasizing about Lauren, he forced those desires from his mind. Michael had long ago learned that discipline makes a person stronger. And he would never gamble their friendship.

When they were on Lauren's boat after Scott's memorial service, however, Michael realized there was now an empty space inside Lauren, and he wanted to be the person to fill it. He was determined to help her put all this in the past. He believed she needed him now, and he hoped she would still need him when everything was over.

Michael smiled at Lauren as he reached to take her hand. He had always known her to be complicated, but she was authentic. It troubled him to think of her crying over a seriously flawed man like Scott Connolly. There were certainly things about Scott he would miss, but Scott's excesses and weakness were not among them. However, even though Michael knew things about Scott which were far from admirable, Michael had never said an unkind word about his friend to anyone.

He noticed that Lauren's attentions were focused on a young blonde woman exiting a clothing store across the street. The woman looked across to the window where Lauren and Michael were sitting before continuing on her way.

"Do you recognize her?" Lauren asked abruptly.

"I don't think so," Michael answered as they watched the blonde walk out of sight.

Lauren frowned then looked down at her watch. "Thank you again for everything, Michael," she said as she quickly reached for her purse. "I just realized how late it is. I can't keep Anya waiting."

"I just don't understand," Michael said, shaking his head. "Why are you so loyal to someone who slept with your own husband? I wish I could be that forgiving."

Lauren abruptly sat up in her chair and stared at Michael. "What in the hell are you talking about?" she demanded.

Michael's jaw dropped open as he stammered, "I just...I thought you must have known." He adjusted his top button and cleared his throat.

"Michael, talk to me!"

Michael took a deep breath then turned to look back at her. "Honey, I don't believe what an ass I am. It never occurred to me you didn't know. It's probably just a malicious rumor. Please forgive me." He rubbed his forehead. "Oh Christ, I didn't mean to hurt you, Lauren."

"It's okay, Michael. But it is just a malicious rumor. Anya would never do that," she said, trying to convince herself. "Let's forget it." Lauren stood up and gathered her papers, avoiding his gaze. "I'll call you later," she whispered as she turned to go.

"Please be careful, Lauren," he called to her gently as she rushed out the door.

Lauren stepped outside and took a deep breath. As she tugged at the black wig, she choked back the raw ache in her throat. While she tried to deal with her mounting confusion, she was completely oblivious to the young blonde woman, who was still watching her very closely from the adjacent parking lot.

However, Tim Mulrooney, parked nearby, sat in his car observing everything.

Chapter 15

Mulrooney circled back toward the bay and drove the few blocks to Lauren Connolly's home. When he pulled up in front, he used his binoculars to look back at Naples. He had a clear view of part of the Rivo Alto Canal, including Anya's house. He had almost missed the visual connection. "If it had been a snake, you would have been lunch," he said aloud, wondering if snakes thought people tasted like chicken.

As he got out of the car, he checked to make sure no one from the media was hovering. He had lost his temper with the media only one hour earlier when he berated them for "scavenging like dingoes on a carcass." He certainly didn't need their company now.

When the area was clear, Mulrooney donned a pair of plastic gloves and withdrew Anya's set of keys from an evidence bag. He tried each key in the lock, one at a time. "Come on," he coaxed as the lock resisted. He was sure he was right. Despite Lauren's firm denial of anyone else having a key to her home, her body language had convinced him she was not telling the truth. "Ah, Lauren, you did lie," he sighed, as the last key turned the lock.

Of course Lauren had given a key to her best friend. Nothing unusual, so why had she lied about it? Lauren was protecting Anya, and Anya was protecting Lauren. "So who's on first?" he mumbled as he dropped the keys back into the bag and entered the residence. "Just why did you fib to your ol' pal Mulrooney, Lauren?"

Mulrooney looked around as he walked through the house to the garage and then backtracked. The crime team had done a clean sweep, but Mulrooney instinctively knew they were all overlooking something. He walked to the bar where Lauren said she had picked up an open bottle of wine then stepped into the kitchen. He then paused at the glass rack before climbing the stairs to the bathroom. 1.5 minutes. He figured Lauren could have undressed, showered, and shampooed in 10-12 minutes. It would have required a minimum of 8-10 minutes or more to dry her thick head of hair. At least 20-24 minutes so far. He walked back downstairs where she said she returned the glass, then back up to the bedroom.

Pausing by the bed, he tried to approximate the time she spent in bed before she got back up to close the French doors as Lauren had later remembered doing. He then walked back to the bed. Roughly 22-26½ minutes. Lauren had approximated being in bed one minute before reaching over to pull Scott toward her, at which point she plunged her hand into his gaping stomach. It would have required less than 30 seconds to run from the bedroom to the middle of Bay Shore, even when taking into account her confused and hysterical attempt to exit through the closet door. Approximately 23-28 minutes total.

Dispatch had received the call at 12:27 A.M. Mulrooney estimated a 1-3 minute response time before the police were called by Anya Gallien. He quickly calculated. If time of death was between 11:58 P.M. and 12:02 A.M. when the phone was taken off the hook, he had to consider the possibility that Lauren was present at the time of the homicide.

What exactly had Lauren Connolly done before getting into the shower, he wondered, and what else could she have done for twenty-six minutes until she exited the house?

He had questioned many murderers who were skilled at hiding deep emotional or mental instability. He had never seen Lauren Connolly cry, not even at her husband's funeral. And he also had some curiosity about the 911 tape, on which there were no sounds of crying even though Anya supposedly had Lauren at her side during the distress call. Was it shock that colored Lauren's emotions, or something else?

Anything was possible, he never doubted that. Psychopaths were even known to fraternize with their lifeless victims. He remembered a case where an elderly woman had put rat poison in her husband's meat loaf. After she killed him, she propped him up so they could continue having all their meals together in front of the TV. When an alert neighbor peered through the window, he noticed the attentive man was tied to his chair. The real giveaway was the victim's toupee, which had overtaken his rapidly dehydrating head. The distraught woman told the arresting officers she thought her husband was just refusing to eat because he hated her cooking.

Mulrooney knew one thing—he had one bird in the cage, and there was room for another. Mourning doves travel in twos, he thought wryly. But he had to get some hard evidence. One woman's life was already on the line. He couldn't allow for more mistakes based on circumstantial evidence. And he couldn't ignore the fact that from the beginning, the coldness of the hit had struck him more as a contract killing, at least in its nature.

As he stood near the bed, Mulrooney stared at the blood-saturated mattress with its macabre stained outline of the corpse. He spotted the pair of pink 12-lb. weights he and Clarke had seen under the mattress frame on Lauren's side of the bed during their initial investigation. Lauren must have some firm arms, he figured, cataloguing his observation in his mental files.

Mulrooney walked out onto the balcony and faced the bay where he could see the dock from which the gondolas operated. He stood very still, formulating entrances and exits to the Connolly house and neighborhood.

After endless tracing of license plates and car owners, he and Clarke were able to determine that each car parked on Bay Shore at the time of dispatch had been there before the time of the homicide and hadn't been moved before police arrived to answer the 911 call. The perp, if he or she left the scene, either would have had to walk the streets, which was too risky, been picked-up, which would have been obtrusive and difficult to time, or escaped via water by boat or by swimming.

No boat activity had been reported in the bay across from the Connolly home, but a strong swimmer would have been able to swim from the bay beach to any of the nearby docks in the Naples canal. Also, the perp could have used a dinghy, which would be easy to hide or pull aboard a larger craft.

Mulrooney was making notes when the sound of a reciprocating saw jarred him like blade on bone. He shifted his gaze to a home under construction at the end of the back alley. Mulrooney suddenly smiled then marked 'dust' off his mental treasure hunt list. He had a good hunch about where the drywall dust had come from.

Evidence had suggested that Connolly's assailant had been wearing cotton gloves; and construction workers often used gloves when cutting drywall. If the perp had been lying in wait near the job site, he could have easily confiscated some gloves. If Mulrooney's hunch was correct, the perp must have known he could find what he needed there, even in the dark. Mulrooney concluded that despite the possibility that Connolly's murder had been a contract killing, the assailant knew the area and the victim very well.

Mulrooney took out his phone and dialed Killackey at headquarters. "It's Mulrooney," he said when he heard Killackey's voice. "Can you do me a favor? Try New Jersey homicide again. Find out if they picked up any traces of drywall dust at the peep show crime scene involving the Long Beach victim."

"So you still think there might be a connection to Doc Connolly, huh?"

"I don't know. But my gut keeps telling me I'm standing on an active fault line."

Chapter 16

Lauren was distracted as she waited for Anya outside the Sybil Brand Institute for Women. When Anya exited the building, she had to run a gauntlet of aggressive journalists to get to Lauren's car. Although Anya immediately embraced her, Lauren barely responded. She averted her eyes and quickly pulled away from the curb.

Lauren's restored white Mercedes 250 SL responded instantly as she adroitly maneuvered past the crowd. She corralled Anya's hand just as Anya was about to flash an obscene gesture at the journalists and then focused her attention back on the traffic. As she sped toward the marina, she noticed something in her rear view mirror.

"What is it?" Anya asked, glancing over her shoulder in the direction of Lauren's gaze.

Lauren slowed to catch the red light for a better look. "I think we're being followed," she replied, recognizing the blonde woman she had seen across from the coffee house.

"Really? See if you can lose her."

As Lauren turned right on Marina Drive, the blonde passed them at the light and continued north toward Pacific Coast Highway. "I think I'm just being paranoid," Lauren said.

When she turned into the lot near her slip, she spotted another group of reporters waiting on the dock near her boat. She abruptly steered her car back toward the road and drove the back way to Seal Beach. After she made sure no one was tailing her, she parked near the beach and gestured for Anya to follow her.

As Lauren felt the warm ocean breeze on the back of her damp neck, she slowly began to relax. Near the pier was an old cafe Lauren loved for its 1940's music and decor. When they entered, her eyes scanned the yellowed Coca-Cola posters of smiling soldiers bussing perky, cream-cheeked girls; and she was able to forget for a moment that she had not yet been cleared as a suspect in her husband's homicide. The pony-tailed hostess led them across the room to a chrome and vinyl booth facing the ocean.

"Thanks for picking me up, Lauren," Anya said as they sat down. Her hands were shaking as she reached out to Lauren. "I was afraid you wouldn't come. We really need to talk."

"Yes, I know, Anya. Perhaps you should start by telling me when you slept with Scott." Lauren listened to her own vacant voice as though someone else was speaking.

Anya looked completely taken aback.

"Anya, answer me," Lauren demanded as Anya silently stared at her. She knew Anya could not mistake the strength in her voice.

"Did Detective Mulrooney tell you that? Has he been trying to turn you against me?" Anya demanded.

"Answer my question."

"You know the answer to that question," Anya snapped as she pounded her hand on the table. "Scott was a friend. And only through you. We had dinner a few times when you were away on assignments, and once or twice when you were separated. You encouraged it, for chrissake!"

"Was there more than that? Did you have a relationship?"

"Lauren, how can you even ask me such a thing? Don't you think we have a few more relevant things to discuss?"

"Tell me, Anya," Lauren persisted, noticing the accent that had begun to color Anya's speech.

"No, of course we never had a relationship. That's ridiculous and disgusting!" Anya blurted. When several people turned to look, she jerked her head to face the ocean. "How could you ever doubt my loyalty after all this?" she whispered through clenched teeth as she watched a trawler dock at the end of the pier.

Lauren took a deep breath then looked down at her hands. "I'm sorry. I had to ask."

"We've been through a lot together, Lauren, and it's not over yet. Don't forget, we were *both* there the night Scott was killed, and we're *both* very much in danger of being convicted. I will never tell anyone anything. I'll stand by you, but I need to know you'll stand by me, and that you won't bend. No matter what. Trust me, Lauren, and I will get us through this."

"I don't know how to deal with the rumors. Nor with the questions, Anya."

"Just remember, you don't know *anything* about anyone, okay? I can handle the rest for both of us. I've faced worse than this."

Lauren studied Anya's face then turned away. She focused on a Jim Young New Zealand 37 sailboat, aware that there were only a few of that model imported to the States. As the boat skimmed the water's surface, it made her long to be on her own boat leaving all the turmoil behind. The women sat in silence for several minutes.

Anya hesitated for a moment before continuing. "Lauren, you were drinking that night-" She quickly held up her hand when Lauren started to protest. "I'm not judging you," she said. "You know I would never judge anything you ever did, Lauren, because I love you. But you become different when you drink. And that night I saw you-"

Lauren cut her off. "Please don't talk about what happened that night, Anya," she pleaded.

Anya reached out and placed her hand over Lauren's. "Lauren, everything is going to be all right,

I promise you. But I must tell you something, even though I don't want to make this any harder for you than it already is."

Lauren sucked in her breath. "What is it?"

Anya waited for the waitress to refill their cups before speaking. "A while back Scott did have a girlfriend. I don't know her name. He was seeing her when you two separated."

"So?"

"And even after you gave up Sam and got back together."

Lauren stared at Anya, and then looked away. For several minutes she sat in silence and watched a group of surfers ride the late afternoon waves, now over four feet high. The surfers looked like seals, weaving and bobbing with the swells.

"I guess I deserved it," Lauren whispered.

"The woman was at Scott's memorial service."

"Do you know who she is?"

"No. But Sam Bennett does."

"Sam does?" Lauren looked astonished. "Why would Sam know her?"

"I saw them at Sam's club before the fire destroyed the place. Sam was talking to Scott and her. When Scott had to leave, the girl stayed, and Sam was very friendly toward her. Other people saw them together also, and that could hurt Sam. Those detectives might suspect that Sam, your ex-lover who hated your husband, and that woman were somehow involved."

"Sam is friendly to everyone, and you know that. I'm sure she was nothing to him, or to Scott either."

"Probably not, but she had reason to hurt Scott, too. Scott dumped her to go back to you even though I heard he still saw her periodically. I haven't told Mulrooney any of this."

"You've been trying to protect Sam?"

Anya shook her head. "Lauren, Sam and the brunette are both a direct link back to you. It could look like you were in cahoots with Sam. Or in a jealous rage over the other woman. I'm protecting *you*. I learned a long time ago that we can't leave our fate to others."

Lauren got up, slid into the booth alongside Anya, and then slipped her arm around her shoulders. "I'm so sorry, Anya," she said. "I should never have doubted you. I've been too overwhelmed to think straight. That night it happened you were-"

"I was what?" Anya interrupted.

"Never mind," Lauren answered as she shoved the images out of her mind. "I think I'm still in shock. I don't know what I really saw or what I imagined. Lauren brushed Anya's hair from her eyes."I could use some time to find out what's going on. But you have to take care of yourself. I don't ever want anyone to be hurt because of me, least of all you, Anya." She kissed Anya gently on the cheek and then sat quietly with her arm around Anya as they waited for the check. "Is she pretty?" Lauren finally asked.

"The brunette?" Anya studied Lauren's face carefully. "So you really didn't know Scott was seeing someone?"

Lauren shook her head.

"Well, she's no beauty like you are, and she's certainly no 'Jackie O.'"

Lauren's jaw went slack. "She was the one in the black veil?"

Anya nodded, then contorted her face. "Her legs are stumpy, and that mole on her cheek looks like road kill."

Lauren's mouth hiked up into a half-grin. She was grateful for Anya's diplomatic offer of balm for her ego.

"We've got to find out her name," Anya insisted, "and what she knows. Preferably before she talks to Mulrooney. If she can incriminate you, I want you to get the hell out of Dodge. Okay?"

"I've got to think this through first. I'll call Sam right away and feel it out. Let's go back to my place and call Sam from there. I think I know where to find him."

"Sam isn't in Australia? He's here?"

"Of course not. You know I would have mentioned that." Lauren thought she heard Anya breathe a sigh of relief as she shrugged it off. "Before I call him, I'll drop you off to do whatever you wanted to do at home, and then I'll pick you up in an hour at the empty garage near your alley. Is that enough time?"

"Make it two hours."

Lauren and Anya exited the cafe into the bright afternoon sun. As the McGuire Sisters sang "Sincerely," the door closed behind them on an era that could never be recaptured. Neither Anya nor Lauren realized that the same could be said for their relationship.

Chapter 17

San Pedro, California
Same Day

The man stared at the battered suitcase on the yellow Formica table and considered what else to pack. He stroked the large protrusion that was his stomach and tried to control his wheezing. After he threw the thumb drive on top of his clothes, he locked the suitcase, checking the lock several times. When he finally sat down to rest, the faded velveteen sofa groaned under his weight.

He glanced at the table to make sure he had his remote control, his Spaghettios, a can opener, and a cold beer. He planned to eat and rest a bit, and then he'd head over the bridge to Long Beach. If all went well, he would make a lot of money fast so he could be shooting craps in Vegas before sundown the next day. Maybe he would pick up a juicy young girl to entertain him on the way, he mused as he scratched his enormous belly.

When his breathing became more labored, he lay back against the arm rest, propped up his swollen feet, and closed his eyes. As the flies buzzed overhead, he tried to focus on what little breeze was coming in from the open door.

In the quiet, he heard a rustling sound and his eyes flashed open. He struggled to sit up as a cold fear crept down his spine into his testicles. He could see his own massive shadow on the stained rose wallpaper just beyond the sofa. Suddenly a dark figure loomed over his heaving silhouette.

Before the fat man could turn to face his intruder, he felt a hot, searing sensation across his neck. "No!" he heard his own voice plea over the gurgling sound that was escaping his throat. As he fell onto the putrid carpet, he thrust out his arms to soften his fall. As he rolled over to fight back, his stomach was ripped open. The last thing in life the dying man saw was the vibrant color of his killer's hair.

Chapter 18

Relaxing on the dock by the gondola launch, Mulrooney sipped a Clausthaler and watched the windsurfers skimming along the cobalt blue surface of Alamitos Bay. He drew the salt air in through his nose, and faced upwind, feeling the breeze on his face and neck.

From his vantage point, he could see the Connolly house to his left, the Second Street bridge directly ahead, the canal entrance into Naples at one o'clock, and the narrow strip of bay separating Naples from the peninsula off to his right.

Mulrooney had spent the past few hours questioning boaters and locals, but nothing new had turned up. He had also learned that Mr. Armstrong, the witness who had verified Lauren's alibi, had taken his boat to Catalina for several days, so Mulrooney would have to wait to question him again. He was 0 for 2 and feeling the frustration.

After leaving the Connollys' house, he had cut across the back alley to the job site of the remodel. With his best broken Spanish, Mulrooney was able to determine that a three-man Mexican crew had been working on the site for a month.

Mulrooney had questioned the men carefully and determined that their alibis were airtight. He observed that they were all right-handed and too short to match the blood spatter pattern, which indicated a perp 5'8" - 5'11" in height. However, the foreman told him someone had recently swiped some gloves from underneath the temporary fencing. From the job site, Mulrooney had a clear view of the French doors leading to the Connollys' second floor bedroom.

Afterward he called his partner to give him the update. Clarke, who usually spoke with the precision of a twenty-one gun salute, had garbled, "Clarke, here," in a remarkable rendition of Brando in *On the Waterfront*. Mulrooney assured Clarke that his now-abscessed tooth had given him thespian potential.

Mulrooney laughed aloud as he thought about Clarke. Even though they had been partners for only two years, they shared an indivisible loyalty. Clarke was happily married with two kids, a psychotic dog named Sybil, a station wagon with stickers of the kids' schools—the whole shot. He had a vegetable garden that could feed a Third World country, and a baby alligator that he and Karen had smuggled home from New Orleans in a Big Gulp cup.

Clarke also had a nasty scar on his abdomen where he had taken a bullet intended for someone else. He had instinctively shielded his former partner when shots were fired during a routine investigation of a domestic dispute. As admirable as Clarke's bravery may have been, the chief had assumed Clarke's move was gender-related because Clarke's former partner was female. Chief Clemente, in his efforts to create a gender-blind work force, had broken up the partnership just before Mulrooney relocated to Long Beach. Mulrooney laughed at the irony. He knew that the small and feisty Clarke would take a bullet for him, too, if he had to. Clarke was loyal. It was just his nature.

He and Clarke had started as partners with definite racial and cultural differences. Mulrooney loved to bust Clarke's chops for eating what Clarke called 'Hood fois gras,' which was pork rinds fresh off the hoof. And Clarke loved to harass Mulrooney about dancing like a "yak on crack." Mulrooney knew they were really two men of one color: L.B.P.D. black-n-blue.

As Mulrooney sat on the dock, he also thought of Lauren Connolly, something he had been doing quite often. She and Anya were obviously as close as he and Clarke. Perhaps closer. In fact, Lauren seemed closer to Anya than to the doctor. Was it because they were women, he wondered, or was it possible that a conspiracy cemented their loyalty? He sensed Lauren had a deep emotional well, and he knew his answers lay at the bottom of that well.

As Mulrooney stood up and tossed his empty bottle into the recycling bin, he saw an old woman drinking water from a fountain near the beach snack stand. He recognized the shock of white hair sticking out from under a shredded straw hat. It was Proud Mary.

It had been months since he had seen old Mary, who had somehow managed to get a shopping cart across the sand to the refreshment stand. Her cart was heaped with an odd assortment of street treasures, including a sign declaring: PLEASE USE REAR ENTRANCE.

"Hey, Mary!" he called as he trudged through the sand to greet her.

Proud Mary looked up at him through milky eyes. The drinking water had left streaks on the soiled and craggy surface of her skin, and one rivulet was caught on her lip where it dangled precariously. She looked skittish, ready to scamper away at the slightest perceived threat.

"It's me, Mulrooney. I'm Officer Kate's friend. You know Kate—she's the pretty cop who always gives you money for food?"

After she examined his face, she abruptly displayed her yellowed teeth in a jack-o-lantern grin. Her chin was so off-set it appeared to be running away from her face.

"Yeah! So how ya' doin,' Malroody?" she chortled. When Mary spoke, she made little fluttering movements with her hands. Like butterflies, they would periodically light on her cheeks, only to flit away again. "You got a quarter for me?" she asked as she made a move to lift her baggy shirt up over her head.

"Yes, Mary, keep your clothes on!" he cautioned while anchoring her shirt with his hand. Proud Mary had gotten her nickname because she proudly like to flaunt her self-described "perfect papayas" to passersby in exchange for money, which was tantamount to extortion in Mulrooney's opinion.

"Your, um, attributes are lovely, Mary," Mulrooney said sweetly as he stared at the bank of hair outlining her upper lip, "but I think women leave something to the imagination when they keep their clothes on, okay?"

Mary cocked her head and placed her fingers on her cheek as if pondering a weighty proposition. "Didja know I was in pic-tures?" she asked, punching the "pic" with a clack of the tongue.

"Yes, Mary, I've heard. Let's see, it was *Sunset Boulevard*, wasn't it? You and Gloria Swanson and Bill Holden." He knew Mary loved to talk about old movies and movies stars from the fifties.

"Thas right," she grinned. Mary lifted her arms dramatically and struck a pose. She raised her brows and snarled, " 'I AM big. The PIC-TURES got small!' "

"Bravo!" Mulrooney clapped, laughing heartily. "I love that movie." He had seen it a dozen times and was always intrigued by the cinematic conceit of having a deceased man tell the story. *Too bad it only happens in the movies.* "I've tried to spot you in that film so many times," he waxed enthusiastically. "I think you said you were in the New Year's Eve party scene, right, Mary? Did you have lines?" He could see her beam as she basked in his attention.

Mary posed coquettishly with one hand beneath her chin and quoted a line from the film. " 'We didn't need dialogue. We had faces!' " She threw up her hand in a flourish.

Mulrooney applauded again. "Ah, I'm going to spot you yet!" As he pulled some bills out of his pocket for Mary, he glanced toward Lauren's house. He knew Lauren had just returned home. Although he couldn't see the garage entrance from where he stood, his keen ear had picked up the distinct sound of her classic Mercedes engine. "Take care of yourself, Mary, and keep your shirt on!" He placed the money in Mary's outstretched hand then turned to go.

"Malroody," she called after him. "A good lookin' gent paid me a whole dollah last week when I showed 'em my papayas." Mary laughed gleefully as she yanked up her top and flashed her two shriveled 'papayas' at him in triumph. "He's gonna be my new boyfriend. He's gonna take me dancin' cuz I just love ta dance."

"You do, huh?" Mulrooney walked back to yank her shirt down.

"Yup. He just went home to change his clothes. He got fish blood all over his fancy suit."

Mulrooney suddenly stopped moving. "Did you say he had blood on his *suit*?" Mulrooney asked, trying to keep the urgency out of his voice. "Men don't fish in suits, Mary. Do you know when that was - when you met your gent, I mean?"

"Last night," Mary said vaguely as she arranged her hair with her hands like a young girl preparing to meet a special beau.

"Are you sure, Mary? Think hard."

"Yes," she answered emphatically. "He was runnin' on the beach. He gave me a buck not ta foller him. The lights from all the police cars lit him up real purty, an' I saw Miss Kate, too."

"Police cars? Do you mean a few weeks back, Mary? Early morning, shortly after midnight?"

Mary shrugged her shoulders. "Maybe. I don't 'member fur sure. Sometimes I mix up my days."

"Do you know where your gent was coming from?"

"Sure, from that there house." She pointed to the large Spanish villa that was the Connolly home.

"You said he had blood on him?"

"Yeah, all over his clothes. We was standin' by that there light, jus watchin.'He dint want me to go with him while he changed. But he's comin' back, ya know. He promised."

"I hope so, Mary. I'd like to meet him. Which way did he go?"

"Thataway." She gestured toward the peninsula.

"Did he get in a boat?"

"I dunno, Malroody," Mary said as her hands took off in flight.

"If I showed you a photograph, do you think you could you tell me if it's the man who is your gent?"

Mary's eyes popped open wide. "Could I keep the pic-ture?" she trilled.

151

When Mulrooney nodded, Mary excitedly jumped around the outdoor beach shower, splashing sandy water all over him. He didn't give a damn. He was so happy to catch a break he knew he'd jump into the shower with her *and* her papayas if she would be able to identify the mysterious gent with the blood on his suit. He grinned at Mary with delight while keeping a close watch on the Connolly home across the street.

* * *

Lauren was trembling as she pulled into the garage and turned off her engine. It was her first time home since the night her husband was murdered. She and Anya sat in the car for a few moments while waiting for the last of the maintenance crew to leave. They both knew it would be difficult to face what was ahead.

"Michael just had everything cleaned. It won't be like, well you know. Help me do this, Anya," Lauren whispered.

As they exited the car and entered the house, Lauren felt a rush of panic. She halted in the doorway that led to the kitchen, unable to move her shaking legs. She had wanted to return home, but now she wasn't so sure.

Anya grasped her from behind. "We're safe. I won't let anyone harm you." Anya took her arm and led her into the kitchen.

Fresh flowers were in a vase on the table. Next to the flowers were several bottles of wine, a stack of books and CD's, and a basket of fruit. A piece of paper with Michael's name and phone number was propped against the vase next to her house key. As Lauren ran her hand along the old pine table which had belonged to her grandmother, she felt grounded once again.

Together she and Anya walked through the house. To Lauren, the house felt only vaguely familiar, like a childhood home in a yellowed photograph. Although the late afternoon sun filled the house as they climbed the stairs to the upper level, Lauren pulled her jacket closer to stop the shivering.

When they reached the bedroom, Anya stopped and held Lauren in place. "Let's not go in there, Lauren. Please stay somewhere else. Please."

Lauren held her ground. "I can't. Everything I need is in there. And I have to face this." With an air of resolve, Lauren stepped into the bedroom. It was immaculate. What shocked her most was how naked the room looked after having been stripped for evidence. It reminded her of a hotel room. It was beautiful but impersonal. There were few signs of life, and no signs of death. When she saw that the mattress had been removed, she finally let her breath escape.

Lauren's chest ached. She thought of the last time she heard Scott's voice. She had called him from the boat that night to apologize for calling him an addict. Although she had tried to downplay the situation to Mulrooney, Scott's continued drug use had become a constant source of worry and conflict.

Now she looked at the empty wall where a painting by Wayne Thiebaud had hung. Scott had sold her favorite painting without her knowledge, supposedly to pay for new office equipment. When their fight escalated that night, she accused him of having sold the painting to pay for his drug habit. His dishonesty and recklessness had seeped into every aspect of their lives.

She had left abruptly after their fight, still hurt and very angry. During their phone call later that evening, Scott was groggy but very apologetic. "I'm so sorry I took something that was yours, honey," he told her. "I wasn't thinking straight, but I'll make it up to you, Lauren," he promised, "because I love you." She knew he had heard her say she forgave him, even though it was far from the truth.

As Lauren turned to look at Anya, she whispered, "It's over now, Anya. It's over." After they packed a few clothes, Lauren closed the door in an attempt to seal off the memories.

* * *

Lauren and Anya returned to the kitchen and opened a bottle of Joseph Phelps Cabernet. "Michael was sweet to do all this," Lauren commented.

"Yes, he thought of everything. It's obvious he's in love with you."

Lauren hesitated. "I've suspected that for some time."

"It's a damn good motive to kill a spouse, isn't it?"

"Perhaps. I admit, in my darkest moments I've suspected every person I know. But he and Scott were friends, and Michael has never even made a move on me, not even when Scott and I were separated."

"Do you think Scott could have owed Michael money?"

"Even if he did, Michael has so much money it's no longer important to him. Michael has amazing self-control, and he's too smart to risk everything he has worked for in his life. I think someone with more volatility did it. It was as if someone snapped. Do you know if the woman Scott dated was in love with him?"

"I really don't know, Lauren. But it's true that jealousy and obsession can drive sane people to do sick things. What about Sam? He was very angry over losing you. Have you talked to him recently?"

"I'm too tired and confused to discuss this right now," she answered, sidestepping Anya's question. She rubbed her forehead with the palm of her hand and then took a long swallow of wine.

Anya watched while Lauren polished off her wine and poured herself another. "Go easy, Lauren, please. You know you don't handle that stuff too well."

"Anya, if ever I've needed a drink, it's now."

"I know, I know. But you know how it affects you."

Lauren reluctantly set down the bottle of wine. She knew her friend was right. Alcohol made her moods darker, maybe even a little crazy. She didn't drink often, but she didn't drink well. A few incidents when her normally even temper had flared out of control had embarrassed and worried her. She also wondered if several recent black-outs were alcohol related. She never admitted to anyone that she couldn't remember anything after the blackouts. Lauren sighed, knowing she would have to face the days ahead sober, or not at all. And Lauren believed she was strong enough to face anything.

"Anya, why don't you get something to eat," she said abruptly. "I need to place a call to Sam."

Anya raised her brows but didn't move while Lauren made a call to long distance directory assistance.

Lauren jotted down the information then turned to Anya. "My hunch was correct. I've located him."

Anya observed Lauren carefully. She could see the telephone shaking in Lauren's hands as she looked at Anya beseechingly. "Do what you have to do," Anya mumbled as she discreetly left the room.

Lauren took a deep breath and dialed with painstaking concentration. She was determined to get answers. When the phone began ringing on the other end, her chest heaved. She was about to hang up when a voice answered. "Gidday, Jazzin.'" It was Sam.

The memory of Sam's voice was as familiar to her as the memory of his warm body against hers. Lauren couldn't speak. She was suddenly so overwhelmed by a wave of conflicting emotions that she hit the off button on the phone and dropped it on the floor.

"Oh, God, Anya, I couldn't do it! I have to talk to Sam in person. That's the only way," she cried as she raced toward the living room. Anya was standing near the television with her back to Lauren. "When I heard his voice, I just didn't know where to begin. I-"

Lauren suddenly stopped in mid-sentence then took a faltering step backwards just as Anya turned around in one slow, mechanical movement. Anya gave Lauren a vacant look then began to walk slowly toward her. Sweat beads had collected above her brow making her face glisten. She was holding fast to a long object in her left hand.

"Anya? What are you doing?" Lauren cried. "No, please-" She reached toward her friend, then her hand pulled back into a position of supplication.

Lauren could see the white light of the television glinting laser-like off the tip of a razor-sharp blade. While Anya moved steadily toward her, Lauren's voice clawed at the tissue of her throat as her screams pierced the surrounding silence.

* * *

Mulrooney was on the beach watching Proud Mary dance in the outdoor shower when he was stopped cold by the paralyzing, high-pitched scream. Mary froze mid-dance. Then, with a long, low wail, she backed away from Mulrooney. She flailed at the ghosts that were bearing down upon her as Mulrooney turned in the direction of the screams. Sunbathers close to the seawall jumped to their feet, alerted by the commotion. Mulrooney knew the scream had come from the Connollys' Bay Shore villa.

"Wait here, Mary!" Mulrooney commanded as he started in the direction of the scream. "Don't leave! Wait here until I get back."

Mulrooney drew his weapon and sprinted through the sand. As he raised his legs high, his heart heaved, and the tightening band behind his knees sent waves of warning. Mulrooney ran faster. Within seconds he covered the distance between the beach and the location of the nerve-scraping screams.

He hurtled the seawall and traversed the street to the house. "Police!" he yelled as he ran past the beach crowd. "Stay back!"

An ominous silence had taken the place of the screams, which Mulrooney knew were Lauren's. *Don't let it be her,* he silently pleaded.

Mulrooney made his way to his car near the sea wall to call for backup. He then sprinted toward the Connolly home and took cover to the left of the large window that faced the bay. With his weapon in ready position, Mulrooney edged closer to the window. From there he was able to view the living room.

He spotted Lauren huddled in a doorway as if sculpted into place. Her eyes were fixed on Anya, who stood in the middle of the room. A knife was extended from her left hand like a deadly talon. Anya suddenly shifted, as though her animal senses picked up the presence of something threatening.

"Freeze! Drop the knife, Anya!" Mulrooney yelled as burst through the door. Anya edged closer to Lauren. As he assessed the scene, his ears automatically analyzed the sound of each approaching car in hopes that a cruiser was nearby. He planted his feet and readied his weapon when Anya swayed slightly.

"Freeze!" Mulrooney screamed again.

Anya's head jolted toward Lauren then in the direction of Mulrooney's voice. She suddenly began to stammer, her now-heavy accent coloring her words. "I...I found it in there," she cried. With the knife in hand she pointed toward the television where a newscaster mouthed words on the silent screen. Several old videos were scattered on the floor around her feet.

"Drop it, Anya," Mulrooney commanded. He had her in a direct line of fire.

Anya stared at the knife in her hand, and then she finally released her grip. When the weapon clattered against the wood floor, she jumped back. Her eyes darted toward Lauren, who was now slumped against the wall.

Mulrooney moved quickly, kicking the knife out of Anya's reach. Keeping his weapon on Anya, he moved to Lauren's side.

"It's not mine!" Anya pleaded. "Please don't shoot me!" She held her hands up as if her defensive gesture could stop a bullet.

Lauren stared down at the knife. When she bent to examine it, Mulrooney barked sharply, "Don't touch that, Lauren!"

Startled by his abruptness, Lauren jerked her hand away so fast she lost her balance. She clutched Mulrooney for support, staring up at him in confusion.

As she leaned into him, Mulrooney could smell the fragrance of her hair mixed with the scent of her flushed skin. He forced his eyes away from her and cleared his throat as Kate and Sanders burst through the door with weapons ready.

"It's under control," Mulrooney said quietly. He turned his focus toward Anya. "Where did you get the knife, Anya?"

"It was in there," Anya repeated weakly, "...in the old VCR." Mulrooney observed how she backed away from the VCR as she spoke. "Lauren still has a collection of classic videos, so I wanted to play one for her. The tape wouldn't go in so I reached in with my fingers-"

"Could you call the Police Lab for me, Kate?" Mulrooney requested while he examined the VCR closely. He could see no visible evidence of prints or blood. The VCR had been meticulously wiped clean, but he could see it was just deep enough to hold a knife if the weapon were put in diagonally.

Mulrooney crouched to look at the knife. It appeared to be handmade. The grip was carved wood and was decorated with unusual, tribal-like markings of orange pigment. The finely ground stone flake was symmetrical in shape with a slight serration of its sharp tip. Mulrooney estimated the blade itself to be about five inches in length, and he could see that it was razor sharp.

"How in the hell did the crime team miss that?" Kate muttered. She led the women aside while Sanders called dispatch.

Mulrooney examined the knife again but saw no signs of blood or tissue. Using his pen, he then shoved open the door of the tape slot on the VCR. When he aimed his flashlight in the slot, the inside appeared to be spotless.

"It wouldn't have been hard to miss, Kate, *if* it had been here that night. Someone painstakingly wiped the weapon clean and then took the time to hide it some distance from the victim, assuming this is the weapon that was used in the commission of the homicide." He turned to Lauren and Anya. "I think someone wanted you to find it, Lauren. Have either of you ever seen this knife before?"

Lauren shook her head slowly from side to side. Mulrooney shifted his gaze to study Anya. She turned to Lauren and hesitated, then she slowly but emphatically shook her head to indicate that she had never seen the knife.

The left corner of Mulrooney's mouth lifted slightly. He had learned from his love of movies that acting was reacting. Otherwise, Lauren's very discreet eye signal for Anya to keep silent would have been almost imperceptible.

Chapter 19

The smell of the fresh sea breeze invigorated Mulrooney as he walked along the dock to the boat slip where the forty-two foot Hattaras was moored. Drops of water on the decking reflected the morning sun, indicating the boat had been recently rinsed clean. Seeing no one aboard, Mulrooney yelled, "Knock, knock." His hand automatically accompanied his voice with a knock-knock against the warm air. He looked around self-consciously. "Ahoy there!" he called, feeling as foolish as a turd hat in his vain attempt to use the lingo of the boat crowd.

"Ahoy there," a voice answered as Mr. Armstrong, dressed in a white jumpsuit with wide pant legs, appeared from the main salon.

"Detective Mulrooney, L.B.P.D.," Mulrooney said, flashing his shield and taking in Armstrong's lounge lizard get-up.

"Oh, Detective, I was expectin' someone else. I need some work on one of the Cummins. It's a 903. Know anything about boat engines?"

"I'm afraid not, Mr. Armstrong. I wouldn't be able to locate the hood." Fortunately, he noticed, Armstrong chuckled.

"If you're looking for Ms. Connolly, she hasn't been around much since that night her husband was murdered," Armstrong said with a look of disappointment.

"Actually, it's you I'd like to speak with," Mulrooney explained. "Although you gave your statement to my partner, I'd like to ask a few more questions if you don't mind."

"Well, I guess I better get used to this. Some Detective named Atilla called to say he wanted to talk to me, too."

Mulrooney was suddenly so furious he wanted to hit something. "Atilla called you?" he repeated.

"Yes, sir," Armstrong nodded.

Mulrooney had no place to direct his anger, so he shoved the matter aside to gnaw on later. "You only need to talk to Clarke and me, Mr. Armstrong."

"Well, com'on aboard. I hope it won't take long cuz I'm expectin' the little woman back 'fore too long. I don't want to talk about Mrs. Connolly in front of her. She doesn't like my lookin' at the young gals, if you get my drift." He winked conspiratorially like a Las Vegas lothario before poking Mulrooney in the arm with a bony elbow.

"I think I understand, Mr. Armstrong. I just wanted to see the view of her slip from here, if you don't mind." He glanced around the salon, mentally photographing the layout. "So, you were watching a passing boat when you noticed Mrs. Connolly that night. Is that correct?"

"Yes, sir, just like I told Detective Clarke." He smoothed back his silver duck tail as he looked out the window toward Lauren's yacht, the Seduction.

"You were here in the main room at the time? Not downstairs?" Mulrooney stared at Lauren's boat as he questioned Armstrong.

"I was here in the main *salon*, yes sir. Not *below*." Armstrong emphasized the words 'salon' and 'below' like the monitor of a spelling bee.

Mulrooney wondered if Armstrong expected him to repeat the words like a recalcitrant landlubber, but he decided to ignore the vocabulary lesson. "Is the wood in her galley the same as the wood in here? Nice stuff," he said, baiting his line.

"'Sure is. It's teak. Hers is finished a lot better than mine though," he complained as he ran his sun-dried hand along a wood cabinet. "Mine needs sanding."

"Oh, yeah, I see." Mulrooney now turned his focus directly on Armstrong. "So have you ever been aboard Mrs. Connolly's boat?"

"No, sir. I only know her to say hello. The little missus keeps me on a short leash, if you get what I'm sayin.'" He winked again as he sucked in his paunch and thrust his chest forward like a spring robin.

Mulrooney was now ready to reel in his catch. "So how do you know what the wood in her galley looks like? You can't see it from here." He watched as Armstrong blinked rapidly, this time with both eyes. Armstrong's cheeks turned so red Mulrooney momentarily feared the old codger would stroke out...or start a flash fire. "You've been watching Mrs. Connolly through those binoculars, haven't you, Mr. Armstrong?" *Can you say 'voyeurism,' Mr. Armstrong?*

Mulrooney waited for a response as Armstrong twitched and coughed. When Armstrong began to wheeze, Mulrooney slapped him on the back. "Christ, don't quit on me now, pal!" Mulrooney said. "Mr. Armstrong, we're going to have to be a bit more honest here, aren't we?"

"Please, Detective, don't tell the little lady. She'd bust my nuh, er, my, uh-"

"Nuts?" Mulrooney smiled then winked as he nudged Armstrong with an elbow as though they were brothers in arms.

"Look here, Detective," Armstrong pleaded, "if you bust me for looking, then you might as well arrest all the fellas around here. Everyone looks at a gal like Mrs. Connolly. There's one guy who stands at the end of the dock on many a night watchin' her. I've seen him myself!"

"Really? Do you know this guy?"

"Nope, he's just some guy with dark hair. He likes to watch her. Been hanging around for months."

"Could you identify him if you saw a photo?"

"Nope. Never saw him during daylight, only night. Never know where he disappears to. I'll watch for him, though."

"Was he around on the night of the homicide? Try to remember, Mr. Armstrong."

Armstrong furled his brow and looked up in the air as if he were waiting for a divine revelation. "Dunno. Maybe, maybe not. Oh, fudge, you gonna bust my nuts now?" Armstrong banged his palm against his forehead hard enough to crack a walnut.

"Let's get a few things straight, Mr. Armstrong. I'm not here to bust you or your nuts. I want information, so take me through what you saw, step by step."

"Yes, sir, Detective. Well, I had my, uh, 'whale' watching glasses out, and I saw a light on in the Seduction. So I happened to notice Mrs. Connolly working that night. The missus was asleep, so I stayed up to read and stuff. Anyway, Mrs. Connolly just read and drank wine for a long time. She seemed kinda agitated. After she made a phone call, she secured the boat and left."

"You told my partner she appeared to be sober, correct?"

"Well, I thought so. But everyone is tipsy on a boat so it's hard to tell. I coulda been wrong."

"Good point. Did anyone visit her that night?"

"No, sir. She came alone and worked awhile, and then she left just after midnight."

"Do you usually wear a watch, Mr. Armstrong?" Mulrooney had noticed that the old man's arms were bare.

"No, sir, I can't cuz I got eczema," Armstrong unconsciously scratched himself. "I can't wear a wedding band either, which ticks off the missus."

"Well then how were you so sure of the time? Time is a very important factor here."

Armstrong smiled as he latched upon a way to save face. He quickly grabbed his binoculars to prove he was an accurate voyeur, seemingly unfazed by the dubious distinction.

"Look," he said as he shoved the glasses into Mulrooney's hand. "Look there."

When Mulrooney focused the high-powered binoculars on the Seduction, he could clearly see the details of the boat. He scanned the decks then focused on the interior.

"Do you see it?" Armstrong asked.

Mulrooney scanned the galley. On the counter was a coffee maker with a digital clock. Mulrooney put down the glasses and reeled around to face the old man. "So that's how you were so sure of the time?"

"Couldn't help but notice." Armstrong flashed a 'twas nothin' grin.

Mulrooney looked at his watch. "Whoa," he whispered. Mulrooney looked at the galley clock in the Seduction one more time, then back at his watch again. "She's ten minutes fast!" Mulrooney closed his eyes as he realized he had one more piece of evidence to prove that Lauren was indeed home when her husband was brutally murdered.

He shoved the glasses at the old man. "Thanks, Armstrong, we'll be in touch. Remember, you don't have to talk to Detective Atilla. And let me know if you spot any other so-called 'whales' in the marina."

At that moment Armstrong's boat listed to port as the three-hundred pound 'little missus' suddenly boarded. She stared down Mulrooney, whose last words about 'whales' had lingered on longer than Generalissimo Franco. After Mulrooney realized his gaffe, he briefly considered drowning himself. Instead, he nodded and bailed ship leaving the explanations to Armstrong. Mulrooney had no time to make nice. He had a perp to catch.

Chapter 20

The old pay phone at the marina had better reception than Mulrooney's cellular phone and provided him with a spectacular view of the yacht basin as he dialed Chief Clemente's office. On the third ring, he abruptly hung up. He decided he wanted to get Clarke's input on this new bit of evidence before consulting with Clemente. Mulrooney had set up a tail on Lauren, so he felt secure about keeping her at close range. And he would deal with Atilla in the morning.

Instead, he rang the Department of Anthropology at Cal. State, San Bernardino. As he waited for an answer, he spotted two enormous starfish in the marina scouring the rocks for food. When it occurred to him that he hadn't eaten, he suddenly remembered his lunch plans with Kate. Dr. James Peterson's greeting interrupted his thoughts.

"Peterson."

"Jim, it's Mulrooney. Got anything for me?"

"Yep. This knife is the most interesting thing you've given me yet, Tim."

Mulrooney enjoyed the excitement in Peterson's voice. "Glad to provide some brain food, Doc. What do you have?"

"Well the knife is definitely Australian. It's aboriginal and hand-carved as you suspected. The quartzite blade is an example of outstanding workmanship using ancient honing techniques. That fancy grip is fascinating. It's made of wood from a gidgee tree and is attached by kangaroo skin and a material we call spinifex."

"That a gum mass, right?"

"Indeed it is. It's strengthened with spiny grass, probably brought inland from the coast. The grip is impregnated with shark teeth fragments, which are usually indicative of northern Queensland; but I'd place it in central or south central Australia due to the type of ocher aborigine markings on the grip. You said there were no prints other than those of your prime suspect."

"That is correct."

"And the blood traces on the knife match the victim, right?"

"Yes, even though it was wiped clean, the police lab found traces up under the grip. The perp should have known we could make a match and that the knife is distinctive enough to trace. Is this some kind of an aborigine message or something?"

"I think your victim got the message intended."

"Good point."

"But I'll do some more research, Tim. I did find traces of something I couldn't identify. When I called Clarke at home, he mumbled something about picking up samples to take to the zoology lab. I think that's what he said."

"Yeah, he is having a hard time talking. He's looks a blowfish—dude has an abscessed tooth."

"Ouch. Well when the samples are done, we'll call you."

"Great. Thanks, Jim. You have my cell number."

Mulrooney hung up and dialed the station. Killackey picked up on the second ring. "Killackey, is Clarke in yet?"

"I was about to text you. He went to the lab, but he told me to tell you he'll be here in forty-five minutes. So will Anya Gallien."

"What?"

"You heard right."

"Why in the hell would someone charged with homicide feed herself to the lions?"

"No idea. But she was adamant that she'll only talk to you and Clarke."

"Tell Clarke I'll be there."

Out of the corner of his eye, Mulrooney saw a platinum Lexus LS500 hybrid pull up near the dock and hesitate awhile before taking off. He recognized the car by its sound. After he slammed down the receiver, he ran to his car and jumped in. He raced out of the marina parking lot looking both ways for the Lexus, which had disappeared from sight. Mulrooney drove up and down Marina Drive and then waited five more minutes. When the Lexus did not reappear, he gave up and headed into Belmont Shore.

As he was driving, he yanked off his constricting jacket and slipped on an old sweater. He turned down Bay Shore and slowed down to look for Proud Mary. She had been scared off when he last saw her, and his informants hadn't spotted her around since then. After a cursory glance at the bay beach, he gave up and turned west on Ocean to take the back way to the Belmont Athletic Club to meet Kate.

Mulrooney parked in the alley off Argonne and ran up the outside stairwell to Murphy's Bar. Kate was seated at the balcony counter overlooking Second Street working on her phone. He crept up behind her and whispered, "Buenas Tardes, my little blue tamale."

"Hasta la Guacamole," she said without turning around.

Mulrooney plopped on the seat next to her and shoved his files and a stack of photos onto the counter. "Sorry, Kate, but I've only got time to chug a beverage. I've got to put the thumbscrews to some suspects."

She put down her phone and turned toward Mulrooney. "Look at that cardigan!" she suddenly roared. "You look like Mr. Rogers!"

Mulrooney grunted as he smoothed his old sweater that looked a casualty of a mugging. "My ex picked it out," he said defensively.

"Boy, Isabella really hated you, didn't she?"

"I'm not officially on duty yet, so comfort is my priority, smartass!" He grinned sheepishly while he arranged the photos on the bar and signaled for a waiter.

"Red Bull shooters, anyone?" the waiter said as he walked up.

Mulrooney turned on his stool. "Kevin, you're back. How was Maui?"

"Great, man! Really great. Hey, I heard there was a murder on the mean streets of Belmont Shore, but I missed all the action. I flew outta here right after it happened, so I must have been at the airport when the shit hit the proverbial fan. Your reputation is spreading fast these days, Detective Mulrooney."

"Yeah, like salmonella. Two root beers, Kevin." After Kevin slapped him on the back and went for the drinks, Mulrooney shoved a photo in front of Kate. "Kate, have you ever seen this guy before?"

"Sure, that's Sam Bennett. He's the Aussie who owned Jazzin' night club downtown. Lauren Connolly's lover, right? Helluva sexy guy."

"What about the guy in this photo?"

"He's a hottie, too? Who are you investigating—the Chippendales?"

"Look again. You're in the singles scene, so I thought you might know him, too. The photo was taken at the memorial for Scott Connolly. He checks out cleaner than a nun's panties, but I'm double-checking. His name is Michael Ryan."

Kate stared at the photo. "No, I don't know him, but as a matter of fact, I do remember seeing him at Jazzin' one night. He was talking to Sam Bennett."

"You're sure?"

"Positive, Tim." She looked at the photo again. "He's a classy looking guy."

"He strikes me as the laid back kind who rides in on a white horse to pick up the pieces. They seldom get dirty."

"Well I would suspect that a jealous type killed Connolly. Somebody with a short fuse. That was one ruthless piece of work."

"If you were going to kill a man, how would you do it?"

"I would drag him into a lengthy discussion about feelings."

"Hell, they'd declare it a suicide," Mulrooney laughed.

Kevin set the drinks on the counter as Mulrooney shoved the pictures aside. "She's a babe, huh?" Kevin exclaimed as he glanced down at the top photo. It was a snapshot of Anya Gallien standing near Scott Connolly's urn.

"She sure is," Kate grinned. "And you should see the other one, right, Tim?" Mulrooney blushed and shrugged it off as Kevin gestured to the photo of Anya.

"I saw that chick when I was leaving work the night I went to Maui."

Mulrooney was suddenly in Kevin's face before Kevin could finish his sentence. "You saw her the night of the homicide? Where?"

"Right down there, on the bus bench across the street." He pointed over the balcony. "The one in front of Midnight Espresso. She was just sitting there alone, having a coffee. I couldn't help but notice her because she's a real babe with that fiery hair and all. But she looked sorta lonely the way she was just sitting there."

Mulrooney stood up and fixed his gaze on the RTD bench across the street. Someone had scrawled Deja Vu on the seat back–two times. "What time was it when you noticed her, do you remember?"

"It was when I got off work at 12:10 A.M. She was still there after I walked down to the ATM for cash, so that was around 12:20 A.M. or so. But she stood up to leave just as I was getting in my car. I remember, 'cause I thought about offering her a ride."

"Kevin, look at this photo closely. "You're sure this is the woman?"

"Hey! Would a hormonal guy like me forget a good-looking redhead? Why? Man, she's not the chick who was charged with the murder, is she?"

Mulrooney looked at Kate and plopped back down on his stool. "One and the same."

As Kevin walked off shaking his head, Mulrooney poured Kate's drink without the usual flourish and took a chug of his own before gathering his files.

"I'm knee-deep in shit," he muttered. "I'll call you later, Katie."

"Get some sleep first," she smiled.

He was halfway toward the steps when he stopped long enough to ring Killackey again. "Lauren Connolly's alibi just went up in smoke," he told Killackey. "Tell the chief I'll need a warrant. In the meantime, have surveillance bring her in for another chat," he directed. "Before Clemente gets too full of himself, you might want to mention that a reliable witness saw Anya Gallien at Midnight Espresso only minutes after the homicide. I thought you'd like to be the one to watch him squirm. It's my way of thanking you for helping me out, pal."

After Mulrooney hung up, he rushed down the stairs and out onto Second Street. He could hear Kate on the balcony above him singing the "Mr. Rogers" theme song, " 'Won't you be, won't you be, my neighbor.' " In spite of his anxiety, he was laughing as he rounded the corner into the alley.

Mulrooney was unbuttoning his sweater when suddenly the earth shifted beneath him. He was thrown against the brick wall a split second before he actually heard the explosion. The ground trembled as lights ignited inside his skull in a dazzling array of color. Just as Mulrooney went down onto his knees, the driver's door of his car shot past his head. He covered his face against a shower of glass that rained down like sparks in the sunlight. Metal fragments screeched as they clawed at the pavement for a foothold, and acrid smoke from melted metal and rubber swallowed the air.

When the echoes in his ears began to fade, the sound of screams replaced them. Mulrooney was reeling from the impact of the explosion. He slowly lifted his head to see his car door imbedded in the alley wall.

Fuck, am I unpopular! He pulled a hunk of glass out of his hair with a trembling hand and tried to gather his wits.

Chapter 21

Anya had just arrived at the station and was waiting in the interrogation room when Mulrooney charged down the hall. As he rounded a corner, he passed Detective Carlos Atilla, who blatantly smirked at Mulrooney's obvious distress. Mulrooney mentally invited Atilla to fuck off, but he kept walking. He slowed down only long enough to hear Killackey report that he had not yet able to reach Lauren Connolly's surveillance team.

Mulrooney couldn't be bothered to change his clothes. He still had glass in his hair, and he was livid. The pipe bomb that had been activated prematurely by an earthquake tremor had destroyed his car. Remarkably, there had been no injuries. Whoever had done it had been watching him. And he or she had worked fast. A team of explosives experts was currently examining the carcass of his very permanently expired automobile.

Mulrooney shook off the pain that threatened to undermine his swollen knees before yanking open the door of the interrogation room. "Hello, Anya," he said.

"Detective," she nodded.

"Is your attorney on his way?"

"No, I fired him. Believe me, lawyers are much more deceitful criminals. I came here to do whatever I can to help you, short of hanging myself for your viewing pleasure."

Mulrooney wasn't sure what her agenda was, but he intended to get the jump on her. "Hanging won't be necessary, Anya. The State has its own methods. Tell me, how good are you with explosives?"

"I beg your pardon?"

"Perhaps you should. But right now I want to know where Lauren Connolly is."

"I don't really know," she answered as she smoothed her coral silk dress. The vivid color, which complimented her features, reminded him of ripe peaches. He took off his Mr. Rogers sweater and threw it on a chair.

At that moment the door opened and Clarke entered. One side of his face was swollen and distorted. He pulled Mulrooney aside and mumbled, "I just heard. Are you okay?"

"I'm just peachy-keen. How about you, buddy?" he winced. "You're looking rather glandular." Mulrooney cut off Clarke's muffled response. "Don't talk, Smokey, or your cheek might explode all over the place, and I've already met my concussion quota for today."

Clarke grunted and handed Mulrooney a slip of paper with a drawing of a balloon on it. Mulrooney nodded then stuffed the paper into his pocket before turning back to Anya. "Anya, with your verbal and written permission, we will be recording our conversation. You may request a lawyer at any time."

After Mulrooney got her signature, he snatched up the consent form and handed it to Clarke. "Okay, Anya, if you want to help us, tell us why you killed Dr. Connolly," he asked abruptly. "You claim you're here to help us, so I assume you want to write a confession." He shoved a pen and pad across the table.

Anya sensed he was baiting her. She folded her hands and re-crossed her long legs, and then she checked her watch. Mulrooney and Clarke watched her closely as she pulled a lock of hair over her temple and rubbed the scar behind her ear.

They waited in silence. Suddenly Mulrooney took a completely different tactic. "What's your game, Anya, and why did you cover for Lauren?"

It was not the question she expected. Anya averted her eyes and sat very still. Mulrooney waited again. *You may have come to me, cupcake, but I'm still running this goddamn investigation.*

"You never drove by Lauren's boat slip, did you? You watched her drive down Bay Shore through your binoculars, so you knew she was already home. You then drove over to Lauren's house, parked, and knocked. When she didn't answer, you let yourself in with your key. You didn't see anyone, so you walked to the back of the house and whistled. When there was no response, you gave up and went for coffee. Upon your return you discovered that your friend had butchered her husband, and now you're covering for her."

He continued to hammer her as she squirmed in her seat. "That makes you an accessory. You know, Anya, we could get the prosecutor to go a lot easier on you if you cooperate with us."

"Lauren didn't kill him!" Anya cried as she jumped up from her chair.

Mulrooney detected the accent that had crept into her voice again. "Yes, she did," he prodded, "she wanted him dead."

"No, she loved that bastard! He deserved to die, but she was too blind to see that!" Anya dropped back down into the chair. Her taut face slowly caved in. Mulrooney could see she was crying, although she made no sound.

He was uncomfortable as he watched Anya try to contain her emotions. It was loneliness that Mulrooney saw in her face, an unspeakable solitary loneliness. Her demeanor touched something in him he couldn't identify. While Clarke handed her a box of tissues, Mulrooney struggled with the familiar conflict between what he thought and what he felt. He wanted to console Anya, but he quickly shoved his feelings back down under his hardened surface.

"You're in love with her, aren't you, Anya?" Anya stared straight ahead, motionless.

"Yes, I am, Detective," she finally whispered. She looked directly at Mulrooney and then at Clarke. "She's all I have left."

"Do you two have an intimate relationship?" Mulrooney asked.

" 'An intimate relationship'? I'm not sure you can even begin to understand that kind of love."

"I'm willing to try, but you have to talk to me."

Anya looked to Mulrooney for assurance that she could trust him with something so precious to her. After a beat, she spoke again. "I love Lauren more than anyone. She is my mother, my father, my dead baby sisters. She is my life. Can you understand that, Detectives?"

"Yes, we certainly can. And are you lovers as well?" The words hung in the air like a life sentence. Clarke looked away as he pulled out a chair and sat down, cradling his jaw in his hand. "No, she is not my lover. Although I prefer women, Lauren does not," she said, lowering her head. She thought about Lauren and smiled. Anya had always deemed it wise to keep a very low profile, but it was difficult, as Anya was not a woman who went unnoticed. However, Lauren had never been threatened by Anya's lifestyle, and she loved Lauren all the more for that.

Anya had suffered a lifetime of guilt believing that her family was executed because she had sought freedom from those who had hurt her. Now Lauren was the only family she had left, and she would stay the course no matter what. This time, Anya decided it would be a life for a life.

Mulrooney interrupted Anya's silence. "As long as you were planning to take the whole rap, Anya," he prodded, "why didn't you admit that you went to Lauren's house earlier that evening to deliver champagne and balloons? We traced the purchases back to you, but you were empty-handed when you arrived there that night after the murder."

Clarke managed to mumble something that sounded like "When Ratso Rizzo rocks."

Mulrooney translated: "When did you last see the doc?"

"I was exhausted from my trip and was afraid I might not be able to stay awake until Lauren returned that night. So I called Scott just as he was going out. He offered to pick up the champagne, chill it for me, and attach the balloons before she returned.

"For obvious reasons, I did not want you to know I had seen him that evening. Besides, I was afraid you'd probably turn up a few incriminating rumors about Scott and me eventually, and I would never want Lauren to doubt me." When Mulrooney and Clarke did not respond, she continued. "It goes without saying that the rumors about Scott and me are completely unfounded. That night I met Scott for a few minutes on the Rivo Alto Canal bridge around nine o'clock. I don't know where he went afterward. But he should have stayed wherever he was."

Mulrooney felt the slow burn. She had made them spin their wheels long enough. "Anya, do you understand what it means in this state if you were to sit back and allow yourself to be convicted on a homicide rap?"

"Yes, I do, Detective, but you have to be able to *prove* I did it. I never really believed that you would be able to do that...and neither did you."

Mulrooney met her stare. "The prosecutor was convinced we could, Anya, but it seems we have indeed located a witness to confirm your alibi." He watched as Anya leaned back in her chair in relief.

"So Lauren made you be her decoy?" Mulrooney said through clenched teeth.

"What do you mean?" she demanded as she bolted upright again. "Lauren didn't direct me to do this!"

"You covered for her because neither you nor Lauren thought we could nail *you* on the rap!" he suddenly yelled. "Do you know what the sentence is for obstructing justice or aiding and abetting? Stop protecting her. We know that Lauren Connolly was home at the time her husband was killed."

"But she has an alibi!"

"Not anymore. It's over, Anya. She's not going to help you, so you'd better help yourself. Isn't that why you came here today? You know something or saw something, didn't you?"

"Lauren could never do something so awful." She leaned in toward Mulrooney. "Scott had a girlfriend. That's what I came here to tell you. But I don't know who she is. That's the truth." When she saw Mulrooney glance at Clarke, she tried to reason with them. "Lauren was not jealous, if that's what you're thinking. She didn't even know about the girlfriend until I recently told her."

"Lauren told you she wished Scott were dead, didn't she? She admitted that to us, Anya."

"You're lying."

"Did she ever tell anyone else that?"

"Please, Detective, please don't do this!"

"Did she tell Sam Bennett she wished Scott were dead?"

"I don't know! Maybe once when she was angry. But she'd never hurt Scott, and neither would Sam. He loves her as much as I do. You don't know him."

"No, we don't. Not yet."

"He would die for her."

"He just might. Anya, you don't need to go to jail to prove your loyalty to Lauren. You are not responsible for the lives of your loved ones anymore. You remember what prison is like, don't you?"

"Of course I do."

"What was that like for you?"

"How do you think it was?"

"I can only imagine. You want us to produce some photos of the jail you were held in? Clarke, can you-?"

"Fuck you!" she yelled. "They were animals! They touched me with their filthy probing hands. They put a gun between my legs. They cocked it and they-" Anya's body began to shake uncontrollably.

Mulrooney walked to the chair, picked up his sweater, and gently draped it over her shoulders. He

crouched in front of her and spoke quietly. "You recognized the knife, didn't you? It's Sam Bennett's."

Her head still bowed, she nodded silently. "Yes, but
he wouldn't kill Scott."

"Did Lauren hire someone else to kill her husband?"

"Why would she be there at the time if she did?"

"Perhaps somebody missed his cue, Anya. Unless
she did it herself. Maybe we should put the ducks
in a row the way the carnivores in the D.A.'s office
will. They will conclude that your friend fought with
her husband that night. And after she imbibed a large
quantity of alcohol on her boat, she called him. The
fight escalated. Was that how it went down?

"She returned home in a state of rage," he continued, "grabbed some gloves from out back–which
implies premeditation–then went inside. She drank
some more wine while she undressed and worked
herself up into more of a drunken rage. Is that right,
Anya?"

Mulrooney's voice was rising in pitch, pushing
Anya even more than he had planned to, but a mush-
room cloud of frustration drove him on. He slammed
his hand down on the table with such force that its
wooden leg split. Anya jolted back in her chair.

"She put on the gloves then took out a knife that
had belonged to Sam, leaving no clues other than
some particles of dust on the vanity. Then Lauren
Connolly ended their volatile marriage once and
for all. She showered again, cleaned the knife, and
quickly hid it in the VCR. Then her best friend Anya

came by and covered for her by disposing of the gloves somewhere between the crime scene and the coffee house."

"If she murdered him, then why would she crawl into bed with his mutilated body?" Anya cried.

"Either the lady drinks and forgets, or it was all part of a damn good act. Your beautiful friend may be a real psycho-cookie, Anya. Believe me, we've seen it all. Truth or fiction, any of the above will provide the prosecutors with enough possibilities to resurrect Freud. And she'll take you down with her!"

Anya jumped from her chair and kicked it so hard it smashed up against the wall next to Clarke. Clarke stood up and riveted her into place with a laser-like glare. Anya screamed at both of them, her eyes dark with anger. "I told you she didn't do it! You can't hang this on Lauren!"

She yanked Mulrooney's sweater off her shoulders and hurled it toward the table before reeling around to face him again. "I DID IT! I killed the bastard because I wanted her all for myself. I used Sam's knife because I knew you'd suspect him."

"Really?" Mulrooney sneered as he bent to pick up his sweater. "After you killed him you went for coffee while covered in blood?"

As Anya hesitated, he could see her grasping for a response. "Of course not. I had hidden extra clothes under the pier on the beach. I changed there and burned my clothes in the beach fire barrel, then I ran down for coffee so I'd have an alibi."

"Anya, Lauren was already home at 11:59 P.M."

"I know. She was in the bathroom drying her hair, so she never knew I was there."

Mulrooney shook his head and ran his hand through his hair. He wondered if Isabella had ever loved him as much as Anya loved Lauren. Anya was willing to die for her. What else would compel her to come to them without counsel, taking maximum risk?

The answer came to him with a rush of panic. If Anya really believed that ultimately they wouldn't be able to pin her with the crime, she might take such a risk in order to buy time so Lauren could effectuate a plan. Mulrooney felt the sweat break out on his forehead. He heard a sudden knock on the door and yanked it open.

It was Killackey. "Surveillance lost Lauren Connolly," he whispered.

"What do you mean, 'they lost her'?" He told himself this couldn't be happening. He had let a suspect get to him, and then he had let her escape. He realized he had been duped by Lauren Connolly from the moment he laid eyes on her. You've been played, Mulrooney. Jesus frickin' Christ, you've been played! "Find Lauren Connolly!" he yelled. "Put out an A.P.B. I want to hear from surveillance the minute she's found!"

When Mulrooney turned back towards Anya, she was discreetly checking her watch again. He looked at Clarke who was studying Anya carefully. Anya slowly let out her breath and shoved her hair back off her face.

* * *

The wheels of the silver Lexus screeched loudly as Michael wheeled into the international terminal at Los Angeles airport. "You have both tickets and ID's I gave you, right?"

Lauren nodded and squeezed his hand.

"Can't I talk you out of this?" Michael said to Lauren as he pulled to the curb.

"No, Michael, and stop worrying. I'll call you when I arrive."

"You're a stubborn one," he smiled. "But you know where to reach me."

As Lauren exited the car, she saw a dark Cutlass veer toward the curb. A blonde woman jumped out of the car and waved a shield at the airport traffic cop. She then shoved a startled skycap aside and followed Lauren into the terminal. As soon as Lauren recognized the woman as the person who had been tracking her in Belmont Shore, she squeezed through a group of tourists and picked up her pace in an attempt to gain distance. The blonde hesitated at the escalator before continuing in the same direction.

Lauren looked over her shoulder as she made her way through the security check. The cop produced her badge again, but she remained a short distance behind.

After reaching the gate, Lauren lingered nervously near a marble column where she could keep a lookout in all directions.

She suddenly spotted the blonde again as the officer took a seat in the crowded passenger area and glanced at Lauren before looking away. Cool cucumber, she observed.

When Lauren noticed a partition that led to the V.I.P. lounge, she stepped behind the partition and waited. Her heart was pounding as she fought her desire to flee. Hidden by the partition, she knew she was no longer in view, but she could see her surveillance in the reflection of the terminal window.

As soon as the cop looked down to dial her phone, Lauren stepped from behind the partition and slipped back into the crowd. As she rushed by the surveillance officer, she was so close she could hear the young cop yelling into the phone, "Goddammit, I wasn't given the authority to apprehend her! Tell Mulrooney she's in the V.I.P. lounge. I think she has a ticket to Sydney!"

Lauren ran through the airport, to the terminal for domestic departures. She flashed her other ticket at security and made it to her gate just as the door to the jet way was about to close. As an attendant hurried her through, Lauren looked over her shoulder. The blond officer was nowhere in sight.

Lauren shook her damp hair free from her neck. Suddenly a chill shot through her. She knew she could be making the greatest mistake of her life. But it was too late now; she had made her decision. Lauren stepped aboard the flight just as the attendant announced their destination. Miami, Florida.

"Would you like me to write a detailed confession now? Anya asked as she looked around the interrogation room.

Clarke remained gravely silent as Mulrooney paced the room. "How long do you plan to keep this up, Anya?" Mulrooney demanded. Anya said nothing as she checked her watch again.

A sharp rap at the door once again interrupted the silence. Killackey stuck his head in to whisper to Mulrooney. Anya watched, trying to read Mulrooney's expression. Mulrooney signaled his partner and then mumbled something as Clarke approached. Anya noticed Clarke roll his eyes in exasperation. He abruptly left the room, leaving Mulrooney alone with Anya.

Mulrooney spun on his heel to face Anya. His eyes were dark with anger. "You've been busted, Anya," he snapped. "We know you covered just long enough for your friend to leave for Sydney, but we've delayed the flight. We have also ascertained that Connolly's insurance policy was worth one million dollars."

"So?"

"I swear to God, you're going down like the Hindenburg for covering her ass. We'll get you for aiding and abetting, interfering with an investigation, trying to file a false report, and planting an incendiary device in my car. And that's just the beginning. I'm going to get you for everything from jay walking to abusing my goddamn Mr. Rogers sweater!"

Anya stared through him. Her mouth moved in a stone face. "As I said, I murdered Scott Connolly. You and your team were right all along, so I assume you can prove it." A smile of relief very slowly spread across Anya Gallien's beautiful face as Mulrooney stomped out, slamming the door behind him.

Chapter 22

Miami, Florida

Lauren sat in the back of a taxi and looked out at the brilliant Miami sun before checking her watch. 10:30 A.M. It was time. Lauren knew what she had to do. She took out a hair clip and distractedly piled her hair loosely atop her head, allowing several strands to fall down around her face.

As the taxi cruised along the row of restaurants and night clubs, Lauren tried to remain calm. A group of Japanese visitors chattered excitedly and snapped photos of a neon sign of a nude dancing girl, which abruptly metamorphosed into a male. Lauren laughed aloud when one animated man who was posing in front of the sign appeared to grow a large, red phallus out of his left ear as the sign switched genders.

The taxi slowed down when it reached the end of the street. After Lauren paid the driver, she stood on the sidewalk with her suitcase in hand, suddenly wanting to flee. Instead, she smoothed her white gauze dress, and then she forced her legs to guide her through the door. When she adjusted her eyes to the dim light, she could see the club was empty.

When she looked around the inviting room, her tension lifted slightly. She could almost hear the music, as if it were painted into the wine-colored walls. An ebony piano overlooked a rose marble dance floor surrounded by black and chrome art deco furniture. Lamp shades the colors of macaw feathers accented the fixtures, and each table was adorned with a black vase in the shape of a clarinet. Atop one table was a box of pink ginger and pale yellow heliconias awaiting arrangement.

The room's crowning touch was a collection of softly illuminated photographs in black lacquer frames. Miles Davis, Dizzy Gillespie, Ella Fitzgerald, Satchmo, and Charlie Parker calmly appraised Lauren as she considered her next move.

Suddenly Lauren's breath caught in her throat. She recognized the sound of his footsteps even before Sam entered the room. He was looking down when he stopped abruptly, as though he had picked up a familiar scent. A shocked look spread across his ruggedly handsome face.

"Lauren?" he whispered as he squinted into the dim light. Unsure of the next move, his feet held fast to the floor while his hungry eyes absorbed her. "My God, babe, is it you?"

"Yes, Sam, it's me." Lauren rasped.

Sam approached Lauren slowly. He stopped to stare into her eyes for a moment, and then he bent down and pulled her into him. Sam wrapped his body around Lauren as if any space between them might allow her to escape from him again. He buried his face in her hair and breathed in deeply.

Lauren pressed her face against Sam's shoulder and held on tightly. His scent overpowered her as his hands stroked her back and shoulders. When she felt his breath against her face, she leaned further into him. "Sam," she whispered.

Sam suddenly pulled back from her and cleared his throat. His jaw stiffened as his mind tried once more to disconnect from her. "Why did you come here, Lauren?"

"I had to. I need to talk to you." Lauren's legs were shaking so much she grasped the back of a chair for support.

"How did you find me here?"

"Most everyone thinks you're still in Australia, which I'm sure is what you planned. But I know you well, Sam. You always wanted to start a club in Miami. And I suspected you'd use the same name, Jazzin,' just as before."

Sam sat down at a nearby table. As he rested his forehead in his hands, his tanned, muscular arms glistened in the soft light.

"I know you need someone now, Lauren. My old contacts in Long Beach told me Scott was murdered. I wanted to contact you so badly to offer my help. And also to tell you how sorry I am." He rubbed his forehead with his strong fingers. "Sorry for you that is."

"Sam-"

"Listen to me, Lauren. These months apart took everything I've got." He turned to look at her, his voice heavy with resolve. "I just can't do this again."

Lauren stared at his face. Even the hard mask couldn't disguise his hurt. She knew for the first time why she really needed to see him again. Lauren knew Sam would either help her save herself, or he would destroy her. For Lauren there were no other alternatives. "Don't turn me away, Sam."

"I told you when I walked out that I will never settle for only part of you."

"Even if that's all that's left?"

Sam's eyes caressed every detail of her face before he sighed with resignation. "Come here, babe," he said, as he reached out to pull her onto his lap. "Christ, I've missed you." Then, he drew Lauren into him with complete surrender.

Chapter 23

Mulrooney felt so vulnerable he had to fight his recurring impulse to make sure his weapon was in place. Clarke, who was standing on his right, inched forward. Mulrooney knew his partner was trying to protect him from the media mob. *No need to go down with me, buddy. Let 'em take their best shot!*

Clarke gently pushed the microphone away from Mulrooney's face. "Give us a little room, will ya' folks?" he suggested, in a manner that sounded downright friendly. His speech was still garbled, but his body language was clear.

The reporter from the *Press Telegram* was not to be deterred. "If Mrs. Connolly is wanted for questioning, how did she manage to flee to Sydney without your knowledge?"

Clarke stepped farther forward. "Because she is only a person of interest, Mrs. Connolly didn't–as you put it–'flee.' And she's not in Sydney. That report was premature. We believe she may be in Florida, most likely trying to recover from such a traumatic ordeal."

"Detective Mulrooney," a female reporter shouted, "rumors suggest you have a history of problematic relationships with women. Did that influence any of your decisions or motivations in this case?"

"No," Mulrooney answered tersely.

"Can you tell us what happened during that well-publicized incident at L.B.P.D. when-"

"No," he said, cutting her off.

"Is it true you abuse women?" she fished.

If that were true, you would be chewing my shoe leather right now, he thought. "No," was the only word he could spit out without an explosion. Mulrooney turned and elbowed his way back through the crowd toward the station.

"Detective Mulrooney," another female reporter said as he passed, "have you been able to determine who is responsible for planting the explosive device in your car?"

"Probably Gloria Allred," he muttered.

Clarke blocked the crowd as they pressed forward. "Blood sports are over, folks."

Mulrooney took satisfaction in the fact that the word 'folks' sounded suspiciously like 'fucks.' When he yanked open the station door, the crowd behind him was reflected in the glass. Detective Carlos Atilla stood nearby, smirking as he watched Mulrooney retreat.

* * *

With great skill, Sam piloted his 48' Camarque, the 'Kookaburra,' out of Key West. Sam owned the boat with several partners who moored it at Key West to take advantage of the fishing and diving. Shortly after Lauren's arrival, Sam had turned over the club to his manager, Biragidji, so he could be alone with Lauren. He also wanted to take no chances in case she was being followed.

The flight from Miami had been short, offering breathtaking views of the coast and the Florida keys. Now Sam could finally relax a little as he felt the warm breeze rush over him. He had been overwhelmed by emotion since she walked into his club the previous day. Although he was thrilled to see her, he knew his hurt and damaged pride had barely dissipated over the ten months since they had parted.

Sam had always landed almost any woman he wanted. He had learned at the knee of an expert, his father Warren. They had lived in a quaint river town in New South Wales, Australia, named Macquarie Post, which was once a trading crossroads for the larger town of Macquarie, host to a gold rush in 1851.

Life in the small town hadn't been easy. His family had been a source of amusement for the locals due to his father's sports of drinking and womanizing. Soon the old man's drinking had depleted what little resources the family had, and the frequent outbursts had made life at home a matter of bare tolerance for Sam.

Although Sam was gregarious and fun-loving, he occasionally instigated fights just so he could tear into someone. Sometimes his anger became so overwhelming he felt as if he were living in a black hole. Often the only way to control his shifting moods was by working to the point of collapse.

Sam deemed it efficacious to combine his work with his social life, therefore, ownership of a pub was a logical choice. After he established and later sold his successful Sydney pub, he had enough money to seek his fortune in the States and leave his troubled past behind.

Although Sam loved America—and American women—he was lonely in the States. When he first saw Lauren, his intent was simply to seduce her. Sam was thrown completely off guard when he found himself falling in love.

Lauren was unique. Sam could listen to her for hours as she related anecdotes from her job-related adventures. She taught him many things. She could be childlike and funny one minute, and passionate and powerful the next. He would often sit aboard the Seduction listening to her classical music, fascinated by the passion in her face. Eventually their relationship consumed him.

Sam was convinced her husband Scott never appreciated what he had in Lauren. But Scott had used Lauren's strong sense of loyalty and her feelings of guilt to manipulate her into coming back to him. However, Sam never stopped believing that one day he would have Lauren for himself. Completely. He was not about to lose her again. Sam Bennett was not a loser.

As Lauren checked out their scuba equipment, Sam turned to look at her, hardly able to believe she was here. He wanted to give her time to deal with the unexpected changes in her life. He needed time also. He was still furious, maybe even bitter, that she had left him to go back to Scott. Now when he looked at Lauren, he could feel a distance. But Sam had long ago resolved to have things his way, and he believed he could make her want him again. It was a matter of time.

As Key West nestled back into the horizon, Lauren relaxed in the main salon fighting images from the previous night, which had been lonely and confusing. After having agreed to spend time with Sam away from the club, she had gone to her hotel room alone, desperate for sleep.

Throughout the night, familiar faces had surrounded her like Mardi Gras revelers. They laughed and threw confetti and trinkets, which turned out to be little blood covered knives that cut her hands each time she tried to gather them. Tim Mulrooney was also there, staring through her as if she were a ghost. When she reached out to touch him, she was shocked to see blood all over her hands and body. Mulrooney grabbed her arm and wouldn't let go. Lauren had awakened in a sweat, unable to sleep again.

As the sun rose, Lauren had sat in bed with the phone in her hand wanting to call Mulrooney to tell him where she was. She needed to explain her need to confront Sam in person. If Sam was a threat, she had to know.

Lauren was ashamed she had betrayed Mulrooney's trust. She liked being near him, even on that awful night they met. She understood the emotional dependence a person can develop on a "rescuer," but she also knew herself well enough to understand that her attraction to the detective went deeper than that. Because of his quiet strength, he was an anchor that held her ship steady and made her feel safe in the middle of sudden, overwhelming chaos.

Lauren perceived what kind of man Mulrooney was from the moment she saw him. She sensed he was not inured to the brutality of his work; and she had unconsciously noted his vulnerability when he had touched her that night. She wondered if he even remembered tucking the afghan around her bare feet, and she smiled at the memory. But in spite of her desire to lean on Mulrooney, she needed more time before calling him.

Now Lauren reclined on deck while the gentle swaying of the boat eased her tension. She dozed on and off until she felt the light stroke of a finger tracing her face and sliding over her lips. Lauren pressed her lips against Sam's finger and opened her eyes.

"You're beautiful," he whispered. "Have I ever told you that?"

She closed her eyes again and held his hand close to her face, which was as close as she dared let anyone be. Although she felt the familiar weight pressing down on her, her eyes still could not release the tears. "You know I killed Scott, don't you Sam?" she whispered.

Sam looked at her closely, then he turned away. "Hush," he soothed, "go back to sleep, babe."

"But I did."

"Lauren-"

"I killed Scott. It was my fault."

"Stop this, Lauren."

"I knew my life would be so much easier if he were gone. That would solve my problems—with him and with you."

Sam brushed the hair off her forehead. "You mean you *wished* him dead?"

"You know I did, Sam. I told you that once when I was drunk and angry. How could I say such a horrible thing?"

Sam avoided her look as he reclined alongside her and pulled her close to him. "You're not the only person who has entertained fleeting thoughts of someone's death, or their own, as a means of escape. But Scott's murder is not a result of the fact that you wished it in a moment of weakness, babe."

"I once thought that if he died I could have it both ways. I wouldn't have to leave him, and I could have you. Well, I got my wish, didn't I?"

"Look, if thinking it made it so, we'd all be guilty of homicide. You would never consciously hurt Scott. You couldn't even leave him even though that arrogant fuckup treated you like shit."

Lauren detected the bitterness in Sam's voice as she watched the blue water push its white caps toward the sky. "I hurt him terribly when I fell in love with you."

"I know, Lauren, but I don't feel guilty. I can't. If I had thought he loved you as much as he loved money and drugs, I would have gone away voluntarily."

They sat quietly for several moments and stared out at the horizon from where the boat was now anchored.

"I loved you, Sam."

"I know," Sam said sadly, noting her use of past tense. "And I love you more than anything in my life. But you also always loved Scott."

"Do you believe a woman can truly love more than one man?"

"Yes. But one love had passion, and the other didn't. I couldn't share you."

Lauren saw the dark look spread across his face again. "Sam, don't close me out," she begged as she reached for his hand. "Tell me what you're thinking."

"I just hate it that you're left with so much guilt. If Scott had been there for you, you would never have gone walkabout."

She grinned in spite of herself. "Do you know you're sounding like an Aussie again?"

"Aw, give me a break." Sam traced Lauren's nose with his finger then smoothed her brows. "Do you regret having met me?"

"No. I only regret not meeting you sooner."

Sam sighed and stared out the porthole to the vast expanse of blue. "Look out there," he said as he pulled her up into a sitting position.

"What? We're in the middle of nowhere."

"Look closely."

Lauren stood up and looked south of where the boat was anchored. Stretching into the distance was an outcropping that looked like an expansive sandbar. Sam led her aft where she could get a clear view. She could see electric hues glistening from below the water like a submerged rainbow.

"What a beautiful reef!" she exclaimed.

"I thought we'd go diving. You'll love it here. There are more than fifteen hundred kinds of fish and hundreds of corals."

"What about sharks?"

Sam grinned. "No worries, babe. None have been sighted in the area. I check the reports carefully each time I dive."

Lauren noticed how Sam's eyes reflected the colors of the ocean, like night meeting day. But beneath his easy smile was a turbulence she could almost feel. As she gazed up at him, the smile left his face as quickly as it had come.

Suddenly Sam grabbed her and pulled her toward him. He leaned into Lauren, breathing heavily. His unexpected passion threw her so off-guard she writhed to free herself from his grasp. Sam abruptly pulled away. He kicked aside a life vest and turned his back to her. While he yanked on his wetsuit, Lauren collected herself.

"I'm sorry, I shouldn't have done that," he mumbled. "I thought a lot last night, Lauren. I want you more than I want anything in this world, but I have to have all of you. Or none at all." He fixed a steely gaze on Lauren. "I know you need someone right now, but I need to take care of myself. And I need to end this." He jerked up the zipper on his wetsuit.

"I understand," she answered softly. Hoping the dive would give her time to think, Lauren pulled on her wetsuit and scuba boots and checked the oxygen valve on both tanks before she slipped into her buoyancy control vest. She made her way to the edge of the boat where she donned her mask and flippers and waited as Sam pulled a spear gun out of the tackle box.

"Are you planning on hauling something in?" Lauren asked tentatively.

"No, it's for protection."

"Now I really feel safe," she said sarcastically. She pulled on her gloves and looked over the side of the boat where a school of yellow butterfly fish fed near the surface.

"What kind of-" She stopped abruptly when she saw Sam strapping a knife onto his leg. Lauren recognized the distinct style of the hand-carved grip that jutted from the sheath and an overwhelming fear overcame her. "Why do you need a knife?" Her eyes were fixed on the blade as Sam wiped it against his wetsuit, and plunged it back into the sheath.

"I'll cut open a sea urchin to attract the fish."

Lauren felt her breath catch in her throat. "Is that the aborigine knife you use for hunting–the one your friend George One-Eye made?"

Sam pulled on his dive vest as he answered. "No, I lost that one. This one is designed for diving. Okay, Lauren, let's go. Stay with me." He shoved his regulator into his mouth and held it with one hand while he held his gauge in the other. Then he sat on the edge of the boat and fell backward into the water.

Lauren sat for a moment, knowing there was no place to run if Sam wanted to hurt her. He could find her anywhere. It would just be a matter of choosing his time. Lauren was determined to face fear head on rather than run from it. That's why she had come. She shoved her regulator into her mouth and followed Sam into the dark water.

Chapter 24

Mulrooney and Clarke sat in Mulrooney's small office trying to avoid looking at the pustular face of a speed freak. Mulrooney noticed that Clarke had slid his chair as far away from the kid as he could get, probably because the kid smelled like infected feet.

"Stop picking at those scabs and place your hands on the desk, Slag," Mulrooney barked. "You're making them worse. And you're making me sick!" The kid nervously complied.

Mulrooney was working a new angle. His hunch about a link between Dr. Connolly's murder and the Jersey homicides had turned something up that morning. The knife Clarence Smolley had been killed with at his moment of ejaculation in the peep show was determined to have had a five inch blade with a serrated tip - like the one used on Connolly. Mulrooney was champing at the bit.

"All we want to know is who Clarence Smolley was hanging out with in Long Beach before he went to

Florida," Mulrooney said to the kid, who could barely stay in his seat.

"I don't know names, man. And I don't know where you got your information from, but Clarence Smolley wasn't no friend. I bought from him once. Only once, man."

"Sit still, Slag," Clarke interrupted. "You keep moving your ass around like it needs wiping!"

"Sorry man," the kid said, "but I think it does."

Mulrooney winced and looked at Clarke, who just shook his head. Slag didn't seem to be worth the time they were spending, and they were both exhausted.

They had been up most of the night trying to trace Lauren. After initially detaining the plane to Sydney to no avail, they had spent hours cross-referencing data on flights showing departure times close to that of the Sydney flight, as well as female passengers traveling alone and last minute scheduling arrangements made from Belmont Shore telephone exchanges. They had finally ascertained that Lauren was in Miami, traveling with a fake ID. An earlier conversation with Miami police had proven fruitless. Now their interrogation of one of their informants was proving to be equally as frustrating.

Clarke stood up to open the door. "You can go, kid," he said.

Slag scratched his crotch and ran a hand through his greasy hair as he stood to leave. "Sorry I can't help, man," he said. "I met Clarence Smolley only once. But I used to see him hanging around in front of Jazzin' before it burned down."

Mulrooney and Clarke stared at each other with raised brows. "Well, well, well, ain't it a small world," Clarke intoned. He nodded at Slag then showed him out the door.

"And a seedy one," Mulrooney added as he kicked the door shut.

* * *

The air bubbles swirled past Lauren's head as she equalized her ears and dropped slowly down the outer face of the reef. She marveled at the colored corals and sea life which undulated in front of her like a 3-D cinema. When Sam tugged at her leg to signal her to level off, she checked her gauge.

As she looked at Sam, she could see where the ocean dropped off into a threatening black abyss beyond him. She kept the depth gauge in hand to control her levels, which could easily increase to dangerous depths due to underwater disorientation.

Lauren eventually relaxed and let Sam take the lead. She stared in wonder as he pointed out elk horn coral and a school of fuchsia colored fairy basselets. As she floated along the wall with the current, she watched in fascination as a sea turtle hatchling swam past, looking for lunch. Hugging the reef, Lauren decreased her depth and swam toward a school of wrasses.

Together Sam and Lauren gradually drifted upward before leveling at about sixty feet. Lauren looked up just as several seabirds dove for a school of anchovies swimming above her head. As the anchovies billowed like a cloud and changed directions in a single move, she watched their synchronized swimming in amazement.

When Lauren turned back to see if Sam had noticed them, she saw that his intense gaze was fixed on her, not on the fish. He stared at her while hanging in suspension, motionless. Suddenly his hand drifted forward, lifted by the current. Lauren froze in horror. Sam held his spear gun in front of him and took aim.

With an explosion of movement, Lauren lunged away from him before he could fire. As she pumped her legs furiously to escape, she had to struggle against the weight of her equipment and against her paralyzing fear. She tried to swim above him, watching in terror as he followed her with his aim, pointing the gun at her head. Lauren screamed into her mouthpiece while she tried in vain to swim against the current.

Within seconds, Sam's powerful legs brought him within reach. Fighting with as much strength as she could, she kicked hard against him, but her flipper caught the tip of the gun. The gun discharged, firing the sharp spear through her fin.

Lauren felt a violent tug on her leg. Sam was reeling in the rope that was connected to the spear. She floundered helplessly as she fought to free herself from her impaled flipper, but his strong hand gripped her leg and jerked her closer. Desperate to free herself, Lauren grasped at the reef, but her gloves tore on the rough coral. Sam's tense body pushed against hers, smashing her into the wall. She cried out again as the coral ripped into her skin. Sam's eyes were dark and piercing. Beyond Sam the black abyss moved closer in its attempt to swallow her. Sam held her against the coral as he tried to reload the spear gun.

She lunged from his grasp, but her regulator caught on a protrusion of fire coral, forcing her head to snap back as her air source was ripped from her mouth. While Lauren sucked water into her lungs, she frantically reached for her extra air hose. As she struggled, she jerked the spear gun from Sam's hands. Sam held her in place with one hand while he expertly unsheathed his knife with his free hand. He loomed towards her with the knife held fast in his clenched fist.

As Lauren rapidly lost oxygen, Sam became large and distorted. A giddy dizziness in her head gave way to brilliant lights and colors. The rush of sound grew louder inside her head. She felt herself floating through a swirl of day-glow fireflies, tumbling faster and faster through the blue brilliance.

Suddenly, she felt a regulator being shoved into her mouth. She vomited seawater into the regulator and pushed it away. Sam thrust it back into her mouth and pressed the purge valve to empty the mouthpiece. Lauren gulped in air before vomiting again.

She realized they were moving together as one body, rising toward the surface as they sucked life from one tank. Sam's body was wrapped around Lauren's, his knife still clutched in his hand. He pointed emphatically at something beyond Lauren. When she slowly turned her head in the direction of the knife, the last thing she saw was a shark shredding the remains of a large tuna.

Chapter 25

Michael Ryan leveled Anya with a cold stare. "You've got to tell me where Lauren and Sam went after they left Miami, Anya. Lauren didn't call me as she promised. I'm worried about her. And she needs to know she's wanted for questioning."

"I'm sure she knows by now," Anya responded dryly. She looked beyond the small bridge that crossed the canal before glancing back over to make sure she and Michael were not being followed.

"I'm not as convinced as you are that she's safe with Sam Bennett," Michael reasoned.

"Michael, she needed answers, and she knows what she's doing. And no one can stop Lauren anyway. You know how stubborn and determined she is. I have to go now before anyone sees me." Anya abruptly turned and walked away, leaving Michael alone on the canal walk.

Michael took out his cell phone and dialed as he watched Anya duck behind the walkway to the small footbridge. "Check with Miami police again," he ordered. "Incidentally, Sam Bennett has always owned a boat of some type. They could be on it, so try to locate it. I've got a bad feeling about that guy."

As he hung up, Michael noticed Anya watching from the small bridge. "He's not the only one I've got a bad feeling about," Michael thought as he shoved his phone back into his pocket.

On the other side of the canal, Mulrooney and Clarke sat inside a vacant house observing the scene. When Michael turned to walk away, Clarke grinned at Mulrooney. "I don't think those two wild cats like each other."

Mulrooney nodded. "But something tells me they like the same thing."

* * *

The warm water eased Lauren's violent shaking as she sucked the ice cube Sam held to her lips. "Shhh, it's okay now," he soothed. Sam had somehow managed to get her out of her gear. They were lying together on the floor of the shower as the hot water ran over them. She huddled against him, unable to get warm enough to stop the spasms.

"Relax ...I won't let anything hurt you." He lifted his head, tucking hers beneath his chin.

"Sam, I didn't see it-"

"I know, babe, but I did."

"What happened?"

"Well, for a while I thought we were the Last Supper. I tried to aim for its head, but you had something else in mind."

"I don't know what to say, Sam. I panicked. I was afraid. You seemed so angry and I thought-"

"God, Lauren, I can't believe you think I'd ever hurt you."

"I didn't see the shark until I was losing air. I can't remember much after that," she said as she sucked at the ice.

"After you lost your regulator, you passed out for a minute there. You were no longer fighting me, so I was able to retrieve the spear gun from the reef and spear a tuna. The shark was distracted long enough for me to get you back aboard."

Lauren shuddered at the memory. She reached out to Sam and buried her face in the dark hair of his chest.

"Come here," he said as he lifted her out of the shower. "Let me dry you off." He wrapped her in a thick beach towel and ran a towel over himself before leading her to the main stateroom.

When Lauren dropped onto the berth, Sam awkwardly moved away and sat on a nearby chair. As he stared at her, the distance between them seemed greater than ever before.

"You seem so far away from me," she whispered.

"Do I? I guess I could say the same of you."

Lauren tried to find the words she had so carefully rehearsed on the plane to Miami, but the words wouldn't come. Eventually she decided her only choice was to be as straightforward as her intent. "Sam, I came here for one reason," she said, "I need to ask you, face to face. Were you the one who killed Scott?"

"How can you ask me that?"

"You threatened him more than once. Answer me, Sam."

Sam hesitated, and then he looked directly at her. "No, Lauren, I never laid a hand on him."

Sam held his gaze for a moment before turning away. "We can't ever go back, can we babe?"

Lauren paused then shook her head. "No, I guess we can't. Nothing will ever be the same again. I'm sorry." Lauren felt the pressure in her eyes once more. She finally allowed herself to cry, feeling the pain of so many losses in her life.

Sam sighed as he watched Lauren bury her face in her hands. As miserable as he felt, he knew Lauren's hurt was even greater. He sensed her complete loneliness and sorrow. He sat awhile longer, clenching the arms of his chair as his last safety net. Finally he let out a long breath, and then he walked slowly to the bed and lay down next to her.

"Let me be your friend," he whispered. Sam pulled Lauren close to him in one desperate gesture of self-lessness; then he held her until she slept.

Chapter 26

Mulrooney stood behind the door to his cubicle and peered through the window into the outer office. Clarke was sitting opposite Anya Gallien, taking his turn at questioning her. Anya, accompanied by a new attorney, was shaking her head and resisting Clarke's efforts to extract detailed information.

Suddenly Anya turned toward Mulrooney as if she sensed someone was studying her. Mulrooney took a long swig of coffee and met her look head-on before abruptly yanking down the shade.

Mulrooney was still pissed about the erroneous information he had originally obtained from Passport Services regarding Sam Bennett's whereabouts. His gut feeling had told him Lauren would go to Sam. When Mulrooney learned Lauren might be in Miami, not Australia, he wondered if Sam had slipped past Passport into Florida. If Mulrooney's hunch was right, Sam was undoubtedly operating under an alias. But why?

He also remembered that Sam's last three businesses contained the word 'Jazzin.' After combing directory information, he and Clarke had pulled up a club called 'Miami Jazzin.' They had called and spoken to a waitress who wouldn't divulge the owner's name, although she inadvertently confirmed he was Australian. Mulrooney knew if he had found Sam Bennett, he had found Lauren Connolly.

Mulrooney sat down at his desk and propped up his legs. The light was dim, just the way he liked it when his head hurt. After another swig of coffee, he popped two Tylenol.

The figure in the corner hadn't moved. Mulrooney looked at the man for several minutes before he finally spoke. "If Lauren gets hurt, you'll be at fault, too. She would have listened to you," Mulrooney said, breaking the silence.

Michael Ryan shook his head. "You give me too much credit, Mulrooney. I don't know where she is; and Lauren does what she wants to do. She refused to listen to me."

Mulrooney thought he detected an air of sadness in Michael's voice. He turned the light up so he could study him more closely. "I can tell you care a lot about her," he said, raising a brow.

"She's my friend. And your concern for her isn't exactly what I'd call impersonal," Michael observed as he stared at a photo of Lauren atop Mulrooney's desk.

"I'm just doing my job," Mulrooney retorted, shoving the photo back into a file.

"I *am* worried for Lauren," Michael admitted as he ran his fingers along the sharp crease in his trousers. "Although her husband was my friend, I was disgusted with him. I'm a wise judge of people, and I knew Scott was going to self-destruct. I have also long suspected that Sam Bennett has two sides. I'm sure he wanted to get even with Scott."

"Enough to kill him?"

Michael shifted in his chair, then shrugged. "I don't know, Detective. Perhaps I've underestimated Sam Bennett. Lauren is an intelligent woman, and I don't think she believes Sam could have done it or she wouldn't have gone to him."

"I disagree. I think she does believe he could do it. That's exactly why she went after Sam. She had to have answers."

Michael looked at Mulrooney and slowly nodded in agreement. "You seem very sure of the type of woman Lauren is."

"It's my job to study people, Mr. Ryan."

"And you didn't consider she might leave town?"

"I not only considered it, I expected it. That's why I had her under surveillance."

Michael nodded and held up his hand. "I'm sorry. I didn't mean to put you on the defensive. You guys get enough abuse. And you're right, I should have stopped her. I wasn't even aware she was a suspect, or I would have advised her not to do anything to make herself look guilty. I've been trying to locate her myself, Detective. I think her decision to go to Sam was a foolish one."

"But a brave one. Lauren has guts. If she's as innocent of any conspiracy as you and Anya contend, then she's strong enough to confront the person who could have murdered her husband."

"We've got to find her."

"We're close. We'll catch up with them sooner or later. You could help make it sooner. You have as many contacts as we do. And a helluva lot more money. I know you know something, Mr. Ryan, or you wouldn't be here, would you? You aren't helping her by protecting her."

Michael sighed in resignation. "Maybe you're right. My sources tell me they're somewhere in Key West," he said quietly. He sat in silence while Mulrooney dialed the phone.

* * *

When Lauren peered out the starboard hatch at a bustling dock, she knew she was back in Key West. She focused on a quaint restaurant at the end of the pier and smiled. The salt air had chiseled at the painted letters of its sign turning The Port Haven into a 'Po t Haven.' Ah, Business must be good, she thought.

"Are you feeling any better?" Sam asked as he entered the stateroom.

"A bit." Lauren sat quietly for a few minutes before she spoke again. "Sam, I have to go back," she said.

"Was that your plan? You came here to turn my life upside down and then waltz right out again?" He did not disguise his bitterness.

221

"That wasn't my plan, but that is what I have to do. I thought I could leave it all behind, but I can't. And Anya needs my help. They're trying to hang Scott's murder on her. She could help herself, but she won't. She knew I needed time to talk to you. I think she believes I saw, something that night. And I suspect she wanted to give me a chance to escape before the police come after me. She suggested I leave the country, but I won't let her go through this alone."

"Why would they link you to this?"

"Because of my relationship with you. They found your knife in the house, Sam." Lauren watched carefully for his reaction.

Sam sat motionless. "My knife?" he repeated. "You think I was there?" Suddenly Sam raised his fist and pummeled the mattress in rage. "Dammit, I told you I lost that bloody knife," he yelled, "along with every other thing in my life. I lost my club, my green card, my money, even my woman! I'm bloody sick and tired of losing the things I love!"

"Please calm down, Sam," Lauren said as she pulled back. "Anya found the knife, but she didn't tell anyone she knew it was yours."

"What makes you so sure?"

"If she had disclosed everything she knew about us, I would never have gotten out of California."

"Are they watching you, Lauren?"

"They had me under surveillance. I lost the woman at the airport, but I'm sure they've figured out where I am by now. Detective Mulrooney knows what he's doing."

"Is this Mulrooney leaning hard on you?"

"Not exactly. He's tough. And complicated. But I like him."

"Just how much?"

Lauren shook her head as she remembered how inept Sam had always been at disguising his jealousy. "I'm just saying he's a good man, Sam. He reminds me of you," she answered diplomatically. "He's handsome, intelligent, and very kind. I trust him."

"So he has an effect on women?"

"Perhaps."

"All women, or just you?"

Lauren felt her cheeks flush.

"This Mulrooney must be one helluva guy," Sam sneered.

"I wouldn't know. All I know is that my husband just died," Lauren said pointedly.

"He died for you a long time ago."

"Whoa, straight for the jugular!"

"I'm sorry, that was out of line. I just want you to stay away from this Mulrooney guy because I don't want you to let your guard down and say or do anything that could look suspicious."

"It's too late for that. I'm going to talk to Mulrooney when I get back. The prosecutor is coming down real hard on Anya, and I can't let that continue. I won't leave Anya's fate, or mine, to circumstantial evidence. Before I talk to Mulrooney, I need to locate a brunette Scott was seeing. I want to talk to her myself to find out what she knows. If she can somehow implicate you or me in Scott's murder, we need to know. I won't go to jail. I'll leave the country first. I would need your help if it comes to that."

"And what if this brunette was involved?"

"That's what I intend to find out for myself."

"That's a dangerous game, Lauren!"

"It's no game, and I'm not afraid, Sam. I have to get to her before the police can. I need to find out what she knows. Anya said she saw you with Scott and the girl at your Long Beach club."

"What makes you so sure you can trust Anya, Lauren?"

"We've been through this before, Sam. Anya loves me."

Sam pressed his fingers against his temple and frowned again. "I just know Anya isn't what she appears to be. You see the good in everyone. Even me," he added with a lopsided smile. "However, I do remember the brunette you're talking about."

"Do you know her name?"

"Donna something, that's all I know. Did you ask Michael Ryan about her?"

"Yes, he doesn't know her."

"Well, she sure was coming on to Michael one night at the club. Of course, she was coked up, so she was coming on to everyone. I thought she left with Michael, but I may be mistaken. Anyway, that was the last I saw of her. It was the night the club burned down, I lost everything that night. All my possessions, my knife, even my photos of you." Sam stared out at the pier, his face clouded with anger.

"Sam, I need to find out where this Donna is. Please help me do so. I scheduled a return flight for five days from now just to mislead the police, but I have to return right away."

Sam's face registered his resignation. She was slipping away from him once more. "Mulrooney will be waiting for you when you step off the plane, babe. We can't underestimate him. If you need time to locate Donna before going to Mulrooney, then let me talk to my man here in town. We'll need a few hours to make arrangements. I'll help you if you promise me one thing. No, two things."

"What?" she asked. She knew she'd do almost anything for Sam. But they both knew their time together was reaching a final ending.

"Call me if you need me."

"That's only one request," she smiled sadly.

"If you ever change your mind, please come back."

Lauren hesitated for a moment, then answered solemnly, "I promise, Sam."

"Blood promise?"

"Blood promise," she replied. She held Sam's gaze until he turned away.

Chapter 27

Mulrooney peeked through the blinds and wondered if Houdini could make him disappear. His lone Lion Fish, aptly named Houdini because of its ability to make all of the other fish vanish from the tank, had just made short work of the guppy Mulrooney had provided for its breakfast.

"They're still circling," Mulrooney said to his fish as he closed the blinds. The media, with appetites more ferocious than Houdini's, had been gathered outside Mulrooney's small condo since his return home.

Mulrooney had inadvertently complicated his life by refusing to discuss the altercation at headquarters that had tarnished his record. Although more than a year had passed since the incident, it was still too painful for him to even think about. He had been juggling media grenades since a recent feature in the *Press-Telegram* had challenged his credibility as a detective on the grounds that his shameful treatment of the woman involved in the incident reflected an "inability to deal objectively with the opposite gender."

Mulrooney had been forced to eat even more crow at the gym when he overheard Carlos Atilla paraphrasing the article and calling him an abuser. Mulrooney was sure it was Atilla who had leaked the incident to the press. When Mulrooney overheard Atilla's commentary, he had to muster up the greatest control since he and Susie Patterson practiced early withdrawal in the tenth grade.

Mulrooney hadn't had a good night's sleep since Lauren Connolly had slipped out of town. He had wanted to give her a wide berth to see to whom she'd turn, but his life would be easier if she had stayed within his grasp. He rubbed his eyes as he stood in front of his easel and inspected his painting, a product of his hours of insomnia. The painting of the sunset looked like a Bertolucci car wreck. He figured he was looking very much the same. Neither he nor Clarke had had a breather since Dr. Connolly was sliced and diced.

They had come up with their own profile of Connolly's killer, which in Mulrooney's mind didn't fit your blue-light-special psychopath. Despite the multiple murders, they believed the assailant had a personal reason to kill. He and Clarke had increased their workload by reviewing every case involving an assault with a knife. They knew any link might provide a break in the Connolly case.

Adding to the pressure were the heated arguments he and Clarke had been having with Chief Clemente.

That morning the chief had personally directed him to keep a lower profile in the Connolly case because of the media coverage. "Suck my sausage," Mulrooney mumbled as he stood at his easel recalling the conversation.

D.A. Perry was practically dancing through the streets in a tutu since hearing of Anya's confession. Mulrooney, however, had the sickening feeling that the real perp was slipping out of their grasp as the D.A.'s office floundered. They were trying to hold the case together while also trying to implicate Lauren Connolly. And because Mulrooney's car had exploded like a Claymore mine, he couldn't forget that he was a target as well.

The District Attorney's publicity machine had managed to get Perry continuous coverage on the Connolly case. One hour earlier, Clarke had called Mulrooney to inform him that an editorial in the *Press-Telegram* had nearly equated Perry with the Second Coming. Clarke scoffed that the only 'coming' the very-married Perry was doing was inside a tarty blond who pulled drinks at Legends. However, Perry had Anya's confession, and Mulrooney knew he and Mayor Howe would see Anya go down before they'd risk public humiliation. Anya was merely collateral damage.

Mulrooney thought Chief Clemente would piss gasoline when he and Clarke told him Lauren had slipped through their fingers. Nevertheless, Clemente had defended his two top detectives in a flurry of tense, media-packed news conferences. Of course, Mulrooney knew he was also covering his own ass.

Chief Clemente rationalized that Anya's alibi still didn't hold up because the waiter at Murphy's could not be exact about the time or identity of the redhead he saw on the bus bench the night of the homicide. Mulrooney, however, knew Kevin was reliable.

Mulrooney also could read Anya. He perceived in her an unconditional loyalty. His profile of Anya Gallien did not include murderer. Lauren Connolly, however, was the source of his unrest. He had been dreaming about her much too frequently; and the dreams were unsettling. Her intelligence and vulnerability had stirred something in him he had long ago compartmentalized.

As he mentally reviewed the facts, he tossed another guppy to Houdini. He knew that even if Lauren had been home when the homicide occurred, there was a major piece of the puzzle missing. In order to get the evidence they needed, he had to be willing to risk everything. Gritting his teeth, Mulrooney turned abruptly and yanked open his front door. He waited for the press to attack him like a school of hungry fish.

Chapter 28

Sam hustled Lauren to the end of the dock. "You'll need to travel under another alias. The authorities will be watching for you. Do you have a photo? I can't give up the one in my wallet. It's the last one I have."

"Here," she said as she handed him a photo of her and Anya, "will this do?"

"Yes, come with me. This place is an Aussie hangout, so we can get some assistance," he explained as he hurried her into Lem's Pub. As Sam and Lauren cut through the crowd of local fishermen to the battered wood plank bar, she was oblivious to the admiring glances of several patrons. When her eyes finally adjusted to the dim light, she looked up to see a salt-streaked canopy of old buoys and tattered fishing nets.

"You a tourist?" a weathered seaman asked her.

Lauren noticed how he rolled his vowels at her like a 45 record on 33 speed. She nodded as she appraised the massive, silver brows that billowed in full

sail when the man's face moved. Even more distract-
ing was the old guy's ill-fitting set of dentures that
goose-stepped each time he spoke. "Sit your lovely
self down," he said as he patted a stool. The man's
face cracked into a blistered mosaic as he flashed Lauren a grin. "How 'bout an iced one and a chat with a
beat-up ol' shrimper like myself?"

Sam spoke over his shoulder, "Sure, two Fosters...and the lady's with me."

"So she is," the fisherman said politely as he
quickly turned back around on his barstool with a
compliant hands-off gesture. Lauren chuckled when
she heard his dentures clank to parade rest.

While she waited for Sam, Lauren surveyed the
hundreds of snapshots of locals posing next to their
suspended catch. A long mirror behind the bar
seemed to double the bar's occupancy, thereby in-
creasing the festivity. The mirror was cut to accommodate an old metal freezer from which the bartender removed two frost-coated mugs. He filled
them until they foamed over the top.

"Where's Lem?" Sam asked the bartender.

"Should be right back. Gidday, Miss," he nodded to
Lauren. "Lem was 'spectin' you. He said to see that
you got this."

Sam looked at the message. It was from Sam's
friend Wyndham with Miami P.D. Old Joe Biragidji,
Sam's Miami club manager, knew Wyndham could
be trusted. Apparently Biragidji had directed Wyndham to call the pub, knowing Sam always dropped in
when he was in Key West. Wyndham had left word

that Detective Mulrooney from California had contacted Miami P.D. to ask for assistance in tracking Lauren and Sam.

Sam shoved the note into his pocket. He had known it would only be a matter of time. "Give Lem this," Sam said as he wrote on a napkin. "Tell him I need it in two hours." Sam pulled the photo of Anya and Lauren from his pocket. He made two sharp slashes to form an X through the face of Anya, then slipped the photo into the napkin before jotting down a few instructions. "And tell Lem I'm borrowing his Jeep. We'll be with George One-Eye."

The bartender nodded and took the note. As he turned to answer the phone, he tossed a set of keys to Sam. Sam took one last chug of his beer then indicated to Lauren that it was time to go.

Suddenly the bartender handed the phone to Lauren. "I think it's for you, Miss," he said.

Lauren was startled. She looked at Sam, and then she took the phone before he could stop her. She pressed her ear to the receiver but said nothing.

"It would be much easier if you didn't make me come after you," the voice on the line said. "You know you'll never get away from me, don't you?" Lauren recognized Mulrooney's voice, calm and self-assured.

"How did you find me?" she asked.

"Experience. And the Miami Police. You're wanted for questioning, Lauren. And this conversation is being recorded, okay?"

"Yes," she whispered.

"Lauren, listen to me; if you're not involved, you can save Anya and prove you're innocent. And if you are involved, you know I'm gonna get you."

"I don't have any doubt about that."

"Your surreptitious exit out of town looks very suspicious, Lauren. And it sure didn't brighten my day."

"I know, I'm so sorry. But I'm coming back."

"You said I could trust you."

"You still can." Lauren heard Mulrooney's steady breathing on the other end of the line. "I'm sorry if I made matters difficult for you and Clarke, but there was something I had to do alone." She noticed Sam observing closely.

"As pissed as I am, I think understand, Lauren," Mulrooney told her. "We know you're with Sam. Are you sure you're safe?"

"I think so." She heard the concern in Mulrooney's voice. "Thank you for your regard. Is Anya okay?"

"She's as well as can be expected of anyone fending off a pack of jackals. You're missing one helluva circus."

"I can imagine. I know you're doing everything you can, Tim. Please keep checking out all possible leads."

"You can count on that, but you've got to trust me enough to let me handle this my way. And I need your permission to enter your house again if I need to. May I?"

"Yes, of course. Anytime until I return."

"Thanks. I want you back here, Lauren. You have forty-eight hours. Miami Police is with you as

233

we speak. We're watching you closely. Be careful. Okay?"

"Okay, Tim," Lauren said quietly before she gave the phone back to the bartender.

As they turned to leave, Lauren noticed the old shrimper glance subtly to a thin man at the end of the bar. The thin man nodded to Lauren, flashed his shield, and then paid for his drink.

* * *

As Lauren and Sam took the back roads away from the harbor, Sam checked his rear view mirror several times. A Chevy was following them at a respectful distance. When Sam gave his jeep some gas, the Chevy also increased speed.

After Sam made several quick turns, he managed to get ahead of a slow-moving pick-up. The driver of the Chevy gunned his engine, but he was forced to drop back, unable to pass the pick-up before the road abruptly narrowed. The pick-up veered right to get out of the way of the impatient Chevy driver, which caused the tailgate to suddenly give way, dumping its load of gravel all over the road.

As the Chevy and the pick-up both screeched to a stop, Sam cut off onto an unmarked dirt lane. He drove awhile before going off-road into a tree-dense area where the land was a blend of sun-parched hues melding into areas so green they seemed painted onto the landscape.

Sam suddenly brought the car to a halt near an outcrop of rocks. When he climbed out of the car and began walking, Lauren followed him into the dense thicket. She breathed in the earthen smell as they made their way up a mossy incline. She could feel the cool moisture from the foliage settling on her skin. Sam abruptly stretched out one arm and signaled her to wait.

"Where are we, Sam? We could get lost out here. No one would ever find us. Except snakes or gators."

"No worries, babe," he assured her a bit too nonchalantly. "Coo-ee," Sam called out, startling Lauren. "Come on," he said, waving her further into the trees. "Don't smile until he smiles at us. It's impolite."

"Who?"

"Coo-ee," Sam let out another bush greeting. "There he is."

Lauren couldn't see anyone. She followed Sam though the trees until they came to a small encampment where a hut of branches and canvas could be seen in the distance. An aborigine abruptly appeared from between two trees like a dark apparition.

"Lauren, meet George One-Eye," Sam said.

"Welcome," George flashed two corn kernel teeth at her. His dark hair poked like fern fronds from beneath a sweat-seasoned hat, and his chestnut skin reflected a deep bronze undercoat.

Lauren shook his rough, warm hand. "I've heard Sam mention you," she smiled. "You've known each other a long time."

George focused on Lauren and Sam with one onyx eye. The other eye was sealed by a band of scar tissue that looked like a night crawler. "Yes, in our home land. You'll be hungry, so I made tucker," George told them. "I thought you would be here sooner."

Sam caught Lauren's curious look. "He must have known we were coming," he shrugged. "In the bush, Aborigines have always communicated by way of telepathy. That's why George insists on living out-doors instead of over Lem's Pub. Lem brought him to the States to work for him, but George keeps his old ways. He won't even get a cell phone. 'Says it would disrupt his ability to 'see' things."

"Here," George said, handing them each a cold beer. "Too much fire destroys the spirit," he cautioned as he popped open an orange soda for himself. George gestured for them to sit on a mat near a tree. "I fixed yams, apples, and wild onions, okey-dokey?"

Lauren enjoyed the way George rolled the 'okey-dokey' around in his mouth like a raw oyster before scuttling over to poke the fire. He sang softly in his own language as he tended to the food.

"What happened to his eye, Sam?"

"He lost it in an accident in the outback. He told his witch doctor he had a run-in with a *twenty-foot* emu," Sam explained. "An emu that flew!" Sam raised his brows at the image.

"Thirty foot emu," George interjected, correcting Sam out of the corner of his mouth. "Flew like a bat out of Hell!"

They both laughed as George flapped imaginary wings. "Anyway, now that's how he got the name 'George One-Eye,' right, George?"

"It did fly, Sam. It was a spirit bird."

"Some say his 'spirit bird' flew out of a bottle of Green Lizard Beer and that George was so full of 'spirit' he poked his own eye out. So no more spirit water unless he's feeling crook, which conveniently occurs every weekend," Sam snickered. "So George, you're cautious now, right?"

"Yes, cautious - I switched brands." George chuckled as he sat down on a red vinyl car seat that was propped against a tree. With the sleight of hand of a magician, George produced a giant, dark green egg. "It's an emu egg. I brought it to America in a coffee can. Maxwell House. I drained the egg and I ate it. Now I have emu spirit, emu strength, emu speed. I'm pretty, too, just like the emu, eh?" After he held the egg aloft for their inspection, George carefully slid it behind the car seat.

"Yep, you're a great old bird," Sam nodded. "George, I brought Lauren here because she needs one of your knives to protect herself." Sam turned away when Lauren shot him a dark look.

"I know," George grunted as he poked at the yams with a stick. He directed his one-eyed gaze, first at Lauren, then at Sam. He handed each of them a long stick with a yam on it and then passed them a plate of apple and onions. "Ancient Djambarbingu clan recipe," he explained, "with Fosters for flavor."

Although he pretended to be engrossed in the fire, George One-Eye observed them carefully while they ate. Lauren sensed he was becoming increasingly agitated.

George eventually spread a cloth on the ground. He reached underneath the car seat and extracted five bundles, each wrapped in a daily racing form. After removing the paper wrapping, he laid out five exquisitely carved knives and sheathes. Lauren shuddered at their similarity to the knife Anya had found in her VCR.

George selected one and handed it to her. She reluctantly gripped it in her hand then turned it over carefully, avoiding its razor-like blade. When she saw the single shark's tooth imbedded in the grip, Lauren gasped and dropped the weapon. George looked on curiously. "Thank you, George, but I'm not sure I agree with Sam that I need a knife."

George shook his head. The thick furrows of skin between his brows formed a hood over the bridge of his nose. "Yes, you do need it," he replied softly. "The bone points at you."

Sam set aside his food and shifted uncomfortably. "We'd better get back to Lem's, George. I'll return alone later."

"Wait, George!" Lauren interrupted. "What did you mean about a bone pointing at me?"

"I can see. Someone seeks to hurt you—to swallow you like the emu egg. Devour you and have you forever."

As Lauren looked to Sam for an explanation, Sam took a final swig of beer and abruptly ended the conversation. "Thanks, George, we'll take this one." Sam selected a knife, wrapped it in a racing form, and tossed down several bills. He grabbed Lauren's hand and pulled her away.

"Wait up," George ordered. He reached into a woven grass pouch lined with bird feathers and withdrew a fine white powder. "Sam, your sheila needs protection," he insisted. George yanked the knife from Sam's hand and looked at Sam closely. He then sprinkled the powder on the knife before handing it to Lauren.

"Thank you," she mumbled.

With a polite nod, Sam spun on his heel and walked away. Lauren looked back at the old Aborigine and hesitated. George fixed his one dark eye on her. He shook his head deliberately from side to side, as if issuing a warning.

Lauren mechanically turned to follow Sam, carrying the knife as though it were a severed limb. As they cut between the trees, she could hear the mournful voice of George One-Eye calling after her in strange aboriginal sounds.

Chapter 29

Mulrooney was feeling sorry for his young informant. Slag, the methamphetamine junkie, had pingponged through the door of his office ten minutes earlier. He was as hyper as a dog with distemper, and was now trying to find a way out the window.

Clarke was talking to him quietly, trying to harness Slag's energy. "Let us help you, son," Clarke said. "Something tells me you came back here because you know you need help."

Mulrooney jotted down a name and hung up the phone. "I've got a spot lined up for you at Exodus, Slag."

"REHAB? No way I'm goin' to any stinkin' rehab!" Slag yelled.

Mulrooney winced as Slag shoved a dirty fingernail into a blister that was eating through his face. "You can do it, kid," he coaxed. "They'll give you something to ease you back down. Com'on, Clarke and I will drive you there in my shiny new cop car."

Slag batted his nose as though there were fleas on it. "Nah, no way man. See, I just came by to tell you I remembered how that Clarence guy who was iced in Jersey talked about some cat called 'Clapp man.' That's all I know, so don't start picking at my brain. My skull hurts. I remembered Clapp 'cause it's like the clap - get it?" he said, scratching his crotch.

Mulrooney and Clarke looked at each other, then Clarke wrote down the name. Clapp was a name even an addict might remember.

"So can ya lay some bread on me, guys? I helped you out, now I gotta score," he pleaded.

"No bread till you're clean," Clarke said as he led Slag out the door by his elbow. "Let's get you off that shit first - and get you into some clean skivvies before you get into the car."

Clarke wrestled with their noncompliant visitor. "I can handle Slag," he said to Mulrooney. "Why don't you stay here and see what you can turn up." Clarke held the kid by the neck and said, "Now walk ... and on your own damn feet, not mine!"

After they left, Mulrooney looked down at a photo of Lauren Connolly and smiled before dialing Killackey's extension. "Killackey I need you to get word out onto streets that L.B.P.D. is trying to catch the Clapp." Somehow, the order gave him great satisfaction.

* * *

When Sam reached out to hold Lauren's hand, she did not respond. Sam pulled the jeep up next to Lem's Pub, turned off the ignition, and turned to face her.

"Your new I.D. should be ready by now. I also left instructions for Lem to book you on the next flight back to L.A. I told him not to cancel your original reservation under the alias you were using because Mulrooney's crew are probably keeping tabs on that one by now. This will buy you some time to get whatever information you need to assist in Anya's defense."

"Thank you, Sam. Now, how about explaining what George was talking about? And please don't tell me you didn't understand. You grew up with aborigines, and you've always employed them. I know you understand them just as they understand the land."

Lauren stared at the sign painted on the pub wall. It announced Lobster races every Friday, with two sweating Lobsters in running shoes, each holding a tankard. She stared at it hypnotically until the lobsters appeared to actually be racing across the weathered clapboard wall.

"George has dreams," Sam finally answered. "He's known among his tribe as a man of great vision. They believe the loss of his eye was a sacrifice for true insight. Maybe it is."

"So was he warning me about you?" She watched Sam push down the sharp response that rose in his throat. "You have a fake passport yourself, don't you?" she pressed. "After I located you in Miami, I just assumed Mulrooney had gotten the wrong information about your whereabouts based on your pass-port activity. But you came back in the States ille-gally, didn't you?"

"I told you I lost my green card."

"Were you in Long Beach the night Scott was mur-dered?"

Sam was angry. He grabbed the door handle and jumped out. After stalking into Lem's, he exited and then hurried down the dock to where the Kookaburra was moored. Just as Lauren was about to follow Sam, he jumped back off the boat onto the dock. With him were several objects, including her suitcases.

"We're going to the airport," he said, as he jumped back into the Jeep.

Lauren yanked the key from him. "This could be the last time I'll ever see you. Tell me the truth about what's going on."

Sam folded his strong arms across the steering wheel then pressed his head wearily against them. "What do you want me to say, Lauren? Yes, I was in Long Beach. And yes, I have a fake passport and Driver's License I use when I need to."

"Why do you need a fake passport?"

"Oh Christ, Lauren," he snapped. "You're not going to let this go, are you? I have a record in Australia. I needed an alias and false papers to get a liquor license and to set up a business in the States."

"You have a record?"

"If you're afraid I'm the neighborhood slicer, you're wrong. I was booked for inciting riots and re-sisting arrest. And indecent exposure."

243

"My God, Sam, what were you doing?"

"It was in Sydney. I was arrested as an activist against deployment of Australian personnel to Iraq. No bloody sense of humor."

"But 'indecent exposure'?"

"We were in our bloomies at the time."

Lauren couldn't suppress her smile as she studied Sam's sheepish grin. For the first time, she noticed the crease above his brow and the brush strokes at the corners of his mouth. She wondered now how many other things she had overlooked during their time together. Had she really ever known him for who he was, or for what he was capable of doing? "Were you at Scott's memorial?" she asked. "I was sure I saw you that day."

"Yes, I was. You should have known I'd be there. I was concerned about you. Did you think that by ending our relationship you could stop me from worrying about you? I flew in as soon as a mate of mine called to tell me what had happened."

"Why did you disappear?"

"Christ, Lauren, you hog-tie me then expect me to dance! You forbade me to contact you. You insisted it would make life harder for you. But do you think I ever stopped watching out for you?"

Sam turned and looked directly at her. "I love you, Lauren. Is that what you came to hear? Yes, I'm still in love with you. My heart and my gut won't let me forget you, and I thought somehow I could get you back. You've just become a fucking obsession for me, like a goddamned *emu egg* that I'm trying to consume—something to have and to own. Maybe I'm as crazy as George One-Eye."

When Lauren reached out to brush her fingers along Sam's cheek, his expression softened. He cleared his throat before gently pushing her hand away. "I can't believe that after what we once were to each other, you would doubt me and yet still believe in Anya. That rips me apart. I know you don't want to hear it, babe, but Anya is unstable; and she's obsessed with you."

Sam grabbed Lauren's face and forced her to look at him. "I think Anya might have set me up. Somebody sure as hell did! I don't know if my knife disappeared before or during the fire at my club, but I sure as hell never found it in the rubble. Neither did the arson investigation team, and they were damn thorough."

"How did that fire start?"

"Who knows? I think it was because I refused to let some local Wise Guys in on the action, but the cops assumed I did it because profits were low. Hell, I was just getting started!" He shook his head in disgust and looked at his watch. "You've got to get to the airport, but I want you to do something for me." Sam reached into the glove compartment and pulled out a thumb drive.

"What's this?" Lauren asked.

"I don't want to hurt you, babe, but you need to see this. Some orange-haired punk named Flint gave it to me one night at Jazzin' Long Beach. He was with a black guy named Clarence Smolley. I never looked at it until I unpacked in Miami. Those thugs must have hoped to use my club as a place of distribution. When you see the tape, you might change your mind about Anya."

"Okay, Sam, I'll call when I get back to Belmont Shore."

Sam took the key from her and shoved it into the ignition. "No, Lauren, just take care of yourself. If you ever need anything, call Old Joe Biragidji, my Miami manager. He'll have instructions to help you in every possible way. I'm going to have to disappear because I'm sure Mulrooney has alerted immigration."

Lauren placed her hand on his arm, but Sam pulled away. "You'll find your answers alone. And I can go on with my own life. I just can't do this dance anymore. As I said before: I want all of you, Lauren, plain and simple. Or nothing at all."

"Okay, Sam, I understand," she whispered, her voice escaping like air from a punctured life raft. Lauren knew she would have to tread water alone in the violent undertow that had become her life, but as she clutched the thumb drive, she felt she was being sucked under.

Chapter 30

Mulrooney was watching the sun come up over the bay from Lauren Connolly's living room when Clarke pulled up outside. Clarke got out of his car and took a bite out of a glazed donut before tossing the remainder back into his car.

"Did you save me a donut?" Mulrooney asked as Clarke entered.

"Nope. My news is going to kill your appetite, bro."

"Lay it on me, Smokey."

Clarke kicked the front door shut with his heel. "Atilla is meeting with Clemente later this morning to try to persuade him to let him take over the case."

Mulrooney shook his head in disgust. "Atilla won't give up until he's carrying my autopsy photo in his wallet. He's probably the maggot who bombed my car."

"Nothing personal, I'm sure," Clarke said sarcastically.

"Fuck him, we're still here, and we have work to do. That's why I got us a fresh warrant. Let's go."

"Let's review our evidence again, dude," Clarke said as he scanned his notes. "Lauren left her boat earlier than she said. Thus, our time line indicates she could have been present during the commission of the homicide. This is further substantiated by the fact that she would have required at least 23-28 minutes to complete the activities she claims to have done before finding her eviscerated husband. But a good attorney, if you'll excuse the oxymoron, could create reasonable doubt by claiming a two minute shower. That would make it possible for her to have come in *after* her husband was iced."

"And we'd both buy that defense, too." Despite Lauren's blown alibi, Mulrooney still had his doubts about her complicity. He wanted to question her, but he knew he couldn't let anything circumstantial confuse his thinking. "You know why I still have my doubts that Lauren knows something, Smokey?"

"My gut tells me it's more than lack of evidence."

"It's her breasts."

"Amen, bro."

"We both know those breast prints indicate she was trying to escape out of an unconscious fear the assailant could still be in the house."

"I know. But you've gotta admit, nothing's lining up."

Mulrooney nodded as they climbed the stairs. When they reached the second level, he stopped. He could hear music in his head. It was Gershwin's *I*

Love You, Porgy. He remembered that he had been in the hallway with Kate and Clarke on the night of the homicide when he had first heard those incongruously gentle notes from *Porgy and Bess.* "The music! He yelled.

"Son-of-a-bitch!"

They turned and ran down the stairs two at a time to the living room and yanked open the stereo cabinet. The compact discs were neatly arranged in a built-in rack. As he scanned the racks, Mulrooney read the titles from the beginning to the end. When he didn't find what he wanted, Clarke pushed a button to release the tray and carefully lifted out a disc. It was a compilation of Gershwin's *Rhapsody in Blue* and other selected pieces.

Mulrooney ran his hand along the top of the stereo until he located the empty C.D. case. Holding it by its edges, he quickly added up the amount of time required for each tune.

He stared at the numbers. "I Love You, Porgy" began playing seventeen minutes and twenty seconds into the piece. That night he had arrived at 12:44 A.M. and had used about two minutes before going upstairs with Kate to the bedroom. *I Love You, Porgy* was nearly over when he noticed that the upstairs speakers were malfunctioning. The piece was approximately seven minutes in duration. Therefore, almost twenty-four minutes of the collection had been played by the time he heard it. Dispatch had been notified at 12:27 A.M., and Lauren Connolly had run into the street at approximately 12:25 A.M. Mulrooney calculated numbers in his head while Clarke examined the buttons on the stereo.

"So either Lauren, or someone else who was here the night Connolly was killed, turned on some mood music sometime between 12:22 and 12:25 A.M."

Clarke whistled. "That's an odd and inopportune time to seek out a little entertainment."

"Exactly. That was *after* the doctor was murdered, but just *before* the 911 call and Lauren's scene in the street. Someone committed a murder and then put on some mood music."

"Unfuckinbelievable!" Clarke exclaimed as he examined the disc cover. "And the repeat button is broken, so there was no loop."

"Either Lauren set the scene with some music, or someone else did-"

"While Lauren was still in the house," Clarke said, finishing Mulrooney's statement. "How fast could Anya have gotten back here from Midnight Espresso? You said Kevin saw her walking."

"It would have been tight. But I know one thing, whoever did it has a taste for Gershwin."

"Yep," Clarke said as he studied the CD cover. "Ah," he nodded when he recognized the Gershwin tune they had heard upon their arrival, " 'I Love You, Porgy!' "

"I love you, too, Bess," Mulrooney grinned.

Chapter 31

Michael Ryan leaned against a Jaguar XJ8 convertible while passengers exited the baggage area at LAX. An attractive blonde, her hair dancing around her shoulders with the same energy as her quick strides, darted ahead of the lagging travelers. She nodded at Michael and smiled before getting into an unmarked police car parked at the curb in front of his Jag. Michael watched her drive away before he turned his attention back toward the terminal.

"You'll have to move your vehicle, sir," a voice said from behind. "There's a five minute parking limit."

Michael extracted his wallet and opened it for the traffic officer to inspect. The patrolman raised his brows, nodded, and quickly moved on.

"Hey, there," Lauren said huskily as she suddenly embraced him from behind.

"Lauren, I've been worried about you!"

"I'm so sorry, Michael. Sam and I left Miami immediately after my arrival so no one would find us. I meant to call sooner."

"Forget it. I'm just glad you're back," he smiled. "Did you sleep on the plane?"

"Barely." Lauren was afraid to sleep. Her nightmares were relentless, and often the same. She was in bed with Scott, covered with blood and viscera. Each time she was about to run, she looked down and saw a knife in her hand.

Lauren looked over her shoulder nervously. "Is anyone following you?"

"No, this car is registered to Futuro, one of my companies. The police won't be looking for it, and they don't expect you to return for three more days, if at all."

"Michael, let's go to your place. I have a thumb drive I need to look at."

"Okay, I'll make us something to eat. I'm sure I can scrape the mold off something or re-hydrate some old pizza."

"And you said you couldn't cook," she chuckled.

Michael smiled at her low, rumbling laugh. "It's good to hear you laugh again, Lauren. Maybe things can slowly get back to normal."

Lauren nodded while knowing in her heart that things would never be normal again. The ever-shifting boundaries of 'normal' had widened to accommodate a dark hole which had become her life.

* * *

From Michael's penthouse Lauren was able to look down on the Queen Mary, serenely moored in the harbor. "I'd forgotten how beautiful the view is from here," she said softly as she accepted a drink from Michael. "You've done a lot with the place. It's lovely."

Lauren walked through the living area, admiring the soft leather furniture and the interesting pieces of art and sculpture. "My God, Michael, you never told me you purchased a Basquiat!" she exclaimed.

Michael flashed a boyish grin as he smoothed his thick hair. "I was lucky. I bought it back when Warhol was first introducing Basquiat around New York. It turned out to be a good investment. If you like it, it's yours. Consider it my birthday gift to you. Please."

"Oh my God, I couldn't, Michael!" she protested, overwhelmed by his generosity. "Besides, I didn't celebrate my birthday this year," she said quietly.

"Well, perhaps you'll reconsider. You'll at least let me feed you, won't you? When you were in the bathroom I called 911 for emergency pizza."

"Thank God. You can barely make toast."

"True, but I'm still a great host," he grinned. "Here, sip this and relax. Let's take a look at your movie or whatever it is until the pizza arrives. We'll have pizza by candlelight."

When Michael reached for the candles above the fireplace, Lauren suddenly gasped. "Michael, where did you get that painting above the mantle?"

"The Thiebaud? I bought it from Scott." Michael saw her shocked expression and shifted uncomfortably. "You didn't know, Lauren?"

"No. No I didn't. He said it was at his office."

"Goddammit! He said you no longer wanted it and that you'd rather have the money. I thought I was doing you and Scott a favor. I don't even know what to say. Please, by all means, take it back."

"No. Thank you, Michael, but it would never have the same meaning for me again."

"Honey, I am so sorry. If you won't take it now, then I'll keep it for you. If at any time you change your mind, it's yours."

Still reeling with disbelief and confusion, Lauren sank into the couch. "Scott couldn't have spent all that money on drugs, Michael. Tell me what you know. Stop trying to protect me."

Michael sat down next to her and stroked her hair. "Scott made some bad investments when you were separated. He told me he had to pay back a few short-term loans to some loan sharks. Apparently he had invested in losing schemes with a number of unsavory people. The more he used drugs, the more foolish he was in business. He took a lot of unnecessary risks."

"He was bent on self-destruction."

"Yes, he was. And you were always the strong one. Don't ever doubt that." Michael stared at her. His eyes searched each feature of her face like fireflies unsure of where to light. Finally he put both arms around her and held her tightly while he leaned back into the couch and reached for the remote control.

Chapter 32

San Pedro, California

Mulrooney stepped onto the dilapidated porch of the flophouse on Magnolia just as Officer Bullock came running out the door and puked into his handkerchief. Johnston, Bullock's partner, was right behind him.

Mulrooney quickly chomped down two Rolaids then washed the residue from his mouth with a swish of strong black coffee. Since his humiliating bashing by the press, his stomach had been at war with his bowels. He had hoped the coffee would combat the effects of his insomnia, but he knew the caffeine wasn't really necessary. If the putrid stench coming from inside the house couldn't awaken him, nothing short of ice in his jock strap would.

Mulrooney winced as Bullock heaved up the remains of his breakfast over the decayed wooden railing. The patrolman then wiped his mouth on his sleeve, his handkerchief having long since been rendered ineffectual.

"Here," Mulrooney said sympathetically as he handed Bullock the Rolaids. "You need these more than I do."

He had been just across the bridge in Long Beach when he heard the report of a homicide in San Pedro where a knife had been the weapon of choice. Although this case was not theirs, Mulrooney called Clarke and then hustled to get a peek at the crime scene before it was compromised. Neither the assigned detectives nor Clarke had yet arrived, but Mulrooney didn't want to hang around any longer than necessary. When he took out his handkerchief and pushed open the door to the flophouse, he immediately started coughing.

A man in a tee shirt and brown overalls stepped forth to greet him. Mulrooney immediately sized the guy up as a junkie. He studied the gummy smile carved into a face that looked like spoiled meat. The junkie was using a pocket knife to scoop Spaghettios from a can, unfazed by the stench of the place. Evidently there were advantages to having burned-out nasal passages, Mulrooney concluded.

Mulrooney was blinking rapidly to control the burning in his eyes when Clarke tentatively stepped through the door. "Jeezuz H. Christ!" Clarke moaned. He yanked out his shirttail and pulled it up to cover his lower face. "Bullock told me between spews that the victim appears to have been decaying awhile. I could smell it half a block away. I can't believe no one reported this sooner."

"There's not much activity around here, Smokey. These buildings are all condemned."

Clarke spotted the junkie leering at him from behind the door. "What's with this character? Is he what stinks?"

The man with the Spaghettios wiped his mouth on his hand before strolling over. He gestured to the far end of the one-room apartment where two feet could be seen protruding from behind a sofa. "I'm the one who found 'im," he announced with undisguised satisfaction. His voice erupted like a series of belches. "I'm the manager, Virgil Peters. I come by to see if he'd done left yet."

"Left for where?" Mulrooney appraised Virgil's sunken face. The tip of Virgil's nose was crusty, and his eyes were wired like faulty light bulbs.

"Well, a few weeks back he said he wuz gonna hit the road fer good. But he wuz s'posed to make a good connection first."

"You mean drugs?" Clarke garbled through a wad of shirt.

" 'Dogs'?" Virgil exclaimed, completely misunderstanding. "Shit, there ain't no money in dogs! Porn. 'Didn't have no friends– prob'ly cuz of the tumor."

"Tumor?" Clarke repeated.

"No, not his 'tooter.' His TUMOR. Clean yer ears! He had a bigass one. That's why he wuz called Tumor. Actually he told me once that it wuz really a hernia. It was pretty disgustin' to see. It was bigger than his head. He used to pet it like a bald dog. Didn't bother me none though."

Virgil chowed down on the Spaghettios while he talked. Mulrooney cringed each time the old junkie wrapped his tongue around the blade of the knife. "I was surprised he wuz still here," Virgil told them between bites, "...what's left of 'im anyway. He was gonna sell some memory sticks he said, but he didn't even pack his bags."

Mulrooney glanced around the room. It was barren except for an old Formica table and a velveteen sofa with its pattern worn to a shine. On the table was a battered suitcase with a pile of clothes strewn about. Mulrooney, sizing up the empty suitcase, leaned in for a closer look. "Check it out, Smokey. The lock has been forced open."

Clarke examined the suitcase and then shot a look at Virgil.

"Tweren't me," Virgil protested.

Mulrooney turned over the name tag on the suitcase. "Whoa," Mulrooney exclaimed, "get a load of this!" He held out the name tag for Clarke to see.

"Lyle P. Clapp himself. Peep Show Clarence's sidekick." Clarke's eyes drilled in on Virgil, carefully articulating each word. "Do you know where Clapp was going?"

"Vegas, with some cat named, uh, I forget. They was gonna stay at the Bellagio, but I guess Tumor crapped out." Virgil laughed at his own quip.

"Bellagio? Nice digs for a guy who lives like this," Mulrooney commented to Clarke through his hand-kerchief, "...real nice digs."

" 'Nice legs'? Hell no!" Virgil interjected. "He had fat ugly legs with big, purple vertaclosed veins."

"Vertaclosed?" Clarke repeated.

"Yeah, vertaclosed. You need a hearing aid, man!"

"And you need Hooked on Phonics, Sparky," Clarke shot back.

"Don't gotta phone."

Clarke rolled his eyes and mumbled to Mulrooney, "Do you think this guy ever tried personality inte-gration for all those people inside his gourd?"

"Not in any of his lifetimes," Mulrooney intoned as he continued to look around. "We better get this over before the crime team moves in, Smokey."

"Yeah, Smokey, get a move on," Virgil prodded, flashing an oily grin at Clarke as he downed another glob of Spaghettios.

Mulrooney saw fire licking at the edges of Clarke's smile and wondered how Virgil would feel about a can of Spaghettios wedged into his forehead.

Bullock and Johnston came back into the house in a last attempt at bravado and followed Mulrooney and Clarke to the far corner of the room. The sofa created a visual barrier between them and the victim. When Mulrooney and Clarke stepped around the side of the sofa, they saw the remains of what had once been a very large man. Lyle P. Clapp's body was dis-tended like a prehistoric blowfish and was glued to the floor by an enormous puddle of caked blood. The vestiges of his eyes stared up at the stained tin ceiling. His throat, which had been slit from ear to ear, was now coated with maggots.

Clarke suddenly grabbed Mulrooney's arm and gestured to the lower portion of the corpse. In one move, they all yelped and backed off. "The fucker is moving!" Bullock yelled.

As they all focused on the enormous hole in the guy's stomach, the dried puddle of blood inside the cavity rose up in a pulsating mound. Mulrooney stared in disbelief until Virgil started laughing. Mulrooney looked again at the enormous, decayed abscess that was once Tumor's tumor. Inside the mass, several large and glutinous rats scurried about in a feeding frenzy.

Clarke immediately headed for the door with Mulrooney close at his heels. The two patrolmen, already too far gone to navigate the distance to the porch, leaned out the windows to deposit what was left of their stomach waste on the tropical overgrowth that surrounded the empty flophouse.

"There's no getting used to some things," Mulrooney grunted as he dropped down on the broken porch step next to Clarke.

Just then the door banged open and Virgil stepped out into the late afternoon sun. He shoved the half-eaten can of food toward Clarke and laughed like a braying mule. "Spaghettios, Smokey?" he taunted.

Clarke's hand, flying upward as if it were spring-loaded, made a direct hit on the bottom of the can.

Mulrooney watched the trajectory of the can as it planted itself squarely on Virgil's mug.

"Oops. Sorry, freakass." Clarke oozed.

"Nice to meet you, Virgil," Mulrooney smiled. "Bon appétit."

Chapter 33

Chapter 33

As Lauren and Michael waited for the images from the thumb drive to appear on the screen, Lauren's body went rigid. She recognized the voices even before the participants stepped into frame. The camera was focused on a treatment table in a pale blue medical office. Little else could be seen except a nearby chair, an overhead light, and the blank wall behind the table. The office was Scott's.

Scott entered the frame first, his back to the camera. Lauren was jolted by the sight of Scott. He was tan and muscular, his sun streaked hair giving him a boyish, innocent appeal.

Scott yanked a hospital gown over his clothes before donning a mask and latex surgical gloves. He then pulled a woman toward him as he laughed and stroked her tousled hair, always conscious of the camera's position. When he stepped aside, the beautiful, oblivious face of Anya Gallien came into view.

Scott whispered into Anya's ear and then stepped back to admire her nakedness. She stood still while Scott slid his hand over her breasts and followed the curves of her body until his hand came to rest in the space at the top of her thighs.

Scott pushed her back on the table. The table was at an angle to the camera and provided a view of Anya while allowing Scott to turn away, remaining faceless. Anya held her hand against his chest. When she started to say his name, he lifted his mask and closed his mouth over hers.

"Oh God!" Lauren screamed. "Oh my God!"

Michael pressed the off button on the remote and clutched her to him. "That's enough," he said. "No more!"

Lauren struggled against the urge to scream again. She sat for a moment while she steadied her breathing. "Turn it back on, Michael," she ordered, staring directly ahead.

"No, you don't have to do this, Lauren!"

Lauren took the remote from Michael's hand and pressed the play button until the images came to life again. Anya and Scott were like two strangers wearing Halloween masks, disguised as people Lauren had once loved. Scott was on top of Anya, fully clothed, struggling with the front of his trousers. After he reached to the side of the table to raise the stirrups, he lifted Anya's legs to position her. When Anya tried to speak again, he put his finger over her lips and thrusted into her.

Scott moved slowly, keeping his head turned aside and twisting his body to expose only hers. Anya moaned and kept her eyes closed while he pushed into her repeatedly. Suddenly he pulled out and spilled his semen over Anya as his entire body shuddered uncontrollably.

Anya lay motionless like an exquisite sculpture atop a funeral bier. She finally opened her large eyes and focused them on Scott. Her hand reached up toward his face just as the image faded to black.

* * *

"What are you doing?" Michael asked as Lauren grabbed her bag.

"I'm going to Anya's. I need answers now!"

"No, Lauren, don't! You don't know what she's capable of doing. This tape is evidence of that." He yanked the disk key out of the computer, and turned to face her. "Why in the hell did Sam Bennett want you to see this?"

"Sam knew I'd never believe this without proof."

"I'm calling Mulrooney and Clarke."

"No. I want to confront her first."

"Then I'm going with you."

"Please, no. She won't talk to me if you're there."

"What good is this, Lauren? You could get hurt. Please call Mulrooney. He's trying to help you. He turned Long Beach and Miami upside down looking for you. I couldn't live with myself if I let something happen to you."

"Anya won't hurt me. She cares about me too much."

"Then why in the hell did she sleep with your husband?"

"I don't know, but I'm going to find out. I want to talk to her alone. If I'm not back in two hours, then come. And bring Mulrooney and Clarke with you."

"I hope you know what you're doing," he warned.

"Not exactly, Michael, but at least now I know the person I'm dealing with." As she stepped into the elevator, she turned to look at him. The doors closed shut, blotting out his dark and handsome face as the elevator began its slow descent.

Chapter 34

"Check with the airlines again, and tell surveillance to stay at LAX," Mulrooney said into the phone. He spun back on his counter seat to face Clarke, who was sipping water.

Clarke groaned, "Jesus! Rats in a tumor!"

"You're definitely a whiter shade of pale, partner."

Sophie set down two menus as she sauntered past. Mulrooney pushed the menu aside. Neither of them had much appetite after viewing the decayed carcass of Lyle P. Clapp. In the few hours since then, Mulrooney and Clarke had reviewed his long rap sheet of porno-related crimes.

"I think we've connected a few more dots, Smokey. According to our informant, the oh-so-ruptured Tumor knew Clarence Smolley, who was killed in the Jersey peep show. Both Clarence and Clapp hung out at Sam Bennett's Long Beach jazz club. They were both slash victims like Scott Connolly, whom we can also link to Sam Bennett."

Clarke nodded. "What's also interesting is that the USB devices that both Clarence and Tumor were peddling had been stolen from each crime scene."

"Besides the M.O., it's the steely execution of those two homicides that makes me suspect a connection to the Connolly case. I talked to the chief investigating officer in the Jersey case on the way over here. He said the perp had pumped a bunch of bills into the peep show money box *after* slicing Clarence.

"How did they determine that?"

"The prints of the victim, who was the first customer of the day according to the security camera, were the only prints on any bills in the box. However, there were bills in the box that had been cleaned of all prints, despite traces of the victim's blood. Apparently the assailant stayed to watch, then he, or 'she' I suppose, finished off the stripper."

"Christ, that's cold. What else did the security camera show?

"Nothing. The tape went black after Smolley entered the place."

"Interesting."

Sophie walked up and set two muffins in front of them. "Did I hear you mention a guy named Tumor?"

"Yes, do you know him?" Mulrooney asked.

"Sure, we dated," she smiled sarcastically. "Hell no, I don't know him, but I know who he is. He came in here once or twice. You couldn't miss him. He had this giant growth that-"

"Please, Sophie, we know," Clarke pleaded, cutting her off. "Did Tumor ever come in here with anybody?"

"No, but one day he was waiting a long time to meet someone. He sat here for more than an hour just petting that enormous growth like he had someone living in there. Oh, sorry, Clarke. Anyway, when the guy didn't show, Tumor told me to tell anyone asking for him that he'd be at home. I think he said he was looking for a guy named Skinfold. No, Skinflint. Yeah, that's it. I don't forget names."

Mulrooney smiled and nodded. "Your memory is as legendary as your list of husbands, woman."

Clarke wrote 'Skinflint' in bold letters on his note pad. "Thanks, Sophie. It's the only lead we've got."

"Is Tumor in trouble?" she asked.

"Not anymore, darlin'," Mulrooney said as he bit into a muffin. "The Tumor has been surgically removed."

Chapter 35

It was just after nightfall when Lauren eased her Mercedes out of the parking garage of Michael's building where she had left it while in Miami. As the fog swept in, she was once again overcome by the feeling she was falling into an abyss.

Lauren drove to Naples where she parked at the foot of the Rivo Alto Bridge and walked along the canal to Anya's cottage. When she crossed under the trellis into the patio, the sensor tripped the lights. While Lauren pounded on the door, she checked over her shoulder for surveillance.

A minute later, the door opened and Anya stood before her. A white satin nightgown clung to her body as she stood in the doorway adjusting her eyes to the light. Anya's serene smile gradually lifted her face. "Lauren," she whispered breathlessly as she embraced her, "I've been so worried."

"Really?"

Anya pulled Lauren inside as she spoke, leading her to the kitchen. She motioned for Lauren to sit while she made coffee. "Of course I was worried! You said you'd call from Miami. But as happy as I am to see you, I don't think you should have come back."

Lauren waited as Anya set out cream and sugar, seemingly oblivious to Lauren's silence. It was no wonder Scott wanted her, Lauren thought as she appraised Anya's lithe body through her slim satin gown. Anya was uniquely beautiful, and she was strong and passionate about everything in her life.

"I hope no one knows you're back," Anya said as she set the cups on the table. "Do you know what's been going on here since you left?"

"Yes, Michael told me."

"I'm sorry you're going through this, Lauren, but we can handle it, I promise. They just want to question you; and I've told them nothing." After she reached for the bowl of sugar cubes, she handed Lauren a linen napkin. "So did Sam know anything about the brunette Scott was seeing while you two were split up?"

"No, but I found out about the redhead."

Anya flinched. "Oh?" As she sat down slowly, she kept her eyes on the sugar bowl. "I was sure the woman had dark hair." Anya heaped sugar into her coffee then stirred more vigorously than necessary.

Suddenly Lauren exploded. "You lied to me, Anya! You were my best friend, and you lied! I trusted you, but I'm the one you murdered. You broke my heart!"

"What are you saying?" With trembling hands, Anya set down her spoon, which missed the saucer and clanged against the tabletop.

"You couldn't have me, so you went after Scott."

"That's absolutely disgusting, Lauren! I refuse to listen to this kind of talk."

"Yes, you will listen, Anya. If you decided to toy with men, why did it have to be your best friend's husband?" Lauren's voice was low and steady. "In spite of our problems, I loved him. You knew that. And I loved you, too!"

"Stop this, Lauren!" Anya cried. She stood up abruptly, knocking over her chair. "I told you I didn't date Scott. We just had dinner–is that a date? If so, I'm guilty, okay? I'm GUILTY!" Anya's voice cracked as she backed against the counter for support.

"Don't lie to me! I know you had sex with Scott."

"Stop! You don't know what you're saying!"

Lauren jumped up. "Tell me the truth!" she yelled.

As Anya recoiled, her limp body banged against the counter like a loose shingle. "Stop it, Lauren! What good is this now? Scott is gone."

"You've been lying all along, haven't you?" Lauren demanded. "Tell me the truth goddammit!" Suddenly Lauren grabbed Anya by the shoulders and shook her angrily. As Anya fell against Lauren, she reached back to brace herself.

"You want the truth?" Anya repeated through clenched teeth "You want all the ugly details? I told you, we had dinner a few times when you were seeing Sam. Although you were separated, you wanted

271

us to remain a 'family,' remember? And that was all I ever wanted–a family. I didn't even like Scott, but I was willing to spend time with him. I was trying to love you in some other way. It was the only way I could."

"So you thought you should have sex with him?" Lauren snapped.

"Are you listening to me, Lauren? We had dinner. DINNER! That's all it was supposed to be. Afterward he took me to his office under the pretense of picking up some files. He made drinks for us there. I had one drink, and then I collapsed on the couch in the waiting room. Scott was suddenly on top of me. It was as though I were outside myself, watching it all take place. I tried to scream, but my screams were trapped in my head. I could barely move. I watched him take off my clothes, yet I couldn't do a damn thing to stop him. I don't even remember how I got from the waiting room to the treatment room."

Lauren let go of Anya's shoulders and jerked the chair upright. "Do you expect me to believe he drugged you?" she whispered.

Anya tried to steady herself. She turned on the faucet, and splashed cold water over her face. "Scott was doing a lot of drugs," she said, keeping her back to Lauren. "I don't know what he did that night. I only know I was unable to fight back. He raped me."

"It didn't look like rape to me," Lauren said bitterly.

Anya whipped around to face Lauren. "What in the hell do you mean by that?"

"He got it all on camera."

"That fucking pervert! That BASTARD! I want that tape!"

"It's at Michael's place, Anya. And it's a damn good motive to kill someone, isn't it?"

Anya was seething. Without warning she picked up a large platter from the counter and slammed it against the cabinet. As the porcelain shattered around her, she didn't flinch. "It's a perfect motive!" she screamed. "God knows I would have ended Scott's life then and there if I were able. Did that filthy tape show me scratching his eyes–the only movement I could consciously command my brain to do? Do you remember his torn eyelid, Lauren? Do you?"

The image of Anya's hand reaching for Scott's face after he ejaculated suddenly loomed in Lauren's mind as her brain scrambled to make sense of it all. "He hurt his eye playing racquetball," Lauren protested.

"Bullshit! I'm the one who scratched his eye!" Anya drove the words into Lauren one at a time. "I wish I had gouged it out!"

"How do you expect me to believe you, Anya?" Lauren yelled. "If that really happened, why didn't you report it to the police?"

"And ruin your life? I thought you had broken free of Scott. When you said you were going to try to work things out, I didn't know what to do. I knew a rape charge would tear you apart. Lauren, I love you. I wanted you to have what you wanted if you could just be happy. I made excuses for Scott's behavior in my own mind, just as you've always done.

273

He was a charmer, Lauren, but he was also a selfish, hedonistic, bastard."

"Shut up, Anya!" Lauren screamed. "Scott's dead. Isn't that enough vindication? You killed him, didn't you?"

Anya raised her hand and slammed it against Lauren's cheek, watching as she reeled backwards. "Maybe you should be a little more honest with Mulrooney about what you were doing the night Scott was murdered," she pronounced with a terrifying calm. "I put my life on the line for you. I've kept silent for you despite my own peril."

"What are you implying?"

"I know Scott hurt you terribly, Lauren. I also know how you react to alcohol. There have been times when you couldn't even remember where you've been...or what you've done. You could easily have killed Scott."

Lauren was completely stunned. She lifted her hand to strike, but Anya caught Lauren's arm in a firm grasp. With tremendous strength, she pressed her fingers into Lauren's arm while she grasped the thick grip of a carving knife that was lying on the cutting board. In one quick movement, she brought the knife to Lauren's chin and pressed the blade against her flesh. Anya kept her tight grip on Lauren as she twisted Lauren's arm behind her back. "Is this how we should end this, Lauren? The jilted lesbian supposedly kills her friend's husband. And then kills her friend?"

"Don't do it, Anya," Lauren whispered.

"Maybe we should die together," Anya replied stonily. She pulled the knife back and held it high above Lauren's head. Lauren struggled to wrench away from Anya's paralyzing grasp, but Anya was too fast. Lauren's screams were trapped in her throat as Anya pulled the knife back and aimed the tip toward Lauren's face.

Suddenly Anya cried out and lunged forward. In one violent motion, she hurled the knife. It sailed across the kitchen and impaled the cabinet with its angry force, ripping the wood apart.

"You should know me well enough to realize that I won't willingly let life take anything else from me," Anya said as she choked back her tears. "I certainly won't ever be a victim again, especially of my own anger. You're all I have in this world. If I lose you, it won't be by my own doing."

Anya brushed back her tears and straightened her spine with steely resolve. "I was willing to cover for you and provide an alibi for you as long as I could. Mulrooney and I both know you were home before midnight, Lauren. You were there when Scott was murdered. Go back to Miami before Mulrooney finds out you've returned, and then go to Australia with Sam. I'm staying here; and I'll protect you until you're safe."

Lauren stood in silence, her face frozen in a mask of confusion. Suddenly she reached out to Anya and tried to cradle her in her arms. "Please forgive me," she pleaded.

"Don't, Lauren," Anya resisted, "please go. I need time to think." Anya turned her back on her friend and braced herself against the counter with shaking hands.

"Anya, I'm so sorry," Lauren rasped. "I'm just so overwhelmed by all that has taken place. I don't think I was drunk that night. But you're right, I don't remember what happened. I've been so confused." Lauren reached out again to touch Anya's shoulders, but Anya remained stiff. "Please, Anya, I can't just walk out and leave you alone," she cried.

"I've been alone for a long time," Anya whispered. She looked around her like an animal in the wild. "You're in danger here," she said. "Please go back to Sam. Go away and leave me alone, Lauren."

Lauren stood very still before clutching Anya one more time. She kissed her hair, turned away, and then she slowly walked out the door.

276

Chapter 36

Mulrooney closed his office door and dropped into his chair. When he grabbed the file on the Connolly case, he spotted three sticky notes bearing Killackey's bold print. The first simply said, NO I.D. ON SKINFLINT. He and Clarke had run every possible variation of the name Skinflint. They had tried Skinfold, Skintight, and even Clarke's creative contributions of Skingraft and Foreskin. Nothing had come up in the computers or on the streets.

Mulrooney glanced at another note: CALL OFFICER KATE AXBERG FOR A GOOD TIME. He grinned and read the last message: CALL DR. PETERSON AT DEPT OF ANTHROPOLOGY, CAL STATE ASAP!

Mulrooney dialed the numbers and waited for Peterson to pick up. "Doc, it's Mulrooney," he said when Peterson came on the line. "You got something?"

"Sure do, Tim. Interesting weapon indeed. Apparently the knife had been soaked in hot water on occasion to clean it. The hot water caused the spinifex around the wooden grip to loosen, allowing traces of debris to collect underneath. We've identified the matter imbedded under the grip. It's grunion skin."

"Grunion? Like the fish?"

"Exactly. And we were able to determine by the decomposition that the knife had been used on the fish sometime within the past month."

"Nice," Mulrooney smiled. "Very nice. Thanks, Jim."

He hung up the phone and shoved aside his notes in search for the *Grunion Gazette*, a neighborhood paper that published the times of the seasonal grunion runs. Belmont Shore locals liked to catch the small silvery fish as they came ashore by the thousands to spawn. To his recollection, the spawning always began the night of the highest tide and continued for two to three nights thereafter. He had often watched as the female grunion burrowed vertical holes, tail first. Just as they spawned, the male grunion would come ashore to fertilize their eggs, thus becoming easy catch for fishermen. Knowing the dates of the season's grunion runs might be beneficial to the time line in the investigation.

As Mulrooney was searching for the newspaper beneath a stack of files, he was surprised to discover a memory stick in a plastic sandwich bag. Mulrooney opened the door to his office and yelled, "Hey, who put this on my desk?" The replies from around the office indicated that no one knew where it came from.

Mulrooney shut his door and popped the flash drive into his computer. Suddenly the face of Anya Gallien, vacant and robotic, stared at him from his monitor, momentarily throwing him off balance. As he watched the video, he immediately knew the man with his back to the camera was Scott Connolly. Mulrooney had studied him so well in death that he almost knew the doctor in an extended form of life. "Holy shit," Mulrooney exclaimed.

While he viewed the tape, he was puzzled by Anya's lack of response. It was odd, because he knew that beneath Anya Gallien's reserved manner was a smoldering passion. After the tape ended, he sat quietly processing the information before removing the memory stick and rushing out of the office. "Tell Clarke to meet me at Vice when he gets back," he yelled to Killackey.

He ran down the hall and burst into the office of Janet Glenn, head of Vice. "Can you please view this ASAP, Janet?"

Janet nodded and shoved it into her machine. "Take a seat."

Anya's face appeared again on the screen. "Not your standard underground fare," Janet observed. She reached for an evidence bag containing a similar flash drive. "You'll want to see this one, too," she said just as Clarke stuck his head in the door.

"What up?" Clarke asked.

"Christmas came early, Smokey. Check it out."

Once again, the images came to life. Clarke's mouth dropped open as Anya and Connolly appeared on the screen before them. "That's one confused lesbian," he muttered. "Where did you get this?"

"Unidentified delivery. Janet, please show us yours." They watched as the second video lit up the screen, clearly showing the office of Dr. Scott Connolly.

"Hi-ho, Silver!" Clarke said as the masked and gloved doctor led a brunette into the scene.

The second tape was much more explicit as the woman responded enthusiastically to Connolly's moves. She took the lead by unzipping his trousers and guiding him into her. Connolly hesitated for a moment before pulling a cloth covered ampoule from inside his glove. After breaking it open, he held it to his nose and breathed deeply. The two then began to move together slowly. Each time the woman looked away from the camera, he turned her head back toward the lens. When the woman approached orgasm, she fought to free her head from his grasp.

"It's 'Morticia' from the funeral!" Clarke sputtered.

Janet pointed to the screen. "See her hair lifting? Hairpiece."

"That's our girl," Mulrooney said quietly. They sat, transfixed, as the doctor stopped thrusting long enough to reach for a long medical instrument.

"What in the hell?" Mulrooney yelped.

Janet pressed the off button. "It gets much more 'medical' than that. And she was definitely into it."

Mulrooney shuddered. "Jesus, there's a market for everything! We need to interrogate her, Janet. We need to find out how she's linked to Dr. Connolly, and to Anya Gallien. Do you have an I.D. on her?"

"First name only–Donna something. Here's a copy of a photo we pulled off the video."

"Thanks. Did you notice the clothes in the corner of Connolly's office on that video, Smokey?"

Clarke nodded. "Designer duds and a very expensive looking woman's briefcase. Business woman?"

"Probably a pipe bomb manufacturer," Mulrooney sneered.

"We have a lead on who's distributing this shit–small time thug named Flint."

"FLINT!" Mulrooney and Clarke yelled simultaneously.

"Janet, can you get us anything more on Lyle P. Clapp, alias Tumor?" Clarke asked. "We know he was from Vegas and peddling pedophile porn. He may also have been distributing Flint."

"We're already tracking Flint because of a new rash of videos involving minors, including snuff films. We're hoping Flint will lead us to the big fish. Organized crime still runs the porn market here. We're after the kingpins at the top."

"If Flint was selling tapes with Anya and Donna in them, is it possible he would know them?" Mulrooney asked.

"It's unusual for a swing man like Flint to know the participants in the merchandise, but our moles say they've seen Flint with Donna. We plan to nab Flint this week. I'll call you if you want in on the sting.

That way you could debrief Flint to find out what he knows about Donna and Scott Connolly."

"We're in," Mulrooney said. "Also, will you see if you've got any connections between Flint and a stiff named Clarence Smolley? He got his throat sliced in Jersey recently. It seems that he, Clapp, and Flint were all working for the same source."

"Will do."

"Thanks, Janet," Clarke said as he stood to leave. "Donna may be our connection to everyone."

Mulrooney nodded. "Yes, and most of her connections end up on ice."

Chapter 37

"You look great," Mulrooney smiled as Kate Axberg walked into The Rib Joint, a restaurant in Naples near the home of Anya Gallien.

"Thanks, Tim," she said sweetly, as she slid into the booth, "And you look like something a stray cat coughed up. What are you doing to yourself?" She watched him dig into an enormous piece of strawberry pie. "You only eat like this when you're angry."

"Hell yes, I'm angry. I've got that asshole Atilla breathing down my neck to take over my case, and I'm frustrated as hell. And we still can't locate Lauren. By the way, do you recognize this woman?" he asked as he flashed the photo of Donna. "I think it's Connolly's girlfriend, the one you heard about when you were at Legends. She was his patient. Connolly's nurse recognized her, but she wasn't sure of her last name. Evidently Donna only came in once or twice. One of his office girls thought it was a 'B' name–'Baer' or something."

"The only Baer I can think of played Jethro on 'The Beverly Hillbillies.'"

"I somehow doubt he was Connolly's girlfriend," Mulrooney said wryly. "We went through every single file but the office manager couldn't come up with a name. However, according to the file numbers, one of the files is missing."

"Interesting. Well, I'm still sniffing around for you. My source says he saw Connolly and the brunette together just two days before the homicide."

Mulrooney rubbed the scar on his chin. "I do know one thing," he continued, "whoever used the murder weapon was in or near California four to eight days before the homicide - the dates of the first and only grunion run before Connolly was killed. There were traces of grunion on the murder weapon."

"Anya Gallien was allegedly in Mexico just before the homicide," Kate interjected. "Are there grunion in Mexico, or in Florida where Sam lives?"

"Leave your brain to science," he smiled. "My exact thought. According to the articles I read, grunion spawn solely on the Pacific coast. They can be found from around Morro Bay down to Baja, and along Mexico's coast, but only as far south as Guaymas."

"I thought Anya was farther south, in Barra De Navidad."

"We're trying to verify that," Mulrooney said as he signaled for more coffee. "So how come you're not with your boyfriend on your day off?" he asked as he speared another strawberry.

"Interesting segue, Detective," she said sarcastically. "We're not seeing each other anymore."

"Interesting answer. How come?"

"He couldn't take the pressure. I'm a cop, even at home I guess. He was ready for a family; and with all I see, I'm not sure I want to bring a kid into this world. Do you want kids, Tim?"

Mulrooney stopped chewing and set down his fork. "I did once...badly enough that I nearly lost my shield over it."

"Are you referring to the incident with your wife?"

"It's never going away, so you might as well know what happened. I was working a lot of nights after we moved up here from San Diego. I should have known the marriage wasn't working when Isabella kept saying how unhappy she was here, but I thought she was just lonely. I tried to convince her to start a family because I thought that's what we both wanted.

"So when Isabella finally got pregnant, I was excited. Then I found out she was boffin' some professor at Cal. State. He was from her hometown in Venezuela. Admittedly, I didn't take it well."

"Oh God, how did you find out?"

"Isabella came to the station one night and caught me in the parking lot. She walked up and suddenly announced that she was returning to Venezuela. Then she told me she had a lover.

"At that point I knew there was no sense in trying to save the marriage. However, I begged her to reconsider anyway, for the sake of the baby. I wanted that kid more than anything, Kate. But she just turned her back on me and walked away. I was so enraged I couldn't see straight. She shut me out like I didn't even exist. So I ran after her and grabbed her by the shoulders and demanded she talk to me.

"Suddenly, with no remorse at all, she informed me that she had aborted the baby. She had been more than four months along! She had paid some quack in Mexico to kill our son. She murdered my child, Kate, and I was absolutely powerless to do a goddamned thing about it. I hunt killers every day of my life, and all I could do was stand there while she told me in that emotionless voice that she had taken our child's life. I felt so damn powerless I just went nuts!"

"Oh God, what did you do?"

"I just lost it, Kate. I yelled, and I pushed her away from me because I couldn't stand to look at her. She stepped back toward me and then lost her balance and fell, but instead of assisting her I turned away. I suppose I wanted her to hurt as much as she had hurt me. When I finally calmed down, I was really ashamed, and completely defeated. So I stalked off like the asshole I am.

"Carlos Atilla was coming out of the station at the time and saw the whole fracas. He reported the incident to the chief and leaked it to the media, complete with his own brand of extreme hyperbole. He said I hit her, so I was nearly suspended."

"What did Chief Clemente do?"

"He said if I got some conflict resolution counseling he'd keep the details off my record and give me another chance. But now everyone thinks my treatment of Isabella is an indication of gender issues. And Atilla happens to be Isabella's cousin, so he also made a racism issue out of the whole mess."

"That explains the ugly rumors."

"No one knows the details except Clarke. I couldn't talk about it. But I think that's when I stopped being objective about the victims in my cases. Losing my kid got me all jammed up. Now it's all becoming too personal; I find myself wondering if the victims liked the Dodgers, or dogs, or Christmas—shit like that. That kind of thinking is real dangerous in our business, Kate."

"Maybe you're just more compassionate now."

"I can't afford to be. That can result in terminal mistakes."

"You're still the best L.B.P.D. has, Tim."

Mulrooney shook his head. "I don't know, Katie...it seems like all we do is bag 'em and tag 'em. Just once I'd like to be able to stop the killing before it occurs."

Kate sighed and shoved her salad aside. "You haven't been with a woman since Isabella left, have you?"

"No. I can't invest that much again."

"Dammit, Tim, you can't stop living. Look at you—you've been in turmoil since I've known you. Why don't you stop being afraid of what you're feeling and admit that you're human, and that you screw up like all the rest of us?"

"I know what passion can do, Kate. Maybe if I'd been alone with Isabella I really could have hurt her.

I still have nightmares where I'm smashing her face. It's ironic that Atilla and I hate each other for the same reason—we each think the other is a mean cop."

"Atilla *is* a mean cop. You're just mean to yourself. Maybe you need to start caring more about Tim Mulrooney."

Mulrooney sighed. He knew he was at a turning point in his life, and he also knew he had lost something irretrievable along the way.

Kate cocked her head and smiled. "Some woman is going to come along who's worth the gamble. And you better go for it, my friend."

"Thanks, Kate. Right now, I'm happy to settle for a buddy. Do you want to go to the beach Saturday night for the grunion run? We can see if any persons of interest are hanging about."

Kate shot him a sly look. "Grunion, huh? God you're dull!"

"Well my self-esteem certainly just sky-rocketed."

"Good. You see, Mulrooney, the world is full of hope, even for a guy like you."

"Only if you're buying," Mulrooney said as he pushed the check toward her.

"Get some sleep before our grunion gig," Kate laughed. She shoved the check back under his pie plate and stood up.

"I plan to dull you to death," he called to her, "if I'm still alive Saturday night."

Kate stopped in the doorway and turned around. "Promise me that's a glib remark and not a premonition."

Mulrooney didn't respond. He wasn't sure of the answer.

Chapter 38

Mulrooney stood in his living room toweling off his peeling, sunburned skin, which appeared to be reproducing. A short while earlier, Janet Glenn had called to alert him and Clarke that the sting on Flint was going down that day, so he had once again cut short his sleep.

After several minutes, Mulrooney surrendered in the battle against his epidermis and tossed the towel on his easel, which had become a bulletin board for the sordid notes, facts and figures of his cases. Suddenly the fine hairs on his neck stood up, and his eyes darted back toward his easel. There, impaled on the wood frame with a push pin, was Houdini. The lion fish was staring at the floor with lifeless, bulging eyes. Mulrooney's still life, slashed to shreds, lay on the floor behind a stack of papers.

He reeled around and reached toward the table for his weapon with one hand while he covered his exposed privates with the other.

Mulrooney immediately dropped for cover behind a chair and scanned the area for signs of entry. He readied his weapon before moving slowly from room to room. With each step he knew he was tactically disadvantaged and far too vulnerable.

After inspecting each room, he moved to the small kitchen. Like all the other rooms, it appeared to be undisturbed. When he looked again, he spotted a dark object protruding slightly from the bottom of the large utility closet. As he backed up against the refrigerator, the cold chrome sent a shock wave down his sweat-covered back.

In one quick move, Mulrooney kicked open the door and took aim. He jumped back against the stove as the ironing board crashed to the floor. He was trying to regulate his breathing when he smelled gas and whipped back around. Mulrooney let out his breath when he noticed two burners that had ignited when he leaned against the knobs.

Convinced the intruder had exited, he waited for his heart to slow down to a normal pace. He felt himself blushing as he stood alone in his kitchen, naked, wet, and panting. *Well done, Mulrooney, you nearly set your ass on fire!*

He looked around and saw no other signs of life. While he had slept, someone very skilled at breaking and entering had invaded his home. He wryly wondered if the coroner would be willing to determine time of death for Houdini.

Mulrooney was so angry he misdialed two times before he finally reached the station; and then he dressed and waited for uniform to arrive. He suspected they would find no more evidence than they had found in the pipe bomb incident. The intruder was sending a warning that whoever wanted him could get to him anytime, anywhere. And they were moving in closer.

* * *

Kristin Donovan was relieved she was no longer pulling double duty on surveillance. The young officer pulled her blonde hair away from her delicate face and gathered it into a ponytail. She was looking forward to the chance to rectify her embarrassing mistake in losing Lauren Connolly at LAX.

Mulrooney and Clarke watched while Janet Glenn checked Kristin's wireless bug. As the surveillance van they were in moved slowly toward its destination, Janet moved about doing the check-out on the equipment.

Mulrooney wiped his brow with a napkin. He was still shaken at the thought of someone invading his home while he was present. He was also pissed that his painting had been slashed. *Everyone's an art critic, he silently groused.* He wondered what might have happened if Janet hadn't called and awakened him when she did.

Janet gave the ready signal. "You two can have Flint as soon as Kristin and Strobe ID him and catch him making a transaction," Janet told Mulrooney and Clarke.

"Roger that," Mulrooney agreed.

Janet's informants had reported Flint was hustling teens to make porn films. A few of those kids had disappeared permanently. Apparently Flint's favorite venue was raves–the underground parties that were a breeding ground for drugs and other illegal activities. Today they all wanted to bring in Flint.

The raves created constant problems for law enforcement. To avoid a bust, the organizers of the raves kept them moving, quite often involving too many jurisdictions for the police to keep them under control.

Vice cops had picked up fliers at a thrift shop in Orange County announcing this one. Telephone information directed the caller to a map point on Fourth Street in Long Beach. There the kids, many underage, could pay twenty-five dollars for a map of the location of the rave. This rave was being held in an abandoned cannery on the bed of landfill known as Terminal Island in the Los Angeles Harbor, in view of Terminal Island Federal Penitentiary.

Mulrooney looked out at the black asphalt piles that dotted Terminal Island. They were headed for the bleak wharf area, a forlorn stretch of rusted out buildings and abandoned ship carcasses.

They stopped the van on a back road to allow Kristin and her partner, Strobe, named for his megawatt smile, to use their own vehicle to drive the last mile to the rave. When the two young undercover cops jumped out, the stench of diesel, rotten fish, and petroleum permeated the van.

As they continued on, the graffiti-covered van stayed at a distance from the old Mustang that Strobe and Kristin were now driving. The van pulled into the lot of an abandoned shipping office, while Strobe parked the beat-up vehicle further up the street in front of a backdrop of skeletal cranes and steel cargo containers.

From inside the van, Janet's team watched Kristin and Strobe exit their car and walk toward the run-down concrete and corrugated tin building where the rave was being held. The music was blaring as crowds of other teens made their way toward the abandoned cannery.

"Tough crowd," Janet commented as they viewed the scene through the holes in the walls of the van. "A lot of gang colors. I don't want to have to bust this up until we get Flint."

Mulrooney and Clarke waited with the surveillance team as they tried to pick up conversation over the rap music throbbing through the van's sound system via the surveillance wires on the undercover officers. They could hear Kristin and Strobe ordering drinks and occasionally greeting acquaintances they recognized from the streets. Suddenly Kristin raised her voice as if to assure her words were coming in clearly. "Strobe, don't you know that guy?" she asked her partner.

"Sure, let's buy him a drink," Strobe yelled over the noise.

Janet gave a thumbs-up. "They've spotted Flint," she said.

The voices faded in and out as surveillance listened to the undercover officers making their way through the rave, which was now jamming. Inside the van, the technician adjusted the sound levels. "I'm getting a helluva lot of interference," he complained.

"Stay with 'em," Janet urged.

Mulrooney and Clarke listened closely. As Kristin and Strobe moved away from the music source, their voices came in clearer. "I'm straight, man," another voice was saying. "That guy in the green shirt looks like he's open for business. Try him."

Janet nodded her head. "They're scoring," she said. They all knew the routine. One man took the money, and then he signaled another who distributed, thereby avoiding being caught receiving money for drugs.

Kristin's voice could be heard over the music: "Hey dude, you look like the guy my friend Donna wanted me to hook up with. Are you Flint?"

"We need to make some bread, man," Strobe interjected.

"Do I look like a fucking employment office?" Flint snapped.

"Donna said you're the man."

"Tell your friend to fuck off."

Janet winced, "Damn, they pushed him too fast!"

"Let's book, Strobe," Kristin urged over the din of music and talking. "This guy looks bogus to me."

In the van, Janet chewed her cuticles as she stared at the recorder. She leaned in when she heard Flint speak again.

"Chill out, man," Flint said. "Donna who? If you're dealing something 'digitized,' I'm not buying any more homemade product."

"We're not sellin' anything. Come on, Strobe, we're outta here," Kristin snapped. "I need to make some bread so I can score some shit."

Flint's voice suddenly grew louder. "Okay, okay, chill little chickie. Maybe I can set you up," he offered.

Inside the van there were audible sighs of relief. "Nice recovery," Janet exhaled. She signaled the technician to increase the volume again.

"Can you hook us up or not?" Strobe demanded.

"Chill, dude. The baby here said she needs to score."

"So what do I have to do?" Kristin asked.

"She ain't turnin' any tricks," Strobe blurted. "She's my lady, so I'm the one you need to be talking to."

"Fuck off, Strobe," Kristin ordered. "You never have enough bread."

"Christ, all right, all right!" Strobe's voice faded in and out like radio static.

"I talk to the babe alone," Flint announced.

Janet stood very still inside the van. "Don't split up," she whispered to the console. "Stay together, guys."

Inside the rave, Strobe could be heard arguing with Flint. "No way man!" Strobe protested.

"Fuck you then!" Flint yelled.

"I can handle myself," Kristin insisted. "So back off. Come on, Flint, it's too fuckin' loud in here; I'm gettin' a headache."

Her words could barely be heard as the pounding music filled the van. When the sound grew more distant, they heard Strobe's voice again. "She's exiting, East door," he said into his hidden mic. "I'm hanging back. Keep her covered."

"They're heading this way," Clarke said while viewing the action through a blacked out window. Activity in the van increased as each officer automatically reached for his weapon. Janet slid the door bolt open in case any fast exits were necessary.

Mulrooney saw Strobe dart behind a truck, keeping Kristin within his view as she and Flint pressed through the crowd still entering the warehouse. She towered above Flint, a weasel type with a gelled shock of blue in his neon hair.

"Nice orange hair," Mulrooney intoned, "I see how Flint got his name." He noticed Flint's hands flopped about when he spoke, like a drunk digging through cotton balls.

"My guess is the kid fried some brain cells," Clarke grunted.

Over the speakers they could hear Flint turn his attention back to Kristin. "Check it out. You're a babe, so all ya gotta do is be real nice to a friend of mine and maybe give it up just to be friendly."

"So you want me to fuck some guy?" Kristin asked.

"Not just *any* guy, sweetheart. He's runs the show. Your friend Donna introduced me to him."

"Do I get paid more if I let him film us doin' it like Donna did? 'Cause I'm cool with that, man."

297

"Did she tell you that? She's a lyin' bitch. Donna fucks for fun, not money." Flint stopped at the side of the road next to a Red Camaro with a dented rear bumper. "Look, babe, I hustle X rated product. Donna sent me her friend–a doctor who needed cash fast. Ironic, huh? So I bought some of his homemade videos and sold the zip drives. Unfortunately Donna found out she was on some of the product I was hustlin' and got pissed. But I figured that was between her and the doc. But the dumb bitch went off on the doc in some club one night when she was loaded. My boss was there and got wind of a moonlighting enterprise."

Flint stopped long enough to light up a smoke before continuing. "So, then the boss dude himself comes after *my* ass. He snatched up all the product I bought from the doc and nearly popped me. It was scary shit. I don't know if he is doing Donna and some of the chicks on the vids or what, but he seriously tripped. It seemed *personal.* I was almost deep-freezed.

"So anyways, I need to get back in good with the dude. I need the big connections again. The boss man will be in town next week. And you could be the one to bail my ass out because he likes your type–classy and hot."

"I'm down for it, but does he have to know who I really am? I've got a legit job I wanna keep."

"Fuck no. I'll just tell him you're a friend of Donna Blair. Just let me know when I can set it up."

"Okay. What name does the guy go by?"

For a moment, Flint was silent. The sounds of Eminem blasted from the rave each time the door to the rave opened. Flint took a drag off his cigarette and scrunched up his face like a mutated rodent as he sized Kristin up.

"First I want to give you something," he said as the cigarette dangled from his pale lips. He unlocked the lid to his trunk and lifted it. "Check out this video to see what the boss digs. He's a walking hard-on for the chick in this one. So study how to dress and do your hair, and all the other details."

Flint's words were suddenly drowned out by the high-pitched screech of tires as a black Mercedes S Class with dark windows shot out from behind a condemned building. It veered onto Tuna Avenue and crossed an empty lot before jumping the curb onto Wharf Street. The sedan increased speed as it careened toward Flint.

Suddenly Strobe's voice could be heard screaming wildly as he ran from his position near the warehouse toward Flint's car. "Get down, everyone!" he yelled. "Cover!"

Startled young pedestrians along the road screamed and jumped back from the street when they saw the car coming at them. The Mercedes tore across the asphalt and slid up close to Flint's Camaro. As the barrel of a gun was leveled through a crack in the window, the .45 Glock locked on its target.

Kristin dropped and tried to take Flint with her just as the sound of shots cut through the air like a whip against glass. Flint exploded from Kristin's grasp and shot upward like an aerialist. With a sickening thud, he fell forward into the open trunk of the Camaro as his feet vainly stabbed at the sky for a foothold.

When the Mercedes sped by the van, Janet, Mulrooney and Clarke bolted from the back while another officer jumped into the driver's seat and gave chase. The Mercedes and the van hugged the shoulder of the road, screeching side-by-side past a shipyard scattered with rusted warships that loomed like prehistoric predators.

The party-goers along the road froze in place. "Take cover," Janet yelled above the chaos to those too shocked to react. She covered Mulrooney and Clarke, who were running full-speed for the Camaro.

Mulrooney bounded past Flint, who lay draped over the back of the car, partially covered by the bullet-strewn trunk lid. As Mulrooney rounded the car, he skidded on the gravel and slid into Kristin. His ankle screamed with the shock of the sharp sideways movement. Kristin barely flinched as she remained in crouched position, her weapon held ready.

Mulrooney forced the pain in his ankle out of his mind as he focused on Kristin, whose face was covered with Flint's blood and brain tissue. Kristin's wrist was spewing blood as she tried to keep her arm aloft. Mulrooney grabbed her wrist and applied pressure while lifting Kristin's arm above her head. Her eyes darted wildly from Flint to the road.

Mulrooney could hear Clarke slide in behind him. "Take her wrist, Smokey," Mulrooney told his partner as he slowly released his grip on Kristin's arm. He was shocked to see the extent of the wound, which was bleeding profusely. Her hand, only partially attached, resembled a piece of raw meat on a skewer.

"I've got you," Clarke said. "Let's get a tourniquet on that. You're doing just fine, Kristin, just fine," Clarke assured her in his mellifluous, calming voice.

"Everybody stay down and keep covered in case they make another pass," Mulrooney shouted to all within earshot.

He then reached up with one hand, shoved the trunk lid open, and yanked Flint to the ground. Clarke pulled Kristin back into him and covered her face as shuddering movements crept down Flint's body blood covered body like ripples in a scarlet pond.

After Mulrooney rolled the body over to check for vitals, he looked at Clarke and shook his head. An extinguished cigarette butt was buried deep in the pulp that had once been Flint's face.

Chapter 39

After cleaning up at the station, Mulrooney and Clarke headed for Donna Blair's house. The home was on a bluff in a ritzy area of Long Beach overlooking a stretch of beach a half mile west of Belmont Shore.

"Is it my imagination, or does everything we touch turn to goat piss?" Mulrooney groaned as he pressed an ice bag against his ankle. He then studied his hands. Blood was caked beneath his cuticles; and large calluses, like antique leather buttons, adorned the knuckles of his right index and middle fingers.

"Did the van ever catch up with the Mercedes?" Clarke asked.

"No, they lost them on the Vincent Thomas Bridge. No plates."

"Fuck. I hope Kristin gets some use of that hand back."

"Yeah, she's a good cop. I wish she'd stop blaming herself for losing Lauren Connolly at LAX. She's too damn tough on herself."

"You two must be related."

Mulrooney grunted as they got out of the car and walked through the garden of the plantation style home. His left ankle felt as if it were connected to his leg with grappling-hooks.

Clarke rapped on the door. There was no answer, so he knocked several more times. When Mulrooney turned to scan the porch, he noticed a silhouette behind the lace curtains of the large front window. As he walked closer to the window, the fabric shifted.

"Open up, police business!" Mulrooney yelled.

The tapping of high heels against a hard surface grew closer, and then the door swung open. A dark-haired woman with frosted brown lid powder and crimson lipstick peered around the door. Her full brows accentuated the frown on her face. "Shhh, don't make a scene," she admonished. "I was gardening in the back. I couldn't hear you."

"Donna Blair?" Clarke asked. Donna nodded and opened the door a bit wider.

"Lovely, outfit," Mulrooney added. He wondered if she always gardened in Chanel suits.

"I was just pulling off a few wilted blooms," she snapped. "I'm on my way to a luncheon. Will this take long?"

"An out of town luncheon?" Clarke asked. He nodded toward an airline ticket and car keys lying on the table in the marble foyer.

Donna hesitated before answering. "After the luncheon I'm taking a short business trip. What business is it of yours?"

"I think you know the answer to that, Ms Blair." Clarke said.

"I'm afraid I haven't time to play hostess," she responded coolly. Donna gestured for them to follow her to the living room. After she perched on a Chippendale chair, she gazed up at the detectives, who remained standing. She seemed uncomfortable as her voice took on a controlled, business-like modulation.

Donna crossed her legs, calling attention to her thick ankles which she tried to flatter with low-cut Italian leather heels. Donna Blair struck Mulrooney as being rather ordinary looking. When she yanked at her barrette to hike the shoulder length hair gathered at the crown, he could see that her hair was two slightly different shades. Hair extension indeed, he thought.

"May I use your phone for just a moment?" Mulrooney asked, seeking an excuse to look around. "Not much cell coverage here."

"I suppose," she huffed. "There's a land line in the hall where you came in."

After Mulrooney made a quick call to the station, he lingered by the wall of glass doors that offered a panoramic view of Palos Verdes and Santa Catalina. He observed Donna carefully as Clarke questioned her.

"What was your relationship with the victim?" Clarke was asking in a deceptively friendly, laid-back tone.

"Just casual friends," Donna explained with a forced degree of civility.

"When was the last time you saw Dr. Connolly?"

"Months ago, really," she answered. "I ran into him at a jazz club downtown. We lost track of each other after that." Her smile was almost a grimace.

"Jazz club?" Mulrooney interjected as he casually bent to sniff an elaborate arrangement of yellow roses. "When I saw your Steinway I pictured you as a classical music buff."

"Well, I also love classical," she responded taking the hook.

"I don't dig that stuffy long hair music," Clarke baited. "Well, not all classical is stuffy. Haven't you heard 'Bolero' by Ravel?"

"Oh, yeah." Clarke began to hum a tune.

Donna shook her head emphatically. "No, that's *Rhapsody in Blue* by George Gershwin. He lacked classical technique in composition, but nonetheless, he wrote beautiful music."

"You seem to know a lot about Gershwin," Clarke said. "How well did you know Dr. Connolly?"

"We were just casual friends."

Mulrooney examined a small oil painting set in a trivet on the walnut credenza. "Nice painting," he interrupted, throwing her off guard again.

"You like art?"

"My partner is an artist himself," Clarke offered. His voice commanded her attention as he kept an eye trained on Mulrooney's furtive movements. "He's no hacker when it comes to watercolors."

"That oil you're looking at is by a local artist - Nick Boskovich, from San Pedro," Donna explained.

"Oh, yes, I know his work," Mulrooney informed her. As he leaned over to examine the exquisite detail of the still life, he slid his hand over a small framed photo near the oil painting, and then he deftly slipped the photo into his pocket. "Unbelievable talent," he said appreciatively.

When Donna peered to one side, Clarke leaned in and distracted her again with a direct attack. "Well, if you and Dr. Connolly were only friends, why did you agree to make pornographic films for him?"

"What?" Donna instantly focused her attention back on Clarke.

Clarke zeroed in on her like a vulture on road kill. "Well, we have this video, so we know you willingly performed with Dr. Connolly. I'd like you to tell me more about that."

As Clarke kept Donna off-guard, Mulrooney meandered over to the wet bar and subtly checked out Donna's liquor supply.

"Those tapes were meant to be private. I certainly didn't know the pig was going to sell them!" she blurted.

"I never said he sold them, Ms. Blair. How did you know that?" Clarke asked.

Donna pulled at the hair on her crown, unconsciously moving the hairpiece up and down like a pressure valve. "I heard he sold some copies."

"Who told you?"

"Fli-" Donna stopped herself.

"Flint?"

"No, I didn't say that."

When Clarke raised one brow, Donna shifted in her chair. "Maybe it was Flint," she snapped.

"What is your relationship with Flint?"

"We have no relationship. I've run into him at the clubs."

"We understand you set Scott Connolly up with Flint to sell the doc's homemade sex merchandise."

"That bigmouth Flint! So what if I did? Scott said he needed the money quick because he was in debt. He told me he had some explicit stuff on tape. However, I certainly didn't know he had taped *us,* or I would have objected. I'm not into exhibitionism, Detective Clarke!"

Clarke caught Mulrooney's smirk and looked down at his notes. "Did you know Sam Bennett?"

"Sure, he owned Jazzin' night club."

"Is that who Scott owed money to?"

"I have no idea."

"What did you do when you found out Dr. Connolly had sold tapes of you two having sex?"

"I demanded he get them back from Flint."

"Flint said someone else demanded them back," Clarke said.

Mulrooney moved to the bar as Clarke attacked and withdrew. Donna suddenly looked very apprehensive. "I don't know anything about that," she insisted as she crossed her arms and pressed her back against the chair.

"Did you know Flint was shot this morning?"

"No. That's too bad," she said insincerely.

"You must have been irate when Dr. Connolly didn't return all the thumb drives."

"But he did."

"Except the one we have," Mulrooney reminded Donna. He tapped a bottle opener against the tiled bar to keep her on edge.

She glared at Mulrooney. "Well I hope you two enjoyed it. Anyway, I quit seeing Scott after that."

"Until the funeral, that is."

Donna jerked her head back to Clarke. "Ah, yes," she said smugly, "I saw you two lurking. I wanted to give Scott a proper send-off. After all, he could be fun, even though he was a fool."

"Why do you say that?" Mulrooney asked.

"Well, he got himself killed, didn't he? He obviously angered a lot of people."

"Do you know anyone besides you he might have angered?" Clarke suppressed a smile as Mulrooney slid a bottle of Tequila back and forth along the counter top.

"Not personally."

Mulrooney noted Donna shifting irritably in her seat. She kicked her crossed legs in time with his constant movement.

"Would you like a drink, Detective?" she finally snapped.

"No thank you, it makes me friendly," Mulrooney answered dryly. He shoved the bottle back behind the others, and then wadded up the cocktail napkins he had used to keep his prints off the bottle.

Donna made a point of looking at her watch. "I have to go gentlemen. So let's cut to the chase. I have an alibi for the night Scott Connolly was murdered, and I have plane tickets and a boarding pass stub for an 12:25 P.M. Delta flight out of Long Beach to Newark. I'll have my attorney provide all of the proper documents for you."

"Thank you, Ms. Blair," Clarke smiled as he stood to leave. "We'll be in touch. We're only trying to get a profile of the victim. You've certainly been of help."

"Yes, thank you," Mulrooney added. He deliberately ran his hand along the back of her chair as he passed by her on the way to the door. "Please keep us apprised of your whereabouts," he requested. "Oh, and by the way, I caught some fresh fish I've been giving away. Do you eat grunion?" He tried not to smile at Donna's look of total exasperation.

"No, thank you. I hate fish!" she snarled, no longer able to disguise her impatience with her two annoying guests. She jerked the door wide open.

"Good-bye, Ms. Blair," Mulrooney said unctuously. He grinned as the door closed abruptly behind him, devouring his departing pleasantries.

After Mulrooney got into his car, he pulled a plastic bag from the glove compartment. In it he placed several hairs he had retrieved from the back of Donna's chair. Clarke prepared a label for the evidence while Mulrooney checked his ankle, which was badly swollen.

"I noticed you found a bottle of Cusano Rojo Tequila," Clarke grunted, without looking up.

"Yup. Did you also notice the agave worm was missing?"

"Sure did. Must have crawled out—in two pieces," Clarke drawled as he placed the bag on the seat. "What else did you nab?"

Mulrooney reached into his pocket and produced the small picture frame for Clarke to study. "Do you recognize this guy in the photo with Donna?"

"Looks familiar."

"I know I've seen this guy, but I just can't place him" Mulrooney said. "I'll check it against the mugs."

"Someone should marinade that woman in meat tenderizer," Clarke muttered as he stared at the photo of Donna.

"She sure is brittle," Mulrooney nodded. "Thanks for providing the distraction in there. I called Janet from the phone in the foyer and got surveillance put on Miss Congeniality. I want her to know she's being shadowed. We're not losing this one."

"Great. I'll check out Donna's alibi with Delta," Clarke said. "I wonder if she flew baggage class."

Mulrooney laughed and started the car. "Fast work, Janet," he purred happily when an unmarked car made a U-turn and stopped on the opposite side of the street. He nodded to the officer as he pulled out.

Hidden from view behind the wall of the alley near Donna's house, Anya Gallien sat in her white BMW convertible. She watched them depart, and then she reached for her gun.

Chapter 40

Anya Gallien maneuvered through rush hour traffic
as she raced from Donna Blair's house toward Shoreline Village Marina. The note from Lauren had been
dropped into her mail slot before dawn, directing her
to slip number 127 at the downtown marina.

Although she was still stinging from Lauren's accusations, Anya had decided to meet Lauren regardless of their painful fight the previous night. She was
determined to get the flash drive. Anya knew she was
in too deep to chance having the video of her and
Scott fall into the hands of the prosecutor.

She firmly believed that witnesses could be broken down by prosecutors, even in America. Her alibi
could fall apart, and Anya knew the video would establish motive for her to have killed Scott Connolly.
And motive was something she indeed did have.

Anya knew the evidence she was withholding was
her trump card. She had seen Lauren arrive home
before midnight, but she hadn't told Mulrooney. She

planned to use that threat to persuade Lauren to give her what she wanted. After all, Lauren's fate was hanging on hers.

That morning Anya had easily outwitted her surveillance. She had ridden her bicycle along the bay walk, which was inaccessible to auto traffic. When she was safely out of sight, she picked up her BMW from the carport of a vacant house where she had parked the preceding evening after losing her surveillance at a Blueline train crossing.

It had been surprisingly easy to put word out on the club scene that a little information would bring a large reward. The information she had received that morning was worth the two thousand dollars she had paid for Donna Blair's name and address. And fortunately, Mulrooney and Clarke had not seen her there.

Getting answers from Donna Blair had taken little time. The .25 caliber weapon she was carrying had been very persuasive. There were five rounds left. Anya knew she had nothing to lose, and she wasn't going to leave her own fate to L.B.P.D. Anya would rather die than live in a cell again.

When Anya pulled into the marina parking area, she spotted Lauren standing near the docks in the shadow of a large lemon tree. After she parked, she quickly placed the gun in her bag and left her purse unzipped.

"I was afraid you wouldn't come!" Lauren said as she rushed to her. When Lauren hugged her, Anya coolly brushed her lips against Lauren's cheek. "I had Michael deliver the note because I was afraid of

313

phone taps," Lauren said. "You're safe. Surveillance hasn't tracked me here yet."

"What do you want, Lauren?"

Lauren blanched at the coldness in Anya's voice and looked at her beseechingly. "First I want to ask you to forgive me. And I want you to know that I do trust you," Lauren assured her as she led Anya to a grassy area across from the docks. Anya clutched her bag tightly to her side as she followed.

"And I want to give you the memory stick I have," Lauren continued. "You can destroy it yourself. It's in Michael's safe. With no motive and a witness to support your alibi, you'll be cleared. I'm prepared to face whatever comes. I'm counting on being absolved of all suspicion, too. After that, I'll leave Belmont Shore for good."

Anya was silent as she looked at the water glistening in the late-day sun. "I admit I'll be relieved to get that back, Lauren," she whispered, "but my fears for your welfare are something I can't ignore, not matter how hurt I am. The prosecutor is looking for a quick fix, and I can't cover for you much longer."

"Cover for me?"

"Lauren, I was using my binoculars when I saw you return home that night... *before* Scott was murdered. When I got there, the door was unlocked, so I didn't use my key. I walked into the living room and called to you, but when you didn't answer, I left. I went to the alley to see if your bedroom light was still on, and I could hear the hair dryer in the bathroom. When it stopped, I whistled like always, but you didn't answer."

"What else did you see?" Lauren demanded.

"It was dark, but the street light from the alley was shining into your room. A few minutes later, I saw a silhouette in the bedroom. I thought it was Sam. I didn't tell Mulrooney, and I never will. But, I know you were there, and I know you weren't alone."

Lauren's eyes darted from Anya to the water. "But it was also possible for you to let yourself in and come upstairs while I was showering!"

"That's true. So what really happened that night? You don't remember, do you? Answer me, Lauren."

"Anya, I know what you're doing. You're trying to convince me I drank too much and that I-" Lauren stopped abruptly and began to pace. "Sam swore he wasn't here." She shook her head back and forth as she tried to fit the pieces together. "But I do remember that when I wished myself Happy Birthday, I had already showered and dried my hair. That always takes me at least fifteen to twenty minutes; and my watch said 12:12." She pressed her palms against her eyes. "If Mulrooney's right about Scott being killed during those minutes when the phone was disconnected, then I *was* there . . . I must have been. Oh dear God, Anya!"

"Let's sit down on the bench," Anya whispered as she wrapped an arm around Lauren.

"You can't sacrifice yourself for me, Anya."

"I did what I believed was right." Anya smiled wistfully as she turned away and looked out over the harbor. "Lauren, I found out the name of the brunette Scott dated, and where she lives. Her name is Donna Blair. She reluctantly gave me a few facts. Mulrooney is on to her, but I was able to use more persuasive tactics than he is allowed. She swears that all the cops have so far is a video of her and Scott."

"Another sex video?" Lauren looked stunned. "My God, Anya, how could I have known so little about my own husband?"

"Scott made those videos for quick money. I found out how much money he owed, and to whom. And with a little persuasion, Donna admitted she had been with Scott the night he was killed."

Anya abruptly stopped talking when she saw Michael Ryan walking briskly toward them. He gave her a warm smile as he slipped his arm around Lauren.

"Hello, Anya," Michael greeted cordially.

"Michael, Anya dug up some information. The name of the woman Scott was seeing was Donna Blair; and she was with Scott the night he was killed."

"I know who Donna Blair is. She used to hang out at Sam's club. She and Sam were very chummy."

"I'm sure Sam only knew her as a customer."

"Are you sure?"

"Yes. Sam wouldn't lie to me. Anya also found out Scott made the videos because he owed someone a lot of money. There's a video of him with Donna, too. Mulrooney has it."

"Busy guy!" Michael grunted shaking his head.

"Let's go back to my house, Lauren," Anya interrupted. "Do you mind? I need to lie down. You can duck down in my car in case surveillance catches up with me."

"Okay," Lauren agreed, "but first I want to give you that flash drive. It's on Michael's boat. I'll get it for you."

"A boat? When did you get a boat, Michael?"

"Two days ago. Come aboard," Michael invited as he took Anya by the arm. "We better duck out of sight; I think I just saw an unmarked car."

"No, she has to wait here," Lauren cautioned. "Anya's terrified around water, remember, Michael?"

Anya looked hesitantly toward the dock. She took a breath, shifted her purse to the front, and then placed her hand inside the opening. "It's okay, Lauren, I can come aboard for a minute. We can talk while Michael fixes me a stiff drink, okay?"

A look of pleasant surprise swept across Lauren's face. "I can't believe it! Don't worry, we'll hold onto you."

Anya took Lauren's arm and focused straight ahead as she accompanied them to the end of the long pier. Suddenly the wake of a boat rocked the dock. Anya gasped, but she kept walking until they stopped in front of a magnificent 40-foot Jim Young design sailboat.

"It's beautiful, Michael," Anya said. She tried to steady her breathing while she appraised the lines of the sleek boat. Her fingers were shaking as she shoved one hand deeper into her purse.

"May I escort you aboard?" he offered, flashing a proud grin.

"Let me admire it from here first. I don't do well on boats, or on docks. This is Lauren's favorite kind of boat, isn't it?"

A self-conscious blush spread across Michael's face. "I was hoping to cheer her up." He smiled as the cool breeze tousled Lauren's sun-streaked hair. "Let's go aboard. The water is shallow here, and very calm. I'll hold onto you, Anya." Michael placed himself between Anya and the water, and then he held out his hand.

Anya looked past Michael to the stern, where the boat's name was neatly scripted in elegant blue letters. She stared blankly ahead for a moment, and then she panicked. "I can't do it!" Anya protested as she unconsciously dug at the scar behind her ear. She imagined the feel the water rising around her, squeezing the air from her lungs.

"I really need to talk to you somewhere other than here, Lauren," Anya urged. "Come home with me. I'll bring you back here to the marina later. Okay?" She took Lauren's arm while her other hand clutched the gun hidden in her purse.

Michael studied Anya's demeanor and shot Lauren a look of warning. "Lauren, I don't think you should go," he warned. "Maybe Anya was followed." He glanced at Anya's handbag as he placed a protective hand on Lauren's shoulder to stop her.

Lauren hesitated. "It's okay. I'll come shortly. Just give me a few minutes to catch up."

"I'll walk you back to your car, Anya." Michael offered.

"No, I'll be okay, thanks." Anya kissed Lauren's cheek and then quickly retreated, making her way down the dock alone.

"Please come as soon as possible, Lauren," she called over her shoulder. Anya kept her focus straight ahead as she distanced herself from the boat. By the time she reached land, she had rubbed the scar behind her ear so hard she had drawn blood.

Chapter 41

"What a cluster fuck!" Mulrooney groaned into the wind as the sun dipped low in the sky. He was still limping as he and Clarke paced the beach bike path two hours after leaving Donna Blair. "Fuck me, Smokey," he yelled above the sound of the surf, "we still haven't located Lauren, and how in the hell did Sam Bennett's record get past us?"

"He paid someone in Australia to expunge his file."

"Well, Atilla found out, which makes us look like a couple of ball-scratchin' inbreeds. Worse yet, if Lauren's not an accessory, and if she's still with Sam Bennett, she's really in danger. In the meantime, Anya could still end up in a state-provided coffin."

"Look, bro, Miami Police lost Sam and Lauren before we could get a warrant. And Atilla has a buddy in Sydney Police who gave him inside info."

Mulrooney was fantasizing about beating the crap of Atilla when Clarke's phone suddenly sounded the first few bars of *Who Let the Dogs Out*. He listened as Clarke relayed the conversation while he spoke.

"The Gershwin C.D. from the crime scene was clean. Dust from the vanity was the same as the dust on the gloves from the construction site." Clarke turned his mouth away from the phone and shot Mulrooney a quick aside. "Nice hunch, buddy." Turning his back to the wind, Clarke pressed his ear against the phone again.

"Got it, thanks." Clarke hung up and turned to his partner. "Sam Bennett used the alias 'Maxwell Barrett' to re-enter the U.S. and establish himself in Miami ten months ago."

Mulrooney sat down on the sea wall to clear his head and process the information. He mentally revisited the crime scene, just as he had done every night these past weeks. He kept feeling some sort of psychic pull leading him through the Connolly house, yet he was unable to zero in on what they were overlooking. It needled him constantly like shrapnel working its way to the surface of his skin.

As Mulrooney sucked in the sea air, he visualized Lauren's bedroom where the victim had stared back in the blank gaze of death. Why hasn't someone invented a way to photographically reproduce the last image on the eyes of the dead, he wondered.

"That's it, Smokey!" he blurted as he clapped his hand to his forehead. "I figured out what doesn't fit. I'll be in the property room. Tell all airlines to detain any 'Sam Barrett' and all travel companions." Mulrooney turned and rushed toward his car. Clarke always knew when his partner was onto something. He was already heading for his own car. "Done. Catch me up later," he yelled.

* * *

Mulrooney was not in a tolerant frame of mind when he passed Carlos Atilla as he rushed into the station.

Atilla shot Mulrooney a greasy smirk. "Mulrooney," he taunted, "you just missed the reporters from the *Press-Telegram.*"

"I'm sure you gave them all the information they wanted."

"The people have a right to know. They wondered how Lauren Connolly slipped out from under your nose. Tough break."

Mulrooney could feel the anger spread over his face like hot wax. He wanted to hit Atilla until his ragged face exploded. But he knew if he laid into Atilla, he wouldn't stop until the prick took his last breath. Instead, Mulrooney stared him down. Unable to provoke a reaction, Atilla sneered and shoved past him.

"Dead man walking," Mulrooney muttered as he watched Atilla saunter away.

* * *

Mulrooney entered the property room, which had once been the jail and now comprised the entire fifth floor of headquarters. While Mulrooney waited at the barred door to the evidence storage area, the property clerk navigated the labyrinthine aisles of tagged property. When the clerk finally returned with a box, Mulrooney took it into a viewing room and sat at a table, propping up his ankle on a chair for support.

As he rifled through the box, he set aside Anya's key to the Connolly house, which he had turned back in. Mulrooney chewed on his knuckle while he examined the victim's gold money clip. Why did Connolly use a money clip if he put paper bills in his wallet he wondered?

He placed the money clip back in the box and stared at the evidence allowing his mental magnet to pull him along. When he closed his eyes, he visualized the room again. The cabinet doors were closed, and behind them was a Samsung television. He could feel his brain struggle to complete the circuit as he pulled a Samsung remote control out of the box.

When he reached into the box again, a sudden calm came over him. It was there—the second wireless remote. He stared at the logo. Sony. Mulrooney visualized the old DVD/VCR in Lauren's bedroom then smacked his hand on the table. The second remote belonged to an older model video camera—not to the Phillips brand unit that was originally logged into evidence.

Mulrooney jumped up and shoved the contents back into their appropriate boxes. He signed for the Sony remote control and the key before he tore out of the room, dialing his phone as he went. "Smokey," he yelled into the phone, "meet me at the crime scene. We finally caught a break!"

* * *

Mulrooney's heart was pounding during the short drive back to Belmont Shore. He knew he had found the missing part of the equation. After he parked in front of the Connolly house, he knocked and waited several minutes before he let himself in with Anya's key. He then climbed the stairs two at a time to the bedroom.

Mulrooney made a visual sweep of the room, which was bathed in warm light from the setting sun. His eyes jumped from left to right like a ticker tape, rapidly lighting on certain points along the walls. He walked to the nightstand on the victim's side of the bed. Once again, he studied the angles from the walls to the bed.

He removed the remote from his pocket and pointed it toward an air vent high on the west wall. Nothing. He paused before aiming the remote toward the cabinet area. He walked toward it and stopped when he heard a low whirring sound.

He determined the sound was coming from within the wall. Mulrooney ran his hand along the bulkhead over the cabinet. What appeared to be pale grey wood was instead a smoky glass panel that reached from the top of the bookcase to the ceiling. It was firmly set into the wood, and its edges were sealed.

Mulrooney headed for the walk-in closet and looked around. He climbed onto a trunk and pushed aside a panel that covered an opening to the attic. Trying to protect his ankle, Mulrooney hoisted himself up and then crawled along the rafters until he was able to pin-point the noise again. Just as he was centered over the sound, the noise cut out. When he paused to listen, he could only hear his own labored breathing. On his stomach now, Mulrooney peered down between the rafters where part of the ceiling and insulation had been removed.

Holding onto a joist for support, he reached down with one hand until he found what he was seeking. "Come to papa," he said aloud. Mulrooney slowly lifted the video camera up from between the joists where it had been planted behind the false front of the cabinet. After backing out of the crawl space, he dropped back down to the floor and limped out.

Mulrooney leaned against the wall and hit replay, transfixed as the images came up on the screen, only partially obscured by the opaque glass which had hidden the camera lens. According to the time stamp, the video was recorded on the same night Connolly was killed. *Bam!*

As he watched, Scott Connolly walked in front of the cabinet and then disappeared from view. After several minutes of viewing an empty bedroom, Mulrooney's heart sank. He listened to background sounds on the video, but they were distant and unclear.

Eventually footsteps could be heard as Connolly returned. This time, he was accompanied by Donna Blair. Connolly kept his back to the hidden camera while he took Donna into his arms and roughly kissed her. She laughed and looked down at the bed as the doctor gestured in invitation. Donna rolled her eyes in mock protest, but she allowed Connolly to undress her, dropping slacks, blouse, and underwear onto the floor, then Donna reclined on the bed and closed her eyes. She placed her hand between her legs and began to massage herself.

Mulrooney watched as Donna performed for the doctor, at first hesitantly, then with more excitement. She moaned aloud while she stimulated herself to arousal accompanied by Connolly's off camera groans. Her body heaved as she brought herself to orgasm several times. When she was done performing, Donna lay still. After a moment, she jumped up, grabbed her clothes, and began to dress. "A deal's a deal," she grinned with self-satisfaction before stepping off camera toward her host.

Mulrooney could hear Connolly chuckle. "You're sexy, babe," he said. His voice trailed off as their footsteps grew fainter. The camera continued to run, focused on the now-empty bed. Mulrooney could see nothing to the left of the night stand, but he could see a digital clock on the table. 11:28 P.M. He fast forwarded until he once again picked up sounds. When Scott Connolly returned, he undressed, crawled into bed and turned off the light.

Mulrooney's hopes disappeared when the room plunged into darkness. The digital read-out on the clock glowed brightly now—11:39 P.M. As Mulrooney stood in front of the vacant screen, he focused on the blackness and listened with the concentration of a blind man. This time he did not fast forward. Instead, he absorbed the darkness, praying for some indication of activity.

Finally a light, evidently from the upstairs hallway, faintly illuminated the bedroom at 11:52 P.M. Although it was still too dark to see the room clearly, Mulrooney could detect a shadow cross in front of the camera lens before moving to camera-left. He squinted his eyes as he tried to physically compensate for the absence of light. Suddenly, at 11:58 P.M, the video abruptly stopped. "Sonuvabitch!" Mulrooney yelled as he frantically pressed the button on and off trying to find an image again.

He ran downstairs when he heard Clarke pull up and park out front. "We have to boogie," Clarke said when Mulrooney opened the door. "I'll drive and you can update me on the way to San Pedro. I just learned that the hair from Donna Blair's house is a match for the black hair found on the victim's remains. And get this: Vice checked out the memory stick Flint had in his hand when he was blasted. It turns out the babe in the video is none other than Lauren Connolly...with her late hubby."

"She's the one Flint said his boss is hot for?"

"It seems so. She may be in danger."

"That video was probably made right here, Smokey, and most likely without her knowledge."

"Damn! I'll check it out when we get back from San Pedro."

"So what's up in San P.?"

"Some guy called dispatch and said he was listening to his scanner when the sting on Flint went down.

He heard the description of the car driven by the shooter and says he's seen the Mercedes and knows who drives it. The informant is going Deep Throat until we meet with him. Dispatch says he got off the phone real fast."

"Seems we're working late again tonight, partner," Mulrooney said as he retrieved the camera and followed Clarke to the car. "By the way, we now have evidence of Donna Blair, wide—and I mean wide—awake in the victim's bed shortly before he was iced. Things are looking up, Smokey."

Clarke hesitated before he turned on the ignition. "Not exactly, Tim. I just heard Atilla's officially on the case as of Monday. Clemente gave that prick the green light while we were with Donna Blair. Our orders are to take a back seat."

Mulrooney sat in silence for a few moments. "Whatever..." he sighed.

"You're okay with this?" Clarke asked incredulously.

"Don't get me wrong, Smokey, I'm not riding into the sunset just yet. But on the way over here I did some thinking. I remembered the time I went fishing with the chief. He liked to talk about how the catch can easily overpower the fisherman when it can't feel the slack in the line. That's when it fights the hardest. It made me think I should cut Atilla some slack and let him think he's getting away. But trust me pal, when I'm ready, I'm gonna reel his sorry ass in."

"Fish fry!" Clarke crowed. "In the meantime, we still have till Monday to do it our way. That gives us three days."

Mulrooney squinted into the fading light. "Let's roll."

Chapter 42

Sam Bennett stood at a pay phone near the corner of Second Street and Bay Shore Avenue in Belmont Shore. He checked his cell phone again for a signal. *Fucking AT&T.* Frustrated as hell, he dialed the pay phone again and waited as the operator placed the collect call to Miami. Meanwhile, he kept his back to a homeless woman pushing a battered cart along the walk.

A voice finally answered on the other end. Sam wiped the sweat from his forehead and spoke into the receiver. "Old Joe, it's me. What did you find out?"

Sam suddenly felt a hand on his shoulder. He spun around and came face to face with the old woman. She grinned out of one side of her mouth as she stared up at him through watery eyes. "Do you have a dollar?" she asked, holding out a dirty hand. She cocked her head like a parrot viewing him from all angles.

"Please, I can't hear," Sam complained. He dug into his jacket for some coins, and then he motioned for her to leave.

Just as he was turning away from the woman, an unmarked car caught his attention. The vehicle, which quickly rounded the corner onto Second Street, was being driven by a black police officer. His partner sat in the passenger seat with his foot propped up on the dash. From Lauren's description, Sam immediately knew it was Mulrooney and Clarke. He also knew they were heading for San Pedro. Right on time, he thought.

The voice on the phone demanded his attention again. "When, Joe? What did she say?" Sam asked. "Did she sound upset?"

The old woman, who had parked her cart alongside the phone stand, was now tugging at his sleeve. Sam covered the receiver with his hand and growled, "Go away!" He tried to bat away her persistent hand until he finally gave up. "Joe, I've gotta call you back later," he said, slamming down the receiver.

When Sam reeled back around, he found himself staring down a pair of World War II vintage breasts, which the old woman was now proudly flashing at him.

"Don't I know you?" she asked coquettishly.

"No," he said as he shoved his cell phone into his pocket.

"Yes, I do," she insisted, her hands flitting about.

Sam stepped past her and darted across the street before the light could change. When he heard the sound of angry horns, he looked back over his shoulder. The old lady was crossing against the light, pushing her cart helter-skelter through the crosswalk in her effort to keep up with him. Sam picked up his pace and finally lost her while she struggled with her belongings on the incline of the Second Street Bridge. When he was sure she was no longer following, he took the back way to the Naples canals.

After he reached the tiny Rivo Alto Bridge, he crouched and looked across the narrow waterway. From his vantage point, Sam could see Anya's bungalow without being exposed. When he was sure no one was within view, he slipped across the bridge. From there he could look between the houses into the back alley.

He immediately spotted the surveillance car behind Anya's house. He knew it would be risky, but Sam Bennett was accustomed to taking risks. And what he had to do could not wait. He ducked into the yard adjacent to Anya's house and quickly hoisted himself over the adjoining wall. After he dropped down behind the bougainvillea alongside Anya's house, he glanced around, and then he pushed open the side door.

"Anya?" he called quietly. "...Babe?"

Chapter 43

As the early evening light cast intricate shadows on the tiled walls, Anya turned the water faucets on full blast. While the hot water streamed into the tub, she stripped off her panties and camisole. She stood naked and stared at her waxen face in the mirror.

"Come on, Lauren," she said aloud, barely moving her lips. Anya had received Lauren's message when she returned from the marina twenty minutes earlier. One hour, Lauren had promised.

While Anya lit several candles, she checked her watch - 7:37 P.M. - approximately forty minutes to go.

She knew Lauren would follow the routine they developed when they were placed under surveillance. Lauren would park near Naples Rib Joint and cut through the alleys on foot. She would then follow the winding canals to Anya's house. Once there, Lauren would create a distraction for the surveillance team by using Anya's spare remote to open the garage door along the back alley. As surveillance waited for an approaching car, Lauren would discreetly enter from the side door, which was shielded from view by the overgrown bougainvillea.

Lauren had been carefully avoiding Mulrooney since her unscheduled return so she could gather more information before placing herself in the hands of the investigators. Anya was relieved that she had managed to convince Lauren to risk being seen in order to meet her alone.

As Anya stepped into the tub and slipped deep into the water, she could feel the bubbles rise around her neck. Strands of her red hair trailed about her shoulders, floating among the bubbles in fiery tendrils. She knew what had to be done, and she had already begun to set things in motion.

Anya checked again to make sure she was prepared. After she glanced at her gun, which was strategically placed on a corner of the tub, she closed her eyes and sighed. *The power one human can have over another is so provocative. And why is power often more evil than benign?*

As always, when unanswered questions left Anya angry and confused, she distilled life to the smallest elements of goodness. She savored the existence of simple things as proof of a greater good. In doing so, Anya made the unanswerable in life seem less threatening. *Strawberries,* she smiled as she tried to focus on a simple joy. *Wild strawberries.*

Her thoughts abruptly evaporated when she heard a noise in the hall. "Hello?" she called, pulling herself up. After several moments, she shook off an inexplicable chill before nestling further down into the tub. As the warm water rose around her, once again, as so many times before, she thanked God for the pleasures of life that usually went unnoticed by those who had never known hunger or pain or deprivation.

Anya could still taste the first ripe banana she had eaten after bribing her way out of the Romanian jail she was sent to for stealing food. She had cried the first night she again experienced a soft pillow, a cup of coffee, and a warm bath at her family's small apartment in Cluj. She had laughed with joy at the feel of soft socks and a tattered flannel night gown. And she had wept at the scent of her mother's hair as she held her close while her young sister clutched her tightly from behind.

Only Lauren had truly understood the things that made Anya cling to life with the desperation of the condemned. Now, as she thought of Lauren, she added the friendship and love Lauren had given her to her list of life's great gifts. *Come to me now, Lauren. Please hurry.*

Sixteen minutes passed before she heard a shuffling noise. She jolted upright at the sound of footsteps on the tiles. "Thank God," she whispered. When Anya surged forward in the bath to reach for her towel, the footsteps stopped.

"Who's there?" she called.

Music from the hall speakers suddenly enveloped Anya with a familiar melody. She recognized the lilting notes of Gershwin's *Rhapsody in Blue* and smiled. "Lauren," she whispered as she let out her breath.

Suddenly a latex-gloved hand clasped her mouth before she could stand fully upright. As the hand pulled her backwards, Anya reached for her gun. She thrashed violently against the hand like a fish caught in a net. Her rigid fingers finally grasped the pistol by its barrel. She twisted her soap-slick body and swung the weapon at the arm that held her.

As she fought with all her strength, Anya's feet slipped out from under her. The gun fell into the bath, and Anya fell on top of it. She sucked in water, choking on her own screams.

Now completely submerged, Anya opened her eyes underwater. She saw her assailant's hand reaching for the gun and struggled to get back up. Her hands were flailing as she tried again to fend off her attacker. Emerging, she gasped for breath. "Please don't!" she pleaded in a soft Romanian accent.

The gloved hand swung violently. Anya heard a snapping sound just before her brain registered the pain above her ear. The blow collapsed the walls of her mind and resonated in her skull as she slipped back into the water. A red heat spread across her forehead, turning the bubbles a delicate champagne pink. *Strawberries*, she thought as a smile parted her lips.

Sinking beneath the water, Anya watched her own hand reach slowly upward like a mechanical arm trying to support the falling sky. The water moved in circles around her, sucking her down as her body was spinning and turning in the bright light. "Papa," she silently cried. The last thing Anya saw through the brilliant pink haze was the black shadow of her blow dryer as it cascaded through the air toward her watery grave.

Chapter 44

"I don't like this at all, Smokey," Mulrooney said to his partner as he looked at his cell phone. Killackey had texted him to say that Anya Gallien had called to say she needed to speak with him urgently. Wanting to meet with her adversaries was odd enough, Mulrooney figured, but now she was not answering her phone. Mulrooney immediately dialed again as he and Clarke sat in traffic with the rest of the late-day commuters as they neared the entrance point to the Vincent Thomas Bridge, which connects San Pedro to Long Beach.

Mulrooney was exasperated. And he wanted a drink. His brain sadistically reminded his taste buds of the flavor of a cold Guinness. He chased away the thought and chewed on his knuckle while he waited for Anya to pick up.

Mulrooney hung up again and sighed loudly. His week had turned into one strategically placed banana peel. Pulling a faceless Flint from the trunk of a Camaro had been unpleasant enough. Then, after following the tip from the telephone informant who claimed he recognized the Mercedes involved in Flint's murder, Mulrooney and Clarke were now returning from San Pedro, having been soundly stood up. Had the informant just gotten spooked he wondered? Suddenly Mulrooney's stomach clenched.

"Goddammit, we were set up, Smokey!" Mulrooney yelled. "Someone knew Anya would try to reach us, so they led us by the balls through San P. to detain us. It's Anya they want!"

"Fuuuck!" Clarke groaned as he stepped on the accelerator and pulled out into the passing lane. He raced around the car in front of him then picked up speed.

Mulrooney reached down with his left hand to switch on the siren and lights. The heavy traffic forced Clarke to weave in and out of the lanes of cars. Mulrooney took in long, shallow breaths as if he could somehow delay the passage of time, but a sick feeling warned him of what lay ahead.

On the Gerald Desmond Bridge, the last bridge before entering Long Beach, the traffic halted abruptly. As they squealed to a stop, Clarke pounded on the steering wheel and hit the speakers, but there was no place for the cars to pull aside on the narrow bridge.

"Call in uniform," Mulrooney yelled. He jumped out of the car and began to run as fast as his ankle would allow up the narrow access walk along the bridge.

When he reached the arc of the bridge, he spotted a two car rear-end collision at the far end of the bridge. The drivers were yelling and gesturing, and the tail end of a Dodge Caravan blocked the left lane preventing traffic from passing.

In a burst of frustration, Mulrooney ran toward the commotion. He darted around several cars which were almost perpendicular to the lanes as their drivers tried to get around the wreckage. "Are you all right?" Mulrooney huffed when he reached the men.

"Yes, but this guy rear-ended me and now he is trying to say it's my fault," the burly driver snapped.

"I'm a police officer, and I don't give a flying fu'-" Mulrooney stopped short, trying to keep his temper in check. "I don't care whose fault it is. Move this piece of shit, now!"

"I can't back up," the ferret-like driver of the second car whined as he backed away. He eyed Mulrooney, who was shifting weight and circling them like a bull in a ring.

"Both of you, come here!" Mulrooney barked.

"Are you going to frisk us now?" the ferret asked hopefully as both drivers quickly followed Mulrooney to the back of the Dodge Caravan.

"Not today, Dorothy," Mulrooney grunted. "Now, lift," he ordered.

The men looked at each other and then at Mulrooney. "I'd like to see a badge," the ferret said officiously as he leaned against the car and pointed a long, skinny finger at Mulrooney.

"Excuuuse me?" Mulrooney growled. "You wanna see a badge?" He whipped his jacket aside to accommodate the trembling man and flashed his weapon in the process. The ferret immediately placed both hands on the bumper of the Caravan.

"Now, lift!" Mulrooney directed. They obediently followed his lead and swung the car's rear end out of the left lane.

Mulrooney then pounded on the hoods in the line of vehicles to get the traffic moving so Clarke could get through. As Clarke pulled up, Mulrooney jumped into the car while it was still moving. Eight minutes later, Mulrooney and Clarke sped over the Second Street Bridge into Naples.

* * *

As they pulled into the alley behind Anya's house, Mulrooney jumped out, startling the surveillance officers. Three squad cars then raced down the alley before squealing to a stop behind Clarke.

"Has anything unusual gone down here?" Mulrooney asked the surveillance team.

"Not really," one officer replied. "There's been no activity other than the garage door opening on its own once in a while. She must have electrical problems. The lights surged earlier."

Mulrooney signaled Clarke before running toward the bougainvillea at the far end of the house. The side door was open offering a clear view of the hallway. Mulrooney unconsciously placed one hand on his pounding heart.

He called out to Anya, but there was no response. Then, he heard the soft, ominous music coming from the stereo. Mulrooney let out a groan. When Clarke caught up, he stopped in his tracks as Gershwin's haunting notes covered their skin like cold sweat. His eyes widened as he turned to look at his partner. Mulrooney's knew they were too late. Perhaps as many as 16.41 lethal minutes too late–the length of *Rhapsody in Blue.*

Mulrooney gestured to the hardwood floors inside the door entrance. Tracks of water lead down the hall, illuminated by a dim light coming from a room at the end, which Mulrooney knew was the bathroom. An odd mixture of scented wax and something more acrid permeated the house.

Mulrooney drew his weapon and stepped inside. While he checked the kitchen, Clarke crossed behind to cover him. Advancing and covering, they made their way down the hall checking each room as they went.

Just as they approached the bathroom, four uniformed officers burst through the front entrance and followed them down the hall. Mulrooney picked up the sound of tires as several other units moved in to surround the outside of the house.

When he looked into the bathroom, the first thing Mulrooney noticed was a layer of water on the tiled floor. Rivulets also streaked the tiles on the walls, glowing in the candlelight like fallout from a fireworks display. Anya had struggled for life until the end.

Something else caught his attention. Scrawled in soap on the mirror were the words "Back Off." Acid flooded into his throat as Mulrooney realized the message was intended for him. *Fuck you! I'm gonna make you die one breath at a time.*

Mulrooney was about to step forward when Clarke suddenly screamed, "Don't move!" Clarke yanked Mulrooney back before he could step into the room. He then directed his flashlight over the water-drenched fabric shower curtain that draped the outer area of the tub before shining his light along the base of the tub. In the light they could see a frayed black cord. From the tub, it snaked around the corner to the vanity area.

Mulrooney grimaced. "We need to find the electrical panel!" He then ran for the kitchen and tore open the cabinets. Clarke rushed out the door barking orders to patrol officers to call in paramedics and the fire department. Mulrooney grabbed a broom from the closet and tore back to the bathroom.

"I couldn't locate the circuit breaker because of the vines," Clarke yelled as he ran back in. "The circuit was probably blown, but we can't chance it."

"We've got to do something," Mulrooney said. He leaned into the bathroom as far as he could while trying to keep his feet from making contact with the water. As he reached for the cord with the broom handle, his body weight pulled him forward. He grabbed the door frame, and fought to regain his balance. "I can't quite reach it. Take my hand, Smokey!"

Clarke looked into the bathroom, then back at Mulrooney. He sucked in his breath and then clasped Mulrooney's hand. Clarke wedged his left foot against the hallway wall as Mulrooney braced both feet against Clarke's right foot and gripped his hand tightly. Mulrooney tentatively leaned forward until he was almost parallel to the bathroom floor. With a forward thrust, he slipped the wood mop handle under the black cord and pulled hard in an upward motion.

There was an explosion of light. A startling spray of sparks illuminated the bathroom just as Mulrooney lost his balance and fell forward. Clarke seized Mulrooney by the seat of trousers and lifted him with superhuman strength, pulling Mulrooney back through the doorway with such force they both crashed into the adjacent wall.

"It was still hot!" Clarke sputtered.

Mulrooney struggled to his knees. "It's not anymore," he rasped. He stood at the doorway and tried to settle his nerves before he stepped back in. When his feet hit the water, he stood momentarily, half waiting for the jolt. When it didn't come, he inched forward as if crossing a mine field. He then reached out and yanked the shower curtain aside.

Anya's lifeless face looked up at Mulrooney with an expression of ultimate sorrow. She appeared to be lit from inside like Christmas candles in a dark house. Her wet hair caressed her face, and her right arm reached upward, as though she were offering an invisible gift to some unseen savior.

Mulrooney tipped her head back and tried to breathe life into the already stiffening body as Clarke felt for a pulse. "Too late, buddy. No vitals."

"Goddammit!" Mulrooney yelled. He stomped into the bedroom and kicked the closet door off its tracks.

Clarke entered and was about to speak when they simultaneously focused on the one thing in the room that was out of place. Mulrooney looked at Clarke then crouched down to examine a phone book that lay on the white satin spread. He pulled a pen from his pocket and slipped it between the pages to where a pencil was wedged.

Next to a column of names was the refined handwriting he recognized as Anya's. She had drawn a figure in the shape of a smile and written the words 'EVIL SPIRIT' inside the smile. Next to the doodle were the numbers 305. Clarke studied the drawing and shot Mulrooney a curious look.

"We need a phone trace," Clarke said.

"Yep. Our girls might have shared more than one man. That's the area code for Miami."

345

Chapter 45

Michael Ryan cradled Lauren from behind while they stood across the canal from Anya's home. They were blocked from view by the overgrown wisteria that separated the neighboring houses along the canal walk. "Shhh," he soothed, "please come with me, Lauren. There's nothing we can do now."

Forty-five minutes earlier they had moored Michael's boat at a vacant dock in the Treasure Island section of Naples. While Lauren bought supplies at a nearby store, Michael had taken on enough fuel to head for Mexico. Afterward they had walked together to Anya's house where they found the area teaming with police, paramedics, a fire unit, reporters, and photographers.

When Lauren saw the activity, she began to sob, overcome by a deep sense of grief and loneliness. She knew Anya was dead. Lauren had tried to run across the footbridge to Anya's home, but Michael stopped her.

Now as they watched, Lauren shuddered when the door of Anya's house opened. A long gurney, one wheel crying out in objection to its load, was pushed through the opening. A bagged, lifeless form lay on top of the gurney.

"I have to go to her, Michael," Lauren cried.

"Listen to me, honey," he reasoned, "please think this through. Anya is gone. And you are the only other person who was there the night Scott was murdered, so you are now the one remaining suspect. And Anya's death could not have been accidental, or Mulrooney and his crew wouldn't be there."

As Lauren's knees buckled, Michael steadied her. "I'm so sorry," he whispered, "but you have to protect yourself, Lauren. If the police knew you were here right now, they would try to pin both murders on you."

"But, Michael-"

"Lauren, there's nothing you can do now. Anya wouldn't want you to jeopardize yourself for her. That's why she protected you until the end."

"I loved her, Michael, and she loved me," Lauren cried.

Michael sighed and shook his head. "I know, honey...but don't you see it's possible she may have killed Scott to have you to herself? I don't think you ever saw Anya for who she really was. And you said she was furious about the video."

"But she didn't know about that video! I knew the minute I confronted her that she was hearing about it for the first time."

Michael shook his head slowly, as if he had serious doubts. "Maybe Sam Bennett gave you that flash drive because he wanted you to believe Anya was the one who had motivation to kill Scott. He had plenty of motivation himself. For your own safety, I'm getting you out of here, Lauren."

"I can't spend my life running, Michael, especially from something I didn't do."

"In time I'm sure Mulrooney will prove that, but meanwhile you could end up in prison. I know you're strong, but you're very vulnerable right now. And I refuse to sit by and watch them hang this on you."

"I have to accept and deal with this. As much as I wish to God I could escape, I can't. I won't run." She looked down the canal toward the bay where her home was now barely visible in the twilight.

"Okay, Lauren, I can see you've made up your mind. I'll get you the best lawyers available. But we've got to get out of here. I hear choppers coming in. You can't implicate yourself further by being seen here. Let's go to Mexico. After a few days, we can arrange an 'arrival' for you at LAX, ostensibly just in from Miami, complete with alibi. After that you can see Mulrooney and make arrangements for Anya."

"Thank you," Lauren agreed as she watched Mulrooney follow the gurney through the garden. As the medics pushed the gurney out of sight, she felt more alone than ever in her life. Her breathing turned to racking sobs as the loss of Anya became final.

"I'm here for you, honey," Michael promised. Lauren squeezed his hand as the door to Anya's house slammed shut, closing her out forever.

She waited for a large sloop to pass on the canal. When Lauren looked back one last time, she gasped. In the passing light of the boat, she could see a dark figure watching them closely from a dock near the bridge. Even from a distance, she knew it was Sam.

Chapter 46

As Mulrooney leaned his head back against his car seat, the damp morning breeze was a cool compress against his face. He was playing his favorite Ella Fitzgerald CD, knowing her voice could soothe his nerves like Valium. Periodically he munched on a fat free, flavor free muffin and sipped a cup of decaf as he watched the cars crawl up Ocean Avenue past Donna Blair's home in the morning traffic congestion.

He was feeling the effects of less than three hours sleep. After popping two Tums, he checked his watch and wondered where Clarke was. They had agreed to meet at 7:30 A.M., and Clarke was seldom late.

As he closed his eyes, images of Anya Gallien filled his mind like a silent film. He considered all the reasons why anyone would want her dead. She must have known too much, he concluded. But what did she know?

He then thought about Lauren. Everything about her had seemed warm and soft. As he pictured her, the pressure in his head was as heavy as the weight in his chest. She had gotten to him alright, and he had believed in her innocence. Was he a chump? He opened a carton of milk and sucked it down to set up a firebreak between his stomach and his esophagus.

Clarke finally pulled up behind him and jumped out of the car. "Sorry I'm late," he apologized. "I stopped by the office. Killackey is on the phone trace to Miami; and in the meantime, it turns out your hunch was right. Jersey Vice confirmed that peep show Clarence was a distributor for Flint."

Mulrooney let out a low whistle. "The same type of weapon was used on all Flint's distributors as on Connolly. And I suspect that the knife used on the doc was planted *after* the crime team finished up. But why leave the weapon?"

"While you ponder that, I need to lay some bad news on you. Chief Clemente cornered me on the way out. He mumbled a few contrite words about Anya–kind of a half-assed mea culpa. And then he told me we'll be off the case altogether come Monday. He needs a public hanging to calm down the media."

Mulrooney looked out at the ocean and sighed. "I feel like the village idiot for losing track of Lauren Connolly."

"Hey, you aren't in this alone, bro."

"We've got one Hail Mary chance to pull this together before Monday. You still in?"

"Does a dog fart stink? By the way, that old codger Mr. Armstrong wants to talk with us again," Clarke added. "He left word he'll be on his boat all day."

"Lucky bastard," Mulrooney grinned.

"Any activity?" he asked as he nodded toward Donna Blair's house. The area was tranquil in the early morning light.

"None yet. Did you get a chance to view the tape of her and Connolly the night he was iced?"

"Oh, yeah," Clarke nodded. "I can't wait to hear her try to talk her way out of that. Let's go have a chat."

As they approached the front door, they saw no signs of activity. Clarke knocked several times and was lifting his hand to knock again when Mulrooney stopped him. They stood still for a moment and listened. Suddenly they both jumped off the porch and tore through the garden to the side alley.

A midnight blue Mercedes S Class was pulling out of the garage when they rounded the edge of the house. Clarke lay to rest the purple azaleas while Mulrooney plodded through a small lavender hibiscus and landed squarely in front of the Mercedes. He held one hand on his weapon and the other hand aloft. "Hold it!" he commanded as his torn ankle reluctantly snapped to attention.

Donna Blair directed a piercing look at him and then at her prized garden. She shoved the gear shift into park, cut the engine, and jumped out of the car. "I hope you're prepared to pay for the damage you've done. And you two macho morons can take your hands away from your weapons. If I had a weapon, I would have used it by now!" She stared down her two adversaries. "Isn't this a bit of overkill?"

"Ironic choice of words," Clarke sneered.

"Let's talk inside," Donna snapped. "I plan to continue living in this neighborhood, Detective Mulrooney, so I'd appreciate whatever bit of decorum you and Barney Fife here can muster up."

They followed her through the door into the large kitchen where boxes were piled high. Donna shifted uncomfortably as Mulrooney read the shipping labels. She had hoped to slip out of Long Beach quietly.

"I thought you said you planned to continue residing in the neighborhood?" Mulrooney prodded.

Donna stood in silence. She was sick of answering to men. She had moved to Long Beach on her father's orders and had been expected to manage one of his many import businesses. Her life had always been controlled by him or by his powerful associate. The sex videos had been her way of proving that she was no longer going to be controlled.

Although she had willingly made the video at Scott's office, she did not expect hers to be among those he sold to Flint. She was furious when she discovered that Scott had used her. She had been nothing but a meaningless pastime to him—a brief substitute for his estranged wife. Scott Connolly eventually got what he deserved.

Donna pulled a chair away from the table and sat down. She leveled her eyes at Mulrooney and spoke through clenched teeth. "You might recall that I told you I was taking a trip. I already had the ticket when you were last here. I always summer in Palermo; that is, unless I'm being arrested for the murder of Anya Gallien. Of course, I hesitate to think that even you two would be so foolish. Aren't you looking pretty bad already?"

"Not quite as bad as you are, Ms. Blair," Mulrooney intoned, returning her accusing look. "Do you want to tell us how you know Anya was murdered? The cause of death has not been released."

"My friend, Libby Martin, is a reporter. She called me last night when she heard the call on the scanner and recognized Anya's address from her investigation of the story. So, I'm afraid you've misled yourselves again. Libby wanted to inform me because she knows how terribly fond I am, was, of Anya."

"And what form did this fondness take?" Mulrooney asked. He moved to the door of the powder room off the kitchen so he could subtly rub his aching gut.

"We were not lovers, if that's what you're asking. My sexual preferences are quite different than hers. I'm all woman, Detective," she said as she ran a hand through her hair.

"Uh-huh, of course," Clarke nodded. "So did you socialize with Anya?"

"No, but I've seen her out at the clubs. And she came here yesterday. She was convinced I had information that could help Lauren Connolly find out who killed her husband. Anya seemed very concerned. She played the part of the wrongly-accused and loving friend quite well. I wonder if Mrs. Connolly knows that her friend slept with her husband?"

Donna picked up on Clarke's glance to Mulrooney. "Scott told me," she explained. "Anyway, I assured

Anya that I had already told you two officials from Mayberry everything I know."

Mulrooney knew she was lying. He stared her down until she averted her eyes. When his stomach made a growling noise, Donna looked up again and smiled derisively.

"Hungry, Detective? I'm afraid I have nothing to offer you on any front," she apologized insincerely. "Feel free to use the bathroom. You'll find room deodorizer beneath the sink," she added to embarrass him further.

Mulrooney was not in the mood to deal with a big mouth on a little trollop. "Ms. Blair," he snapped, "we have proof you were with Dr. Connolly at his house the night of the murder. That makes you a prime suspect. Would you like to call your lawyer?"

Donna's jaw dropped. She wordlessly traced a finger along the carved table leg until she regained her composure. Finally she bestowed a tight red slash of a smile upon her interrogators. "There is also proof that I left town at 12:25 P.M. that night. And I didn't just appear at Long Beach Airport like a poltergeist. It takes time to get there and check in."

"What time did you leave the murder scene?"

Donna kept her gaze fixed on Mulrooney. He was now her chosen adversary and the target of her venom.

"I left there around 11:25 I think. Would you like the name of the person I was meeting in New York?"

"Rudy Giuliani?" Clarke hissed. "Incidentally, Doctor Connolly taped you performing a sex act for him that night."

Donna's face exploded from behind its stone mask. "That disgusting pervert!" she yelled. "He never learned when to back off. His damn arrogance was what got him killed!"

"You said you had quit seeing him. This is in direct conflict with your earlier statement, Ms. Blair," Clarke reminded her.

"Okay, so I did see Scott that night, and for good reason! That bastard sold the video of us having sex in his office, even though I was the one who set him up with Flint to distribute his kinky little porn in the first place. When Flint told me I was on the video, I insisted that Scott buy it back. Scott said he'd take care of it—for thirty thousand dollars! He promised me he had made only one copy, which was bullshit."

"So what happened that night?" Mulrooney prodded.

"First he came here and we had a few tequilas, and then we argued about the video. He said he was going home, but that I should drop by while his wife was out if I changed my mind and wanted to bring him thirty thousand dollars. He said I could have the memory stick, but I also had to perform for him. When I dropped by on the way to the airport, I did what he asked. After I gave him the money and got what I wanted, I left. I didn't know the maggot had a video camera at his house, too."

"Why didn't you tell the police he was blackmailing you?"

"I was embarrassed!"

Mulrooney noticed the corners of Donna's mouth twitching, but she quickly regained her composure. "Where did Scott put the money, Ms. Blair?" he asked.

"He had left a money clip here, so I returned it with the bills. He put the money clip in his pocket."

"Did anyone else know about this?"

"Of course not."

"Do you know to whom he owed money?" he pressed.

"No, I stayed out of his slippery business. He should have stuck with pap smears."

"Did you or Dr. Connolly turn on any music before you left?" Clarke interjected.

"Why would I put on music and leave?"

"Seems to be a trend," Mulrooney grunted. His pager went off just as his stomach growled again. Mulrooney stepped into the bathroom and chomped down more antacids. His teeth felt like they were wearing chalk socks.

"Yeah, Killackey?" he announced into the phone as he stared at a photo on the wall. It was a photo of a younger Donna holding the hand of the same man who was in the photo Mulrooney had pilfered from her living room on their first visit. Both were smiling against a backdrop of a small Mediterranean town.

"We've got info from the airlines," Killackey was saying. "Sam Bennett slipped into Long Beach sometime yesterday under a new alias. We're trying to track him."

"Was Lauren Connolly with him?"

"No, he came in alone. And another thing: According to airline records, Donna Blair's alibi checks out."

After Mulrooney hung up, he turned back to study the photo again. He and Clarke had spent hours trying to identify the older man, but in this photo the guy was younger. Mulrooney held the photo up to the light. "Holy shit!" he exclaimed. He raced back into the kitchen and loomed over Donna like a hungry bear. "Show me your passport," he demanded.

"What?"

"Show me your passport!"

Donna reached into her bag to produce the requested document, but Mulrooney snatched it from her hand before she could offer it up. He flipped it open and held it under the light. "Nice fake." he snarled. "Clarke, meet Donna Maria Bonanni."

Clarke's eyes widened like two hatching eggs. "This party just keeps getting better."

"What's your point?" Donna snarled.

"Daddy is an organized crime boss, that's my point."

"So what? My father's business is none of mine. Or yours. You have nothing on me, so either arrest me like the fools you are, or get the hell out of my house!"

"Okay," Mulrooney said, "but I'm taking your passport. You're not going anywhere. If your daddy has any complaints, tell him to feel free to call me. Goodbye, Ms. Blair."

As they walked out, they heard the door slam loudly behind "I'll check to see what we've got on Vic Bonanni in this area," Mulrooney said as they headed for the car.

"He'd have a good reason to avenge his little cannoli."

"True. I'll also see if any of Connolly's other acquaintances can be linked to Bonanni. A guy like Bonanni would use someone else to do his dirty work. Catch ya later, Smokey."

As Clarke watched his partner get into his car, a feeling of trepidation washed over him. "Hey, be careful, big guy," he yelled to Mulrooney.

Mulrooney held up his hand in a wave. He then checked to make sure his weapon was in place.

Chapter 47

"You told me to give a shout if I saw anything unusual," Armstrong said as he and Mulrooney stood on the pier. "Well last night I saw some guy down by Mrs. Connolly's boat again." Mulrooney stared at the slip where Lauren's boat, Seduction, swayed tranquilly in the wake of a passing schooner.

"I saw a guy around midnight," Armstrong continued. "Dark hair and stood about six feet, six-two. I couldn't see his face though." When Mulrooney raised one brow, Armstrong whined, "I really couldn't–the little missus took away my binoculars, even after I explained how I was only using 'em to help you out."

"Thank you, Mr. Armstrong," Mulrooney smiled, "Is there anything else you can tell me?"

"Well, I don't know if the guy was the same guy as before cuz this time he didn't stand up here," he said, gesturing to the marina walk. "He went down by the boat, looked about, and then left, just like that!"

Armstrong snapped his fingers so loudly Mulrooney feared the old guy might sustain a compound fracture.

"Did you see what he was wearing?"

"You betcha. Jeans, jacket, and sneakers."

"Well, please call me if you see anyone else, including Mrs. Connolly. Thank you, Mr. Armstrong."

"Aw, you can call me 'E'. It's short for Elvis. It's what the missus calls me," he bragged as he thrust his pelvis forward to justify the moniker. "I'll keep an eye out for Mrs. Connolly all right," he promised, flashing a lascivious grin.

"Why, thank you very much, 'E,'" Mulrooney drawled, rolling the syllables from the back of his throat in his legendary Elvis impression. Mulrooney left Graceland and headed for the station.

* * *

Clarke intercepted Mulrooney the moment he entered the building. "The team is checking out mob connections," Clarke said, keeping up with his partner's pace.

"I smell New Jersey."

"Who doesn't?" Clarke sneered. "Killackey's on the Miami phone trace; and we're still tracking Sam and Lauren. Donna Blair, according to surveillance, is still at home, probably sticking pins in her Mulrooney doll. Her reporter friend verified Donna was home at the time Anya was murdered. Also, the computers from Connolly's home and office were searched for video uploads, but nothing turned up.

He must have destroyed whatever computer he was using after Donna busted him, so no break there."

"Smokey, I want to look at this video again with Wizard." Mulrooney and Clarke had dubbed Will Keller "Wizard" because of his editing skills, and the name had become Will's identity around L.B.P.D.

"I've been thinking," Mulrooney continued as they headed for Wizard's office, "the battery was still good in Connolly's hidden video camera, so the camera didn't go off by itself that night. Someone had to turn it off. However, the remote control was in view of the camera lens. Even though the room was dark, we might still be able to pick up an image."

They turned into an office where the Wizard himself, donned in his trademark saddle shoes with no socks, was busy at work.

"We're two souls in need of aid," Mulrooney announced.

"I don't do exorcisms," Wizard grunted as he took the camera from Mulrooney and connected it to his state of the art computer. "Okay, let's see what this baby can do."

Wizard manipulated the image as soon as Donna's face came up on the screen. "Who's the chick?"

"The president of Mulrooney's fan club," Clarke quipped.

When the light on the video eventually faded, Wizard tugged at his beard and scowled, "Whoa, this looks bad. You may need to go to U.S.C. for help, guys. They have some prototype image enhancement equipment that works miracles."

"We just need the last minute of the tape, Wiz." Mulrooney pleaded. "See what you can do."

Wizard fast forwarded the video until the digital clock on the nightstand read 11:58 P.M. "Let's see if I can enhance the resolution. What piece of image do you want?"

"Zero in to the left of the clock radio," Mulrooney directed. "There's a video camera remote there somewhere." He watched Wizard adjust image, trying to increase the exposure.

"That looks like crap," Clarke complained.

Mulrooney squinted to try to make out an image. "It's getting worse, Wiz," he groaned.

"Do you two always prematurely ejaculate? Give it a chance, dudes!" As they waited, a glint appeared on the screen. "Relax," Wiz purred, "and see what a genius can do." After several attempts, a blurred image of the remote control and the edge of the clock finally appeared on the screen. Wiz grinned triumphantly.

"Holy hard on!" Mulrooney exclaimed. He and Clarke looked on with shocked expressions. The picture was pixilated, but the image was unmistakable–the tip of a blade was suspended over the remote control on Connolly's nightstand. "Someone used a knife to push the remote control button!"

"The perp must have heard the camera rolling," Clarke nodded as he moved closer to the screen. "Can you get a hand or arm in there, Wiz?"

Clarke moved closer as Wizard managed to zero in on a hand and wrist just before the hand went out of frame. "The subject is a lefty, and wearing the same kind of gloves picked up from the construction site. The sleeve doesn't tell us much though."

"See if you can get a piece of image as close to left of frame as possible, but down on the floor," Mulrooney directed.

Clarke nodded. "Farther left. Right there!"

When Wizard adjusted the resolution again, a foot and ankle instantly came into view. The shoe in the image was wrapped in a clear plastic baggy.

Mulrooney whistled. "That explains the blood smears on the floor where there should have been footprints. Can you get any of the leg, Wiz?"

Wiz worked his magic until the hem of a pair of dark slacks could be detected just within frame. "Take it back to the foot, Wiz...there. Are you thinking what I'm thinking, Smokey?"

"Yup. That ain't no Cinderella, unless she plays for the Lakers. Not with those feet. We're looking at a perp who's at least six-two, I'd guess."

"Wiz, I love you!" Mulrooney hooted as he leaned down to plant a loud kiss on Wizard's cheek.

"Cut him some slack, Wiz," Clarke laughed, "that's the most action he has had since his blow-up doll left a suicide note."

Chapter 48

After returning from Wizard's office, Mulrooney sat with his head propped in his hands and stared at a photocopy of Anya's doodles found in her phone directory. The smile with the words "evil spirit" seemed like a contradiction. *Just like this whole friggin' case.*

His memory was grasping at something when he was suddenly overtaken by the pervasive odor of sweat, grime, and cheap perfume. When he looked up, he saw Proud Mary standing with Detective Noodles Nardo outside his door. Mary seemed shy and nervous until she spotted Mulrooney. She flashed a large grin.

Mulrooney jumped up and rushed out of his office to greet her. "Mary!" he said as he shot Noodles a curious look. "Where have you been?"

"We found her in an alley down on Loma. It seems she *owns* a bungalow there." Noodles' expression indicated that the house was a case for the city inspector.

"A homeowner, eh? Mary, my girl, you've been holding out on me."

"Hiya, Mr. Malroody," she blushed. "This fella here said you might have some nice pic-tures for me." When Mary spoke, the words clacked along the top of her mouth like tap shoes.

"Yes, I do. But I've been worried about you ever since you disappeared. Have you been off doing another film, my dear?"

"No," she demurred, flashing two buttery teeth at him, "but I was in *Sunset Boulevard*."

"Really?" Mulrooney exclaimed as if hearing the news for the first time. Mary nodded gleefully as Clarke strolled over to greet her.

While Mary was chattering to Clarke, Mulrooney saw Atilla enter his office cubicle. Atilla picked up part of the Connolly file from Mulrooney's desk, held it up for Mulrooney to see, and then walked over to the water cooler. He shot Mary a look of disgust as he turned his back on them.

A slow burn crawled up Mulrooney's neck. He forced his attention back on Proud Mary just as Clarke was struggling to make her keep her shirt down.

"I 'member you," Mary was saying to Clarke. "You were with Detective Malroody last night when I met my gent."

"You have a wonderful memory," Clarke proclaimed, ignoring the time lapse.

"Come on into my office and look at some photos, Mary. Can we get you a beverage?" Mulrooney added gallantly while leading her back into his office.

"I gotta git back to the set," Mary hesitated, shaking her head. "But can I getta pic-ture of my gent?"

Mulrooney quickly pulled out several six-packs of photos and arranged them on his desk in front of her. He slipped Sam Bennett's photo among them.

"He came back, ya know—I saw 'im again," Mary said excitedly.

"You did?" Mulrooney, Clarke, and Noodles exclaimed in unison. Mary's eyes blinked like a camera shutter at their animated response. She immediately turned toward the door.

"Relax, dear. We just want to hear more about him. Do you remember when you last saw your gent?" Mulrooney gestured for Clarke and Noodles to stand back by the door of his cramped cubicle so that Mary would not feel threatened.

"Last night," she answered emphatically. Mulrooney chuckled as Clarke rolled his eyes in exasperation.

While Mary perused the photos on the desk, she paused to stare at some longer than others. Mulrooney could see a similarity in the mug shots over which she hesitated - an indication that she had a firm mental image of someone.

"Where did you last see your gent?" he asked nonchalantly.

"Horny Corners," she explained using the nickname for the bay beach area across from the Connolly home. "He wuz in a dinghy-boat acrost from that house that you and that lady cop, Miz Kate, and this nice little Nigra fella here was in."

Clarke flashed a tolerant smile as Mary turned to gesture his way. Noodles and Mulrooney both stifled their laughter at Clarke's magnanimous expression.

"Was that on the night all the police were there...the same night you saw all the cars with lights, Mary?"

"Nooo," she answered impatiently. "I told ya already that it was *last* night—'fore dark."

Mary suddenly jumped up. "He ain't here. I hafta go," she announced. She shoved the mug shots aside and pushed past Mulrooney.

"Mary, dear," Mulrooney soothed as he tried to prevent her from leaving, "can't you spend a little more time with us? We don't know any other movie stars."

Proud Mary smiled modestly, hesitated, and then shook her head. "Gotta go," she insisted. She rushed toward Clarke and Noodles, who were blocking the door.

"Wait, Mary!" Mulrooney called as he reached for his iPad. "Do you remember that scene in *Sunset Boulevard*, where Gloria Swanson and Will Holden dance? Wasn't that romantic? You once told me that you just love to dance."

Mary pirouetted toward Mulrooney and grinned with delight. He quickly turned on some music, and then he bowed dramatically as the train whistle of *Chattanooga Choo-Choo* blared through the office. All heads in Homicide Division turned in unison to see what Mulrooney was up to.

Mary began to twist slowly. She added a sliding step before snaking her way toward Mulrooney. "I call that the 'Anaconda,'" she announced flirtatiously. She continued to slither while Mulrooney managed a few dance steps with surprising alacrity.

Several detectives gathered near the door by Clarke and Killackey and began to clap in time with the music. "Com'on, join the train," Mary urged the men as she grabbed Mulrooney by the hips. Mulrooney immediately lifted his brows in silent persuasion to Killackey, who was standing nearest to where the "train" boarded.

With a rumbling "choo-choo" sound, Killackey grabbed Mary by the waist and followed along. Just as Clarke was caboose-ing himself to the weaving line of dancers, the song faded, melding into the opening notes of *Moonlight Serenade*.

When Mary sighed with pleasure, Mulrooney held out a hand and pulled her into his outstretched arms. She closed her eyes and swayed back and forth in time with the music, smiling serenely. Mulrooney hummed along as he peered over her head. Then, with a series of fancy steps, he waltzed her to his desk. He kept moving as he reached down with one hand and quickly rearranged the photos.

Clarke, Noodles and Killackey were watching silently when suddenly Atilla's voice boomed from behind the ever-expanding group of detectives. "Why is that stinking-"

Before he could get another word out, Clarke turned on him. "You say one insulting word about Mary, and I'll kick your ass so hard you'll be shitting out of the middle of your forehead." When Atilla opened his mouth to retort, Clarke got up in his face like a rabid dog. Re-thinking the wisdom of taking on Clarke, Atilla shrugged and stalked away.

"Oh, Mr. Malroody, you're such a gent," Mary cooed. "Ya wanna know a secret?" With her eyes still closed, she let out a giggle. "My gent isn't in your picture pile." Mary continued to sway as she leaned her head against his chest. "But that's him in that there pic-ture near the phone."

Mulrooney stopped abruptly. "I knew you'd find him. Show me which one," he smiled triumphantly. While the other detectives closed in behind Mary, she pointed to a photo that was partially exposed near a stack of forms on the desk. Mulrooney had deliberately placed it where she could see it.

"Well kiss my cajones!" Killackey exclaimed as Clarke gave a salute to Mulrooney.

"Are you positive?" Mulrooney asked.

Mary continued to sway her hips until the music ended. "I'm sure, Malroody. Ain't he dreamy?"

"Man, he came up cleaner than Mother Hubbard's cupboard!" Clarke said shaking his head.

"Someone please get my lovely dance partner here a copy of this photo. And a hot meal, too," Mulrooney added.

"And how 'bout some brandy?" Mary grinned.

Mulrooney laughed and pulled out a wad of bills. "Mary, I want you to order the best brandy there is. You're a star!"

As Mulrooney handed the photo to Killackey to photocopy, he looked down at the image into the beautiful, soulful eyes of Anya Gallien, caught unaware at Scott Connolly's memorial. She was standing in front of the jade urn that held the victim's remains. In a casual pose next to her, looking toward the camera with piercing eyes, was Mary's handsome gent–Michael Ryan.

Chapter 49

Mulrooney tapped his pencil nervously while he waited for Ted Riordan in the Organized Crime Intelligence Division to run a computer search. "Try 'Futuro.' It's an import/export business in Los Angeles."

Mulrooney kept his eyes fixed on the computer. As Ted typed, #SS07302005 popped up on the screen. Ted opened the file and leaned back in his chair. "Hot damn!" he exclaimed.

Mulrooney whistled. They were staring at the file of East Coast crime boss Vic Bonanni, Donna's father. "What's his connection to Futuro?" he asked.

"Nothing solid. Bonanni's West Coast businesses include drugs and pornography. We've been trying to nab them for years, but they've got better legal protection than the U.S. government. Bonanni is slippery as hell. We've been chasing a lead that he's a silent partner in Futuro and could be using the company to launder money. That's why Bonanni's file is cross-referenced with Futuro. But we don't have anything solid."

After several more keystrokes, a photo appeared on the computer screen. "Is this your guy?" Ted asked. Mulrooney nodded as he stared into the intense eyes of Michael Ryan.

"Do you know if he was in town when Connolly was killed?"

Ted glanced over a detailed report of all Michael Ryan's reported activities. "We check in on him periodically, but he's basically an altar boy. He was last spotted in New Jersey a week before Connolly was murdered."

"How did he do that? We already confirmed his flights to Buenos Aires. He was supposedly on business there."

"That's odd. He has a private plane."

"Hmm... I suppose he could have arranged for someone who could pass for him to fly commercially *if* he had reason to keep his whereabouts secret. When did he return from the East Coast"

"His scheduled return was three days after the date of Connolly's murder, but because Ryan isn't a top priority, we had no one on him to confirm he was on his plane when it returned. If he's Bonanni's West Coast beard, I hope you have better luck than we've had trying to pin something on the guy."

"He may be slicker than a turd in a shower, but if he committed homicide, he won't get past us again. Thanks, Ted."

On his way back to his office, Mulrooney rushed past Clarke and gestured for him to follow. "It's possible Michael Ryan is laundering for Bonanni's West Coast enterprises, Smokey."

"Your hunches are newsworthy," Clarke said as they entered Mulrooney's office. "I just confirmed that Anya Gallien *did* phone Miami just before she was murdered–to an unlisted private line at Sam Bennett's club. Let's ring them."

Mulrooney nodded and then dialed the number. "Is this Miami Jazzin'?" he asked as soon as he heard the line pick up.

"You've reached a private number, sir," a female voice answered guardedly.

"Police business. Don't make me come down there," Mulrooney snarled.

"What can I do for you?"

"I need to speak to whoever answered this phone last night around 7:00 P.M."

"Well this is a private area, sir. The only other person allowed phone access besides me is Biragidji, the manager."

"Do you or this Bearded-Gigi guy know where I can reach the owner?"

"Biragidji," she corrected. "Hold on please."

"Gidday," a man's voice answered after a short pause.

"Hello, Mr. Bira-"

"Just Old Joe."

"Old Joe, I'm Detective Mulrooney from Long Beach Police Department in California."

374

"Ah, the home of Mickey Mouse."

"Close enough. Did you take a call from a woman named Anya Gallien on this line last night around 7:00?"

"That would be me," he answered in a strong aborigine dialect. "She called for Mr. Sam, but he's gone. No idea where. She said to tell Mr. Sam to call her. Urgent, she said."

"Did she say anything else?"

"Yes, she asked if I'm aborigine."

"Do you know why?"

"Yes."

"Well, can you *tell* me why?"

"She asked the meaning of a word. She speaks many languages, and she thought the word is aborigine because it's a word she heard once from Mr. Sam. He's also from down under. He hired me-"

"That's nice," Mulrooney interrupted impatiently. He had a strong hunch he knew where Joe was going if he could just guide him there. "Can you please tell me the word she asked you?"

"Yes."

"Well, then tell me, please!" Mulrooney said as he tried to control his exasperation.

"The word was 'cunci.' Not my tongue. I'm a different clan—Dalwongu–but I know words of other clans. It means evil spirit. Very bad."

"Thanks, Old Joe. Thank you very, very much."

"Gidday," he replied as he hung up abruptly.

"Somehow I doubt that-" Mulrooney said as he placed the phone back on the hook while Clarke waited.

Mulrooney stared at the paper with Anya's doodle. "If 'Cunci' means evil spirit, which is what Anya wrote on the paper, what in the hell is this drawing?" He turned the doodle around on his desk to observe it from every direction.

"Bro, it's not a smile. I think it's a friggin boat!" Clarke reached for the phone before Mulrooney could move. "Christine, Clarke, here," he barked into the phone. "Pull up any numbers you've got on a boat registered as the Cunci, will you?" He paced in front of Mulrooney's desk as he waited.

"Really?" he said into the phone. "How do you know? I see. Thanks, Christine."

Clarke hung up and turned to Mulrooney. "The Cunci wasn't registered until ten days *after* the homicide. That's how we missed it. However, one week *prior* to Connolly's murder, a citation was issued to that same Jim Young designed New Zealand 37 sailboat for not having been registered upon arrival. It was purchased in Florida by Futuro. Slip 127, Shoreline Marina."

"Michael Ryan could have easily slipped in and out of the bay the night of the homicide," Mulrooney said as he adjusted his holster. "If he did, he probably docked at an empty slip and then used a dinghy to get to shore. And that's where Proud Mary would have spotted him."

"And when Lauren came home, she would have surprised him," Clarke added. "In the video, a hall light came on just minutes after her arrival according to our time line."

"It's still circumstantial, but let's play it out: If our hunch is right, Ryan could have whittled the doc while Lauren was in the shower and Anya was outside trying to get her attention," Mulrooney said. "He took the thirty thousand dollars back for Bonanni's little minotaur and exited around 12:22 A.M.."

"But not before he put on a little Gershwin for mood music. That's the part that's throwing me. 'You think he acted alone?"

"Dunno. Sam Bennett could be involved. Futuro's legit side does a lot of business in Florida where the boat was purchased."

"Sam Bennett couldn't have been too broken up about the doc being murdered. And maybe Ryan had something on him?"

"Could be. My guess is that Anya Gallien was outside with her binoculars the evening the doc was murdered. She would have noticed a unique boat like the Cunci if it entered the bay," Mulrooney theorized.

"And if she saw it again, she would have remembered it and thus called Old Joe for info."

Mulrooney bit his knuckle as he looked at Clarke. "If Anya saw the boat a second time, she must have seen Michael Ryan. And I doubt she'd be with Ryan unless-"

"Lauren Connolly is back," Clarke said jumping to his feet.

Clarke was already heading for the door when Mulrooney rushed past Atilla and snatched the Connolly file off his desk. "You won't be needing that."

"You're chasing down a lead based on a photo I.D. from a dim-witted homeless woman?" Atilla sneered derisively.

"You let us worry about that," Mulrooney shot back. He turned around in one move and headed for the door.

"If you find Lauren Connolly are ya' gonna slap her around for making you look bad, Mulrooney?" Atilla yelled to his back.

When Mulrooney stopped in his tracks, Clarke placed a hand on his arm to keep him from losing control, but as Clarke looked back over his shoulder, the smug look on Atilla's face sent him into a slow burn. He withdrew his hand and snarled, "Go ahead, bro, get the cocksucker!"

As Mulrooney slowly turned to face his tormentor, his expression relaxed into a broad smile. "I believe in a fair fight, you malignant parasite, and you're too full of shit to go a few rounds. However, I'll tell you what—I'll bet you our 'dim-witted' witness is on the mark. Michael Ryan is somehow involved. If I'm right, you'll take Proud Mary out for a first-class dinner. And afterward, you'll take her dancing, like a fat-ass Fred Astaire—a real, honest-to-God night on the town with all of us in tow to make sure you mind your manners."

"And if you lose, Mulrooney?" Atilla asked cockily.

Mulrooney hesitated, and then he yanked his shield off his belt and threw it to the floor where it skipped like a stone along the wooden floor, creating an echo in the silent room.

Clarke turned to Mulrooney with a shocked expression on his face. Suddenly he reached into his pocket and threw down a wad of bills. "A hundred bucks says my partner is right, asshole." He grinned as one by one the other detectives followed suit with a flurry of greenbacks.

"Start planning your retirement," Atilla sneered.

Mulrooney shot him a clench-jawed grin. "Right after you order a corsage for Mary, Fat Fred."

Chapter 50

The Cunci basked serenely in the late afternoon sun, unfazed by the group of police officers that guarded her from the dock and from the deck of an adjacent boat. The officers waited while two Port Police boats quietly slipped up to her starboard side.

"Come out on deck with your hands raised," an officer bellowed through speakers on the police boat.

Mulrooney and Clarke silently crouched behind the gear boxes on the dock, their weapons reflecting the sun onto the hull of the boat. After several failed attempts by the Port Police to illicit a response, Mulrooney rolled to the edge of the dock near the port side of the Cunci as Clarke moved in behind him. They crawled along the dock, cautiously peering into the cabin windows. Back-up covered them as law enforcement moved in from all sides.

"I think we missed them," Mulrooney whispered, hoping Lauren wasn't already dead. Through the window, he could see the cabin was empty, but he recognized the angora robe that was hanging on the open door to the head. It was hers.

Mulrooney turned and signaled. The team entered the cabin cautiously and secured the area section by section. When two officers climbed back out of the engine compartment and gave an all-clear, Mulrooney and Clarke investigated the cabin.

"Lauren's back all right," Clarke said as he inspected an airline ticket. "The name's an alias, but it's a return ticket from Miami."

"Check it out, Smokey," Mulrooney said as he gestured to a table in the main cabin. "Michael Ryan is seriously courting her. He's got candles, flowers–the full monty."

"How do you know the lady didn't buy those?" a young officer asked over Mulrooney's shoulder.

"Because they're not sleeping together yet, Tom," Mulrooney said patiently. He nodded toward two hastily made-up berths in the main stateroom. "Michael Ryan seems to be taking his time. He's setting up the seduction."

Mulrooney pulled open the door of the closet. Hangers with expensive men's clothes were almost obsessively spaced, and several pairs of Italian leather shoes were in exact alignment underneath. A stack of Armani sweaters, perfectly folded, lined the top shelf.

"Lookee here, bro," Clarke interrupted as he held up a handful of compact discs. "We've got your standard Tony Bennett, ol' Blue Eyes, and the ubiquitous George Gershwin."

"Thank God it wasn't playing when we came aboard," Mulrooney responded as he examined the drawers in the galley. "Check out the custom can opener and scissors. Ryan's a lefty."

"Oh, this isn't good." Clarke held up an empty Glock case that had held a .45 caliber firearm.

Mulrooney shook his head. After a cursory glance at the refrigerator, he opened the freezer door and tore open several packages of carefully wrapped food. He let out a long whistle.

Clarke stared at the package in Mulrooney's hand and raised his brows. He then passed Mulrooney an evidence bag while the young officer looked on.

"Frozen fish?" the officer asked blankly.

"Evidence," Mulrooney nodded. "It's filleted grunion."

Chapter 51

Lauren sat in her living room staring out at the bay where shadows danced along the water like spirits of the deceased. She knew what she had to do. Michael and Anya were right—she could be the one accused of killing her husband. She couldn't bear this nightmare any longer. Michael had dropped her off on the peninsula so she could sneak home and pack to go to Mexico with him, but she would be gone by the time he returned.

She planned to pilot her own boat to Guadalajara where Anya's friends could arrange papers to get her to South America without being noticed. If she could make it through the next few hours, she knew she was strong enough to go it alone.

As she reached for the lamp, she noticed a police car pass slowly by the house. Despite the waning light, she was able to distinguish Kate Axberg and her young partner, Sanders. Lauren pulled her hand away from the lamp and took a candle from the drawer. By candlelight she went upstairs to pack.

She entered the bedroom, walking quietly as if fearful of disturbing her dead husband. Although the room had been cleaned, Lauren avoided looking at the bed as she went to the dressing closet to begin packing, selecting the few pieces of her life she would take with her.

When she reached for her bag, the knife crafted by George One-Eye, still wrapped in its used racing form, fell to her feet. She stepped out of the closet and set the knife next to the flickering candle on her vanity in the bedroom before continuing to pack.

Lauren suddenly heard music. Startled, she stepped back out into the bedroom, but all she heard was her own breathing. When Lauren returned to the closet, she heard the sounds once more. She crouched to place her ear near the air vent.

The memories of the night Scott was murdered suddenly flooded over her in a punishing wave of images and sounds. As the Gershwin composition filled the closet like a heavy perfume, Lauren finally remembered the music she had heard as she ran from the house that night, covered with the blood and flesh of her husband. It was the same music she heard now—Gershwin's *Rhapsody in Blue*.

Lauren dropped to her knees, and her body began to shake uncontrollably. She steadied herself against the closet wall as she fought against the terror.

Suddenly she felt a hand on her back. Another hand clasped her jaw as she opened her mouth to scream. She smelled the rich cologne and felt the coolness of the smooth, commanding fingers. As her head was yanked backwards, she looked into the piercing eyes of Michael Ryan. He was crouched behind her, his hot breath stroking her ear.

"Shhh," he cautioned as he slowly released his hand. "Honey, I'm sorry. I didn't mean to frighten you. I'm surprised you didn't hear me call out to you." Michael gently stroked her cheek with the back of his hand. "I was afraid if you screamed the neighbors would hear. The police are looking for you. I heard it on the boat scanner, and I saw them pass by."

"I've decided I'm not going with you to Mexico, Michael," she whispered hoarsely. "I'm going away by myself."

"Lauren, don't do this, please. They're looking for you. You'll be caught." Michael leaned against the closet wall as he tried awkwardly to find the words he needed to say. "Lauren, I'm doing my damnedest to protect you. Don't you know I'm in love with you?"

"Yes, Michael, and I'm so very grateful for all you've done ... but I'm not in love with you."

Before she could rise, Michael crouched down and pulled her into him. He kissed her passionately, covering her mouth with his. When she tried to pull away from him, he pressed against her even harder. Lauren, unable to maneuver in the cramped space of the closet floor, finally quit fighting.

When Michael felt Lauren's body became limp, he quickly turned away and stood up to smooth his clothes. Without looking at Lauren, he offered her his hand. When she mechanically reached out, he gently pulled her up from the floor. "I was out of line," he said. "I'm sorry Lauren. Please forgive me."

Michael squeezed his eyes shut and pressed his fingers to his temples. Then, without warning, he lurched forward again and sealed her mouth with his strong hand. "We're not alone," he whispered. "Don't make a sound–you've got to trust me." He lowered his hand then quietly pulled the closet door shut plunging them into darkness.

"Lauren?" The voice was coming closer. "Lauren?"

Michael suddenly kicked the closet door open. Lauren was startled to see they were standing face to face with Sam Bennett. Michael removed his hand from Lauren's face as Sam stood still and cautiously appraised the situation.

"Sam!" Lauren whispered. Lauren stepped toward Sam, but Michael reached out to hold her in place.

"Stay back, Lauren," Michael warned. "He's dangerous."

Lauren stared at Sam. As his eyes flitted around the nearly dark room, the candlelight created dark scars on his face. "Let her go, Michael," he ordered. "She's walking out of here with me, and you're not stopping us."

When Lauren tried to pull away from Michael once again, Michael restrained her as he gave Sam a warning, "You better come clean, you bastard. She needs to know who you truly are!"

Lauren turned to confront Sam. "Come clean about what? What does he mean, Sam?"

"Sam killed Scott, Lauren," Michael said through clenched teeth. "He would do anything to get you back. Tell her, Sam."

Lauren gasped. She tried to shut out the images of her bleeding, lifeless husband as she stared at the man who had once been her lover. Sam lowered his eyes and glanced to his left, focusing on the oblong package with its distinctive race form wrapper.

"Don't believe him, babe," Sam pleaded.

When Lauren turned back to Michael in bewilderment, Michael shook his head sadly. "How long do you plan to keep this up?" he asked Sam. He looked directly at Lauren. "Listen to me, Lauren, and listen carefully. I *was* here that night. I work for Vic Bonanni, Donna Blair's father. He's not a reputable person, but the businesses I run for him are legitimate. And Donna's welfare is my responsibility. When Scott blackmailed Donna for thirty thousand dollars for the return of a sex video he had distributed, the situation put me in a precarious position.

"Scott was so foolish he was shaking her down to get money to pay back what I had loaned him from the business to cover his drug debts. That's why I have your painting–as collateral. I tried to warn Scott. But I didn't kill him. That night I came here to get Donna's money back, nothing more. I left his own money in his wallet and left. It was business."

Sam glared at Michael as Lauren stood in silence. Suddenly Sam lunged for the vanity. He grabbed the paper bundle and ripped the knife free of its loose

387

wrap. "Let her go," Sam ordered as he moved in on Michael. Lauren's body trembled uncontrollably as she looked from Sam to Michael, and back again.

With a calm, even voice, Michael spoke into her ear. "Lauren, I saw Sam leaving your house when I arrived that night. You were in the shower, and Scott was already dead. Sam unloaded his knife in the VCR before he left."

Lauren searched Sam's face as she tried to process the information. She could feel her knees weakening.

"That's bullshit!" Sam yelled. "I haven't seen that knife since your mafia goons burned down my club. You took it because you planned all along to set me up. And you set up Anya. You gave that flash drive to Mulrooney so Anya would fry, didn't you? You wanted to get rid of everyone who separated you from Lauren. You never learned the difference between winning and owning, Ryan." Sam turned to Lauren. "You've got to believe me, babe," he said quietly.

"Drop the knife, Sam," Michael warned.

Sam kept his eyes on Michael as he spoke. "I spotted the Cunci docked in Naples on the day Anya was murdered. I've been staying out of sight in San Pedro, so I left word for Mulrooney and Clarke to meet me there so we could talk. I was headed for the bridge when I got word Anya had tried to reach me regarding the Cunci. That's when I put it all together. I went back to her house hoping you might be there, but no one answered. I heard the bath running, so I waited on the dock. I saw Michael exit her house, babe, and shortly after that there were cops everywhere. Then I spotted you both across the canal." He glared at Michael and moved closer as he spoke.

"Lauren's too smart to believe that," Michael said.

Lauren raised her face toward Michael as all the broken pieces of her life finally came together. To Lauren, the reality of knowing was no worse than the horror of wondering. A sad smile crossed her pale face as she turned to Sam. "I believe you, Sam," she whispered.

"Lauren, how could you-" Michael pleaded.

"Because I know you're lying, Michael, I never told you that Anya found a knife in the VCR." Her words remained hanging in the silence that followed. Lauren choked back a sob, and then she reeled around and slapped Michael hard on the face.

In one sudden move, Michael pulled a gun from his waistband. He aimed it at Sam as he grabbed Lauren by the throat. "Put the knife down, Bennett," Michael ordered as he shoved Lauren toward the bed. "If either of you makes a sound, I'll kill you. Lauren, I'm sorry this is necessary," he said quietly. With one hand, he shoved her to her knees, keeping the gun trained on Sam while he reached into a drawer in the nightstand.

Sam quickly sized up the situation. The bed was between him and Michael-too far to lunge before Michael could get a shot off. Sam tried to keep his cool as he waited for the right minute to make his move.

Michael pulled out a gauze scarf and tied Lauren's hands behind her back as she knelt, and then he stretched the scarf to bind her wrists to her ankles. He then removed a pair of silk panties from the drawer and stuffed them into Lauren's mouth. Using another scarf, he tied her gag in place.

"It won't work," Sam warned. "Even your hench men won't get you out of this."

"Shut up and get down on your knees with your hands behind your head!" Michael ordered. After Sam reluctantly complied, Michael pulled a silencer from his pocket, attached it to his gun, and walked up behind Sam. As Michael lowered his gun, Sam suddenly rolled back on the balls of his feet and sprang upward driving his head into Michael's chin with tremendous force.

Lauren screamed silently into her gag as Michael's jaw snapped shut and he reeled backwards. Sam spun around, but before Sam could attack again, Michael recovered and drove his head into Sam's stomach. As they fell onto the bed struggling, Michael shoved the weapon into Sam's gut. Sam rolled quickly, pulling Michael on top of him as they hit the floor.

Lauren watched in horror while they fought for the gun. There was an explosion of glass as Sam rammed his foot through the door of the book case, dislodging the bookcase from the wall and slicing his leg. He struggled to extricate himself while using his free foot to kick the gun from Michael's hand. The weapon slid along the floor and slammed into the French doors.

Sam clutched Michael's legs, but Michael struggled to his feet and attempted to pull the bookcase down on top of him. The heavy piece swayed each time Sam tried to yank his foot free. As blood soaked through his pants, he writhed awkwardly. He cried out in pain as the contents of the bookcase fell on top of him, but he kept a firm grip on Michael's legs.

Michael finally wrested free. He maneuvered to the side of the cabinet, slipped his powerful arm behind it, and tipped it over.

Lauren watched in horror as the bookcase teetered for an instant before falling. Her choking cries were drowned out by the muffled screams that echoed from beneath the shattered cabinet. Lauren heard Sam's bones snap, and then Sam lay silent.

Lauren arched her back in a desperate effort to see over the top of the bed. Sam eyed her wordlessly from beneath the cabinet while she sobbed silently into her gag. Lauren could see he was barely breathing, and blood was trickling from the corners of his mouth.

Michael straightened his clothes and then smoothed his hair with his fingers. "I'm sorry, Lauren," he apologized as he wiped blood from his mouth. "I hoped it wouldn't come to this."

He walked toward Lauren, leaned down, and rubbed his lips along her wet face as though drying her tears with a linen cloth. "I've been a gentleman long enough."

Suddenly he slipped his hands between her thighs, sighing as he felt her warmth. Michael then closed his eyes and smiled while his fingers stroked her. After a long silence, he reached for his zipper. "Your boyfriend there took you from me, Lauren, and now I'm taking you back. I want this to be the last thing Sam sees before he dies."

Chapter 52

Michael gently stroked Lauren's thighs. He prided himself on his patience. For years he had prepared like a master chef, planning each course, selecting each cut, and timing each step until it all came together to his satisfaction.

There had been many beautiful women, but Lauren was the one he wanted. And Michael Ryan always got what he wanted. He believed he had acted gallantly, even encouraging Lauren to try to make her marriage work. The complications had only increased the challenge for him. But the longer the wait, the greater the pleasure. He had learned that many years ago.

The home where Michael and his Aunt Grazie had lived in the Chambersburg area of Trenton was one of many row houses adjoined to the neighbors' houses on each side by a common wall. After years of ostracism as the Yid Kid, Michael found a way into the world of his neighbors, even if it was without invitation.

He bored a small hole through each common wall, creating a vantage point from which to see and to listen to his neighbors like specimens under his microscope. They were as powerless as smashed bugs on a windshield. In his mind, he now controlled them. However, many years would pass before he would get the ultimate revenge. During that time, he learned to savor the anticipation that comes with waiting.

When Michael was ready to leave the 'Burg to set up business in New York City, he needed extra cash. Although still an outsider, he had invested well for local clients, including neighborhood boss Vic Bonanni, so he decided to borrow from Bonanni to capitalize his plan. He knew the price would be high.

Bonanni, who by that time was running most of his operations out of New York, knew a financial genius when he saw one. He eventually turned over many of his investments to Michael's new company, and Michael earned more money and respect than he had ever imagined. And even more power.

For all practical purposes, he was Bonanni's equal, and Bonanni soon came to acknowledge him as such. But as a result of that trust, Michael was often saddled with cleaning up the messes Bonanni's daughter Donna made—a task he detested. But he did Bonanni's bidding, and he did it well.

Michael prided himself on being a practical man with an ability to assess the exact moment to make a strategic move. When he was young, he mastered the board game *Risk*. No one could beat him, not even the adults. He learned to win by patiently amassing supplies and a formidable strike-force while others seemingly progressed in battle. When Michael would finally choose his time to strike, no opponent could recover.

As an adult Michael played his own version of *Risk*–for high stakes. When the New York branch of Futuro was thriving from Michael's astute investments in the Caymans and South America, Michael returned to the 'Burg and purchased the entire block of row houses where he had once lived, displacing all the nearly life-long tenants, including Grazie. With cold satisfaction, he watched as they left, like peasants on a death march.

He sat in the back of a Lincoln Town Car listening to Rachmaninov the day the building was demolished. He had won once again at *Risk*. And for his opponents, there would be no recovery. He had proven the rule: the longer the wait, the greater the pleasure.

* * *

Michael appraised Lauren as she stared at him with contempt. Although he believed her anger would pass, Lauren's resistance excited him even more than he expected. He knew she needed a man who could control her, not a weak man like Scott...or a dying one like Sam Bennett.

Michael smoothed his hair. The self-control had become such a drug to him that he would almost miss the anticipation. Lauren would learn to love him eventually. Every woman he had ever known had learned to respect, and love, his power. And he would use his power to take care of her the way she deserved.

He had often stood on the dock observing Lauren as she worked alone on her boat. One night he watched with excitement as Sam Bennett pushed Lauren against the wall of the cabin and made love to her. As she wrapped her long tan legs around Sam, Michael smiled. To him, it was a promise of what he would one day have for himself. For ten years he had wanted to sleep with his head buried between her thighs. He would no longer be denied; and he would take his time.

The Cunci had been insurance in case he was being watched, and he was sure it had been discovered by now. He and Lauren would head for L.A. via speed boat where they would board a private jet to Buenos Aires. He would run his businesses from there.

Each detail had been neatly tended to, and he had done his job well. He had taken care of Bonanni's *enfant terrible*, retrieving her money and restoring her dubious honor. Scott had been easy, and Clarence Smolley and the peep show employees had been a necessity. He had forced Flint to do the honors on the repulsive Tumor shortly before taking out Flint himself.

One of Michael's few mistakes was allowing Flint to work the pornography end of Bonanni's Long Beach interests as a favor to Donna. He also knew he shouldn't have let Donna talk him into letting Flint live after he discovered the punk was selling Scott Connolly's amateur porn on the side.

Scott had learned too much about Michael's business; and Michael wasn't going to lose what he had because of Scott Connolly. Although Scott had been as much of a friend as he had ever had, Michael didn't need friends. He only needed respect. Scott had opened his eyes when the knife entered him. He died knowing who was in charge.

Now as Michael appraised his prize and savored the ache of anticipation, he suddenly heard the sound of footsteps below. He listened carefully for several moments before moving soundlessly toward the bedroom door. He glanced at Lauren and reached for his weapon. Soon he would have Lauren over and over again—any way he chose. However, there was something he had to tend to first.

Chapter 53

Mulrooney's instincts had come knocking like the Grim Reaper. Shortly after he and Clarke left the Cunci, they had gotten a call to meet uniformed police at Lauren's slip where Sam Bennett had been spotted. Clarke had headed for the docks, but on the way to the marina, Mulrooney felt an overwhelming anxiety.

He knew Sam Bennett was a self-made man, a maverick who had loved Lauren enough to let her go. Michael, on the other hand, was an owner and a collector—a man who would win at any cost.

Mulrooney stared at the traffic light, trying to anticipate Michael Ryan's next move, as if he were still a Marine on enemy soil. If Ryan's mission was to overtake Lauren Connolly, then Mulrooney had to determine the location of the target.

He knew Lauren was a woman who wanted to regain control of her life. And she was also gutsy.

"Lauren would go home," he said aloud, "and Michael Ryan would go after her."

It was time to stake everything on his belief in his ability, win or lose. If he was wrong, his shield wouldn't be worth much to him anyway. Worse yet, if he was right and didn't act on it, Lauren could end up dead. When the light changed, he made a sudden U-turn and headed back in the direction of Lauren's house.

Mulrooney texted Clarke then stepped on the accelerator. He wove through the streets of Belmont Shore, laying rubber as he took the corners as fast as the narrow streets would allow.

When Mulrooney pulled up in front of the Connolly house, the house was dark, and there were no signs of activity. As he pulled around the back alley behind the house, his stomach heaved. Kate's unoccupied squad car was parked behind the house. He knew Kate and Sanders must be checking out the premises.

Mulrooney shoved his car into park, jumped out, and made his way along the dark passage that separated the Connolly house from the vacant bungalow next door. He moved rapidly with his light off, ignoring the sweat that was streaming down his neck. "Kate?" he whispered as he squinted into the dark, "Katie?"

Suddenly his foot jammed into something that felt like a large sandbag barricading the narrow sidewalk. There was an agonized moan. "Holy Jesus!" Mulrooney yelped, startled by the sound.

He crouched down and snapped on his flashlight. As he directed the light toward the mound, he was shocked to see Sanders lying in a pool of blood.

Mulrooney immediately grabbed one wrist to check for a pulse. He could see from the way Sanders' head sucked up the sidewalk that part of his skull was missing.

Sanders moaned again and opened his eyes. "Hold on, Sanders," Mulrooney soothed as he flashed his light around the walk area. "I'll get help. Can you talk, son? Where's Kate?"

"In ga-garage, sir," Sanders whispered hoarsely. "The d-door was open..." Sanders stammered and licked his lips as he stared up at Mulrooney.

"Sanders, hang in there," Mulrooney pleaded. He could hear the helplessness in his own voice.

"Nine-seven, s-seventy-five, sir."

"What? Just try to relax. Stay awake." Mulrooney stood up and yanked off his shirt as Sanders' moans became one prolonged gurgle. "Nine, seven..." Sanders' lips continued moving.

Mulrooney crouched down and gently pressed his shirt against the gaping wound that opened each time Sanders moved his head. "Don't move, son," Mulrooney ordered as he reached for his phone, "and keep talking to me!"

Sanders pressed his fingers against Mulrooney. As his lips struggled soundlessly over blood covered teeth, he tried to force something into Mulrooney's hand.

Mulrooney knew Sanders was moments from death. He gently removed the piece of crumpled paper from the officer's fist and trained the light on the paper. It was a real estate listing sheet with a photograph of the bungalow next door. Mulrooney's chest ached as he read: BEAUTIFUL BAY SIDE BUNGALOW—REDUCED–NOW ASKING $975,000.

"Thanks for remembering, Sanders," Mulrooney rasped. "You're great, kid, and you're a damn good cop. Relax now, son."

"C-could ya' call my mom for me?"

"You bet I will." Swallowing his emotions, Mulrooney rose to his feet. His eyes burned as he tried to hold back his anger and sorrow. Suddenly he felt the stunning blow from the butt of a pistol. Mulrooney's knees folded beneath him as his brain erupted in a sparks.

Chapter 54

Mulrooney choked back the contents of his stomach as the intense pain in his skull brought him back to consciousness. He looked down at his bare chest and tried to remember where he was. Using the back of his right hand, he wiped his mouth. When he tried to lift his other hand, he realized he was on his knees with his left hand secured behind him, bound tightly with gaffers' tape to his ankles. His hand and ankles were then bound as a unit to the foot of a bed frame. When he floundered with his free right hand in a futile attempt to extricate himself, he became dizzy and disoriented.

When Mulrooney looked up, his eyes slowly focused on Michael Ryan. As Mulrooney blinked to push back the intense colors that filled his eye sockets, he saw that Michael's mouth formed a black slash. The slash smiled.

"I knew I'd enjoy watching you attempt to free yourself," Michael said. "I gave you a bit of line, so to speak."

Mulrooney looked slowly to his left through the blood-and-sweat-covered hair that poked at his eyes. He was overcome with dread when he saw that Lauren Connolly was tied to a night stand nearby, with a gag shoved into her mouth.

"I know you won't make a sound," Michael said as he loomed over Mulrooney, "or I'll kill you all, one at a time."

Mulrooney noticed a slight movement to his right. When he focused his eyes, he saw a fallen bookcase. Sam Bennett lay underneath, distorted by blood and broken bones. With the last of his strength and consciousness, Sam was still helplessly trying to free himself.

Michael shook his head. "I'm surprised he's still breathing. He should save his strength. Actually, I'd prefer that he were dead, but Lauren has had enough to deal with recently." As Michael looked sympathetically at Lauren, she turned away from him in disgust.

"Too bad about the cop," Michael said. "He was careless."

Mulrooney contorted his body and tried to dig at the strips of tape with his free hand while Michael studied him as though he were a fascinating specimen. He was suddenly aware he had no idea how long he had been there. "Officer Axberg will be here with back-up any minute," Mulrooney threatened in a thick voice as he worked at the tape.

"No, I don't think so," Michael said shaking his head. He walked to the bedroom closet and yanked the door open. Lauren's clothes lay on the closet floor in a heap. Kate was hogtied, suspended from the clothes pole like skewered meat. She choked on her gag as she stared at Mulrooney with wild eyes. Mulrooney was horrified.

Michael calmly observed Mulrooney's reaction. "This is your fault, Mulrooney. You were warned to back off. Obviously the car explosion taught you nothing. It's unfortunate that you didn't take it seriously. Unfortunate for your Lion Fish, too."

"Please," Mulrooney pleaded with Michael, "just let the officer down and loosen the gag."

Michael shook his head. "I'm afraid I can't accommodate you, Detective."

Mulrooney forced the panic from his head and tried to evaluate his captor. He knew Michael Ryan had a distorted sense of propriety. Ryan had shown up at Scott Connolly's funeral, and he had waited to make his move on Lauren. Mulrooney suspected that Ryan needed to believe he was a fair opponent.

"Lauren was wrong about you, Ryan," Mulrooney baited. "She described you as a gentleman with a sense of fair play. That police officer is a woman. Where is your respect? I thought you had more class than that."

Michael studied Kate for several moments then turned back to Mulrooney. "I know you're trying to manipulate me, Mulrooney," he smiled, "but I'll play along." He walked toward the closet and loosened

Kate's gag slightly. After a moment's hesitation, he lowered Kate's feet to the floor before slamming the closet door shut. "Now don't push for anything else, or I'll kill her," he said in a mock-friendly voice.

"They'll be cops crawling all over this place in a manner of minutes. What do you intend to do?"

"I intend to take what's mine," he answered simply. "You want her too, don't you Mulrooney? The only difference between you and me is that I know how to get what I want."

"That's not the only difference," Mulrooney said angrily.

"We'll see."

Mulrooney could feel his chest pounding as Michael walked over to Lauren and crouched in front of her. He began to kiss her cheeks and forehead, and then he ran his fingers over her lips, which were stretched to accommodate the gag.

"We could have done this privately, Lauren," he said softly, "but you need to know who is boss. And they need to know to whom you belong. I'll give you everything you've ever wanted. I love you," Michael said gently as he cupped her breast, "and I'm going to show you how much." Lauren choked into her gag.

Mulrooney's dread was almost unbearable. Desperate to free himself, he yanked at the tape until he felt it cutting into his wrist. It took all his self-restraint to keep from yelling, but he feared the repercussions. It was Michael's game, and Mulrooney was losing ground.

"Nobody refuses me, Lauren," Michael calmly reasoned. His lip curled as he eyed Sam, who was barely hanging on. "Sam learned that when he refused protection for his club. And I'm sorry about Scott, too, but I warned him. He gave me no choice. I had to dispose of him, as I'll have to do with Robocop here."

Mulrooney tried once again to free his legs from the bed frame. The searing pain from his old injuries intensified each time he moved. Although his knees and ankle felt as though they were on fire, he continued to struggle.

Michael shook his head at Mulrooney before focusing his attention back on Lauren. When she turned away from him, he hesitated for a moment, and then he slapped her hard across the face. "Don't ever turn away from me again," he said angrily. In one quick move, Michael ripped her blouse open revealing the ivory lace bra beneath. He slid both hands into her bra and lifted her breasts to expose them. As he traced her curves with his finger tips, he stared down at her possessively.

"No, stop!" Mulrooney begged as he tried in vain to lunge at Michael. Although the bindings held him in place, he struggled again to get to Lauren. He locked eyes with Lauren, who was looking at him beseechingly. "Don't do this, Ryan," he pleaded. "You and I can work this out alone, just let her go."

"I told you not to make a sound." Michael warned menacingly.

"If you love her, don't hurt her."

"I would never hurt her. This is what she wants, Mulrooney. Don't you, Lauren?" As he stroked her breasts, Lauren threw her head back and glared at Michael defiantly.

Michael pressed his mouth to her cheek and spoke. "I've watched you with Sam...you want someone who can control you, don't you?" He squeezed her breasts even harder and smiled as she arched her back in pain.

Mulrooney looked at Sam, who was writhing beneath the cabinet as Michael assaulted Lauren. Sam had worked his hand from beneath the bookcase and was inching it toward the knife, which lay on the floor nearby.

Michael suddenly spun toward Sam. "Aren't you dead yet?" He walked toward Sam and picked up the knife. "Is this what you want?" Michael asked as he put his gun down. He lifted the knife then drove it through Sam's outstretched hand, crudely affixing his hand to the floor. When the screams came, Michael covered Sam's mouth. "Remember, any noise and everyone dies," he said through clenched teeth.

Mulrooney felt a chill go down his spine as Michael reached for the corner of the bedspread to wipe Sam's blood off his hand and shoes. When Michael returned to Lauren's side, he left the gun on the floor near Sam's pinned hand, and out of Mulrooney's reach, deliberately tantalizing them both. Sam stared helplessly at the gun as his hand disappeared in a wellspring of blood.

Michael stood over Lauren. "I wish you could hear the music from here, Lauren. It's Gershwin–one of your favorites. I played it for you on your birthday. When you came downstairs that night, you were naked. I watched you from the den..." he smiled and closed his eyes. "You're beautiful." Michael bent to press his lips to her mouth once more, and then he slowly removed her gag. "Shhh," he warned as he unhooked his belt.

Mulrooney watched Lauren turn away with repulsion. As she choked back sobs, Mulrooney exploded. "No!" he yelled. "Don't do anything you'll regret, Ryan!"

"Shut up!" Michael said. He reeled around and slammed his fist into Mulrooney's jaw. "One more sound and your friend in the closet dies first."

Mulrooney pressed his eyes shut and sucked down blood and bile as he tried to contain his fury. His silent rage fed his will to live. *Today is not my day to die, you motherfucker.*

Mulrooney opened his eyes and forced himself to stay in the present. He was a man facing the terms of his own death. Every one of his senses was on alert. Suddenly his ears could hear the music clearly, in spite of the broken speakers. The crowning measures of *Rhapsody in Blue* covered him like death sweat. As he felt his blood pumping through his veins, his breathing became steady. The tape that cut into his skin grounded him, and his mouth relished the musty taste of his own blood. He looked around him, laying bare all his senses.

Suddenly Mulrooney jerked upright and riveted his eyes on Lauren. He silently commanded her to look at him again. But as Michael continued his sadistic foreplay, Lauren squeezed her eyes closed.

Look at me, Lauren, Mulrooney's mind screamed. *Look at me!*

Slowly Lauren opened her eyes. She turned away from her tormentor and focused her eyes on Mulrooney as if she could hear him calling her.

Mulrooney lifted his brows, widening his eyes with painful intensity. Silently, he guided her attention to the space on the floor between the nightstand and the bed.

When Lauren turned to look to where Mulrooney had indicated, Michael immediately grabbed her face and yanked it toward him. "I told you to never turn away from me again."

"I'm sorry, Michael," she said softly. "Maybe you're right. Maybe, maybe a man like you is really what I need."

Lauren winced when she heard Sam sob. Mulrooney glanced at Sam, whose dull eyes remained focused on the gun.

"Yes," Michael whispered. Then he pressed his groin against her face so she could feel his hardness. He lifted his face toward the ceiling as he absorbed her warmth.

Mulrooney slowly stretched his free arm as far as he could. He was short of reaching the discarded gun by only one foot.

As Michael continued to press his erection against Lauren's face, Mulrooney was startled by the moans of pleasure that suddenly escaped from Lauren's throat.

"Michael," she whispered huskily. "You're exciting me. I have fantasized about you for a long time. Let me give you pleasure."

"I knew you'd come around," he smiled.

"Free just one hand. I'll give you what we both want. I do want you. And I don't care who is watching."

Michael looked over at Sam and smiled with satisfaction, before leaning down to untie one of Lauren's arms. When her hand was finally free, she slowly unzipped Michael's pants. Michael groaned as his excitement mounted.

Suddenly Lauren yanked her hand away. In a split second move, she grabbed for one of her hand weights, which were near the edge of the bed where Mulrooney had indicated. She swung with all of her strength, driving the dumbbell upward between Michael's straddled legs. A dull thud could be heard as the weight sunk deep into Michael's groin with tremendous force.

Michael let out a high pitched scream. Stunned into immobility, he clutched at himself in agony. Lauren drove the weight into him again, this time even harder. When he reeled backwards, Lauren hurled the dumbbell at him. A sound like crackling firewood could be heard as the weight connected with his ribs. Michael grasped feebly at the air to stop the onslaught before doubling over.

At that moment, Sam yanked his impaled hand free of the knife. His scream became an aching howl as the knife sliced his hand into two pieces. With his final breath, Sam swung his splayed limb in a bloody arc along the floor, knocking the gun toward Mulrooney.

Mulrooney reached for the weapon just as Michael was coming at him. As the two men struggled, Mulrooney heard the second weight connect solidly with Michael's spine. Mulrooney grabbed for the gun with his free hand. He could taste Michael's sweat as he wrested the gun from his grasp and shoved him backward.

Mulrooney had the gun by its barrel. Before he could change his grip, Michael came at him again. Mulrooney drove his head upward into Michael's chin. In one deft move, he flipped the weapon in his hand and pulled the trigger.

Michael stumbled backward and gave Mulrooney a bewildered look. His hand clasped his chest where his breath ruptured through the angry hole made by the bullet. He made a futile attempt to fasten his trousers before smoothing his dark hair with a bloody hand. After he propped himself against the wall for support, he nodded in defeat.

Suddenly Michael's eyes widened. Mulrooney followed his gaze to Lauren, who was using her free arm to remove the scarves that held her in place. She broke free and dove for the knife.

"No, Lauren! Mulrooney yelled as she yanked the knife out of the floor. "He's done."

"Well I'm not!" she screamed as she raised her arm and hurled the knife. A dull sound could be heard when the knife impaled Michael Ryan's temple. A startled expression settled on his face before he slid slowly to the floor. His head dropped to one side, and then a low rattle escaped from his lungs.

Lauren sobbed and threw herself at Mulrooney. As he pulled her close to his chest, Lauren closed her eyes and clung tightly. He held her in his arms as a welcome calm washed over him.

Chapter 55

"I was coming in the door just as you fired, pal," Clarke grinned as he stood on the jetty and stared out to sea.

Mulrooney and Kate sat on a large rock nearby. "Perfect timing," Mulrooney razzed him, "but I would have enjoyed seeing you a little sooner."

"What, I'm psychic? Your text never came through. It's just 'cause I know you so well that I figured out where you were. That was great work on your part, buddy; but next time wait for your ol' partner."

"You got it. By the way, thanks for backing me up in my wager with Atilla."

"Another hundred bucks says that fat fuck will leave town before he'll ever make good on his bet to take Proud Mary to dinner."

"Too bad," Kate added as she adjusted the sling that stabilized her dislocated shoulder. "Mary would be the classiest date he ever had."

"And the cleanest," Mulrooney laughed.

"Word is out that Mayor Howe was so far down in the polls he decided to scuttle his campaign plans," Kate reported. Clarke hooted with glee. "And Clemente is retiring now that the D.A. is being investigated for taking bribes."

"Ain't life grand?" Mulrooney smiled. "It's finally starting to feel good again."

Mulrooney suddenly got to his feet as the Seduction pulled into a slip in front of the yacht club. Lauren waved to them as she tied up the boat.

"I promised you a surprise," she called to Mulrooney, "and you can't say no." She leaned down and picked up a fishing rod and a box of lures and handed them to him. "Clarke told me you like to fish, so I thought you might want to get away to Catalina some time."

"Thanks, that sounds great," Mulrooney beamed as she stepped onto the dock. "Lauren, we're all very sorry about everything that you've been through."

"I know," Lauren said sadly. "And I'm sorry about Officer Sanders," she added as she placed a hand on Kate's arm. "Kate, you and your partner did everything you possibly could. You'll never know how much I respect and admire you. And you, too, detectives," she smiled, "you both have been wonderful." Lauren's smile lingered on Mulrooney.

"Should we give her a line about us just doing our jobs?" Clarke grinned.

"I already feel like The Mod Squad with the three of us fools standing here together," Mulrooney grumbled.

Lauren laughed as she stepped back aboard. "See you soon," she waved. She smiled at Mulrooney, then she deftly maneuvered the boat back out toward the channel.

Mulrooney knew Lauren was planning to go to Catalina for a while. As he watched the breeze lift her hair around her face then drop it back onto her tan shoulders, something in his chest reminded him that he was alive again. He suddenly realized he had wasted too much time alone.

"You've got her cell number, Tim," Kate smiled. "Call her."

"Maybe I will..."

"Let's go get pie while you think about it."

Mulrooney helped Kate into Clarke's car. He was still clutching his fishing pole as he noticed Lauren watching them from the deck of the Seduction. When she saw the grin spread across his face, she turned the boat back around and slowly edged it back toward shore.

"If you two don't mind, I'll skip the pie," Mulrooney drawled. "I'm going fishing." Then, with the saunter of a heavyweight champion, Mulrooney headed in a straight line for the jetty.

Dear reader,

We hope you enjoyed reading *With Wanton Disregard*. Please take a moment to leave a review, even if it's a short one. Your opinion is important to us.

Discover more books by Gwen Banta at
https://www.nextchapter.pub/authors/gwen-banta

Want to know when one of our books is free or discounted? Join the newsletter at
http://eepurl.com/bqqB3H

Best regards,
Gwen Banta and the Next Chapter Team

You could also like:

Inside Sam Lerner by Gwen Banta

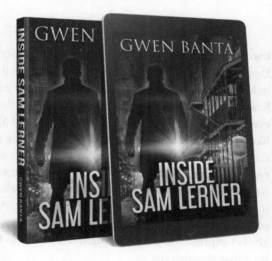

To read the first chapter for free, please head to:
https://www.nextchapter.pub/books/inside-sam-lerner

Acknowledgements

I would like to express my gratitude to Jan Pastras, Denise Carver and Jay Markanich for being the first independent "eyes" to help guide and encourage publication of this book. Ann Connors, you were there every step of the way, and you still are. I would also like to thank Dr. Dmitry Arbuck, who never lets me forget I am a writer, Buddy, who keeps me company when I burn the midnight oil, and my publisher, Next Chapter, specifically Miika Hannila for believing my work is worth the time and investment. And of course my deepest gratitude is for my family, who always express the pride that motivates me and the love that sustains me.

About the Author

Born in Binghamton, NY, Gwen Banta received B.A. and M.S. degrees from Butler University and earned a language certification from The Defense Language Institute in Monterey, California. Her first novel, published in 2016, is a coming-of-age story set against the backdrop of the racial and social unrest of rural Indiana in 1960. Filled with humor as well as pathos, "The Fly Strip," received the Opus Magnum Discovery Award for New Literature-Honorable Mention. Her second novel, "Inside Sam Lerner," is a chilling crime thriller set in New Orleans. It was published by Creativia in 2018 and has received great critical acclaim.

The author has received numerous awards for her fiction in multiple book festivals throughout the nation and abroad: Great Northwest Book Festival, Los Angeles Book Festival, Pacific Rim Book Festival, San Francisco Book Festival, and the Great Southeast

Book Festival. Gwen resides in Los Angeles with her dog, Buddy, who is a major fan of her work.

With Wanton Disregard
ISBN: 978-4-86750-903-6 (Mass Market)

Published by
Next Chapter
1-60-20 Minami-Otsuka
170-0005 Toshima-Ku, Tokyo
+818035793528
17th June 2021